Ac

'O
po
inc

'Ar

'In
a snappy re...                            ...ations with...

*Irish Independent*

'Compellingly written'                    *Dublin Evening Herald*

'I never realised Irish romantic fiction read as juicily as this!'
*Sunday Tribune*

'A thought-provoking read'                *B Magazine*

'She is adept at creating convincing characters'   *Bookseller*

'Purcell's attention to detail, the off-screen change of light or
emphasis, explains her mastery of one of the most difficult
genres of them all'                       *In Dublin*

*Also by Deirdre Purcell*

A Place of Stones
That Childhood Country
Falling For A Dancer
Francey
Sky
Love Like Hate Adore
Entertaining Ambrose
Marble Gardens
Last Summer in Arcadia
Children of Eve

# TELL ME YOUR SECRET

# SECRET

Deirdre Purcell

**headline**
**review**

First published in 2006
by HEADLINE BOOK PUBLISHING

First published in paperback in 2006
by HEADLINE REVIEW
An imprint of HEADLIINE BOOK PUBLISHING

1

A format 0 7553 2417 X (ISBN-10)
A format 978 0 7553 2417 0 (ISBN-13)
B format 0 7553 3335 7 (ISBN-10)
B format 978 0 7553 3335 6 (ISBN-13)

Typeset in Bembo by Palimpsest Book Production Limited
Printed and bound in Great Britain by
Mackays of Chatham plc, Chatham, Kent

Headline's policy is to use papers that are natural, renewable and
recyclable products and made from wood grown in
sustainable forests. The logging and manufacturing processes
are expected to conform to the environmental
regulations of the country of origin.

HEADLINE BOOK PUBLISHING
A division of Hodder Headline
338 Euston Road
LONDON NW1 3BH

www.reviewbooks.co.uk
www.hodderheadline.com

For Suzannah Allen

Whose courage and cheer against desperate odds has inspired me more than I can ever tell her.

# ACKNOWLEDGEMENTS

My last novel, *Children of Eve*, was the tenth and I used the occasion to thank family, friends and colleagues, past and present, who have helped me on this journey. I hope they will know I remain profoundly grateful for all their support.

This time, I would like to pay particular tribute to my patient colleagues at Headline UK, and Hodder Headline Ireland, who pulled out all the technological and editorial stops to ease this book's difficult passage to publication on time. Marion Donaldson, Kate Burke, Breda Purdue, Ciara Considine and Ruth Shern could not have been more sympathetic towards my IT struggles. Hazel Orme is a brilliant copy editor – and I can barely imagine how the production team accommodated the problems with which I presented them. Thank you all.

In addition, I'm grateful specifically to Mary O'Dea and her parents, Helen and Frank, for information about Dublin city in the mid-forties; also to Carol and Roger Cronin for helping with other reasearch.

Finally, I have to thank my calm and stalwart agent, Clare Alexander. And as always, Kevin, Adrian and Simon, it's all for you.

# 1

# THE TOWER ROOM

The days pass. Whatever you do, however much you struggle, the days pass.

At the beginning, during those first terrible months spanning the end of 1944 and the beginning of 1945, disbelief turned to rage and then despair. It was some years before I accepted they would never release me and that I would most likely die without ever again stepping outside the tower room at Whitecliff.

In our family, we had always called it the tower room. This was fanciful since it was merely the largest of the attics, which in centuries gone by had accommodated maidservants and potboys. As children, my brothers, sisters and I had been allowed to use it as a playroom. It was so far away from the main rooms inhabited by our parents that we could make as much noise as we liked, so we never worried about playing tig, or about the rumbling of marbles on the bare boards. We rummaged through the trunks we found up there but, truth to say, found little of interest, just old garden implements, worn kitchenware, maps and books about Africa, Asia and South America that had belonged to Grandfather – a tea

1

merchant who had taken advantage of all opportunities to travel to his suppliers' plantations.

At some point in the past before our family came here, someone had knocked through into the windowless room next door to install a rudimentary lavatory and we held water fights up there, thrilling to the danger, because we knew we would be in trouble if Mother or Father were to catch us. We never feared Nanny – well, not so much – for it was to Nanny, a big, kind-hearted woman from Rathlinney, our local village, we ran for comfort in the event of skinned knees or other childish crises. She did spank us, but half-heartedly, always with a light hand and – should our parents be within earshot – a conspiratorial wink that encouraged us to shriek as though we were being keel-hauled. Nanny's employment in our house suited her well. A spinster with one bachelor brother, she suffered from an unfortunate facial disfigurement that had been with her since birth (she called it a strawberry mark, but in my memory the puckered skin from hairline to jaw on one side of her face was a vivid purple). She stayed with us until I, the youngest of our family, had turned fourteen and our parents deemed that her services were no longer required.

I think of her often, even now.

There were never any cast-off toys in the tower room because any we had outgrown were distributed to 'poor children'.

The division between 'poor children' and ourselves was something we never understood. Our father, trading as Rathlinney General Stores, was the district's grocer, victualler, fuel merchant, vintner, general outfitter, haberdasher and purveyor of hardware, farm implements, fine footwear and millinery: we knew that. We had Nanny, and Whitecliff was a very big house: we knew that too. To us, however, our lives seemed even more parsimonious than those of our school-mates. Whitecliff was draughty, freezing and damp in winter: we all had chilblains and constant colds as we clumped along our acres of stone-flagged or bare wooden floors. The house was furnished, not with the cosy settees and turf fires we glimpsed through the windows of the cottages in Rathlinney, but with big, lumpy chairs and sofas, vast brown tables, monu-mental, half-empty china cabinets and display cases.

Father, a healthy, God-fearing man to whom the desire for physical comfort was somehow letting the side down, limited the amount of fuel we could use in the fireplaces, warning us that wanton waste made woeful want, and constantly turned the gas lamps so low that it was impossible to read.

At mealtimes, we had to eat every scrap we were given 'because you children might never see such good food again', while my sisters and I could never play dress-up: Mother was an adept seamstress, maintaining her own and Father's attire in apple-pie order and turning the boys' shirt collars until the fabric was so worn they were useful only as dusters. As for we girls, she mended or altered our clothes as we grew; as the youngest, I never once had a brand-new shop dress or coat.

So, to us we were as poor as everyone else in the area and it was a mystery why, at school, we were mocked for our accent, for being posh, for being 'twopence ha'penny looking down on twopence'. Once I mentioned Nanny and got such an uproarious reaction I never made that mistake again. It can be lonely coming from the Big House in an Irish village.

When the time approached for me to be confined to the

tower room, they removed the trunks, old hallstands and other items and began to furnish it with strange care. Father had the water closet fitted out with a basin, a toilet with cistern and chain pull and a half-sized bath.

Unwittingly I participated in the refurbishment, believing we were doing it for guests. In retrospect, this could only have been fantasy: we Shines had few visitors other than those business acquaintances of Father's who were occasionally invited to supper. Nor were we children encouraged to bring our schoolmates home. So, when I was asked to choose wallpaper from the sample book Father brought home one evening, I was happy to be included. I was more than happy: I was ecstatic because it signified that perhaps I was to be forgiven.

The room measured eighteen feet by twelve – I have paced it often enough, God knows, to be accurate about this – with one window running from half-way up the wall almost to the ceiling, so high I had to stand on my chair to see through. It was barred on the outside for reasons that to this day are not clear: Whitecliff stands three storeys over its cellars, with the addition of the further attic storey running the width and depth of the entire house under its eaves. Any intelligent burglar or intruder brave enough to defy Father's shotgun would have taken the easy way in through the ill-fitting front door or the ground-floor windows, whose wooden frames, even before I was incarcerated, had been so softened by salt-laden rain and wind that it would have taken only a few pushes with a sturdy screwdriver to lift them out of their sockets.

As for the rear of the house, my purview, no one was ever determined enough even to ramble past underneath my window because our land, fenced on both sides with barbed wire, ran right to the edge of the cliff, which was sheer and seventy or eighty feet high. (I think today that is thirty to thirty-five metres – I find it difficult to get used to modernisms.)

Whitecliff is more than two hundred years old and I have mulled over many theories as to why the barring of this particular window, the only prison window in the entire house, was thought necessary. Perhaps, despite the difficulty of access from the outside, the room had once contained a family's treasures. Perhaps it was feared that if this window were left undefended, local swains would shimmy up a rope of twisted sheets to have their way with the maids.

Or perhaps a mad aunt (or a mad first wife) was shut up here because she was considered a danger to herself. Or to her family's reputation, should she throw herself to her death.

What may sound odd, even questionable, given the circumstances, is that, over time, I came to think I had quite a nice place to live and when finally I decided to accept my situation, I discovered that in a heartbeat – yes, it was as quick as that – I was free.

I remember the moment, although I could not tell you what day or even year it occurred.

For a long time, many years, I had faithfully wound the watch Uncle Samuel had given me for my sixteenth birthday, but little by little, it dawned on me that when you have no control over your life, time ceases to matter. So I put the watch aside and, from then on, lived by cycles of light and darkness, warmth and cold, storms and calm – and the prompt arrival of my food tray.

Whitecliff's gardens were to the front and sides of the

house. The narrow terrain between its rear and the edge of the cliff was covered with stones and scutch, offering minimal changes of colour or growth. As a result, from my chair, I had to rely on the sky, the sea and the position of the sun to follow the seasons. In that place I learned from experience to find the position of the sun on all but the dourest of days. I learned also to follow the tilt of the earth on its axis by the location of sunrise and sunset relative to my window. The sun and the sea became my friends.

The actual moment of liberation was unexpected.

It took place in midwinter, close to noon on a day when sea horses raced the raggy clouds above. I had taken my customary position on my chair by the window, and was straining to pick out activity among the stones at the edge of the cliff. I was sure I had seen movement. A vole? Fieldmouse? A feral cat or even a rabbit – rare at that time of year? I was holding my breath so that I made not the slightest motion.

But yes – there. I became excited. There again – a rabbit! Definitely a rabbit . . .

As I watched, the creature sat upright on its haunches, ears relaxed but twitching against its back, little paws hanging close to its chest . . . It was facing Whitecliff. Surveying our grey walls.

I concentrated hard, endeavouring to pick out individual features, eyes, the busy, nibbling mouth.

Maybe it wasn't a rabbit. Maybe it was a hare, a small one – turn round, little thing, so I can see your scut, the length of your legs – please turn round . . .

But then the clouds split and I had to shut my eyes. My window faced east and, when it rose during the short days, the sun glared.

I waited until the light receded behind the clouds to open my eyes. But, no matter how carefully I scanned, I could no longer see the rabbit, or hare. It was gone, or its camouflage was effective.

When you are in a situation like mine, the smallest setback can become a catastrophe. I flounced from the chair to my bed. Fuming, I picked up my water carafe to throw it at the window, caring not a whit what noise I would make or for the fate of the glass, then realised that losing my temper was absurd, of value as a weapon only against someone with whom one is angry. The person has to be physically present.

Who could react here? The wallpaper? The walls themselves? The only quasi-human in the room, encased for ever in his cheap wooden frame, was the Laughing Cavalier. We caught one another's eye. He continued to laugh. I laughed too and the tantrum drained like hot water through a colander.

I had been given fresh linen that morning and, as I lay on my pillows, became aware of the scent of the lavender bags Mother hung about the airing cupboard. It was soothing and pleasant.

I saw my room as though it were new to me. I saw plaster flaking like butter shavings off the ceiling, the faded but still merry posies of forget-me-nots on the wallpaper I had chosen, the subtle colours in the Oriental silk rug on the floor, my blue velvet hassock with the silk tassels, my table and chair, my writing materials and embroidery hoop with its riot of coloured threads, the glowing red scarf I was knitting as a future Christmas present for a recipient as yet not identified.

My bird books, atlases and dictionaries stood upright and waiting in the bookcase. Down there was the graceful iron footpiece of my bedstead, and beyond it the blue Delft tiles of the fire surround.

There was my oil lamp – that magic lantern I could employ at will to throw shadow wall-pictures of kangaroos, elephants, bunnies, even gentlemen with tall hats, twisting and turning my fingers for hours on end to make them dance to my tune.

I could even appreciate the skill that had gone into the neat carving out of a serving hatch, latched from the outside, through the solid oak of my door. At one time, near the beginning, I had harboured urges to shake it loose from its hinge and wriggle through. I had even tried but it made too much noise and, distant though I was from the rest of the house, I knew they would hear. The latch, too, appeared very strong. They had overlooked nothing.

That day of my liberation, I surveyed the other pictures I had been permitted. Above and behind me, a pair of tabby kittens batted at multicoloured spools of cotton. The wall beside the door sported an autumnal forest scene; and in his niche beside the chimney-breast, the pastel guardian angel smiled like a dotty uncle from between spread, protective wings. It had been a present from Nanny.

I felt detached, Violet floating above Violet's earthly body.

Then I heard it. I promise you. As clear as the shush of the sea on the shingle below the cliff, I heard a whisper: 'Rest now, Violet Shine . . .'

But the sky outside darkened abruptly and all was as it had been before. I was lying on my bed, in my ears the squall of a hail shower against the bars at the window and the only images in the tower were the reproductions and prints I have described.

I was not alarmed that my mind played such tricks. I was

used to them. Sometimes, when I could not sleep, I heard the wallpaper rustle, initiating an argument with the floorboards that creaked back a reply. Sometimes I spoke aloud to these inanimate objects, just to prove I still had a voice. (Sometimes I even heard replies. In this twenty-first century, I would be curious to meet someone else who had endured 'solitary' for decades. I would like to compare notes about these mind aberrations and illusions.)

But something about this latest episode made visceral sense. Why don't you rest now, Violet Shine?

Why not indeed?

After all, I was not the worst off in the world, or even in Ireland. I had adequate food, light and comfort. No one oppressed my thoughts or curbed my imagination. My wants were catered to in every respect except one only: I could not leave.

The idea of rest from constant fretting was attractive. It meant one thing, surely: that the worst had happened. I had no control over what lay ahead and there was no longer any point in harbouring resentment about the past.

Senses sharpened by the combined scents of lavender and the carbolic soap Mother used on her washboard, I became conscious that something previously unyielding was giving way. I was as free as I wanted to be, and although they had won the battle, I had won the war.

Unnerved, but exhilarated, I hopped off the bed and up again on my chair to gaze through the bars and the slanting hail at tumbling kittiwakes, at hardy dippers and ducks facing confidently into the dark grey chop, at sea-water gravid with seals.

## 2

# THE SONG OF THE
# WHOOPER SWAN

Get to know the neighbours at Cruskeen Lawns: Whooper swans, Brent geese, shy foxes and silverfish – yecch.

Concentrate, Claudine!

Anyway, isn't a silverfish some kind of beetle or earwig? As for the wildlife in Cruskeen Lawns, well, there'll be plenty of that. Of the rodent variety. Last time I was out at that site, there was nothing to be seen except mud to a depth of five feet and nothing to be heard except pumps pushing trillions of muck-brown gallons from the foundations back towards the estuary. No wonder I'm concentrating on birds and bees. I'm trying to keep the poor mugs' eyes raised to the sky.

Damn, there goes the mobile. 'Hello? Oh, hi, Tom, I'm working on the Lawns brochure. What's up?'

For the next three minutes I can't get a word in edgeways. My boss, Tommy O'Hare, wants me to check out some old pile that he believes might come on the market in the next while. 'If I go up there myself, I'll tip off the competition, but nobody'd suspect you.'

I can feel my face and neck getting hot. Thanks a lot,

Tommy, I think, thanks a bloody lot for the vote of confidence. I've only been working in the business for the best part of ten years . . .

The name of the pile turns out to be Whitecliff and I pay attention. 'I know that place. But it's derelict. Where did you hear it's on the market?'

'I have my sources.'

'It's been empty for years – it must be a shambles inside – and isn't there some story—'

'Forget about stories. Forget about the house, kiddo. There's nineteen acres with it.'

I can almost hear him salivate. Nineteen acres of coastal site in North County Dublin is a developer's dream. Closer to Dublin than Cruskeen Lawns? 'Who owns it?'

'Not quite sure about that but I should be able to access the title through the Land Registry. Some old codger or old dear in the West of Ireland, I heard. But as a matter of urgency, as soon as you're finished with that paperwork, I want you to get up there, have a good sniff round, see how the land lies. You know what I'd look at myself?'

'I think at this stage in my career—'

'Good girl, good girl. I'll leave you to it, eh? Give us a bell as soon as you've been up there, all right? This could be the big-time.' He's off again.

Tommy O'Hare is originally from Dublin city where his parents ran a tiny greengrocer's shop on Camden Street. He retains the patois, not only because he's proud of his origins but also because he believes that punters warm to a Dublin accent – 'A real one, Claudie, like me da's and me ma's, not your new-fangled, half-California type.' He is unmarried because, I'm always telling him, any woman would be mad to take him on.

In a profession dominated by national or regional groupings and even multinationals, he is that maverick: a sole operator who wants to remain thus. Nevertheless, he has always wanted a bigger slice of the action. O'Hare Property Consultants – OHPC – subscribes to the sellers' and buyers' online Bible, myhome.ie, but in the Dublin region's frantic property climate all of us get thousands of hits on that site so our firm still relies mainly on word of mouth and local advertising. We snagged this Cruskeen Lawns project because Tommy went to school with one of the lead players in Greenparks, the consortium developing the place, and it's by far the biggest we've undertaken. But while the percentages are not to be sneezed at, we won't make anything like the big money the developers will. So if we did manage to whip the Whitecliff property from under the noses of the big boys it might be the start of better things. As of now, we don't even have a shopfront or office: each of us operates mainly from home.

'You know, Claudie,' he's still talking, 'if we pull this off, depending on the state of the main house, we could even do one of those luxury-hotel things, with satellite bungalows for self-catering, and good landscaping. We'd make a fortune. Hey! We could even put in a pitch-and-putt course. So while you're at it, kiddo, check with the Heritage people if the place is listed or anything like that.'

I'm no longer irritated: he's a roundy little chancer but he's my roundy little chancer. He has political ambitions, does Tommy, is a member of the local *cumann* of Fianna Fáil, goes to every funeral within a twenty-five-mile radius of the office. He's also a softie who cuts OHPC's percentages when faced with tearful first-time buyers. 'I will go up there, but I've to finish this brochure and I've a viewing of that cottage in Rush at half past two.'

'Screw the viewing. I'll do it. As soon as you've got that Greenparks stuff off for approval, high tail it up there to Whitecliff. Don't forget, I have a *cumann* meeting at half seven, so ring me before that.'

'I get the message, Tommy.'

'Sorry, sorry, sorry. Gotta run – cheers.'

'Don't you want to know the name of the client for the Rush viewing?' He has to be really turned on by Whitecliff if he forgets to ask for the name of a potential sales target.

'Oh, shit! Yeah.' I can hear the rustle of newspaper. He writes notes to himself in the margins, on tissues, on anything handy, including his sleeve. 'Give us it here.'

When he's finally signed off, I sigh and get back to my copy. How do you make twelve blocks of apartments, duplexes and so-called 'townhouses' sound desirable and romantic? Or, at least, different from the other tens of thousands of identical homes currently on the market. For instance, at right angles to Cruskeen Lawns, a second swathe of the boggy landscape bordering our estuary is filled with cranes and diggers busily putting in foundations for a rival development, of more or less the same density, to be known as NorthWater Plains.

Right. Here goes again. 'Fly as free as the seabirds at Cruskeen Lawns . . .' Nope. That'll just remind the punters they'll have mortgages like anvils hanging round their necks . . .

'Tired of breathing traffic fumes every time you open your front door? Fed up with two or three-hour commutes? Why not wake to the song of the Whooper swan and in the quiet evenings hear nothing but the cry of seabirds and the chatter of roosting starlings as a golden sun sinks below the rosy western horizon – there's room to breathe both in and outside these larger than average apartments . . .'

Hmm . . . Maybe . . . But do Whooper swans sing? As for western horizons – Where else would the bloody sun sink? Anyway, the development faces east. And 'larger than average apartments'?

Sometimes when I'm doing viewings I wish I had the courage to shove a tape measure into the hands of the poor goms who are so desperate to buy they can't see that, in some cases, the furniture is custom-made, miniaturised to make the rooms look bigger. I feel like such a heel in the face of all that hope. Those shining eyes and surreptitious hugging when they think I'm not looking . . .

And what the hell am I doing writing this crap anyhow? I'm forty-one, with a 2:1 in English. I wish Tommy would agree to my suggestion that this part of the job should be given to a professional PR or marketing firm, but that would squeeze the margins. 'You're great with the words, Claudine. A terrific wordsmith. Now me, I have a heart-attack if I have to write a simple letter . . .' His flattery is wearing thin.

I stare gloomily at my copy-writing efforts. What else could I do if I got out of real estate? I don't want to teach – and my BA, good and all as it is, wouldn't be enough anyway: I'd have to go back to college to do an H.Dip. Perish the thought. I'm only semi-literate with computers, can use them on a need-to-know basis, but am not interested in expanding my knowledge there, so no office job, at least nothing more demanding than what I do with OHPC. And Bob would have a fit if I suggested working in a sandwich bar or a newsagent's. I'd quite like that: an undemanding little job where I could spend the day, chatting and organising – I'm a good organiser, I think. How would it play with The Guys?

'How's the missus these days, Strongy?' Our name is Armstrong.

'Actually, she's gone into the – er – the retail business . . .'

'You mean she's opening a shop? Good for you, Strongy!'

Oh, for God's sake, Claudine, just write the damn copy. And what would Daddy say if he saw you still wearing your dressing-gown at eleven thirty in the morning? He was a natty, meticulous dresser and after eight o'clock he hated to see anyone in his household, including Pamela, less than fully dressed and ready for the day.

# 3

# LOOPING THE LOOP

Greenparks and Cruskeen Lawns can look after them-selves for a while. I fax the sales copy when I'm dressed and ready to leave, and don't wait for a response.

It's a lovely day and, actually, I'll enjoy being out in the fresh air, playing sleuth. Whatever its present condition, Whitecliff is in a gorgeous location. Prime, we'd call it, and for once the description is accurate. But my ears had pricked up at its name not because I'd heard it bandied about from time to time in the property world or because I'd seen the place from a distance, but because I'm curious about that house.

I have one of those ragbag memories that forgets impor-tant things but files away the odd – sometimes trivial – detail of casual conversations and Whitecliff had come up one Sunday morning years ago, when Daddy, Pamela and I were having a 'treat' breakfast in the Royal Marine in Dun Laoghaire. Eating breakfast in plush hotels on Saturdays and Sundays was something we did a lot. Daddy felt that for busi-ness reasons he should be seen out and about in public ('You never know when a friendly "hello" will turn into a sale, chicken!') but, a gregarious character, he enjoyed it too.

I was fifteen or sixteen, I think, a teenager anyhow, so we'd have had that breakfast in or around the late seventies. I wasn't paying much attention to the conversation but perked up when I heard Daddy and Pamela resume an argument that had been bubbling in our house for months.

At the time we were living in Glenageary, but there had been talk for a while about a move to a better house – Pamela had never liked ours. 'There's nothing at all wrong with the northside, Christy,' she had said that morning, mascara flashing over the baby blues, blonde ponytail wagging. 'There are some really lovely houses there. For instance,' she threw down her knife and fork, foraged under the table and pulled a piece of paper out of her handbag, 'what about this place here, Whitecliff? It sounds perfect for us, gorgeous sea views, huge reception rooms – think of the parties we could have, honey – even rooms in the attics. It's been empty for a while and it clearly needs refurbishment but that's not a problem, surely? It has acres and acres around it. You could build garages for your vintage cars to your heart's content . . .' She stopped. She had been going on so enthusiastically she had failed to notice Daddy's reaction until then. I hadn't.

'Are you finished?' He was getting irritable.

'Christy—'

'Out of the question. The subject is closed.' He glanced at me and smiled. 'Everything OK, chicken? Enjoying that?'

'Grand, Daddy, it's lovely. And I agree with you, Daddy. I certainly don't want to move to the northside. But if we do have to move house, Sandycove would be lovely, wouldn't it?' I gave him a Colgate smile and, when he returned to his scrambled eggs, lowered the wattage to snigger at Pamela.

Yes, I was a spiteful, spoiled brat. But – understating it –

17

Pamela and I did not get on. To be fair, I never gave her a chance, and although I had convinced myself she had married Daddy for his money, the bottom line was that I couldn't forgive her for forcing me to share my father. On day one I decided I wouldn't give her a chance and never deviated from that vow. (Don't believe that such decisions cannot be made by four-year-olds – I'm the living proof that they can.) Daddy had created such an enchanted, self-contained fort around the two of us that when she breached its defences I spent the rest of his life trying to kick her out and shore up the gaps.

She came into my life on my fourth birthday: 'Hey, Princess, how would you like to go to the circus with Daddy and Daddy's friend?' Young as I was, I recognised a set-up when I saw it and resented it with a depth of passion I can still remember. Worse, she married him three months later – in Barbados, with only me and two hotel staff as witnesses. Despite the bribes of 'a great holiday' and a miniature bridal dress, complete with veil and little bouquet, I was a pretty sullen flower-girl.

I stored up the Whitecliff incident to ask him what the problem was, but over the next few days I never had him alone and for a time it went out of my mind. Then, maybe two months or so later, he announced, with her at his side, that we were going to move to 'a magnificent house in Sandycove, twice the size of this one, Claudine, and right by the sea. You'll love it. You'll be the envy of your friends.'

At some later stage I brought up his odd reaction to the other house but he blanked me ('What reaction? Don't know what you're talking about, chicken!'), which confirmed my belief that he had to know the place. By then, however, we were installed in Sandycove so I parked my questions and forgot about them until I was working in real estate and heard the place mentioned – when he was no longer around to answer them.

There's talk of little else among estate agents but properties and from time to time I'd heard Whitecliff referred to speculatively as a plum ripe for development, although never as a real prospect and usually in tandem with lurid rumours: the wife there went mad and was locked up in an asylum, she cursed it, the house is possessed and needs to be exorcised by the ecclesiastical authorities before anyone can live in it.

No, she didn't go mad, she wasn't locked up in an asylum and, anyway, it wasn't the wife, it was the daughter: she committed suicide, and on nights when there's a full moon you can hear a woman screaming. I'd even heard that the outwardly respectable family, who were merchants in Rathlinney, one of the North County Dublin villages, was engaged in a cult – I've had this sort of stuff from middle-aged professional men, who were being perfectly serious. One told me from behind his pint and his horn-rimmed specs that, in his opinion, the place was haunted by a banshee.

The rumours might have put Daddy off but, on the other hand, the motor trade at that time wasn't as cut-throat and segmented as it is now and he was at the height of his success. It was possible, even likely, that he had sold cars to the merchants of Whitecliff: he dealt at the high end, and his reputation extended not only to the city but to the whole of Leinster. Maybe he'd had a bad experience with them.

It's interesting that Tommy thinks the estate might be on the market now. If it had sold when Pamela flashed that sales brochure at Daddy all those years ago, the new owners had done little with the place during their stewardship. Last time I was out that way, I could see that the land was half buried in a jungle of thick bramble, bracken and gorse. Ivy and buddleia had started to consume the house – that huge house – to such an extent that it was impossible to say whether or not it was sound, certainly at the distance from which I could see it on the beach below.

As I whiz on towards the coast these ruminations bring me back squarely to Daddy.

I adored my father, there's no other word for it, and even still, alongside my sorrow at his loss, I can get furious with him for deserting me, not only emotionally but also temporally. He died suddenly, and it transpired, in the dreadful days and weeks that followed, that although he had been in the process of changing his will (he had even told me so: 'Better late than never, chicken, eh? I've just been too busy and, anyway, who's going to die any time soon? Not me!') he hadn't completed or signed the new document and the only valid one, bequeathing everything to his 'beloved wife', had been drawn up many years before.

Wild with grief and anger at him, Pamela, the whole world, I fought her through the courts for what I felt was my rightful share but with only partial success: she had been his wife, I was twenty-one and the judge ruled I had been fully educated, with proper provision made for me during Daddy's lifetime. He did allow that I should be able to buy a house for myself in keeping with the 'standards' to which my father had accustomed me. And he made an order that both sides' costs of the court action should come out of the estate so – spiteful to the last – I had ensured that she didn't get everything her own way.

This all sounds crass, I know, but that was how it happened and I can't undo it. I also know that I should, long ago, have grown out of thinking like this but the sad fact is that, although she is no longer a permanent burr under my skin, any mention of Pamela, by Bob, for instance, brings on a flush of renewed dislike. I seem to need her as nemesis, as punch-bag to alleviate the frustration and loss I still feel, and no matter how much I exhort myself to 'let it go' or to 'put light around her', and all the rest of it, I haven't been able to accomplish it. But I will. Soon. Honestly. I'm already making progress of sorts, in that I can admit shamefacedly now that I scapegoated her; and at dead of night, I can further admit that, where the will was concerned, it was I who had forced confrontation. If I hadn't been so headstrong we might have come to some arrangement.

To be fair to me, my suspicions about her gold-digging seemed justified when, within a year of Daddy's death, she had sold both the car business and the house in Sandycove and had moved to Miami. The first I heard of this was in a letter she sent, enclosing a cheque for five thousand dollars, wishing me and Bob well. I threw the note and the cheque into the bin, but Bob retrieved them, pointing out that we could do with the latter. 'It's conscience money, Bob!' I protested. 'Five thousand dollars? Out of an estate worth millions?'

'Conscience money or not, Claudine,' he said, 'we owe our overdraft,' and I had to give in. At the time, although the house had come free, running it and paying our bills had not and we were pretty skint. My only form of redress against Pamela, therefore, had been (horribly) never to thank her for her gift.

When I think about the years immediately following Daddy's death, the only way I can describe them is in terms of the picture in my children's Bible where Lucifer, the chief archangel, was falling from a bucolic place of light and glory into a roiling mass of darkness and shrieks, illuminated by flames. When Daddy died, I was that angel. Over-dramatic, perhaps, but that was truly how it felt.

They say you should never make any major decisions within two years of a significant bereavement but, tormented as I was, I was taken by some mad notion that I should get away from my previous life altogether and make a fresh start. I decided to leave Dublin and, interpreting the judge's housing 'standards' for myself, quickly found a substantial home, split-level, with reception rooms, kitchen and two *en-suite* bedrooms on the ground floor, master suite, family bathroom and two more bedrooms upstairs. It had been built as the residence at a former stud farm, whose land had been sold separately, and was tucked in against the brow of a hill in the countryside between Garristown in North County Dublin and Ardcath in County Meath. From the front garden, the view is of fertile countryside rolling to the sea, a platinum shimmer beyond the cranes of Drogheda port; and on a clear day such as this, the vista is framed by the Mountains of Mourne and the hills of the Cooley Peninsula. As soon as the deeds were handed over, Bob and I married quietly, moved in and, for a while, I tried to heal myself with frantic activity, making a home for us and discovering the undoubted joys of sex. As Bob and I learned the ropes, we made our bed sing and, for me, it blotted out the ache.

Travelling at speed across the motorway bridge over part of the Malahide estuary, I can see not only the busy flocks of birds we exploit as sales tools, 'our' cranes at Cruskeen Lawns and 'theirs' at NorthWater Plains but, beyond the skyline of the apartments at Malahide Marina, the wide, free sea. Weirdly, my vision of Daddy's life after death has always involved him and my mother flying and looping in the sky above the sea. Some sea. Any sea . . .

I need to stop the car. Because, after all this introspection, here it comes again, that rush of grief. More than two decades after Daddy's death it still catches me unawares. My vision blurs so I put on the flashers and pull on to the hard shoulder to regain control.

Lately, I have found these rushes double-edged: while mourning him, my feelings are for her too, the mother who, at only forty, died giving birth to me. It's odd to think that, had she lived, she would now be an old lady of eighty-one; I always think of her as she was in her black-and-white wedding photographs, happy and smiling in her forties' suit and pillbox hat.

I wish now I knew more about her and her family, but beyond answering childish questions about what she looked and smelt like and assuring me that she loved me from Heaven, even in later years, while Daddy had clearly loved her, he had never been all that forthcoming about her or her family. I'm sure he had his reasons – I can only guess they had to do with his own grief and remarriage to Pamela who, in my view, might have been jealous that he had loved someone other than her perky little self. (Do continue to bear in mind that my opinions in this matter are pretty suspect!)

Daddy had been a lot older than my mother, and while he still had a few cousins scattered across the country, whom we never saw, everyone in her family was gone, he said. And while he could produce a stash of grainy old photographs from his side, he had none from hers: 'She didn't bring any of that stuff with her, chicken, just those snaps I showed you from her college days.'

He did maintain that I'm a ringer for her, and in my early teens, in an effort to see the resemblance, I went through phases of studying those wedding photographs, the studio portraits taken on their engagement, the snaps from their honeymoon in the south of France and the tiny number, just four, from college, one of which had obviously been taken during a party – because there are a lot of people in the background – when she was clearly having a great time, smiling flirtatiously over her shoulder at the camera. Yet, hair and height excepted, I could see little of myself in her.

They'd got married in Paris – 'We asked a waiter and barmaid from the café we'd had breakfast in that morning to stand for us, chicken. We had to use sign language because they didn't speak English. It was fun!' – and, in retrospect, from something he let slip, I believe my mother's family did not approve of the marriage. 'They wouldn't have come to the wedding anyhow, even if we'd had it here. I don't think they liked me.'

'Why not, Daddy?' I was outraged at the notion that someone might not have liked my wonderful father.

'They thought I was too old for her, I know that, but sometimes grown-ups have no reason for being stupid.'

So, I danced through my first twenty-one years with him doting on me and acting as both father and mother. He was enough for me and, to be truthful, I wasn't all that interested in her until it was too late. From time to time as I got older, however, I did make half-hearted decisions to start researching:

Daddy had told me that her family had had a farm, for instance, so a good place to start might have been with the farmers' organisations. And I could quite easily get a copy of her birth certificate. But somehow I was always busy with other things and didn't have the commitment to follow through. Maybe this might be the year to begin, I think now, as I root in the glove compartment for tissues.

I'm disoriented by this recent phenomenon of missing her and, as a matter of fact, can't even put words on it since, having little insight into who or what she was, I have only the vaguest notion of what I miss. I have her wedding and engagement rings and a gold neck chain, all of which I wear all the time, but other than these, little else. A cardigan, a pair of shoes or a handbag might have helped me identify with her, but Pamela had been thorough and there was nothing personal of my mother's in the house. As for furnishings, in the terrible aftermath of Daddy's death, young, anguished and impetuous as I was, I brought virtually nothing except the snap albums from Sandycove to my new house and my new life – a decision I now thoroughly regret.

Yeah, I'm an orphan, I think, laughing through a gush of self-pitying tears, but for once my efforts to snap myself out of it with derision don't work.

The day Daddy died, at my twenty-first birthday party, became the day against which I've measured all others. At his funeral service a few days later, I felt as though I'd been isolated on a sandbar in a fast-flowing river. To my right, the future flowed towards danger and the unknown. To my left, bundled, rushing history – life with Daddy – sucked at my feet, intent on destabilising my feeble grip on life.

Bob, tweedy in one of the salesman's suits that hung off

his bony young shoulders, was in the church that day. We had been dating but now I upped the ante. It's a familiar story. College girl meets handsome junior salesman who works for Daddy, flirts, falls in love, and a short time later, in personal crisis, begs him to marry her because she cannot stand the pain of loss. A husband, a lover, fills the chasm, as the fairy-tale goes, and for a while, as I've said, it did for me, certainly in the bedroom.

From time to time I imagine I can see disappointment, as thick as smog, hanging about my husband's face and put it down to disillusionment: that in marrying me he had assumed he'd marry the business too. After Pamela's clean-out, however, he had found himself looking for another job. Although he still works in the trade, it is as a managing director, rather than a proprietor, but to give him his due, he never whinges, just gets on with it. This year he has cheered up consider-ably because his company has moved from its plush but dilap-idated premises in Dublin city to a state-of-the art showroom at the new motor mall at Airside in Swords. The complex is still at building-site stage, but Bob's gaff is complete and gleaming and a lot of the credit for being among the first dealers off the blocks goes to him. It's closer to home too and he no longer has to sit in the vast car park that every morning constitutes Dublin's so-called commuter belt.

Once or twice recently I've found myself wondering what keeps us together. Now, maybe because I'm feeling so maudlin, it strikes me that I might have misinterpreted his disappoint-ment, if that's what it is. It might have less to do with his career than our marriage. Does either of us any longer know what the other dreams?

When I was young, with a sentimental view of marriage

(not, obviously, Daddy's and Pamela's!), I visualised it as two boats tied together to float down a wide river called 'hope' towards a destination called 'happiness'. Perhaps it's no such thing. Perhaps in the most stable marriages there are two boats on two separate streams that meander along at different speeds, coming together only occasionally when by chance they enter a placid lake.

Oh, hell, Claudine, I think, you read too much! Get a grip. So you're an orphan – big deal at your age! You're healthy and comfortably off, with a husband who's a good provider and with whom you get along reasonably well, a lovely house and, while it's not going to set the world on fire, a job that doesn't tie you to a desk. Half of the world's population would give a lot to be so lucky.

I blow my nose as, boom, boom, boom, the traffic shoots by with a wink of mirrors and a flash of hubcaps, no one casting even a glance at me.

Ah, well, I think, I wouldn't look at me either, snivelling bundle of contradictions that I am.

# 4

# WAVING AT MATTHEW

After some months in my tower room, I asked for – and received – my violoncello. It was February, coming up to my seventeenth birthday and, as I told you, at the beginning I did not settle or accept, and spent many of my days in denial and bitterness. Perhaps, I thought one morning on waking, music might help.

Here is – or was – my family.

My father was Roderick Shine, who, an only child, inherited Whitecliff and the family business from his father. Fiona, my mother, inappropriately nicknamed 'Fly', was born in Dundonald in the North of Ireland. I have no idea how they met: their private affairs were never discussed in front of us children and we were not encouraged to enquire. Both sets of grandparents had died before I was born and, as far as we knew, we had only one other close relative, my mother's unmarried brother, Uncle Samuel – after whom my brother, Young Samuel, was named.

Uncle Samuel, a publican, was my godfather. We children looked forward to his annual July visits to us, not only because he always brought generous presents but also because of the breezy good humour he injected into our quiet household. In personality he was as unlike our mother as it was possible to be. They were both short but while she was slight and usually expressionless, he was portly and red-faced with a booming voice, eyes that vanished into the surrounding creases when he smiled, and a hearty laugh that rode out to play on a saddle of beer breath. As you will see, I had reason later to be grateful to him.

Perhaps it was this paucity of relations that led our parents to have seven children.

My eldest sister was Johanna, who latterly became my best friend. After her came, in descending seniority, Marjorie, Young Samuel, then James and Thomas, who were twins, Matthew and finally myself, christened Violet Jane. Oddly, we children were all born in January and February: Johanna, the twins and Matthew in January, Marjorie, Young Samuel and I in February. Nanny used to say it must be something in the water at Whitecliff!

By the end of the war in 1945, we had lost three of my four brothers.

Matthew succumbed to tuberculosis when he was only six. He died on 22 February 1933, and because we children had been quarantined, I spent part of my fifth birthday, two days later, watching through a window as undertakers carried his coffin from the house.

It was my first encounter with death or a corpse. I had had no dead grandmother or grandfather to kiss or mourn, I had never even seen a chicken's neck stretched, or heard the squeal of a stuck pig. Some of our land was tilled for vegetables, we had an orchard and glasshouses for tomatoes, but we kept no livestock, not even hens for eggs. Given the frugality by which we lived, this might seem strange, but Mother abhorred dirt and could not see the point in having to perform all the tasks associated with animals and fowl when, as prime retailers in the village, we had access at cost to every supplier within miles. We did have cats, but they were strictly forbidden in the house and were not pets. Even outside in the garden, if they approached us, we were not to give them milk or stroke them, as this would encourage them. Mother tolerated them only because she felt they discouraged mice and rats. Fed infrequently, they were expected to fend for themselves on the land.

Like most children, we had begged for a dog but she was adamant: 'This family does not need a dog since there is nothing of interest to thieves in the house.' Father had once considered keeping a horse since we had plenty of grazing land and could take back some of that rented to locals for their cattle. We even had a small, tumbledown stable block of three stalls, but Mother vetoed the horse too.

So, when poor Matthew died, the shock to me was profound and the days surrounding the obsequies still play like a slideshow in my imagination.

For instance, I can describe in detail how, before he was brought back from the sanatorium to the house on the day he died, Nanny stopped the two pendulum clocks. 'What's wrong, Nanny? What's wrong?' Whining, I followed her from the hall, where she had stilled the grandfather clock, into the drawing room where she was about to still the granddaughter. She picked me up and laid her disfigured cheek against mine. It was wet, I remember. 'You have to be the goodest, bestest little girleen in the world for the next few days, Violet,' she said. 'Oh, Lord, Lord – your poor misfortunate parents . . .'

Father entered then and, bewildered, I could see that his arms were filled with bundles of black fabric. Nanny wiped her eyes on the sleeve of her dress and put me down. 'Run along to Johanna now,' she said to me. 'She's in the kitchen and she'll give you a bowl of milk. And remember, you must be as quiet as a little mouse.' She took some of the drapes from Father, and while he hung one over a picture on the wall above the big sofa, she dragged a chair to the fireplace so that she could cover the mirror over the mantelpiece.

Instead of going to the kitchen, I ran upstairs in search of Mother. If I wish, I can re-create the hum of thick silence behind her locked door within the thicker silence blanketing the rest of the house; I can still feel the grain and growing warmth of the wood against my face as I pressed it to that door.

The situation was no better downstairs. I found Johanna, tear-stained and stiff-backed, scouring the sink as though it was not already as clean as a new china plate. I ran to her and clutched at her legs: 'Nanny says you're to give me a bowl of milk,' I sobbed, not knowing why I was sad.

'Sit at the table, Violet,' Johanna said gruffly. Then, instead of picking me up as I had expected, she hurried to the pantry, removed the muslin from the top of one of the big white jugs and poured milk into a bowl. 'There,' she said, putting it on the table.

'I don't want it,' I mewled.

'Then don't have it.' She removed the bowl, threw the contents down the sink and resumed scrubbing. This behaviour was so unlike what I was used to in Johanna that I stopped crying and felt something cold and slimy wriggling in my chest. It must have been my first conscious recognition of fear.

Although Matthew had died on a weekday, it felt like Sunday. My other brothers and my sisters had been taken home from school. Father had closed the store in Rathlinney and Nanny had been instructed to dress us in Sunday best.

Also, instead of eating with Nanny in the kitchen, which we did every day except the Sabbath, we were instructed to go to the dining room where she had lit a fire and laid the table for luncheon. The scent or taste of an apple still reminds me of the crackling that defined our doomy silence that afternoon because we were burning apple logs from a fallen tree.

We were confined to our bedrooms while the undertakers delivered the body from the sanatorium later that day. In the meantime, Matthew's bed had been carried downstairs to the drawing room, which we seldom used. When, clutching Nanny's hand, I went in with the others to see him, all the sofas and easy chairs had been pushed to the walls and Father, dressed in black, was sitting unnaturally still in an upright chair beside Matthew who was all in white: white nightshirt, white pillow, snowy coverlet. It was not Matthew. I stared, transfixed, at what he had become: projections of bone under stretched, grey-white skin; a thin blue line where his lips should have been; filmy, transparent eyelids sunk in dark sockets so deep they could not have contained my brother's eyes.

In the draughts, the flames of what seemed, to my childish eyes, to be hundreds of white candles flickered, causing the wax to spit. I felt their heat and my serge dress itched. Although the morning had been fine, the weather outside had turned and rain, driven by a gusting wind, flailed now at the french windows at one end of the big room and then at the bay windows at the other, so that our family, our house and poor

Matthew seemed caught in the centre of a violent circle. 'You should kiss him, Violet,' Nanny, bending low, whispered in my ear. 'Good girl. That would be the proper Christian thing to do.'

I could not bear the prospect and wept, raising my arms to her to be lifted up. 'Ssh,' Nanny soothed me, while my brothers and sisters took turns to kiss Matthew. Thomas and James were openly crying. Young Samuel, as the eldest son, betrayed himself only with a hiccup. Johanna and Marjorie were silent, but tears streamed down their cheeks.

Meanwhile, I had buried my head in Nanny's soft fat neck. She always smelt of roses (from this perspective I assume the scent was of her talcum powder). 'Go on, Violet. It's the right thing to do,' she whispered.

'No!'

Yet I was an obedient child and, after further persuasion, agreed not to a kiss but to touch him just once. Clutching Nanny's blouse with one hand for safety, I leaned down and reached for one of his, intertwined with the other on the coverlet. I recoiled: I had not touched my brother's fingers but something as sharp and hard as kittens' claws.

If I had been fearful before, I panicked now. This was not the ruddy-faced brother, closest to me in age, who had used an old broomstick to ride a cockhorse with me through the tower room. I screeched with fright and Nanny had to remove me from the room.

I do not recall any church service, but in spite of my then tender years and that it happened such a long time ago, I can clearly remember the small, awful procession of Matthew's last journey some time the following day. The trees were in full leaf under a high, bright sun; our lawn had not been mown for a couple of weeks and the glossy tips of the grass rippled in the light breeze.

Mother had decreed that none of us children was to go to the cemetery so the cortège consisted of just three vehicles: the hearse, silver furbelows glinting, our clergyman's old black car, and Father's, which was an incongruous yellow. I could not see Mother's face in the passenger seat: she was veiled.

As the three motors inched down the driveway towards the gate, I was confused. The day before, even as lately as that morning, Nanny, now sitting beside me on one of the three window-seats in the drawing room bays, had assured me over and over again that Matthew would go straight to Heaven. However, I could see no sign of his taking to the sky: he was still enclosed in his white box, travelling along in the hearse as if it was any old tractor in the district.

I knew that he was nailed into that white box. How was he going to get out? Panic, like a ball of ice and fire, threatened to explode inside me. 'When will he get out, Nanny?'

'Ssh, dote!' She picked me up and hugged me. 'Say goodbye to him now. Say it with your whole heart and soul. But don't worry about how he'll get to Heaven. When the sun goes down this evening and nobody's looking, God will take Matthew in His arms and carry him straight up. He does this secretly with children. It's so good up there, Violet. No school, no rules, no chores, just fun all the time. God knows, everyone wants to go to Heaven and he doesn't want to upset all the little sisters and brothers on earth who have to wait their turn.'

Although I was still watching the slow progress of the cars, I considered this. 'Who'll he play with, Nanny? I want to go with him.'

'You have to wait your turn. There are so many little children already there, and so many great games, Matthew won't have a minute to himself. If you're a good girl here on earth, when God does come for you, Matthew will be there at the gates of Heaven to show you all the best toys and the best places to play. He'll have marked it all out for you. He'll be delighted to see you, child.'

It sounded reasonable, even thrilling, and my panic eased. 'How'll God know where to find him this evening when the sun goes down?'

'Tsk! Tsk!' Nanny chided, then had to blow her nose on the big white hanky she always carried. 'What are they teaching you at that Sunday school, Violet Jane Shine? God can do everything. You should know that by now.'

The cars were almost at the bend in our driveway. 'Should I wave, Nanny?'

'That's exactly what you should do. Wave bye-bye to your brother now, Violet dear.' So while my siblings wept aloud and held each other on the other two window-seats, I waved excitedly from where Nanny and I sat. I pictured all the toys, even train sets, all laid out and waiting for Matthew in Heaven.

James's funeral came next, eleven years later. It took place in the late summer of that fateful year of 1944. The twins had signed up together in Belfast after their eighteenth birthday the previous February, persuaded to wait until then by Father. Like many other young men, prepared to lie to the recruiting officer about their ages, they had wanted to go earlier.

I said goodbye to them only perfunctorily when they were called up because by that time I was in love with Coley Quinn – and, other than how to evade surveillance in order to see him, I could think of little else but his hair, his eyes, his hard strong mouth, smooth white shoulders and broad back. When James and Thomas came to say they were off to fight for freedom, I hugged them, told them how handsome they would be in their new uniforms and, having been assured they'd get a furlough after training, wished them luck and said I'd see them then. 'Anyway, you probably won't see any action. Everyone says it'll be over by next Christmas.' I was airy, parroting what I'd heard from grown-ups and Coley Quinn. Coley, whose family rented grazing land from us, worked in the creamery and was therefore in a position to hear all the latest news.

Mr de Valera had kept us Irish out of that horrid war, and before we were directly affected, it was merely an irritant to us at Whitecliff: it meant we had to go about at evening pulling blackout curtains or blinds over the windows, and that, as purveyors, we could not get enough tea, sugar, bicycle tyres or lamp oil to satisfy our customers' or even our own needs. Coley could have smuggled me some butter but that would have alerted my parents to our liaison so I pretended outrage: 'Not when our soldiers are going hungry, Coley!'

The man's republican ideals excepted, Father was an admirer of Mr de Valera. He believed they shared social and moral aspirations for our country. By chance, on the previous St Patrick's Day in 1943, he had twirled the dial of our wireless away from something he thought dull on the BBC and found Mr de Valera in scratchy full flow, making the case for his vision of Ireland. If I have it correctly Mr de Valera revealed that he wanted us to 'live the life that God desires that men should live', and that our countryside should be bright with cosy homesteads and ringing with the cries of athletic youth. Father quoted this often and there was a brief period when, given what Coley Quinn and I were up to, I used to shudder deliciously at the thought of how Mr de Valera, or indeed Father, would feel about it.

I had plenty of time later to regret my superficial farewell to my twin brothers: James, excited in anticipation of a great adventure, Thomas, the quieter one, pretending to be equally jaunty. They were not identical and had very different personalities. Thomas always followed his more extrovert twin's lead and I suspect now that he joined up only because James had thought it an awfully good idea.

After their departure for the front, three months after their training, poor James saw just two days of action before he was killed at dusk during shelling of his position. I wept many tears when I heard but was still, I think, in shock at my incarceration. That, with the loss of my lover, was my daily obsession, superseding all outside disasters.

It was no easier for me when Thomas, too, died in action, in the closing days of the war in 1945. Locked in with life and loss stretching into infinity and no distraction offered by Coley Quinn or anyone else, I fell to copious, even histrionic weeping. On the night I heard this latest news, there was a full moon and, at that impressionable age of seventeen, swollen eyes raised to the empathetic light streaming through my prison window, I was convinced I would go mad.

By then I had my violoncello, and for some days after Thomas's funeral, I tried to put my endless leisure to some use by composing a set of laments for my three lost brothers and that other, about whom I shall tell you presently. Compounded by my own hopeless situation, the turmoil was intense, yet I wanted for skill and experience in composition, and all I could produce from my instrument was the howl of a banshee.

# 5

# A PET MORNING

That last day of ours, Daddy's and mine, started so gaily. Although I didn't as yet have my results, I felt I'd done well in my finals, so could concentrate on having the best time of my life.

Even the weather conspired with me: I'd been too excited to sleep and was awake and alert as the rising sun flooded my bedroom at ten past five in the morning. I jumped out of bed. Twenty-one! I thought, as I took a deep breath and pulled back the heavy curtains.

Our house was directly across the road from a curved bay; we could see James Joyce's Martello tower on one promontory and, in the other direction, the long finger of Dun Laoghaire pier pointing sternly towards England. The world passed my window, and if I stood there long enough on any day, I would see not only the native shoals of yachts from the clubs up the road but sea traffic from all over the globe, giant car ferries and container ships, coal boats and other cargo or passenger craft steaming in and out of Dublin port.

But that morning there was no Golf outside our gate.

I gazed out at the empty road and beyond it to the flat,

primrose-shaded sea. I was a teeny bit disappointed: I'd been dropping naked hints that for my birthday I wanted the racing-green Golf I'd seen on Daddy's forecourt. It would have been just like him to have it gift-wrapped outside the railings that morning.

Plenty of time, though, I thought. He probably wanted to fill it with cases of champagne or balloons.

I didn't feel guilty at having asked for such a big present. After all, I was going to be twenty-one only once and, anyway, lots of my friends had had trophy cars for their twenty-firsts; one had even got an apartment in one of the modern blocks that were beginning to appear in some parts of Dublin. I threw up the sash window and inhaled the still, salty air. Twenty-one! I tried it out again. It seemed like only a couple of years ago that Daddy was dropping me into big school for the first time, yet here I was, a crone. An adult: Daddy's little grown-up, on the threshold of the best day of my life, with greetings, presents and pleasure, culminating with the party tonight. From time to time in the past I'd suffered pangs of envy when hearing of swarming family occasions in my pals' houses – they never lasted long when I heard about the rows! – but tonight my lack of family was going to work in my favour: since we had no old aunts or uncles, or any other decrepits that we simply had to invite, the party would consist only of my own friends and we'd have a ball. With the brief attention of youth, I wondered for a moment or two how my real mother would look, or behave, if she were here, but the thought was gone virtually before it arrived. Since I'd never known her . . .

I'd gone for a black-and-white theme so the Snow Whites could shine and the other lot could come shredded if they liked. Daddy would be there, of course, and Pamela, and a couple of big clients he'd felt it would be advantageous to invite: 'Are you sure you don't mind, chicken? They won't stay long. They won't cramp your style.' We had flowers and caterers and hired chairs in the marquee in the back garden – that was for the sit-down meal – and the entire downstairs area of the house had been cleared and rigged for the disco. It also looked as if the weather was going to co-operate. That morning I was virtually sick with excitement.

First, though, there was to be lunch with Daddy and Pamela in the big, clubby dining room at the Berkeley Court.

He had been surprised at my choice of venue for my birthday lunch: 'Are you sure, chicken? We've been there a lot and a twenty-first is a real big event in anyone's life. I'll take you anywhere – Paris, even. If we left on an early-morning flight, we could be back in time for your party.'

'Leave it with me, Daddy. Maybe I should think about it some more.' I pretended to look concerned and, for the next few days, had teased him that since it was time for me to take the world seriously, far from allowing him to whisk me off to Paris, I should probably start dealing with the real world. We should choose somewhere where people not as privileged as ourselves were forced to eat: a right-on, bare-tabled dive at the end of a grotty lane.

Despite all the teasing, though, I'd never had any intention of going anywhere but the Berkeley Court Hotel for my birthday lunch. It was 'our' place, Daddy's and mine, and I knew it would please him if I opted to celebrate one of the major occasions of my life there. He had always taken me, or me and Pamela, to the Berkeley for big days and celebrations. Great big wodges of roast beef with marbling like a road map, black on the outside, squidgy and bleeding in the centre. As well as the mangetout and ratatouille, there were old-fashioned vegetables, like turnip and cabbage. Cutlery so solid it'd give you a hernia if you tried to lift too much of it. Even as a small child, I had never felt in the least over-awed by the high hush, the palaver with silver domes on the plates, the massive sweet trolley, the murmuring waiters; instead, I felt secure, cushy and glamorous, as if nothing could ever harm me through the thick walls and draperies.

It was still too early to telephone anyone. I left the window and sat on my bed, hugging my knees. I counted my bless-ings, not least among them rude health, my super-generous daddy and my very handsome boyfriend, on the up in his career. Not to speak of my own good performance at uni.

I had no illusions about the privilege of my upbringing, especially where my degree was concerned. Frankly, I didn't know how some of my fellow students made it through their courses. English was no doddle at University College Dublin, and it took a fair amount of effort to keep up, but in addi-tion to attending lectures and tutorials and meeting essay deadlines, some had to slave for a pittance in greasy spoons or other places so that they could eat. When I'd think dark thoughts like that, though, I'd remember the parable of the beloved child for whom the fatted calf was killed. I was equally beloved, and it was hardly my fault, was it?

When I was younger and on days off or holidays from school, Daddy had taken me with him everywhere, even on business trips. Once we had a glorious weekend in London, and before we came home, he took the afternoon off from business and we trained it to Brighton, 'Just for the experi-ence,' he said that morning, laughing in that whistling, wheezy way he had. 'We're an island people, and it should be compulsory to see the sights of the world. Our government should give us grants to go and see the Eiffel Tower, the Taj Mahal, the Great Wall of China and the Grand Canyon. Brighton pier isn't in that league, chicken, but it's a start.' I would have been about eleven.

I turned on my bedside radio and lay back on the pillows to enjoy the anticipation of a wonderful life ahead.

I wondered if Bob was awake yet, and what he had in store for me later. I was going to meet him for coffee in the Royal Marine later that morning. I hoped he'd have my present with him.

We hadn't done 'it' yet. We had necked and petted, of course, but hadn't gone the whole way. It was my fault: something held me back, I wasn't sure what. Maybe being a Protestant was the problem – we're a little reserved that way; I think it's because we're in such a minority in Ireland that we feel we have to be extra careful about our reputations. For whatever reason, I just felt it wouldn't be right to go to bed with my boyfriend before we were married, and I was always conscious that Daddy would be disappointed in me if he found out. And he would: Daddy found out everything.

That day I couldn't wait to see Bob. Maybe he'd pop the question. Have the ring with him in the Royal Marine, take it out of his pocket or drop it into a champagne glass or hide it in a sandwich. Wouldn't that be something to show the girls tonight? I thought happily. I wouldn't come right out with it, make an announcement or anything. I'd just wave the sparkler and dazzle them with it.

I let the fantasy run a little. If we got married we'd manage OK. Daddy had promoted him to the senior sales force a couple of months ago so he'd had a big jump in salary and his commissions were growing. And even if I couldn't find a high-powered job, one that would pay well, Daddy wouldn't see us stuck. He'd give us the deposit on one of those new apartments. Even a house – although living in an apartment sounded so exotic and New Yorkish . . .

In some ways, I admitted to myself, a little guiltily, it was great to be an only child, especially a girl.

That, of course, was on 1 June 1983, the day everything went pear-shaped.

# 6

# A SLASH HOOK

Away from motorways, national and regional routes, North County Dublin – or Fingal, as it's been called since the county was sliced into three administrations – is a maze of narrow, winding roads, boreens and cul-de-sacs. At this time of year, despite the best efforts of the council, the hedgerows and grass margins encroach to the extent that, to the unsuspecting visitor, they all look the same, as if a gang of mad road planners had conspired to lead him or her astray.

There's an upside to this, of course: on the verges the grass, interwoven with foxglove, celandine, dog daisy – even sheaves of crimson poppies here and there – is impossibly green. Behind are thick banks of yarrow, green willow, whitethorn and hazel. Growth is rampant. In fact, the year has been unusually clement so far. Wet, I grant you, but warm too. So-called global warming, no doubt. Bring it on!

At present I'm lost. I know Whitecliff by sight only from a distance, hulking from above us on its cliff when Bob and I are out walking the beaches below it with Jeffrey, our mutt. (I know, I know! The name was Bob's idea. When we got the dog he was reading *Kane and Abel*, one of maybe three novels he's read in his life. I hadn't had the energy to argue.)

I had already bumped down two cul-de-sacs to find myself first at a farm gate and then in the junk-infested yard of a garage-cum-machinery workshop. Although mindful of Tommy's warnings – 'Make sure nobody knows what your interest is, Claudie. You know what country people are like' – I was tempted to ask for directions but held off to make one last solo try.

Tommy can be melodramatic but this is not a problem for me: it can keep things interesting and, right now, if I'm honest, I'm quite enjoying behaving like a spook in enemy territory.

I slow down and attempt to get my bearings. Hedges to the right of me, hedges to the left, one of those squiggly signs in front, warning of tight bends ahead. The hell with it, I think. Might as well take a breather. I pull the car up on the margin, turn off the engine and roll down the windows to be assailed by that complex scent of rural Irish summer. It's simultaneously rancid and sweet: silage, slurry and warm cowpat combined with virgin grass, tree sap, wild flowers – and, so near the sea, a cut-through of ozone.

No wind. No cars, tractors, JCBs or diggers, as everyone within spitting distance is at his or her dinner: this pocket of the country is the kind of place where those left behind by daily commuters still eat their main meal in the middle of the day. There isn't even much birdsong, just the occasional subdued twitter. At this season, the birds are busy and don't have time to sing, so the loudest sounds are from bees thrumming in the hedges, bluebottles and flies buzzing over rugs of dung on the shimmering Tarmac.

I watch as two cabbage moths alight on the same white

blossom and fight gently for possession. This is the life, I think, and start on my own lunch, a packet of sweet Thai chilli crisps. I should give up the hurly-burly, OHPC and all who sail in her, in favour of my garden, plus-fours, walking-boots and a pair of nice Labradors.

I pick up the Ordnance Survey map spread out on the passenger seat. Whitecliff, marked and named in the centre of a dense, spidery network of roads and small fields near and around it, is at the edge of a townland called Maghcolla. The problem is, I don't know where I am now – I might be within a hundred yards of the entrance, I might be four miles away. Maybe I should go back to Rathlinney, where I'd stopped for petrol, and start again.

I hadn't been to Rathlinney village for a few years. It is, or was, one of those little places off the beaten track that you'd never pass through if you were travelling from A to B, if you get my meaning. You'd have to want to go to it.

Although OHPC hadn't been involved in any new developments there, I knew that, like most of the small settlements in Fingal, it, too, had morphed into Commuterland, but driving in, I was startled at the extent and scale of the changes since last I'd seen it. From what used to be rich grazing land, it is now besieged by acres of sprawling new estates, identical houses built in long, straight rows – because it's easier and cheaper for the builder to lay services that way rather than in curves. Rathlinney used to be a sleepy, one-donkey place, and 'besieged' might be the wrong word to use in the context of its new residents because this village sure has embraced change. As well as a new school, it now boasts a florist, coffee shop, Montessori crèche and tarted-up post office.

As for the shop, which used to Rathlinney General Stores

– I think, although I couldn't swear to it – its expansion was staggering.

In my memory it had been one of those old-fashioned sell-all places with a single petrol pump, a yard at the back, and displays of galvanised buckets, Wellingtons and enamel dishes alongside the groceries and drawers labelled 'Women's Knickers OS' in its dark brown interior. Today, from its pastel, modern interior, I could have brought home not only staples for my larder but cash from an ATM, a newspaper or magazine, a greetings card for any occasion, hot coffee, a complete fried breakfast, 'continental' breads, a bottle of wine from my favourite region. I could even have rented a DVD. What the original owners would make of it I cannot imagine.

I throw my head back and tip the crisps bag upside-down to funnel the last crumbs into my mouth. If I hadn't done so, I might have missed the way into Whitecliff. Because a few crumbs have fallen on to the shoulder of my jacket, and when I turn to brush them off, something pale catches my eye. An old notice on its back in the ditch, half buried in vegetation.

Private Lands.
No Thoroughfare.
No Trespassers.

I'd been beside it all the time!

Upright, the sign might once have been forbidding; lying on its back on a mound of nettles and scutch, it whispers something about how the mighty have fallen, not least because the thoroughfare in question is now a shadowy tunnel. Floored with a lumpy grass track, it is pocked and puddled even on this warm, dry day. By the look of it, no vehicle has passed along it for many years, and without a machete gang travelling in front of it to cut back the long, trailing brambles, I don't want to risk my car's paintwork.

I grab the map again, trace inland from the house and discover, if I'm right and this is the way in to Whitecliff, the track is short, maybe less than half a mile.

Nothing for it but shanks's mare. I take my notebook, make sure the camera is in my handbag, secure the car and plunge in. The things I do for Tommy O'Hare! Within two minutes I have a painful scratch to the side of my face and my leather-soled boots are slipping and sliding on wet moss, and slime of other types that I do not care to think about.

When I come back into the merciful light, across from me, less than ten yards away, I see a pair of lopsided, rusted iron gates between two stone pillars, spattered with yellow lichen. They are secured by heavy chains, locked together with a huge, newish-looking padlock. To the right and left of the pillars are the remains of what must have been an impressive boundary wall. Lots of it has fallen but in places it is still about two metres high.

The house is not visible but, then, I didn't expect it to be. I had always seen it from beneath the cliff and the topography lines on the Ordnance Survey map show a rise in the landscape to its front.

I walk over to the gates. Affixed to them is a notice:

TRESPASSERS WILL BE

Some wag had aerosoled out the next word and substituted

## NEVER FOUND.

I have to smile. There might once have been a double-width driveway leading from these gates but it's in evidence now merely as an overgrown track in imminent danger of extinction by a pincer movement of thick, thorny bramble, broken here and there by crowns of bright yellow furze or a windblown tree. How am I going to get to the house? For the sake of it, I give the heavy chains on the gates an experimental rattle but, as I'd expected, they don't give way.

I set off along the perimeter wall, stopping at every gap to see if there is a possible way through. Whoever owns this place must make at least some attempt from time to time to check its condition. And if, as Tommy says, the owner lives in the West of Ireland, wouldn't he pay someone up here to keep an eye? Well, if he does, he's being taken for a ride, I think, as I trudge along the wall for maybe half a mile – ten or eleven minutes anyway – with no success in finding an entry point.

At one of the bigger tumbledown gaps, beyond which the bramble barrier seems more formidable than ever, I decide I've had enough. Maybe I could try again another day by approaching from across the cliff. I put my notebook on one of the fallen stones, then pull out my mobile to call Tommy.

It is fresher than it was in the labyrinth of little roads that led me here but it's still very quiet and the pinging of the mobile's buttons is loud.

Tommy's goes straight to voicemail. 'Hello, this is me—' I begin, but then I get such a shock that I drop both notebook and phone, which disintegrates on impact – phone, battery, battery cover – but its fall is cushioned by the thick moss that covers most of the stones.

A man has appeared, just inches away. He has materialised out of the metre-thick mat of brambles.

His chin is stubbled, his thick hair, although short, is uncombed and his clothes are in shreds. His trousers are held up with a frayed piece of blue rope, the kind you see on the quays of fishing harbours. He is old, at least I think he is: his face is as lined as my map. That gives me comfort but then I notice that, within their wrinkled framework, his eyes, a faded sailor's blue, are fully alert. He is carrying a slash hook.

We stare at each other.

I want to run as fast as I can but calculate that, old as he is, he is tall, straight and wiry and could probably run faster than I. 'You gave me a terrible fright.' I don't recognise my voice.

'Who're you?'

'My name is Claudine Armstrong. I'm – I'm a tourist.' Did that slash hook just twitch in his hand? 'I – I was out for a walk and came across this wall. I was just wondering where it led. How do you do?' I hold out my hand to shake his. He ignores it. He's frowning.

'Are you new from the social? Where's the other one?' It's a beat before I realise what he's on about. 'No. I've nothing to do with Social Welfare.'

'What's this for, then?' With his free hand he picks up my notebook and brandishes it. 'If you're from the social, tell them I'm all right. All I want is to be left alone. I'm as healthy as a trout.' He's still looking at me very strangely – as if assessing, even interviewing me.

Ah, the hell with it, I think, this is ridiculous. 'I assure you

I've no intention of disturbing you.' I hope I sound author-itative, even bossy. 'I'm sorry if I have. And could I have my notebook back, please?' I hold out my hand.

He cocks his head to one side, still studying me. It's a stand-off.

'Check through it, if you like. You'll find what's in it has nothing to do with Social Welfare. Or anything official.'

'What are you doing here, so?'

'I told you. I'm just a—'

'I don't believe you.'

'That's not my problem, Mr . . .'

He lowers the notebook a little. 'You're a good-looking woman. D'you know that?'

This is surreal but I'm no longer frightened. 'Could I please have my notebook?'

Instead of giving me back my property, the man turns on his heel and, using the curved, non-lethal side of the slash hook, beats at the brambles nearest to him. Astonishingly, they fall aside for a few moments to reveal a narrow pathway, wide enough for one person. It has been so cunningly camouflaged that no one could ever have found it except by accident.

He tucks the notebook inside his ancient jacket. 'Would you like a cup of tea? Pick up that oul' phone yoke there and follow me.' He surveys me up and down. 'You needn't look so worried. Sure can't you ring 999?' and he laughs, showing an intact set of teeth.

A cup of tea? This is more than surreal, it's off the planet – and I'm torn between running for my life from this lunatic and my roaring curiosity. Curiosity wins. Anyhow, I can't abandon my priceless OHPC notebook filled with client phone numbers and vital information on various properties, not to speak of my exquisite marketing prose. 'Thank you. That would be lovely.' I try to smile as I gather up the pieces of my mobile.

'Ready?' He turns so his back is to me. 'Stay close or you'll get a fair scratching.' He watches over his shoulder, waiting until, making an act of faith, I come right up behind him and am mere inches from his back. Where the pungency of his jacket overcomes even the sharp scent of the bracken. Then, with him as majordomo swinging his slash hook right and left, me trying not to step on his heels, we make a poor man's marching band as we progress jerkily towards where the house should be.

## 7

## THE HAWTHORN TREE

I met Coley Quinn in the early afternoon of Friday, 17 March 1944, St Patrick's Day.

After breakfast and church, Mother took to her room, Johanna went to a neighbour's house to visit a former school-friend who had come home from Dublin for the day and Father, taking advantage of the rare free weekday, shut himself into the dining room to do some paperwork.

Having left national school in July of the previous year, I had been travelling since September to Balbriggan to study French, Latin, English literature and geography at the private school that had educated Johanna and Marjorie before me. Reports on me from the Misses Biggs, my teachers, were favourable, and Father had told me that if I continued to progress at my present rate, he would consider sending me to France for a year when the war was over to enhance my fluency in the language.

I was thrilled with this, but it was only March and in the meantime I was not at ease in Whitecliff. The house seemed bigger than ever, with no one but my dearest Johanna for company, apart from Mother and Father: Marjorie was living in Dublin, the twins were in the north for a few days' holiday at Uncle Samuel's house before reporting to the army for training and Young Samuel was also in Dublin, studying at Trinity College.

In particular I found mealtimes excruciating, since my poor sister, a quiet, shy person, had always struggled with general conversation and since Father had taken to reading his newspaper while he ate.

The first time this happened, Mother had been taken aback: 'Roderick, surely you know that it is not done to read at table?'

He had lowered his newspaper and said, in tones of icy tolerance, 'Perhaps not, Fly. But when one of you women introduces a topic of conversation that interests me, I will reconsider.' She had flushed, but from then on had focused on me. I, however, frequently ran out of replies to her desultory enquiries about my studies so our meals were taken mostly in silence, punctuated by the tiny polite noises of cutlery on china.

With Johanna missing that St Patrick's Day, the house was quieter than ever. In my own room I tried to write some geography exercises for school but could not concentrate. Perhaps it was that the economic decline of the tin mines in Cornwall was of little interest to me but it was more than that: it was the atmosphere. The day stretched ahead of me like a dreary brown bog. These feelings of dissatisfaction and restlessness had been occurring with some frequency. I found them difficult to overcome.

That afternoon, I gave up the struggle with the tin mines, threw aside my exercise books and, after a futile attempt to write to the twins – what cheery news could I give them from this strangled house? – went downstairs to the drawing room in search of a novel I had not yet read or some other reading matter. Once there, though, my gaze was drawn to the light outside and I went to sit in one of the window-seats. Hugging my knees, I looked out at our 'crowd', our 'host of golden daffodils'. Planted by some forebear many years ago, they had long ago naturalised under the beeches and stretched right to the gates along both sides of our curving avenue, bobbing and chatting like a merry guard of honour awaiting the arrival of an important visitor.

In front of me, two sparrows pecked busily at the gravel outside the windows. Yes, they had short lives but at least, unlike me, they were at liberty. I was sixteen now and should not only be allowed the freedom but also given the respect to make my own decisions. It was neither fair nor just that I should be buried in this – I struggled for an apt descrip-tion – this living sepulchre.

I looked around the drawing room, penetrated by the early spring sunshine, which was not kind to the furnishings and accoutrements that, except when Matthew had lain here in his whiteness, had stood since time immemorial in exactly the same spots. Everything seemed shabby, even when it was contrasted with the simplicity of the old-fashioned classroom at the Misses Biggs's. As for the books: they were more than shabby. They were dead. I had read everything I wanted to read from that selection.

Yet I had to find something constructive to do for the afternoon because if Father or Mother found me idling I would be put to work again on the family opus, this year's Shine Quilt.

In other years, I had toiled without a murmur of protest

on it but now I chafed against my enforced contribution to the fête run by our parish each July, and not to be cancelled because of a mere war. Our family donation had always been a patchwork quilt for raffle; Mother's stitching was exquisite, the patterns different each year, so the raffle was one of the highlights of the fête and always well supported. However, at Christmas, Mother had caught a chill that she could not shake off and this year had sought more assistance than usual from Johanna and myself.

Even here I was treated unfairly. While my sister was allowed to help with the substantive work of sewing the patches to the pattern Mother had drawn on a piece of butcher paper, my task was to use a running stitch to back each one with pieces of cotton cut from old sheets. Patch after patch after repetitious, tedious patch.

I made a quick decision. I was not going to spend our national holiday stitching a quilt, however worthy the cause, so I ran back upstairs, put on my woollen coat and gloves, then wound a scarf round my head. I was going out. Somewhere. Anywhere.

I knocked on the door of the dining room and, without waiting for invitation, popped my head round it: 'I'm going out for a walk, Father.'

He did not look up from his spread of ledgers and invoices. 'Don't go far, Violet.'

'Don't worry, Father, I'll stroll along the cliff. I might go down to the beach. I could do with some fresh air. I have a headache.' This was a white lie.

'Very well, very well.' He removed his spectacles to rub his eyes, and I noticed that he seemed older than he was and, for the first time ever, that his big hands were stained and rough. This was not from the shop, although I suppose his work there had contributed: had he not inherited the business, Father might have been a craftsman. He loved joinery – and, indeed, performed many of the repairs around the house; he would have made a good living as a cabinet-maker and, as time permitted, shut himself up in one of the outhouses with his lathe and planing table, producing on one occasion a hall bench fashioned from an old yew felled by a storm in the church graveyard. It took pride of place inside our front door and was much admired by visitors, rare though they were. 'Don't be too long. Your mother might need attention,' he said now, and as he continued to rub his eyes, I noticed also that his shoulders had become stooped. The combination of these indications of ageing, even weakening, shocked me. Although my parents continued to order my life, I rarely saw either of them as persons in their own right.

'Be careful going down those steps to the beach,' he continued. 'They're worn and becoming dangerous. I shall have to get them seen to one of these days. More money! I'll end up in the workhouse – you'll see.' He sighed, put his glasses back on and bent again over his papers.

A big man, well over six feet tall with a physique to match, Father rarely betrayed any vulnerability, certainly not in front of his family. As I saw him pore over the columns of figures, however, I felt sorry for him. Perhaps, I thought tenderly, I should offer to help him with his calculations. 'Father . . .'

With a backhanded wave, he flicked dismissal at me. The gesture stifled the tenderness so thoroughly that, as I stared at the back of his large white head, I had to suppress the startling urge to put out my tongue at him. Or to announce that I was running away to join a harem in Morocco. Of course,

I did neither. 'I should be back in less than an hour,' I said.

Outside, under the whistling wind, the surface of the sea glittered hard with sun-diamonds, beautiful but cold. So, instead of venturing down to the beach, I set off along the cliff, holding the collar of my coat to my chin with gloved hands. The gale tore at my headscarf and it became too much trouble to hold it on so I untied it, stuffed it into my pocket and invited the wind to do its worst.

When I came to the limit of our land, a barbed-wire fence running along the northern line of the sea field, as we called it, I had been buffeted so much that I was out of breath; my hair had come loose from its braid and was whipping against my face. But I had been out for only twenty minutes and was reluctant to go back so soon. I pulled my collar tighter and lingered for a few moments in the corner of the field to watch a pair of small fishing-boats not far offshore. They were busy doing whatever fishing-boats did at sea; I could make out the men working on deck, stick figures, bent double. Odd, I thought, that they should be out on St Patrick's Day, but then I remembered the wretched war and the food scarcities. They were probably fishing for their families.

My walk might have been of some physical benefit but had not improved my mood. Why should I feel so often out of sorts? Why could I not be grateful and accept the way we lived? Why could I not count my blessings, as Nanny had always urged when I was fretful? After all, I was more fortunate in a material sense than most other Irish girls, as Mother never ceased to point out, and far more fortunate in every way than the poor suffering girls caught up in the war in so many countries. I was pretty enough, or so I had been led to believe by Johanna and Nanny. Even Marjorie, when she was in a good mood, would hold my face up to the light and tell me I had been blessed with the best looks of the family.

The enumeration of my blessings was of no assistance now, though, and I felt like breaking into a fast run, to run and run and never stop until I arrived in London, Paris, Florence, or even New York. Not for the first time, I felt it was bad luck to have been born a girl in Ireland; I had read of Karen Blixen, Amelia Earhart, even Florence Nightingale, but none of them was Irish. None of them had had to live in a huge, gloomy house like Whitecliff, or if they had, they had found the gumption to escape. None of them had had to live in a country where the number of books, even Irish books, on the banned list grew and grew, or had to watch jumpy films because the kissing had been cut out. None of them had had to live in a country that this very month had been sealed off from the outside world by a blockade of our ports. This was because of our continuing neutrality and now we were not allowed to travel even to England. Father had warned Johanna and me that, in conversation with locals, we should never, but never, bring up the subject of the twins having signed up for the British Army: 'You would never know what reaction they might have,' he said. 'We must be prudent. It is not only for political reasons. After all, we depend on their custom.'

It occurred to me that everyone in the district already knew about Thomas and James joining up; it was hard to keep a secret in Maghcolla but I did not argue. My arguments would have been dismissed – unlike Young Samuel's, for instance.

Yes, to be a girl in this country was a distinct disadvantage. Unlike boys, who could make their own decisions and set out to see the world if they felt so inclined, we girls had to fill in time, however mundanely, until some man came along. What lay ahead for me between now and when I got married? On no account did I want to become an unpaid housekeeper, like Johanna.

Since Nanny had left us, I had had no one with whom to discuss these sentiments. Johanna was a lovely, gentle person but it would not have been kind to confide in her. It would have made her anxious about me. More than that, she would have been fearful I might be about to do or say something that would disturb the equilibrium of the household. To Johanna, a calm environment, whether natural or assumed, was all.

I might have talked to Marjorie, who had become far worldlier since her move to Dublin for her secretarial course, but I rarely saw her now. Her visits home had become infrequent because, I suspected, she was having such a good time with new friends.

I had never been good at making friends. In the national school, the other girls were either standoffish – in awe of our position in the community – or cruel, teasing me and pulling my hair when the teacher was not looking. They taunted me that I was too ladylike to get my hands dirty or even to put them in water. As well as mocking my accent they jibed about the words I used: 'Look who swallowed a diction'ry, look who swallowed a diction'ry,' was the jeering chant in the school playground if I used a word of more than two syllables. Although I was quick at lessons and almost always knew the answers to the teacher's questions, I learned never to volunteer one by raising my hand: the worst sin of all in that school was to show off.

It was better for me with the Misses Biggs, but by the time I entered that academy, it was too late. The habit of reticence was ingrained, and although one or two of my new class-mates made small overtures, I tended to respond with some-thing inappropriate or inane. As a result, I knew – or suspected – that, behind my back, these girls, too, laughed at me. But whether they did so or not it was irrelevant, because the more I desired to make friends, the more tied up I became.

Out at sea, the fishermen had finished whatever they had been doing on deck and, trailing a tattered canopy of seag-ulls, set the boats on a parallel course. I watched them for a few minutes but became restless (again!) and, since there was nothing else of interest to see, decided I had no choice but to go home.

On turning, however, I was arrested by the sight of a tall, thin boy, a wilting cigarette hanging from the corner of his mouth, regarding me from the other side of the barbed wire. He was familiar: one of the boys from the village? However, I could not immediately place him. He had wiry, sandy hair, so unfashionably long that it brushed his collar, and his eyes were blue, but of a lighter shade than mine, with a fringe of pale lashes.

His gaze was insolent.

'What are you doing here?' I blurted, before realising that the boy was on the far side of the wire and therefore not on our land. I had lived up to my lady-of-the-manor reputation. He gave me no time to recover or apologise but shot back, 'I might ask' he pronounced it 'aks' 'you the same question.'

I was stung. 'I live here.'

'I know that. We take conacre from you. Nine and a half acres.' The boy pushed some of the hair off his forehead, exposing a prominent widow's peak. I placed him then: he was one of the Quinns from Rathlinney. I had met him a few times when he came with his father to pay the annual rent for the grazing land. Colour, like hot punch, rose from beneath the collar of my coat. 'I apologise. For a moment I forgot that this was our boundary.'

I had made things worse – the heat grew until it was a conflagration against my cheeks. I wanted one of those Cornish tin mines to open and swallow me but something about the boy's pale, unwavering gaze steadied me. I stuck out my hand. 'I was rude. Could we start again? I'm Violet Shine. You are?'

'I know who you are and where you live,' he interrupted me, and instead of taking my hand, removed the cigarette from his mouth and carefully extinguished it by running it along the side seam of his corduroy trousers. 'I have every right to be standing where I'm standing. This is not your field I'm in.'

I recovered my nerve. If I had been rude, he had been *very* rude. 'I know that.' I withdrew my hand. 'I have just said so, but perhaps you were not listening. I have apologised but it is obvious you do not have the manners to accept.'

Still holding the extinguished cigarette, he cocked his head to one side: 'You're forgiven, Violet Shine,' he said, so gravely and with such a penetrating look that I felt heat reignite at the base of my neck.

Just then – I thanked God for His benevolence – the wind blew vagrant strands of hair across my face. I used both hands to uncover it and saw that the boy was smiling. 'It's a windy day, Violet Shine,' he said. Then: 'Since you've given me your name, my name is Coley Quinn.'

# 8

# THE TIN MINES OF CORNWALL

Coley, Coley, Coley Quinn – Coley, Coley, Coley!
I no longer resented being a girl and, far from feeling gloomy and restless, I felt so energetic and alive that in the classroom at the academy I could not keep still in my seat.

Classes run by the Misses Biggs were to finish for Easter on the final Friday in March and, revising for our spring examinations, we were once again dissecting the decline of the wretched tin mines but instead of boring me (Boring? Mines?) the subject caught every fibre of my imagination – I could single-handedly have reinvigorated Cornish tin-mining. No matter how atrocious the weather conditions, I would work my hands to the bone at the head of my mine as one of the bal-maidens who sorted the ore brought up by the boys and men.

Better yet, I would be the first girl miner in the industry. Caring not a fig for my own safety, I would go down those stinking, suffocating shafts to the deepest and most inhospitable caverns and extract every last tumbler of cassiterite that contained the metal. I would wade waist deep in water to find new deposits and, despite the suffocating 100-degree heat, would exhort my fellow miners to keep up their courage so that we could resurrect the economic fortunes of tin. When my efforts bore fruit, I would be a Cornish heroine. People would put up statues of me in their town squares.

I would be modest, of course, refusing a royal offer of a title. In the front courtyard of Buckingham Palace (to where, through cheering Cornish crowds, I had been carried by relays of brawny miners in a white silk palanquin), I would curtsy to those people's king. As the wind blew the hair off my fetchingly tanned face, not willy-nilly in thick, unflattering strings but in a perfect halo, I would curtsy. 'No, thank you, Your Majesty. While I am overcome with gratitude at the honour you propose, and came here to tell you so in person, I am but a simple Irish girl and we are a republic. I have been happy to assist in the economic recovery of the tin mines of Cornwall but the deed was sufficient unto itself. I am affianced to an Irishman. After our marriage, we intend to rear our children to love and cherish our Irish nation, so what you propose, I'm afraid, is out of the question.'

Then the king, admiring more than ever my spunk and selfless philanthropy, would turn to his nearest courtier: 'Zounds! What a girl!'

'Violet! Violet! Violet Shine!' Miss Sarah Biggs cut crossly into my reverie. 'Please pay attention!'

'Sorry, Miss Biggs.' I was back in our green and beige class-room. It was raining outside and my seat companion was shaking our desk with her energetic use of an india-rubber to erase a mistake she had made in mapping the mines. Miss Biggs, not mollified by my contrition, was wearing her sternest expression. 'You must know so much, Violet Shine, that you obviously see no reason to learn any more. Therefore would you give us the benefit of your knowledge and enlighten the class as to the meaning of the word "allotrope" as it applies to tin?'

'Of course, Miss Biggs. Allotrope is any of two or more physical forms in which an element can exist. Tin is an allotrope of cassiterite.' I could have sung it. I was whizzing through my exercises at night. Love, it seemed, had enlarged my brain as well as my heart.

Miss Biggs, or Bumpy, as we called her behind her back, because of her unfortunate complexion, peered at me. I could see she was surprised but she did not give up. 'Very good, Violet, but you could have learned it by heart from any book. Another example, please. A practical one.'

'A diamond and a piece of graphite are both allotropes of carbon.'

'I am impressed.' She looked disappointed.

Half an hour later, we had English literature with the other Miss Biggs, Lucy, a quieter, gentler version of her sister. Having been told to read Emily Brontë's *Wuthering Heights* we were now discussing the author's style and narrative technique.

With my newfound insights into love, however, I found that our teacher's concentration on structure and format, her embarrassed skittering across the depth of passion between Catherine and Heathcliff, made a travesty of the book. So when my turn came to read aloud a passage, the one concerning Heathcliff's admissions to the housekeeper of his attempt to disinter Cathy from her grave, I invested the performance with such energy and drama that Miss Biggs was astonished. 'My goodness, Violet, that was excellent! In fact, I have never heard you so animated.'

'Thank you, Miss Biggs.' I smirked and, amid an amazed

silence from the other girls in my class, resumed my seat. Miss Biggs looked around: 'It is not often we are so entertained. I think we should ask Violet to read some more, girls.'

There came a ragged chorus of 'Yes,' so I stood again. The teacher ran her finger down the open page, then looked up: 'Ah. Here it is, Violet. Why not give us the paragraph, further down that section, where Heathcliff describes the feelings that never leave him? Start with "When I sat in the house with Hareton".'

'Thank you, Miss Biggs.' I took a deep breath and 'felt' myself into the passage, using the onomatopoeic battering of the rain against the classroom's rattling sash windows to underpin the drama: '"When I sat in the house with Hareton, it seemed that on going out, I should meet her; when I walked on the moors I should meet her coming in. When I went from home, I hastened to return, she must be somewhere at the Heights; I was certain! And when I slept in her chamber – I was beaten out of that – I couldn't lie there; for the moment I closed my eyes, she was either outside the window, or sliding back the panels, or entering the room, or even resting her darling head on the same pillow as she did when a child. And I must open my lids to see. And so I opened and closed them a hundred times a night – to be always disap-pointed! It racked me!"'

'Thank you, thank you, Violet,' Miss Biggs cut in – rather hastily, I thought, for, understanding how the poor man felt, I was just getting into my stride.

Having thanked me again and told me I could sit, our teacher turned to the blackboard. 'Now, girls, with Emily Brontë's text and Violet's splendid interpretation of it, I think we have learned enough for tonight's composition topic.' Then she wrote, in her looping, flowing script, '*Did Heathcliff's behaviour after Cathy's death demonstrate a descent into madness?* Discuss.'

As I said: a travesty.

That class was the last of the day, and as we congregated under our umbrellas by the bus stop afterwards to go our various ways, I saw, or thought I saw, new respect in the eyes of my classmates. 'The way you read was extraordinary. Did you prepare? Did you, perhaps, have some training in reading aloud, Violet?' This, jealously, was from the girl who always came top of the class in examinations.

'Oh, leave her alone, Mary Quigley!' Mary Kelly snapped at the Brainbox, then turned to me, smiling sweetly: 'Would you like to come to tea some evening, Violet?' Mary Kelly was a dunce but very beautiful, and because she had three older brothers, an invitation to tea at her house was much in demand. This was my first.

'Thank you. That would be lovely, Mary.' I smirked sideways at the Brainbox. I had become a serial smirker. I was no longer shy. I was in danger of becoming popular too.

'Terrific, Violet.' Mary smiled her gorgeous, Barbara Stanwyck smile at me. 'That will be peachy.' Mary Kelly went to the cinema regularly and her speech was peppered with such words. 'My family and I are going to Wexford for Easter, Violet,' she added, 'but I'll write to you and we'll make an arrangement.'

As events unfolded, her invitation, if it ever came, was one I could not fulfil.

That first meeting with Coley Quinn had resulted in a deliberately casual agreement to meet again at the same spot. 'I like talking to you, Violet Shine. Could we do it again some time, d'you think?' he asked. 'How about Sunday?'

I had little fear of being refused the opportunity to go for another walk on a Sunday so had no hesitation in agreeing. 'That would be lovely.'

'Grand.'

'Yes.'

'I'll see you Sunday.'

'Yes.'

'Sunday.'

'Goodbye . . .' Yet we lingered and talked some more. So much so that I miscalculated the time and was almost discovered by Mother when, panting and dishevelled, I attempted to slip back into Whitecliff via the back door. She was in the pantry off our kitchen, where we kept food and the larger, more unwieldy pots and pans. As I pushed open the door, she dropped a pan with a loud clatter and did not hear me enter, so I was able to close the door again and wait outside, peeping through the window, until I saw her leave. Fate was with me that day. Or perhaps not. Although it was two floors below, the window where I waited beside the back door lay under that of the tower room.

That first evening, the evening of St Patrick's Day, Johanna, who knew me best, asked me more than once if I was sure I was not sickening for something, and as I bade him good-night, even Father took note of the rosiness in my cheeks. 'You look as though you have a fever, Violet. Are you well in yourself?'

'I am very well, thank you, Father.'

'I hope you are not worried about your examinations?'

'Not at all, Father. I have worked hard and am quite confi-dent. Thank you for asking.'

He had been right to ask. I was suffering from a fever of

sorts – a giddy heat in the blood, which was to continue throughout my association with Coley.

Our second meeting on the Sunday was, as you might expect, quite complicated from my perspective. In my imagination, I had invested it with such theatricality – would we kiss? – that I felt I was in danger of bursting with excitement and nervousness. What if he did not come?

My brain buzzed, my whole body frothed impatiently, yet I had to sit quietly during Sunday luncheon and feign interest in the local tittle-tattle Nanny brought to the table on one of her Sunday visits: since retiring from our service, she was occasionally invited to join us. To avoid attracting attention, I ate everything on my plate, even forcing myself to swallow the leeks I detested.

There was one dangerous moment. Lost in my imagination, I was chewing steadily when I realised there was a lull in the conversation. Everyone was looking at me.

'Nanny asked you a question, Violet.' From his place at the head of the table, Father was frowning at me. I glanced at Johanna, but she widened her eyes, indicating that she could not help.

'I'm sorry, Nanny.' I made myself sound humble. 'I was thinking about something.'

'She's been like this for the last few days, Nanny.' Mother clucked. 'The sky could fall and Violet wouldn't notice. What shall we do with her?'

'Oh, she's a young 'un.' Nanny smiled at me. 'You must remember what it was like to be young yourself, ma'am.' In all the years she worked for our family, Nanny had never called Mother anything else. 'Don't worry, lovey,' she said to me then. 'I was only asking after your lessons.'

I rushed to reassure her, and everyone else at the table, that my lessons were peachy. They raised their eyebrows at each other but let the slang go uncorrected.

Coffee – we used a wartime substitute, roasted chicory or Irel – was always taken in the conservatory, even in winter, and thank goodness I was still judged too young for it. So as usual, having helped Johanna clear the table, I was excused. 'If you don't mind, Mother, I have some exercises to do but later this afternoon I think I'll go for a walk.'

'Good, good.' Mother waved me away. I kissed Nanny's good cheek and made my escape.

Coley and I were to meet at the same little windblown tree in the sea field, on our side of the fence this time, at four o'clock. I should not be missed from the house if I got back before supper at six thirty. So we would have two hours.

He was waiting for me, crouching in the grass, one hand cupping the stub of a lit cigarette. 'Are you sure I'm allowed on this side of the wire?' His expression was cheeky, yet I could see he was as nervous as I.

'Of course! Please don't start that again ...' Should I remain standing, or sit beside him? If I did, wouldn't I get grass stains on my good coat, or even my skirt, and then Mother or someone else in the house would know that I'd been up to no good? I had dressed with supreme care that morning, putting on and discarding outfit after outfit – Johanna was scandalised when she came to see why I was keeping everyone late for church. 'For goodness' sake, Violet dear! Your bed looks like the nearly-new stall at a jumble sale!'

As I dithered under the hawthorn tree, Coley reached up and grabbed my hand. 'Take the weight off. We're not looking to attract attention, are we?' He pulled me down beside him.

Although the tree sheltered us from the stiff north-east breeze, the ground was cold. But I felt no discomfort. Neither did I care a whit any longer for stains: I would deal with that problem when and if it arose.

Although there was at least a foot between us, I could feel the warmth of Coley Quinn's body, like heat reflected from a mirror, against my own. 'I'll have to be back before the blackout,' I blurted, 'but half past six should be plenty of time.'

'That's grand.' Coley busied himself with making one of his little cigarettes. 'Sure we've plenty of time so.'

My experience of interaction between the sexes was based entirely on books or the occasional visit to the cinema so nothing had prepared me for the storm of feelings that were now unleashed. Playing with my brothers had been no help either. I had no idea what to say or do next.

Coley, on the other hand, seemed to know exactly how to behave. He lay back on one elbow as if he was on a beach or beside a Hollywood swimming-pool and, pulling on his little cigarette until there was nothing left of it, embarked on a long story about someone he knew in the village who had been arrested for stealing money from the poor-box in the Catholic church and put away for five years.

I listened while not listening at all. I was watching Coley's lips as he talked and smoked: the way they swelled and tightened round the butt, then pursed to blow out the smoke; I was watching the way the skin round his eyes creased when he squinted into the sun; as he gesticulated, I was watching the unexpected delicacy of his long, nicotine-stained fingers. Nanny, not to speak of Mother and Father, would have been appalled to see them. No one in our house smoked. The idea was unimaginable.

'So, Violet Shine, what do you think of that, eh?' Coley
finished his story and peered up at me. I had remained primly
upright. My back was beginning to ache. 'Five years in gaol,'
he continued, 'for someone who, you could say, needed that
money a lot more than some of the so-called needy in this
parish. Do you people have a poor-box in your church?'

'I – I think so. I'm not sure.' It had never occurred to me.
'We people' were charitable in other ways, I supposed. 'We
have a parish collection and a fête. Does that count?'

'Dunno.' He shrugged. 'So what'll we talk about next?' He
sat up and turned so that we were face to face. 'Tell me about
your family.'

Although I searched his face, I could see no hint of irony
or sarcasm. 'I thought you knew all about us?'

'Only what I hear in Rathlinney creamery.' Now his accent
coarsened considerably: 'I heard that yiz eat off of gold-
rimmed plates. And that yiz eat partridges from yeer pear
trees.' His cheeks had crinkled.

'We eat exactly the same as you do,' I retorted. 'At least, I
think we do. Does your family shop at Rathlinney General
Stores?'

'We have our own vegetables,' he acknowledged, 'but other
than that . . .' He was staring at me openly now.

A strange thing happened: I saw myself through his eyes.
I saw my box-pleated blue sateen dress with the white belt,
cuffs and collar, my black T-bar shoes and 'good' stockings
(they were lisle, but transparent – silk and nylon was impossible to get during those years), my apple-green shawl, a
Christmas present from Mother, knitted in a complex basket-
weave pattern from two different grades of wool.

Let me deviate to describe what the mirror in general

reflected. I was a girl of slim build and above middling height, and at that time was of sufficient vanity to believe my eyes quite fine: they were, I fancied, larger than average and of a very dark blue. I also boasted good, well-shaped ankles. I was not so proud of my nose or mouth. I thought the former too snub and the latter too wide and full. That Sunday, however, watching myself through Coley's eyes, I feared his scrutiny of me was critical. I put my hand to my hair. 'Is there something wrong? My hair . . .'

Slowly he shook his head. 'Do you ever let it loose?'

Dark, almost black, and very curly, the despair of Nanny who had had to wrestle with it when I was little, my hair was as usual confined to a heavy plait. Johanna had hair like Mother's, fine and fair, but Marjorie and I had inherited Father's, which, had he not kept it cropped, would have made his already large head seem even larger. Today I had taken particular pains to confine every single unruly strand. 'Let it loose? S-sometimes,' I stuttered.

'It's satiny, like a horse. Can I touch it?'

My heart did something in my chest, an up-and-down swoop, then wheeled and yawed. 'All right.'

Coley Quinn did more than touch my hair. He asked me to turn my back to him, then unbraided it, taking his time, smoothing each strand as it came free. The sensations running across my skin were indescribable: I felt as if my whole body was being dipped alternately in warm and cold water. I think I began to tremble.

When I was all undone, Coley Quinn turned me round to face him, reached both hands round to the back of my neck and, using his spread fingers, lifted the hair off it. I felt helpless, unable to resist and bent my head forward to accommodate him. 'It's so beautiful,' he said huskily, letting the hair cascade round my shoulders. 'You're lucky, Violet Shine. Half the women in the country are spending their husbands' hard-earned wages on crimping and marcel waves.' His voice cracked, and before I could guess what was to come next, he let go my hair, placed a hand gently on my breast, then kissed my mouth and my life changed for ever.

# 9

## LILIES-OF-THE-VALLEY

'Claudine? Sure what kind of a name is Claudine? Is it French or what?'

'Yeah. My mother died when I was born and it had been her choice.' The old man is watching me with sharp eyes, expecting more, but I'm at a loss for what to say next. Yet for the second time today I'm engulfed by sadness. This time it's accompanied by a vision of her dying while I'm being born. I clear my throat. 'That's what Daddy said anyway. Obviously I never had a chance to ask her.'

My host, who had said I should call him Pat 'because that's what they called me across the water when I was working at the building', continues to watch me for a few seconds longer. Then, seeing something that warns him not to press on with this line, he continues to minister to his Volcano Kettle. I've never seen one of these until now. Made of tin and about two feet tall, it is a conical, double-hulled object – in effect, two cones, one inside the other with a gap between, surrounding a hollow core. I watch, fascinated, as, from an old milk can, he pours water into the compartment between the two hulls, then stuffs torn-up paper and a few little sticks into the hole at the centre. He leaves a flag of paper and one twig sticking out of the top. 'Stand back!' He strikes a match and touches it to the kindling.

Within seconds, there is a high flame and although he has placed the contraption on a low platform constructed from two planks laid across two little walls of brick, to me the blaze looks pretty dangerous. I can already hear the water surrounding it beginning to sing. 'Would you not be worried that some of that lit paper might blow into the bracken and start a fire?'

'I'm careful. Sit down there and take it easy.' He jerks a thumb towards a beat-up armchair covered with yellow fisherman's oilskins. 'This won't take long. I hope you don't take sugar. I don't keep it. It attracts insects.'

'But you've only one chair. Where'll you sit, Pat?'

In reply, he stomps across to what looks like a small, but tidy, personal dump and extracts three faded lifebelts; he lays them on top of one another, then straightens up. 'There y'are! Good for the piles, eh?' He laughs. He has a distinctive laugh, a startling dog-bark.

The handbag between my fingers feels reassuringly solid – this is not a dream or a fantasy. I am at present sitting in the open air with an old man who is making me tea but who has a slash hook.

Too late now to do a runner, though. I remove the oilskins and sit. The chair, though threadbare, is comfortable and while I continue to watch his deft, quiet movements I conduct a survey of what is evidently this man's home.

We're in a clearing, maybe seven metres by ten, surrounded by what in other circumstances might be called litter – black plastic sheeting from silage bales, driftwood, semi-rotting planks of all sizes and types, heaps of anonymous plastic bags, even a rusting fridge – but everything has a purpose. The silage plastic has been folded and stands in neat symmetrical piles under weights of rock, the bags are knotted at the neck and bulge with their contents, the wood is stacked according to size – some has been cut into logs.

Beside the Volcano platform a large barbecue grating has been laid across a fire pit. Beyond this is a home-made tent, a sort of tepee: less than three feet high, it consists of a tarpaulin, like those seen on soft-sided lorries, draped across a framework of branches, every inch of the skirt secured to the ground with a double row of large stones. The entry flaps are open, revealing a sleeping-bag on a ground sheet, an old-fashioned pastel print of an angel propped at the head.

At the side of the tent I can see a rough table, constructed from planks and held together with nails that have long ago rusted and stained the wood; around the fringes stand the rest of the household furnishings. A huge steamer trunk serves as a rudimentary toolshed. Stood on its end with its lid at right angles, it has been fitted with hooks and shelves, both in the body and lid, to hold saws, a hammer, an axe, a mallet and various boxes containing nails, screws and screwdrivers, baling twine, lengths of wire and some objects I can't name. Another piece of tarpaulin, at present rolled up, serves as the door.

Butted against it, a fridge, door wedged open with a brick, is the old man's larder-cum-cookstore and contains a frying-pan, a battered aluminium saucepan, three delft mugs, a bowl, two plates, a few pieces of cutlery in a jam jar, three can-openers in varying degrees of sophistication, beans in tomato sauce, sardines, long-life milk, tea-bags, a sliced pan, two tubs of Flora, apples, a large packet of cornflakes and a bunch of blackening bananas.

'You're impressed with my happy home?' Hunkered in front of the Volcano, he is decanting boiling water into a white china teapot decorated with lilies-of-the-valley and rimmed with gold. An unusual object, I think, in the context of everything else. 'I certainly am. And that's a lovely teapot by the way. Is it a family heirloom or something?'

Immediately I've said it I know I've dropped a clanger because he flicks me a stony glance. 'No.'

From now on I'll keep my mouth shut. This old guy doesn't want to reveal anything personal – if he did, though, there's got to be a lot there.

I clamp down on my inquisitiveness and watch while he places the teapot on the ground in front of me, 'Let that stew for a minute,' then sets us up, table, mugs, long-life milk, two spoons. 'Sorry I've no biscuits. I wasn't expecting visitors.' He sets himself on his little heap of lifebelts, picks up the teapot, swirls the contents, then pours an experimental few drops on to the ground. 'That'll do.'

As we drink, he sits in that position adopted by confident men: head low, knees far apart, free hand relaxed and dangling between them (I notice he has long, finely shaped fingers). He doesn't seem to need conversation but I do. 'This is very good tea. How long have you lived like this, Pat?'

'Oh, a good while. Since I came back from over.'

'Over in England, you mean?'

'Aye. London. Manchester. Coventry. At the buildin'.' His accent is local but there are echoes of urban England.

'So, why this place?'

'It's private,' he says, his tone indicating nothing. He might

78

have meant either his motives were private or the place was; I decide on the latter. 'I can see how nobody'd bother you here.'

'That's right.' He looks off into the distance. 'Nobody bothers me here.' He is at ease, balanced on his ridiculous cairn, and I remind myself why I'm here and, while I'm intrigued by the man, my purpose isn't to learn his history.

'Isn't it a lovely day, Pat?' The smell that the sun brings from the earth is dank yet sweet, almost musky, and unlike the dense silence in the boreens and laneways, the air vibrates to the song of a lark.

'It is, it is.' He's still looking away.

'So,' I take a mouthful of the cooling tea and then, deliberately casual, 'this house. Whitecliff. It's a pity it's been left to go to rack and ruin, isn't it? Who owns it these days?'

'Who owns it?' he repeats, looking at me again in that intense way of his. 'Damned if I know who owns it now.' He shrugs. 'Probably some fat-cat developer. But mebbe not. Mebbe nobody owns it.'

'Somebody has to own it. How long has it been derelict?'

'Haven't seen anyone next, nigh or near the place for years.' He shrugs again. 'This is the kind of place you hear stories about, the kind of oul' guff that people go on with. Frightens people off, I reckon.' He's gazing at me from under shaggy eyebrows.

'Stories? Oh, yeah – I have heard somewhere a story about the place. Something about a ghost, or it being haunted or something?'

We have another staring match. He breaks it: 'What was your name before you got married?'

This is such an unexpected twist that it throws me. 'How'd you know I'm married?'

He points at my wedding ring. 'Oh! Yes, of course. My name was Magennis.'

'Who was your father?'

'I beg your pardon?'

'His name!' He's impatient. 'What was his first name?'

'Christopher. Chris.'

He nods. 'Car dealer.' It isn't a question.

'How do you know that?'

'Sure everyone knew Chris Magennis. Magennis Motors, right? All the nobs in the county dealt with him. Now he's looking at the ground. What an odd man.'

'The people in this house here?'

'Might have. Can't be sure, mind, but I don't think so. They got theirs from the north, as far as I know. Kept 'em for years, ran 'em into the ground.' He looks up again. 'So, you're Chris Magennis's daughter. It's a small world, eh?'

'Sure is.' I'm disappointed I can't make this small connection with Whitecliff. It's time to go home, I think. I'll come back another day and approach the house a different way, the most likely route being via the cliff. 'Thank you for the tea,' I begin.

But he interrupts me: 'What's your interest in Whitecliff anyways?'

I don't underestimate this man. All right, he's a tramp living rough, but his eyes spark with intelligence. 'If you open my notebook, you'll see that I work for a property company. And before you get on your high horse, we're not fat cats. There's just my boss and me. We heard that this place might be coming on the market and he sent me to suss it out.'

He seems to consider this for a few seconds. Then, slowly,

80

still thinking, he empties the dregs from his mug on to the ground. 'You'll want to see the house.'

I almost drop my own mug. 'Do you have a key?'

He stands up. 'Come on. We don't have all day and it's going to rain.'

I look up at a brilliance of blue sky. But I mimic him, emptying what's left in my mug on to the earth.

# 10

# LOUGHSHINNY

It was the beginning of April 1944 and I was happy-hearted. School had risen for Easter; my duties in the house were light; Young Samuel was due home from Trinity for a visit and would divert much of the attention my parents currently paid to me.

I had done well in my spring examinations and, as far as Father and Mother were concerned, awaited only the end of the war to go to France. Of course, they did not know that the last thing on my mind was travel away from Whitecliff. With the blitheness of youth I dared hope that somehow our isolation from the rest of Europe would continue. This, of course, was tempered with guilt because of the twins. I loved my brothers, but during that period I'm afraid I thought about them very little. In fact, I thought about nothing and no one except Coley Quinn.

Through the latter half of that March I knew by the puzzled look her face showed from time to time that Johanna sensed something different about me. As usual, however, she kept her own counsel, for which I was grateful.

All over the townland, in the hedges and fields, hawthorn

trees sagged under an uncommonly early burden of creamy blossom. When I viewed it from one of our higher fields in Coley's company, the pattern of irregular green squares with white borders seemed magical. 'God's draughtboard', he called it, demonstrating what I knew, with every fibre of my heart: that this was no ordinary boy but someone possessed of fine sensibilities. While almost anything could in that period seem magical or significant to Coley and me, the people of Maghcolla did not share our views about the hawthorn. 'There's too much of that thorn blossom this year,' Nanny said, when she came to visit us on another Sunday. Then, shaking her head, 'And I never saw it come so early. No good will come of it.'

Perhaps it's different in these modern days, but at that time, thorn trees were associated with spirits, fairies, graves, pagan rituals; farmers who wished to plough their land would not dig up a solitary specimen, no matter how inconvenient or wasteful its location. Also, it was said that Christ's torturing crown had been woven from its branches so it was considered unlucky to bring the flowers indoors. Not that Mother paid any attention to that: she regarded it as Roman superstition and persisted in decorating our house with it whenever she felt so inclined. It was not until many years later that I discovered hawthorn was also associated with doomed lovers. If I had known this, perhaps Coley and I would not have chosen such a place under which to leave messages for one another and to snatch our meetings. At the time he and I cared little about ancient beliefs.

It was a continuing miracle to me that, in those weeks of late March and early April so far at least, my trysts, now almost daily, had not been discovered. Coley, it seemed, had little difficulty in accommodating my schedule. He was on short time at the creamery and his boss was generous with permissions to leave if he said he had to take time off to see to the family's cattle.

At home I, too, had invented a story, telling Father and Mother that the Misses Biggs had encouraged me to get more fresh air: they had noticed I was looking a little peaky. Father in particular was all for health and fitness so, after a little close scrutiny, neither parent queried why I had so suddenly and enthusiastically taken to the outdoors. In any event, they knew I could not go far. I had no money of my own for buses or hackneys and, anyhow, wartime fuel restrictions and shortages meant that transport was infrequent. So, as often as I could, I flew to our hawthorn as straight and fast as a swallow homing at dusk.

On the face of it, the location was ideal. The field in which our tree stood was at the time fallow and rarely inspected. It was right at the cliff's edge so we could observe anyone approaching from at least three sides, and because of the undulating lie of the land, it was hidden from Whitecliff.

That spring I neglected my food, even my prayers. By contrast, my diary lengthened to the size of a novella.

It was not a proper diary, with clasp and lock, but first one, then two, ordinary scholar's notebooks. I kept them hidden in the patch pocket of an old winter coat of Marjorie's, encased in a calico cover at the back of my wardrobe.

Coley, Coley, Coley Quinn, I wrote in this exercise book, repeating the name in varying script. Instead of conjugating French or Latin verbs, I fantasised about lace veils and vases of flowers in country churches, while printing: 'VIOLET QUINN', 'VIOLET JANE QUINN', 'VIOLET SHINE-QUINN', 'VIOLET

QUINN-SHINE' – or even 'VIOLET JANE SHINE-QUINN', which even I thought a little unwieldy.

I spent hours printing out the letters of our two names, crossing out those common to both, to play Love, Like, Hate, Adore, Kiss, Court, Marry. To achieve the desired outcome I cheated, of course, by manipulating them, adding my middle name or Coley's (which, to his embarrassment, was Norman), but nothing I could do would produce 'Marry'.

I could, however, achieve the next best thing. 'COLEY QUINN' printed above 'VIOLET JANE SHINE' showed that he Adored me and I Loved him; 'COLEY NORMAN QUINN' above 'VIOLET JANE SHINE' reversed this, with him Loving me, I Adoring him. Either was satisfactory because Loving and Adoring were two sides of the same face, were they not?

I was ecstatic at this outcome and, thinking myself on a par with the monks who had laboured over the Book of Kells, spent hours embellishing both sets of letters with little roses, daisies and other flowers of indeterminate species in differently coloured inks.

In the meantime I had to be careful that My Love, as I thought of it, was not discovered. So I acceded to every request of Father's and every command of Mother's and was determined, in the house at least, to be an exemplary daughter.

If I could keep it up, I felt, it was possible that during the run of the coming summer I would be trusted to go off alone from Whitecliff, even – although I thought this unlikely – to take a jaunt as far as the seaside resort of Bettystown. How Coley and I could enjoy ourselves in the sand dunes at the beach's northern tip! Even if Johanna and/or Young Samuel was sent to chaperone me, I dared to hope that either or both could be bribed to let me go off unaccompanied for an hour.

Johanna came unannounced into my room one evening and found me busy drawing hearts and arrows round Coley's name. I had been too absorbed to hear her knock or approach until she was behind me.

I hid the page with one hand then sprang to my feet to confront her. 'What are you doing, Johanna, sneaking up on me like that? This is my room. I will not have people spying on me!'

'I knocked, Violet.' Her eyes were wide, their expression troubled.

'You did not! Don't lie to me!'

'I did. Honestly I did.'

My bedroom overlooked the garden at the front of the house and the sun was setting in spectacular, rose-gold fashion that evening, gilding the little butterfly slide in my sister's long, straight hair. She always parted it to one side and kept it from falling over her face with one in a collection of these slides, a style that made her seem younger than her age. I threw my arms round her. 'I'm sorry. I'm sorry I shouted at you, Johanna.'

Instead of accepting my apology, though, she disentangled herself, then backed away to the door as if she was afraid I would hit her. 'Don't go.' I followed her. 'What did you want me for?'

'Nothing important. I forget now.'

'You startled me. That's all.'

She smiled, but as she left the room, her expression was still clouded. How much had she seen and understood? I had to have faith that she would not say anything to Mother and Father. I did have faith. I had faith that nothing in the cosmos could affect my sublime happiness. It had been ordained. It was bigger than any petty concerns of family.

Poor Johanna, I thought. I had begun to see my sister through the filter of a new, heightened sensitivity. At twenty-three, having finished her own education seven years previously, she had never expressed the desire to become a secretary or anything else and her life seemed dull to me. She helped with the shop accounts, but Mother considered it *infra dig* for her to serve behind the counter. So, when it was deemed no longer necessary for Nanny to be part of our household, many domestic duties had devolved on Johanna.

It seemed to me, therefore, that my sister's only hope of escape from Whitecliff was the emergence of a suitable husband. So, again from the lofty perspective of my sixteen years, I pitied her: I thought it hardly fair that she was forced by happenstance to live a Jane Austen life while My Love and I whirled around in one imagined by a Brontë.

Although, as yet, we had never declared it in words (and I doubted that Coley would have read the novel) the depth of Suppressed Passion between Catherine Earnshaw and her Heathcliff described to a T how he and I felt about each other. In fact, the novel was so accurate in this regard I found it difficult to believe it had been published in 1847, the olden times, almost a century before I had devoured it. Since I had discovered it through the Misses Biggs, I had read and reread my favourite passages until, even when the book was closed, they were distinguished from the rest by discoloration at the edges of the relevant pages.

Apart from the Breadth of Our Love, there were many striking similarities between the fictional story and ours. For instance, her disfigured face notwithstanding, it was not beyond imagining that loving, sensible Nanny had been the model for the empathetic housekeeper, Nelly Dean.

As for the pull of the moors on Catherine and Heathcliff, our flat, grassy landscape might look tame by comparison, but that was only to the superficial gaze. During a storm, when the spume and spray-laden gale rattled our windows and howled so that conversation at an ordinary level proved impossible, when waves ate up our shingle beach and crashed so powerfully against the cliff that the foundations of Whitecliff seemed to shake, I could well believe I was not living in Maghcolla townland but in the shadow of the high crags of North Yorkshire. My love for Coley had opened my eyes to the natural world and, as he and Catherine might say, much else besides.

When the Misses Biggs released us for the Easter holidays at one thirty on the last day of term, some of the other students, including my new friend Mary Kelly, had arranged to go to a film. I declined to join them and raced, not to the usual Balbriggan bus stop but to the next along the route, which, with a different bus, served Rush, Skerries and Loughshinny. Coley and I had planned an illicit jaunt.

I had not told Mother we were being let off earlier than usual that day and she would be expecting me home off the five o'clock bus as usual. So, Coley and I could have more than three glorious hours together. He had a bicycle and would take me home on his crossbar, letting me get off well away from our gate.

At that time Loughshinny was a tiny, tranquil harbour with a scattering of thatched cottages and a curved sandy beach. (It may still be. My visit there with Coley six decades ago was my last.)

He was already there when the bus let me off and I ran to him. We were acquainted with no one in that village, as far as I knew. And even if we were, so what? That day I felt invincible.

The afternoon was still, even at the water's edge where, holding hands, we walked and talked, accompanied by the lap-lap-lap against the shore of a single, recurring wavelet. The tide was ebbing and the only activity was on the harbour wall where a couple of men were tinkering with ropes, buoys and lobster pots.

It was fascinating to me how I could suddenly have so much to say, so many inner thoughts to express, about my own circumstances, the world and everything in it. I realised that, for the first time since we had met, we were behaving not with such nervous energy that the encounter left us exhausted but like friends as well as lovers.

We climbed up to a little plateau of sandy grass overlooking the beach, sat down to rest and I found myself telling him funny stories about the Misses Biggs, especially Bumpy, then this and that about my family. 'We expect Young Samuel to take honours in his degree—'

'That's his name? Young Samuel?' He raised an eyebrow.

'Well, it's really Samuel, but we have an Uncle Samuel so—'

'Do people call him "Young" for short?'

'Cheeky!' Playfully I hit him (or smote him, as Emily Brontë might say). 'This from a person whose family names all end in "ie" or "y" – what is it now? Coley, Bridgie, Ginnie, Florrie, Millie? And what's your mother's name again?' Like me the youngest in his family, Coley had no brothers, only four as yet unmarried sisters so he lived in a house dominated by women. He smiled. 'I told you. My mother's name is Monnie. Monica to you.'

'Monnie. Hmm.' I pretended to consider. 'And you have the temerity to laugh at us having a Young Samuel?'

'Hey! Not fair. What's "temerity" when it's at home?'

'Sorry.' I had forgotten our pact: no big words. 'It means you're very impertinent, Coley Quinn!'

He grabbed me, tickling me under the arms, and we rolled over and under each other, laughing and laughing and laughing. Of course, the laughter turned into kissing but I called a halt when I feared we might go too far.

We sat up again.

Over the weeks we had told one another just a little about our families. Unlike me, Coley did not want for relations but had uncles, aunts and cousins all over the world. The impression I received was that, whenever they managed to get together, for a christening or a funeral, for instance, they were an argumentative group. Coley had confessed to me that he loved being in the fields with me, not only because of Our Love but also because of the quiet. 'Tell me about your brother who died.' He was playing with my plait, which had become a habit.

I confided my sorrow to him. Although it had happened so many years before, as I talked about my little brother's funeral, I found it was as if it had been only yesterday. The pain could still draw tears. I had to stop.

Coley cradled me in his arms and allowed me to cry. After a short while I regained control. 'Thank you, Coley. I'm so sorry. I hope I didn't embarrass you.'

'You didn't embarrass me.' He kissed my cheek. 'Nothing you did could embarrass me, Violet. Ever.' He drew back and we looked at each other. I felt icy, with no breath in my chest, and a sensation I can describe only as a sort of drilling started up in my stomach. I could see Coley was going through something of the same nature.

Without saying a word, we both knew that this was It.

We scrambled to our feet. Coley took my hand and we walked out to the headland where there was a field of winter barley, already knee-high. On the way, we disturbed a pheasant, which ran, hopped and intermittently flew across the field. We craned our necks to follow its progress by watching the ripples in the vegetation; we were both behaving as though the flight of this panicked bird was the most important project on our minds. As if we were not approaching our destiny.

When Coley was sure we had found a place where we would not be seen, he stopped and looked me straight in the eye. 'Are you sure you want to do this with me, Violet?'

'Yes. No. I mean yes.'

'Are you absolutely sure?'

My breath hung in my chest like an expanding balloon. 'Yes.' Then: 'But I haven't done it before.'

He smiled slightly but his expression remained serious. 'I haven't either.'

'We'll learn together. It'll be all right.' I felt brave. I would have trusted Coley Quinn to rescue me from a sinking ship. To risk his life for me.

Making love to him was all I had been dreaming about, although I was hazy about the process. In fact, I was completely ignorant and, even reading between the lines, none of my novels had been very informative. Ignorance, however, had not prevented night-time fantasising.

Since I had met Coley, these flights of fancy had reached new intensity. I had found sleep difficult in any case because of the amazing energy I had somehow acquired. So, as I tossed and turned, I had created a series of scenarios.

Coley and I were riding muscular white horses across a wild, romantic desert somewhere in North Africa. With no one else in sight, we dismounted and shed our clothes to stand naked and proud before one another. He took me in his arms, his skin against mine—

Coley and I were in a small open boat in the middle of a vast, quiet sea, both of us naked – the boat was piled with cushions. Coley kissed my mouth, then rolled on top of me so my soft naked stomach pressed against his—

There were others, but as soon as I shut my eyes to re-create either of those two, I was unable to prevent myself touching 'down there', provoking sensations I would not dare to describe. Of course, I knew there was more to making love than naked bodies touching, however potent the sensation – but what?

There had been no point in asking Johanna, even in a roundabout way, and I would not have dreamed of asking Mother, but since meeting Coley, I had many times wished Marjorie, with her bobbed hair and fashionable shoes, was home. She even smoked – I had discovered as much when I found her puffing away in one of the outhouses.

Earlier on, when I first began to speculate about love-making, I had summoned up the courage to ask Nanny directly. But she had become inexplicably woolly. 'When the time comes, you'll know everything. But, remember, you must save yourself for your husband. It is the greatest gift you can give any man and no man would like to think his bride had given it away to someone else. Once it is given away, Violet, there's no taking it back.'

I am not a stupid or superficial person, I think, and Nanny's general meaning was quite clear. Yet she would not elaborate so I was no further along in discovering the details of what exactly lay in my gift.

That day in Loughshinny, however, I could think of no better person than Coley Quinn on whom to bestow it.

# 11

# SURGICAL PRECISION

Moses striding through the Red Sea.

That's the image that springs to mind as I follow the tramp because brambles seem magically to part before him as he swings his slash hook in easy motion – right, left, right, left. It's hard going on the uneven ground; my suit jacket is sticking to the silk blouse underneath and I can tell by the strain on my calves that the land is rising. When I look west, a significant bank of cloud is billowing towards us. The old man might be right about imminent rain.

We crest a little hill and there in front of us is the house, windows blind, snaggletooth chimneystacks puncturing the sky.

He stops to let me catch up.

When I had seen it from the cliff or the beach, at a distance of perhaps half a mile, Whitecliff had seemed romantically sad. A what-a-pity house. An I'd-love-to-get-my-hands-on-that sort of place. Up close, I can see that a person would need very deep pockets indeed to bring it back to a habitable state.

We have come out to face the padlocked double doors at the front, sheltered inside a peeling, pillared portico and flanked on each side by three deep, shuttered bay windows. Although they have made good progress, the brambles are still at the early stages of weaving their carpet here because in places I can see traces of gravel; at one point there must have been a half-moon parking area or turning circle.

Weathered to bare wood, the double entrance doors, complete with frayed bell-pull, might be the sturdiest component of the house. The window-frames are rotting, the house's fretwork of chimneys sprouts healthy crops of buddleia and, like discarded crutches, many of the gutters and downpipes dangle from rusted supports. More seriously, some of the roof trusses are visible where slates are missing, and a lot of mortar has crumbled away so there might be a question about how much longer the walls will hold together. Without checking inside, I'd say Whitecliff is riddled with wet rot, dry rot and anything you're having yourself. Any developer would take less than a second to decide it had to be knocked.

All of that being said, while the old house looks sad, it wears its age gracefully, a dowager fallen on hard times but whose aristocratic bones, including the bell-pull at the door, gleam through her rags and tatter. I love her.

'There used to be big beeches on this avenue and daffodils under them.' This confirms my suspicion that the old chap's choice of Whitecliff as a squat wasn't random and that he has some emotional attachment to it, but his tone is odd and he's watching me, almost as though he is seeking a reaction. But, I remind myself, I have neither the time nor the inclination to play amateur psychologist: I have to keep business in mind. So, rather than delve, I settle for a sort of half-way house: 'What happened to them? Beeches should last for centuries, shouldn't they?'

'Felled. I heard they went to a sawmill.' He's still watching me. I smile, which seems to disarm him. He looks up at the sky, where the first cloud has rolled over the sun. 'We're in for a sup right enough.'

'So, Pat, could we go inside?'

He looks down at me, considering. 'I'm not cracked, like some probably thinks, and I well know that some day I might have to let them take care of me. I might break a leg or get cancer. I'll be seventy-nine next birthday, but as long as I can put one foot in front of the other, I want to stay here.'

'It's not my call, I'm afraid.' I feel sorry for the man, but what can I do? 'If the owner sells it or wants to develop it, I have to be honest – I doubt you'll be left here, Pat.'

'But . . .' he hesitates '. . . by the time they get me through the courts . . .' He looks bleak. 'Please. I'm snug here.'

'I can see that.' But I'm puzzled. It's almost as though he thinks I'll have influence over his fate. 'Look, it wouldn't be fair to you if I didn't try to make you understand that it's probably only a matter of time. This house is attracting attention. We're a small outfit. If my boss has heard it's likely to come on the market, you can be sure others have too. He sent me here as a matter of urgency to try to get ahead of the posse.'

'Mmm.' He considers this. The temperature has dropped a little, and I'm chilly now. 'I'll have to take my chances, I suppose,' he says slowly, 'but on the other hand I might up sticks in the morning and go back over. I still have friends there. You could come here in the morning,' he shrugs ostentatiously, 'and you wouldn't find hide nor hair of me. I travel light as a sparrow.'

'I hear you. You're telling me you're a free man.'

'As long as you remember that.'

'I will.' I look upwards along the grey height of the house while something nags at the back of my brain. 'I know it's been a good while, but exactly how long have you been living like this?'

'Goin' on eighteen years. Since I came back for good from over.'

'And no one has tried to get you out?'

'The social tried a few times.' He glances sideways at me, then hawks and spits. 'They gave up, though. A person can't be forced into a place they don't want to go.'

I try not to look towards where the spittle landed. 'How do you manage for water and all that, and if you get sick?'

'I manage.' He is curt. 'There's good water on this land. And I don't get sick.'

'And no relatives, eh?'

'My generation's gone. Buried all over the world, Chicago, Perth in Australia, Scotland, cities in England.'

'What do you do for money?' I'll have time later to consider this conversation. 'That food back there at your camp?'

'They send the pension to Rathlinney post office and I go in there to get it and me few messages every week.'

It's on my tongue to point out that his seclusion isn't very watertight, that he's already admitted that the authorities are aware of his existence, and if the post-office people in Rathlinney know about him, everyone does. But I know I've gone about as far as I dare. I gaze up at him, shabby for sure, but in many ways admirable, and the information that has been nagging at me comes right up to the surface. 'You know, you might have squatters' rights here. It's called "adverse possession" and although I'd need to look it up to see what claim you'd have on this land, I think that under the law you only have to occupy a place for twelve years. And actually, now that I think of it, there's another law that applies if a place can be designated officially abandoned.'

'Officially abandoned, eh?'

He's staring at me again with the inscrutable expression that unnerves me. 'We have all that information back at the office,' I plough on. 'I could easily find out for you.' Some property negotiator you are, Claudine Armstrong. If Tommy ever finds out what you've said to this man he'll murder you.

But Tommy needn't worry. 'I ain't a farmer,' the old man says. 'I don't care about land. I don't want no squatters' rights nor nothing. I want to be left to live out me days owing nobody nothing, nobody owning or owing me. How many times do I have to tell you? I want nothing from nobody. Now, do you want to come inside this house or not? There's no furniture, mind, only an old stick here and there.'

'That doesn't matter at all, Pat. Listen, I don't want to keep calling you "Pat" – what's your real name?'

He weighs up his answer. Then: 'Colman. But nobody calls me that except the social. This way.' He moves off.

I feel obscurely chuffed that he has trusted me as we walk across the half-circle and, still on relatively open ground now, round the side of the house, past the blackened remains of a long-dead tree right at the corner. 'Another beech?'

'Yep.'

'It looks burned.'

'Probably lightning.' He doesn't alter his stride.

We've come round to an open space on the cliff top. The back of the house is, I'd say, less than twenty-five metres from the rim. I can see fence posts and wire at the edge, leaning outwards at a crazy angle. 'Erosion?'

'Yeah.' He grins. 'We'll be safe enough for another fifty years, maybe a hundred. It's going at about half an inch a year, some years two inches, some years nothing at all.' We're standing beside a water pump that looks to be in good condition – now I know where he gets his supply. I walk across and touch the meat safe fastened to the wall alongside the back door; the wood is rotting but the wire door, while rusted, is sound. Then I look upwards.

From this angle, without the portico and curves of the bay windows that soften the front, Whitecliff appears high, sheer and rather severe. Right under the eaves there is a barred window. 'Are the attics habitable?'

'Don't know.' He's short, cutting off follow-up questions as he produces a keyring from a pocket in his trousers and unlocks what seems to be a recently fitted padlock. Is he some kind of an eccentric caretaker? He pushes in the creaking back door, which results in the sound of tiny claws scrabbling on the flagged floor.

Mice.

I stop dead and close my eyes to give them a chance to disperse. I hate them but if I don't have to see them I can manage. OHPC's beat encompasses a lot of old properties and if I were to get jittery at every little furry creature I encountered, I'd be a very nervy – and in front of clients a rather unsuccessful – negotiator.

'You can open your eyes, Claudine.' He barks his laugh. 'The coast is clear.'

We're standing in a large, old-fashioned kitchen, empty of furniture except for a huge table, constructed from deal so thick it looks indestructible. It's in very good nick and, unlike the manky iron range, is very clean and supports several rows of cornflake boxes, packet soups and clumps of tea-bags, each one secured in a plastic wrapper with a wire tie. It's obvious that the Belfast sink is in use too – there's another milk can beside it, with a bottle of Cif and a scrubber sponge on the windowsill above it. I turn back to the table. Search for something neutral to say. 'You eat a lot of cornflakes?'

'Yup.' He casts a look round. 'As you can see, this here's the kitchen.' His heavy workmen's boots ring as he crosses to fling open the top portion of a half-door fitted with an old fashioned up-and-down latch. 'And in there's the pantry. It's dry enough.'

I peer in. It is dark, but there is enough light to see that it is not empty. There's no food, but its shelves and hooks hold old kitchen utensils, pots and pans, another meat safe, wooden spoons, whisks, very large milk jugs, pudding and mixing bowls, a huge metal basin, probably tin although it's hard to say – humble objects that once were so useful. I reach in across the half-door and pick up an old colander, enamel over metal, of a type you don't see any more and that would probably sell for a small fortune in a Dublin antiques shop. Whoever cleared this house forgot, or ignored, the pantry. That seems poignant for some reason as I turn the colander in my hands: it's dented and the enamel is badly chipped.

'Why don't you take it?'

'I beg your pardon?' I'm surprised.

'Take it home with you for a souvenir.' His old eyes, having caught whatever light there is from the open back door, appear to glitter. Now I know where the teapot came from.

'Are you sure it would be OK?' I don't want it, yet I do.

'Who's going to say it's not?'

'All right.' I tell myself I'm taking it to please him. And it does feel ridiculous to carry it as I follow him across the flagstones of the double-height entrance hall, semi-dark because the doors to the rooms off it are all closed and the portico windows are shuttered. The only furniture is a dusty coatstand (*circa* the nineteen fifties and incompatible with the house), although I can see, against the faded wallpaper, the more vividly coloured outlines of furniture, the open rectangle of a hall table, for instance, and a rather odd crescent shape near the double doors. As well as taking everything in, I'm marvelling at the change in my guide who, after closing the pantry door, has beckoned me almost imperiously to 'come this way, please'.

His protests about not needing or wanting property rights are all very well but it occurs to me for the first time that, in fact, he might not be Whitecliff's caretaker but its proprietor. It's not beyond the bounds of possibility and he's now behaving with the pride of an owner showing a visitor his home. In the property business, you come across all sorts of unconventional and weird people and maybe Tommy's 'old codger' is not living in the West of Ireland after all.

The kitchen, however, has turned out to be by far the best-preserved room at Whitecliff. The drawing room must once have been splendid, I think, as we clump in, sending dust-balls rolling. Although it wears its abandonment like widow's weeds, with its three bay windows, parquet floor – most of the blocks buckled and lifting – and massive fireplace in cream marble, it's not hard to envisage it hosting smart parties, even balls, in days gone by. 'This has to be very valuable.' Amazed that it has survived so long without being stolen or vandalised,

I walk over and touch the fireplace's cold magnificence. It is of a type I have never seen before – or have I? Some dim recollection tugs at my brain but refuses to clarify. What's significant is the mantel: it curves upwards at both ends, like a Balinese dancer's arms. Had it perhaps been imported from the East? 'Was the family very wealthy? They owned the shop in the village, didn't they?'

'Mmm.' He, too, fingers the fireplace.

'You knew them?'

'Everyone in this district knew them. They were the local nobs.'

We leave the drawing room and cross the hall again. 'We'll go upstairs now but you'll have to be careful. These steps can be slippy.' He has to raise his voice because the house is being attacked by a fusillade of the rain he'd predicted. 'I'll show you the dining room and conservatory on our way back out, all right?'

'I'm in your hands.'

The wide, curving staircase is of stone. It is somewhat worn – even in the gloom, I can see the sag and shine at the centre of each step. It's wonderful.

'Wouldn't be surprised if we have a belt of thunder,' the old man, already ten or eleven steps ahead of me, shouts back over his shoulder, his last words echoing because, as suddenly as it had started, the rain stops.

We come off the staircase on to a wide, balustraded landing, big enough to hold a party independent of any in the reception rooms below. If I was selling this house, I think, with the bays, the fireplace, the double-height entrance hall – and certainly the staircase – I'd style this landing as one of the major features of the house. I'd call it a minstrel's gallery and, although not directly illuminated, if the shutters on the seven tall windows set into the second-storey wall of the house were to be opened, this whole area would be flooded with natural light. Now, that's a brochure I'd like to write, I think, yet apart from professional appraisal, I have a strong urge to throw everything wide open. I want to give the lungs of this house, this *grande dame*, a breath of air.

As I've said, I'm used to old, even very old, properties and I'm not intimidated by size or potential value but there's something about the atmosphere here that I just don't get. It's not the shutters or the dust or even the melancholy feel of any house left vacant for a considerable amount of time. It's something more. A kind of expectancy or pull, as if Whitecliff is poised on the brink of something. Destruction or redemption?

Talk about whimsical – what's got into me today? While I don't consider myself superstitious or susceptible, Whitecliff is definitely getting under my skin.

With my free hand, I push cautiously at a couple of the balusters. They don't budge. I push harder, still no movement. They're sound. 'You don't get workmanship like that, these days.' Spieling to myself now? 'Well, thank goodness the rain's stopped anyhow,' I add, for the sake of saying something. 'It was only a shower, after all.'

'Not much point in going into the bedrooms.' The old guy is watching me again. In fact, his constant scrutiny is becoming a little creepy. 'They're much of a muchness, anyways, although the main one is a bit bigger. I wouldn't be too sure about the floorboards either.'

'How many bedrooms?'

'Seven.'

I am aware of something deep in the pit of my stomach, half-way between a rustle and a crunch. I recognise it because I've experienced it twice before, but never at this intensity. Excitement. I want this house. 'Could we at least see the master?'

The old man walks away towards one end of the landing and I notice that he keeps to the side, avoiding the ancient runner set along the centre of the bare floorboards to avoid dirtying it with his boots. The bedroom he shows me turns out to be as I would have expected in a place of this size, with a pair of tall sash windows, wallpaper drooping sadly off the walls and dark hillocks of mould flourishing along the skirtings and near the ceiling. But he'd been only half right about the floorboards. They're oak, and while they're dusty and dull with one or two needing replacing, they're beautiful. The pressure in my stomach expands. I am wearing a silk, Fortuny-pleated dress as I sit by the hissing log fire in the grate of my marble fireplace downstairs. The drawing room, painted apple green, is accented by cream sofas and cream damask curtains at the windows, with splashes of colour here and there in cushions, art on the walls, the new fabric covering the window-seats. Maybe a pattern of red poppies. My dinner guests are due shortly and, over the piano sonata discreetly issuing from the house-wide sound system, I can hear the faint clatter from my distant kitchen where the caterers are putting the finishing touches to the food they will serve in my candlelit dining room.

A carriage clock chimes the hour. I take another sip of my cocktail, glistening pinkly in my lead-crystal glass, then put the glass on its coaster and stand up. I am ready. The house is ready.

'Well, if you've seen enough, we should go,' the old man breaks in.

'Sorry. I guess I was daydreaming.'

'I guess you were!' He ushers me out, closes the door and makes for the head of the stairs.

'Just a minute. I want to get a bit of perspective here.' I walk to the opposite end of the landing and turn to look back along its length. As I do so, I see beside me a door I haven't noticed before. It is set back a little in its own alcove and is narrower than the others. Probably a linen closet or storage cupboard, I think, and push at it before realising that it opens outwards. I tug.

I stand there, puzzled, trying to make sense of what I see.

Imagine all those American movie scenes where someone pulls open a door to a basement: you're looking at a narrow staircase running downward between two tight walls.

Reverse the direction and you get the idea. But that's not all that's interesting.

I can see where a set of stairs used to come out on to a landing above. I can see the join where the last step met the floor of that landing. I can see sky between the exposed roof beams and joists above a hole in the landing's ceiling; I can hear the drip-drip-drip of rainwater through the timbers and I can see those drips gather momentum as they fall ten metres to bounce in front of me.

I'm looking up towards the attics, access to which has been removed with great, even surgical precision. Although there are marks and deep dents on the walls, there is no sign of rotten or fallen wood. All that remains of the staircase now are two steep steps going nowhere.

# 12

## SILVERY FISHES

I tried to excuse myself from supper that evening when I came home from Loughshinny because I wanted to be alone in my room. Mind and body, I was awash with the momentous events of the afternoon. Now that Coley Quinn and I had become of one flesh, I had to have quiet to work out how it felt to be a real woman.

Excited and fearful all at once, I was caught in desperate conflict. I wanted to hug my precious, exhilarating secret to myself but at the same time found it difficult not to scream, 'Look at me, everyone! Everyone, look! I've changed! I've changed! Does anyone see?'

Yet when I got home at the time I was expected, thanks to Coley having strained every nerve and muscle to get me there on the crossbar of his bicycle, I had to stroll calmly along the avenue from the gate as though nothing had happened and that my only emotion was satisfaction that the Easter holidays were upon me.

I was far from calm. Much of my agitation arose from the discovery that the act itself had not been what I expected. Not having known beforehand what was to take place, I had imagined lovemaking to be dreamy, slow, and so romantic that we would float like silvery fishes within our own skins. Despite Coley's best efforts to hold himself in check, however, I had found things to be rather quick and even a little violent.

Coley seemed to guess at my confusion because as we held each other afterwards, hidden by the waving vegetation, he kissed me a hundred times or more, asking me over and over again if I was all right. 'You're not sorry, Violet?'

'Of course not, Coley,' I said tenderly, while trying to disregard the stinging between my legs. 'It was wonderful.'

I was not sorry. It was just that I had questions.

'Are you sure?' He stroked my face. 'I didn't hurt you? I promise it will be better for you the next time.'

'It couldn't possibly be better,' I lied. 'And I am absolutely sure I am not hurt.' I gazed upwards at the solitary seagull, wings outstretched, serene on the trapeze of the wind. Then I took a deep breath and, with every ounce of passion I could summon, kissed my lover. 'I love you,' I declared, the statement more profound and stirring to me than what we had just done together.

'And I love you.' He gathered me into him and hugged me so hard my back hurt. Then he drew back, looked into my eyes, said, 'Remember this. I love you, Violet Shine,' and for a whirling, exploding moment, I thought I might disintegrate, a firework shot like spangles towards the stars.

I could not tell you what route we took back to Whitecliff, and although Coley kept as far as possible off the normal tracks, I was afraid that some acquaintance of Father's or Mother's might recognise me. What I do recall, as we rattled through the seaside lanes, is my lover's strong breathing on

107

my neck and against my cheek and the grip of his upper arms holding me steady on the crossbar.

Although the urge to 'recollect in tranquillity' was overpowering, Mother would not hear of my missing supper when I suggested that I have a lie-down. 'I'm rather tired, Mother. As you know I've been studying very hard and I am not at all hungry. I think I should like to go to bed early this evening. Right now, in fact.' I yawned showily.

'Nonsense.' She looked up from her work on the Shine Quilt. 'You must eat, Violet. But, yes, I can see that you do look flushed, I think you may be overdoing this fresh-air business. A good meal will settle you and you can sleep all you like tonight. But after supper, I shall need you and Johanna for the quilt. We are rather behind, you know.'

'But, Mother—'

'You may lie on in the morning.'

I hesitated. It was urgent that I get to my room. I could not think of what else to say.

'Are you ill, Violet?' She put down her piece of the quilt, folded her hands and adopted what Johanna and I referred to as her glinty look. 'It's not your friend, is it?' In our house, our time of the month was referred to thus.

'No.' I was afraid that if I seized on this excuse for my flushed appearance, someone, perhaps Dr Willis, would discover things I would prefer to be kept secret. I'd heard doctors could tell instantly if a woman was no longer a virgin.

'Then it's settled. We're having eggs. Please go into the kitchen and help Johanna with the salads.'

'May I at least have the opportunity to change out of my school clothes, Mother?'

She looked closely at me. 'I do not appreciate your tone,

Violet. Perhaps it is as well that you have some time off school and we can keep a closer eye on you. You may change. Quickly.' She picked up the quilt again.

I rushed up to my room and, locked the door. Then, half ecstatic, half guilty, I threw myself on to the bed and closed my eyes to recall the feel of Coley's warm, energetic body thrusting on my own.

Somewhere in the recesses of the house I heard the door-bell ring: we had one of those clanging types attached to a rope outside the door, so loud that it could be heard in every part of the house. I, however, was far from worried as to who might be calling late on a Friday afternoon . . .

I had felt a little false in my efforts to match my lover's wildness: I had been excited, of course – what we were doing felt brave and grown-up and daring – but not to the degree that had possessed him. If I had not been doing it with Coley, I might even have been frightened when his kisses and caresses grew less and less solicitous to become perfunctory, when his face creased as if he was in agony, when he groaned as if in pain . . .

Unexpected physical sensations and fears had intervened in the experience for me: that unexpected soreness, for instance, combined with apprehension that this furious activity might tear me apart. More mundanely, I was conscious of the earth beneath me and that the back of my skirt might be stained with grass or blood or other fluids which would lead to the discovery of my wantonness.

I mention the more negative side of what happened only because it mixed me up at the time and I feel I should be truthful. I certainly do not want to give the impression that I was disappointed or upset. Far from it. Coley Quinn was

My Love, we were Making Love, and nothing on earth would dim what we should be feeling together – so while it was going on, I determined to concentrate on the heat of his skin, the hardness of his stomach and thighs, the potent smells we created . . .

I had been too shy to look at his body that afternoon but had kept my gaze on his face, on the high cheekbones I had come to love, and the somewhat wolfish teeth, the unruly hair, the widow's peak that I fancied might have come from the illustration on an Etruscan vase. Now I realised I was longing to see more.

I decided that, next time, Coley Quinn and I must find a more secluded place because we would be fully naked. Lying there on my bed that evening, I felt my blood race at the thought.

I knew I had not much time but I was addicted to what my imagination decreed. So, while Martin, our part-time workman, whish-whished his gravel rake just beneath my open window and the smell of frying eggs rose from the kitchen a floor below, I rushed to set the scene.

I would put us in a bosky glade somewhere. No, better – we would stand facing one another on a high, rocky moor. Heedless of danger, unable to control our mutual passion, while the wind screamed and tore at our heads, we would scrabble at one another's clothes until they fell away like flags in a battle—

No. I would take the lead. I would make Coley slow down. I would force him to keep his hands behind his back while I undressed him, shirt button by shirt button, right down to his underwear. And when he was standing there, chest glistening in the sunshine – it would be windy, but sunny and warm too – I would look at him from under blowing strands of hair and ask him to undo my braid as he had done before. 'And when you have done that, Coley, may I ask you to unbutton my blouse, please? My breasts in their satin pouches of scarlet await the caress of your hands. They long to be freed from their ruby shells to be kissed by your lips—'

The fact that I possessed not a thread of satin underwear, scarlet or otherwise, seemed irrelevant. I would have satin for Coley. Somehow.

Lost in these images, I failed to hear Johanna knocking at my door until she was hammering and calling, 'Violet! Violet? What are you doing in there? It's suppertime and Mother is getting very cross – and there's news. She wants to tell us something . . . Violet!'

'Sorry,' I called. 'I fell asleep for a few minutes. I'll be down right away.' I sprang off the bed.

'Please hurry,' she called.

'I'm coming, I'm coming.' I pulled off my skirt and left it in a crumpled heap on the floor.

Then I remembered it might be Evidence, picked it up and bundled it to the back of my wardrobe.

When I rushed into the dining room they were waiting for me at table. Mother and Father cast disapproving glances in my direction but in response to my apologies and explanations, surprisingly did not scold me. 'We are all hungry. Sit down, Violet.' Mother shook out her napkin but, despite her tone, there was something unusual, a gaiety, about the way she did it and I noticed that her cheeks were pink. She was a pale woman who kept her emotions firmly in check and it was unusual to see such a sparkle.

I remembered the ring of the doorbell and Johanna's

announcement about news. 'What has happened?' I looked at both my parents as I took my seat.

Mother glanced at Father. 'We've had a telegram,' she said, smiling.

'A telegram?' Despite her smile, I was alarmed. We had received only two telegrams in my lifetime, both concerning the death of obscure relatives. And lately, in our locality where, besides James and Thomas, other boys and men had joined the Allied war effort, telegrams more than ever meant bad news.

'Yes, Violet,' Father said patiently. 'We've had a telegram from James. He and Thomas are coming home next week for a few days' leave prior to mobilisation.'

'That's wonderful!' In my current state of elation, it would not have taken much to tip me over into ecstasy but this was surely a marvellous development. Life in the house. Noise. Activity.

Camouflage.

'When are they coming?'

'A week from today apparently.' Father cut into one of his eggs.

Mother followed suit. 'That gives us just six days. It is as well you are on holiday, Violet. You two girls will have to rally round. We need to get supplies, bedrooms aired and so forth. And,' she continued, flicking another glance towards Father, 'I have decided something else.'

'Oh?' We all looked at her.

'We will hold a party a week from tomorrow for Young Samuel's twenty-first birthday – and also to celebrate the twins' homecoming. We do not have much time so I propose to ask Nanny back to help us. She is getting old but she is still strong, and I am sure her organisational skills will not have deserted her. I hope you agree that we should ask her, Roderick. We do not have long.' Her voice had risen throughout this speech until it was almost defiant. We all knew that it was not Nanny's temporary re-engagement that was the cause but the party.

We had never held parties at Whitecliff. Not even for the twenty-first birthdays of Johanna or Marjorie. I supposed that, although it had not been discussed, Young Samuel, as the heir apparent, had always been destined for one on his coming-of-age.

'But his birthday is not until next February,' Father said faintly. 'And supposing I do agree? It's wartime, Fly. How are we going to cater for a party? And shouldn't we wait until he is actually twenty-one? Isn't that the more normal thing to do?'

'It has to be next week. The twins will be here. And as for supplies, we will make do. Everyone will understand.' Mother's tone brooked no argument. 'We should get a message to Young Samuel at Trinity and to Marjorie at her flat, Roderick. Will you see to that? Make sure they have no choice in the matter.' She looked down at her plate and toyed with a lettuce leaf. 'Only God knows where we will all be by the time the actual twenty-first comes round next February.'

Silence descended on our table as we all realised why she had decided to have the party now.

Father lifted things with an announcement of his own. 'Well, since we're all so full of surprises, I have made a decision too. We are going to have a telephone installed in the house. We cannot be relying on telegrams to hear from our children.'

'Won't it be expensive, Roderick?' Mother frowned.

'I hope you see the irony in what you say, Fiona.' Father raised an eyebrow sardonically. 'How much do you think we need to find to throw a lavish party? If we can afford that, we can afford a telephone. Anyhow, I can make some adjustments to the use of the telephone in the shop. We rely on it far too much. We have become lazy, using it instead of our feet or our bicycles.' He had installed the instrument in Rathlinney General Stores as soon as the line reached the village. We were Rathlinney 3, third in order of precedence after the post office and the Catholic presbytery.

What an eventful day. I thought it all over as I cut into the fried egg to let the deep yellow yolk run over my plate. It was wonderful that the twins were coming home for a visit. It was even more wonderful, amazing, even, that we were planning a party on the very day I had become a woman.

In that context, however, it was not so wonderful that I would be tied to the house, skivvying, for the next week. Then a delicious thought struck me. 'Whom shall we invite to this party, Mother? Are Johanna and I allowed to invite our friends, for instance?'

Johanna looked up. 'Yes, Mother. I could invite Shirley. I am sure she would come for the weekend.' As far as I knew, Shirley, my sister's old classmate, was the only friend she had.

'Perhaps.' Mother smiled at her. All this good humour was positively unnerving. Then she looked at me. 'Whom do you have in mind, Violet?'

'Oh, you know,' I said airily, 'some of the people from Misses Biggs's. Mary Quigley, Mary Kelly. And a couple of boys, of course. If it's to be a real, proper twenty-first for Young Samuel, if there is to be dancing, for instance, we have to balance the numbers, don't we?' I held my breath as all three of the others looked at me in surprise.

'What boys?' Father asked.

'Well,' I improvised, 'Mary Kelly has nice brothers. And now and again I have run into some of the boys I used to know in national school.' I cast around for a few names. 'You know, people like Peter Cronin from the chemist's and John Milford, whose father runs the creamery, Coley Quinn – people like that.'

Still they looked at me. I avoided Johanna's eye.

'I didn't know that any of the Quinns were in your class at school, Violet.' This was Mother. 'They're good people, but—'

'Look, Mother, Father, Johanna,' I interrupted, to head her off the path of the Quinns being decent people but not exactly of our class, 'it would not necessarily be Coley. He was a little ahead of me in class anyway, and his name just came because I do run into him occasionally. The same way I run into others. I do not plan it. It just happens. We live in rural Ireland where people know each other.'

I was in full flight and could not seem to stop. 'Actually, now that I remember, Mary Kelly and her family have taken a house in Wexford. So there's not much point in asking them, even if we knew their address. I should probably ask Coley Quinn to bring one of his sisters. I think one of them was in the twins' class. Wouldn't that be a good idea?'

I had not known I could be so creative.

'I worry about what has got into you lately, Violet.' Mother glanced at Father. Both were frowning but, I guessed, more in perplexity at my garrulousness than at what I was suggesting.

I pulled back a little. 'I'm not a hermit, you know,' I said, in a more conciliatory tone. 'I have been going to school, which meant travelling into and out of Balbriggan on public buses. You have allowed me on occasion to go to the cinema. I am sixteen. Would you not agree I have a point? It is not as if we have a wide circle of friends and relatives to choose from, so if we are having a party it should be a proper one, yes? I am sure the twins and Young Samuel will be allowed to invite anyone they like. So should it not be the same for Johanna and me? Marjorie too. Maybe she has a beau in Dublin.' I risked all.

My parents again exchanged a glance. 'We shall think about it,' Mother said. 'But – and please remember this, girls – if we agree to your request, numbers cannot be unlimited. Parties are expensive, especially in these straitened times, and, contrary to our reputation around here, we are not wealthy. Now, hurry up and finish your supper. There is still a great deal left to do with the Shine Quilt, you know.'

'Yes, Mother.' I took a mouthful of almost cold fried egg. I glowed.

# 13

# CARBUNCLES

'That didn't turn out too bad, now, did it? She's a grand old bird really, eh?'

'No, it was fine.' Bob and I are standing in the doorway of our house, waving at his godmother, his eighty-four-year-old aunt Louise, grand-aunt to be accurate, who is climbing inch by inch into her little turquoise Daihatsu. Special order. All Louise's cars have to be turquoise – good vibrations, apparently. 'She's in great nick.'

He looks at me, seeking an undertone. Bob is an only child, like me, and with his parents both gone too, his aunt Louise is important to him. 'I mean it!' I continue, waving, as Louise grinds down our driveway. She goes through at least three clutches with every car she buys. She's a standing joke in the workshop at Bob's dealership. 'She's terrific for her age.'

'Will you feed the dog?' Bob asks, after his aunt has turned out of our gateway.

'Sure.'

'It's just that the match is starting—'

'I said OK.'

He hesitates. 'You were very quiet this evening.'

'Was I?'

'You hardly said a word during dinner. Is there anything wrong, Cee?'

Shortening given names and using nicknames is part of our pack ethos, Strongy'n'Cee, Slats'n'Jo-Jo, Pick'n'Dairine, Muddle'n'Clare, joined at the hip in pairs. 'Sorry, Bob.' I close the door. 'I had a few things on my mind.'

'Lord help us all. I hate it when women think!' He smiles but, from experience probably, does not think it prudent to ask what I'm thinking about and I can see he's itching to get to the TV.

'Go on. I'll clear up in the kitchen.'

'Are you sure you don't mind?'

I can see his mind is already elsewhere. 'Go on.' I give him a little push, and as I watch his retreating back, find myself harking back to my introspective examination of our relationship. I'd begun to notice that closed look on Bob's face more frequently, but any time I asked if anything was wrong, he answered that he was thinking about work.

I'm not stupid. In any long-lived marriage, there have to be peaks and troughs – or, to resurrect the watery analogy, perhaps our individual boats are not connecting just now.

Bob is a good-looking man who has kept himself in great physical shape, and while he can be offhand, overall he is generous and kind, unlike me: I can be unkind about him in my thoughts. And while he does have his self-centred moments and while – a new development – there have been several occasions recently when, citing the entertainment of clients, he has turned in late stinking of booze, I have to acknowledge that he's easy to live with and never constrains me; I suspect that if I told him I wanted to start a business importing yak butter and needed money to travel to the source in Nepal, he would have shaken his head in comic disbelief and written the cheque. I suppose the best way to describe his outward attitude to our marriage is that he is casually decent. So, to my shame, any negativity about him comes from within myself.

So why? What's wrong?

I'm not sure. Let's just try and see it from his perspective, I think, as I walk slowly into the kitchen. What do I bring to the party?

I'm faithful. Although I've picked up signals from various people over the years, and will admit that I have flirted now and then, I have never been tempted to have a full-blown affair. I'm waxed and highlighted and use the exercise bike, so I've kept my figure. Although our sex life has slowed down a lot – no one could have kept up the pace at which it started! – he has expressed no dissatisfaction there, overtly at least.

I bring in a little money. I keep our house the way he likes it to be kept: at any time of the day or night, Bob Armstrong could invite a client in for a drink and he would find no cushion unplumped, no floor tile unsparkling.

I sit down at the half-cleared table in the kitchen. We eat in here unless we have company – Aunt Louise doesn't count as 'company' – which is seldom these days. With the new morality on drink-driving, Bob's friends and colleagues dislike travelling out from the capital; anyhow, since we're all so prosperous now, eating in restaurants is no longer a big deal. And who has time any more to cook large, elaborate meals?

I lean down to pat poor patient old Jeffrey, who is lying under the table with his soft blond head sticking out so I cannot miss his imploring doggy eyes. 'I haven't forgotten you, kiddo. We'll get you your dinner in one minute – OK?' As I straighten up again, my eye falls on the old colander I took from Whitecliff. I've washed and scrubbed it until the scourer disintegrated, but it has stubbornly refused to shine and sits like a squat, reproachful little dinosaur on our island unit, under the woks, bunches of garlic, dried herbs and lavender I've hung from my 'Victorian' clothes-airer.

That colander is a carbuncle on the perfection of the kitchen. I look away from it towards the stainless-steel splash-backs, the side-by-side fridge-freezer that can practically talk, and the Belfast sink – a modern, inferior copy of the one at Whitecliff. Isn't it a howl that nowadays, the more affluent we become, the more we ape the frugal past?

Why don't I throw out that colander right now? I'm half-way out of my seat to do just that when, suddenly and unreasonably, I hate perfection. I want rumple and untidiness, a place where it doesn't matter if the cutlery isn't heavy in the hand or that some of the plates might be chipped. My home, I think, as I stand beside our set of Wedgwood serving dishes in a glass cabinet, could be a metaphor for our marriage: glossy, attractive, user-friendly, hollow at the core, probably because there are no children to fill it.

This is merely an observation, not an issue. It never was an issue between Bob and me; nor was it that horrible modern phenomenon, a lifestyle choice. We would have liked to have children, expected to have them and certainly would have welcomed them. But when nothing happened over the years, we simply drifted into acceptance. Perhaps, given all the books and newspaper articles out there about women moving heaven and earth in their efforts to conceive, we might be seen as unnatural, even cold, in this acceptance. I don't feel we are, but if that is the case, so be it.

'Shit!' I shoot to my feet: I'm sick of all this navel-gazing. 'Come on, Jeffrey! Dinner?' With him padding an inch behind, I fill his bowl with a mixture of dried food and the remains of our steak dinner. Bob and Jeffrey love steak. We have it at least three times a week.

While he lollops into his meal, I empty out his water-bowl and refill it; I should have tried the taps at the kitchen sink at Whitecliff. I should have asked the old man if the house has mains water – but it shouldn't be a problem, especially if the surrounding land is to be developed . . .

I put down the second bowl and lean against the sink to watch my dog enjoying his food. Long-haired, stumpy-legged, with a lineage based somewhere around wheaten terriers, he is not perfect. But he could teach me a thing or two about how to live and I envy him his uncomplicated little life. Eat. Walk. Sleep. Eat. Sleep. Walk. Permanently reasonable and uncomplaining, Jeffrey is thrilled when one of us picks up his lead. He is thrilled to see us coming into the house. He is thrilled when we throw a ball for him or open the back door to let him out to chase birds or cats. For him, the dawn of each new day is Christmas renewed, full of amazing potential, at the very least full of more great eating, sleeping, chasing, drinking, walking – and love.

He loves us. It does not matter whether we love him or not, he loves us just the same. Sentimental tears prick at the back of my eyes. Good God! Crying about a dog now! I leave him to it and go up to our bedroom, where the bed is, of course, perfectly made, where the fitted wardrobes are bespoke and the pots and potions on my dressing-table are regimented by size. I open the drawer to take out my hair-brush and, staring through my reflection towards whatever might be beyond, begin vigorously to apply it.

What lies on the other side? More of the same? More cheery smiles while I talk clients into selling or buying prop-erties on behalf of OHPC? More steak dinners and Sunday walkies with Bob and Jeffrey? More rugger-bugger outings with our gang to pubs and fashionable restaurants in Dublin?

I rely on Bob too much. I need a friend.

At the age of twenty-one I moved from Daddy's protective arms to Bob's and, in the process, somehow abandoned all the pals I'd made during my school and college years, and even at the time, grief-stricken and panicky as I was, I had known at some level that this was dangerous. But over the years I had persuaded myself that things were fine: wasn't I lucky to have a nice home and a handsome husband who had equally hand-some friends with well-groomed wives and girlfriends?

I stop brushing and stare at my reflection. Of those girls and boys who had been at my twenty-first, how many of them had made real efforts to keep in touch after Daddy's funeral? None, was the dispiriting answer. But, on the other hand, had I made any effort? Had I reached out to any of them or asked them for help?

No.

By the time I had raised my head out of that swamp of loss, complicated by the legalities involving money and Pamela, I was married and settled miles from Dublin. I do have vague memories of certain occasions at the beginning when the phone would ring and someone or other would ask tentatively how I was doing. I was always (brightly) 'fine', and we always wound up the conversation by making promises to meet some time, and to keep in touch. I knew this would never happen and within two years of my fateful twenty-first birthday, the calls had fallen off, and where social life was concerned, I was Bob's adjunct.

With a gleaming home and a very active sex life, the next thing was to integrate into my community. After all, Bob was gone all day, and while I still loved sex, he was frequently – and reasonably – too tired at night. To start with I joined a local choir, but this hadn't worked out as I had hoped, although I have a decent voice and was recruited in my youth to the alto line of my school outfit. All I'd wanted was a quasi-creative outlet and a modicum of social intercourse. Quite soon, however, I became fed up with the subcutaneous power games I detected among the would-be leaders of the group and quietly let my attendance fall off.

Then I joined the charity circuit – tea-parties for Alzheimer's, coffee mornings for the hospice, dinner-dances and pub quizzes in aid of a trip to Disney World for a kid with leukaemia, Cancer Care, river blindness – you name it, I collected for it. However, after seven or eight years I found this wasn't enough either and one day, in the local Centra grocery shop, while scanning the community noticeboard, I spotted a handwritten ad:

> PA wanted for local business MD.
> Must have full clean driving licence.
> Admin experience desirable but not necessary
> as training will be given.

On impulse, I rang the telephone number and met Tommy O'Hare.

Our (Bob's) group celebrates birthdays together. We are invited to each other's housewarmings and kids' First Communion parties. We women accompany our men to golf tournaments in the South of Spain and Miami; occasionally, we get together without the men for girly outings to various spas or to make trips to Avoca Handweavers in Wicklow where we have lunch and finger the gorgeously hued rugs and blankets, quirky housewares and filmy dresses. We caw with half-guilty, half-defiant the-hell-with-'em delight as we hand over our supplementary credit cards and vow that we must do this more often.

But we are not friends. We know nothing of what friends should know about each other. Proof of this is that a marriage separation within the group always comes as a shock. We recover quickly, however, and welcome the man and his new woman (it's always the man who remains), she who must be integrated as quickly as possible so that the incision in our corporate underbelly can be stitched up.

From below, I hear a triumphant roar: 'Yes, yes, yes!' Bob's team has scored. I go to replace the hairbrush, and as I do, my gaze alights on the wilted envelope containing the four college-days photos of my mother. I stare at it, pick it up and, with shaking hands, remove the four little snaps. My mother is crossing O'Connell Bridge, holding on to her beret so it won't fly off; she is standing, one of four girls, in front of some kind of brick building in Dublin; she is sitting in a chair, a book open in her lap. But the one I choose to examine is the one of her flirting with the camera in that over-the-shoulder party pose. As a well-to-do grocer/farmer's daughter (I had never imagined that Daddy would marry anyone from an income stratum other than his own), she was probably part of a set that went to house-parties all over Ireland. At this particular one, however, she is standing beside a fireplace – one end visible, curved upwards like the arm of a Balinese dancer. If there's another fireplace like it, I'll eat Tommy's Rolodex.

My mother had attended a party at Whitecliff. My family had a connection with that house. I don't care if it was as tenuous as having attended parties there – anyhow, she was bound to have been there more than once: the fact that there is only one snap means nothing. Cameras were not as ubiquitous then as they are now . . .

No wonder I felt that house call to me.

Oh, God, I'm getting superstitious in my old age: I don't care. I need urgently to talk to that owner in the West of Ireland: even if he doesn't remember her precisely, maybe he could steer me in the right direction, towards someone else who was at it and might remember her. He'll definitely recall the party. While old people have difficulty with short-term memory, their recollection of events long ago improves. Isn't that the case?

Another roar from the lounge. Bob's team has scored again. Now would be a good time to buttonhole him and not only because they're winning. He'd just had Q1 results for the business and, so far, Q2 is looking good too. He'll be in for the half-year bonus. I slip the photograph into a pocket of my wallet and, having returned the other three to their envelope, race down the stairs, forcing myself to slow down before I enter the lounge. I don't want to scare him.

He's sprawled on the sofa and while the TV, at yelling volume, is making that irritating whistling they use to indicate an instant replay, he's rattling round in the sports pages of the *Irish Times*.

125

Jangling with excitement, I sit beside him. 'Are you totally involved in this, Bob?'

He looks up, surprised. 'You know I am. Why?'

'I want to ask you something.'

'Uh-oh! I'm not going to like this, am I?' But he is distracted by another screaming rally from the sports commentator. 'Sorry,' he says, when things have died down a little. 'What did you want to ask me?'

'Should I wait until the match is over?'

He groans. 'Don't do that to me, Cee. You know I hate it.'

'All right. I want you to listen to me for five minutes. Five minutes only. Then I'll take questions, OK?'

He looks at his watch but I don't take offence because I can see I have his full attention. 'How much do you like this house?' It comes out in a rush.

He puts down the paper. 'Oh, God. Here we go. What kind of a question is that? Would I live here if I didn't like it?' He waves expansively, taking in the whole caboodle, inside and out, the segmented couch in aqua leather, the plasma screen, the one-off coffee-table from Germany constructed from a single piece of sandblasted glass, the cobble-locking on the driveway outside complementing his black Beemer. 'We've sure spent enough on it.'

'You might live here for all kinds of reasons. This house is lovely, but it's inconvenient in some ways. None of our friends will come out here, for instance – no matter how often we invite them, they make excuses. And there's no public transport. But you might put up with all of that because you might think it's too much trouble to move.'

'Is it the nesting season again already? How long before you get over it this year?'

'I'm deadly serious, Bob. The timing is coincidental.'

'You were serious about it that last two times we went through this, Cee. Could we talk again about this, maybe over the weekend? But in the meantime, to answer your question, I do like this house. And it is too much trouble to move.' With an indulgent shake of his head, he shifts his gaze to the TV, where things are obviously under control. Then he goes back to the sports pages.

I have to admit he's right about the nesting thing. Nothing to do with my job, but come January or, at the latest, February every year, I do start perusing 'interiors' magazines and property supplements the way other women read fashion and gossip. I've twice gone as far as paying for architectural and engineering surveys on properties, resulting in my attendance at two auctions but, on both occasions, I balked at the last hurdle. Bob tolerated it until he saw a pattern: he has every right not to take me seriously.

But not this time. 'I want you to listen.' I shove up beside him on the couch and take the newspaper from his hands. 'This is different.'

'It's always different.' He groans again. 'It's an annual ritual with you. I thought you loved this place, Cee.'

'I did love it. I do. But don't forget that this house was an investment too. My guess – and Tommy agrees – is that it's put on at least twenty times its value since we bought it. Maybe even more.'

'It's a chain, Cee. Everything else has gone up too.'

'Not the place I'm talking about. I asked for five minutes. It's not up yet. And can I turn this down?' I glance at the TV screen. 'Your match still has half an hour to go and you're leading.'

'You sure know how to pick your times. All right.' He glances at his watch again, but half-heartedly.

I grab the remote control and lower the volume to a manageable level, then, as quickly and succinctly as I can, tell him about the house. I outline my suspicions about wet rot, dry rot, the roof, the need for insulation and new windows, the brambles, the whole thing. I make it personal. 'I don't want to be running around the country for Tommy O'Hare for the rest of my life, Bob. This could be a great opportunity. Tommy's interest will be in the land, I'll bet on that. He did say something about a boutique hotel but when he sees the state of the house he'll immediately send for the wrecking ball. He's not into details. I'm the detail person. The place is a wreck, sure, but for that reason he'd give it to us cheap. I could do amazing things with it.'

'How much would it cost to restore the place?' He's staring straight ahead.

'One, one-five tops. That would do it.'

'A million and a half?' That brings him round. His eyebrows have shot into his hairline. 'Plus the cost of buying it? Cee, are you cracked?'

'There are perfectly ordinary semi-ds in Dublin city changing hands for one point five and a lot more.' I won't be stopped. 'We'd get that easily for this house here. Come and see Whitecliff with me. Please?'

'Whitecliff?' He's scandalised. 'That's the place you're talking about? It's a complete ruin.'

'It looks it and I suppose it is. But it can be restored. I'll bet my soul on it. It has views to die for. The basic structure is sound – sort of. It has seven bedrooms. You should see the fireplace in the drawing room. Six bay windows on the ground

128

floor, Bob. Six. A wonderful minstrel's gallery. Huge. Could take a symphony orchestra. Think of the parties we could have.'

'Wait a second. You've already seen this dump? What's the point of talking to me about it?' He's getting angry. 'Anyhow, we're not in that league. You're talking too big—'

'And it's closer to Dublin than we are here.' I don't give him time to go further. 'There's a railway station only two miles away.'

'Oh, Claudine,' his use of my full name shows how dismayed he is, 'just when things were going really well.'

'You have your business and it's still a challenge to you,' I press on doggedly. 'I need something better in my life than trying to act as an intermediary between two people who are inching up a grand, or even a few hundred, on the price of a tiny little cottage at the back of beyond. You never know, I might even like to run a B and B' – I'm coasting here – 'one of those luxury country-house places—'

'A luxury B and B? What do you know about the hotel business?'

'What did I know about the property business before I joined OHPC? Please, Bob. I really want you to consider this. When have I ever asked you to do something for me? Something real?'

'What about those last two places you were absolutely convinced about and then didn't even put in a bid?'

'I accept that. You've every right to say that. But I keep telling you, Whitecliff is different.' I'm not sure I want to reveal this next bit yet, but then I do. 'It – it called to me, Bob.' I tell him about the photograph taken of my mother by the fireplace. 'I know I'm not superstitious, and I know you certainly aren't, but could you understand why I feel this house is for us?'

He gazes despairingly at me, and then through the picture window at the Beemer. At the manicured lawn, greenness itself, the beech hedge, the box borders and the ovoid flowerbeds where the solar lights, like fairy toadstools, are beginning cheerfully to glow in the dusk. 'I accept that you would be affected by any connection to your family. But she just went to a party there.'

'Daddy might have been there too.' Suddenly it has occurred to me that this might have been the source of my father's disquiet. Maybe there'd been some kind of incident at that party. Maybe my mother's parents threw him out or something like that.

Bob is staring straight ahead. 'So what? They were at a party there. You've made up your mind about this place on just one visit? A few poxy minutes spent in this bombsite?'

He's made a mistake. He's stepped on to my territory. 'It's not unusual to make up your mind about a property so quickly. It's been proven scientifically that decisions on buying houses are made within fourteen and seventeen seconds of a prospective buyer crossing a threshold. Something like that. Seconds anyhow. That's why we make sellers light fires, burn candles, make coffee and bake bread. We want them to hit all the senses. We try to convince them they're selling not a house but a lifestyle, something intangible, the prospect of happiness. I know this place is for me without any of those props or that staging. I know Whitecliff. I know it in my bones.'

He gazes at me, his expression haunted.

'There's one other thing,' I go for broke. 'There's this old guy we'd have to accommodate. We could build him a little bungalow or something. He's not all that house-trained but I kind of admire him. I couldn't just throw him off.'

'What old guy?' His voice is faint.

'He's a sort of sitting tenant. He lives outside among the brambles.'

Bob slaps his knee and explodes with helpless laughter. Even to my own ears that last bit had sounded quite barmy. And that's without mentioning the chopped-off staircase. I start laughing too.

I settle down beside him to watch his match. As long as we can still laugh together, I think . . .

And it's just as well we're in good humour because, on the telly, the other side scores.

# 14

# HIGH NELLIE

The fuss and tumult at Whitecliff during the days following Mother's announcement was not only animated but as happy as I had ever experienced, and even Father got caught up in the party preparations. He called in favours from his suppliers and customers, securing for us not only a small supply of white flour, but some tea, some real, proper coal for the drawing-room fireplace, and two very precious slabs of chocolate.

The flour was reserved for bread but there was still the dilemma of the birthday cake, for which even Father could not get enough flour, let alone the quantities of dried fruit and sugar we would need. Nanny, though, offered a solution: she had a friend of a friend, a woman in Drogheda, who specialised in creating and decorating realistic-looking wedding and celebration cakes from cardboard. 'Needs must, ma'am,' she said to Mother. 'You'd never know the difference unless you tried to eat it, of course. It's what everyone's doing these hard days.'

'I suppose people would understand.' Mother tried to be philosophical but she fretted about other restrictions: for instance, since the blackout curtains would have to be drawn at six thirty or so, our party had to start at five o'clock so we could make the most of daylight.

I gained the impression that her idea of a proper party was one that ran all night under a blaze of chandeliers. I was no doubt romanticising this: I saw everything in a shade of pink now that I had become a woman. 'We'll have plenty of light, Mother,' I said kindly to her. 'We have lots of lamp oil and tallow candles.'

But she was not appeased: 'I hate this horrible war. How much longer are we going to have to put up with this kind of thing? One gets so tired of being inventive and making do.'

When Mother had asked her, Nanny had gladly agreed to help out and to stay with us for the duration so that she did not have to travel in and out of the village.

That was what she called it: 'the duration'. I found this very funny, in the same way I found it funny that what the English *Times* called War, the Irish newspapers referred to as the Emergency. Alongside romance and pinkness, I found humour everywhere and, when safely alone in my room, I was prone to fits of giggles.

As the days passed, however, my elation had become tempered with frustration: during Nanny's duration Coley Quinn and I managed to see each other only once, and for just a few minutes, because from the day after Mother's announcement, Johanna and I had been put to making the house ready for the homecoming and the party. Working even through the Sabbath, we washed ewers and scoured baths, beat every rug in the house, pegged out eiderdowns to air. We dusted picture rails and chair legs, polished tables, swept bedrooms, shook out and aired feather mattresses and changed linen on the beds. We spent the whole of one day cleaning the parquet in the drawing room and dining room, and when we reported that done, we were given tins of Cardinal polish and told to use it on the quarry tiles under the portico. Every time we finished a task, Mother found three more for us to do. We were putting off scrubbing and buffing the flagstones in the hallway, which was very big and would probably take a whole day.

What was more, except for the periods just before sleep, I had little opportunity to dream about Coley in my room, because after the day's physical work was done and the blackout curtains secured each evening, instead of being allowed to escape, I had to slave over my patches for the Shine Quilt. We were sparing the paraffin too, to have as much as possible for the party, so while Mother stitched the body of the quilt spread over her relatively well-lit work-table, Johanna and I had to work close together within the dim circle of yellow light cast by a small, secondary lamp. We were always getting in each other's shadow, and by the time we were released each evening, I was nearly seeing double.

How I hated every single one of those patches. I also hated the silence of those evenings, broken only by the ticking of the clock or the occasional cough. Father wished us to be protected from war news, as broadcast by the BBC, and the Irish station sent out only a limited amount of music from Athlone. I found it staid and old-fashioned, but I would have welcomed even that. Mother, however, insisted she needed to concentrate absolutely on her sewing and forbade us to turn on the wireless so, over and over again, as I stuck my needle into the fabrics or bent close to the lamp mantle to thread it, I vowed resentfully that next year, somehow, I would find a way to wriggle out of this tiresome task.

I never uttered a word of complaint, however, and what sustained me throughout was the thrilling knowledge that, after further strategic nagging, Father and Mother had agreed that Johanna and I could indeed invite friends to Young Samuel's party.

Yet on the Monday morning after the Loughshinny outing, with just five days to go to the party, I was seriously chafing. Johanna was upstairs, writing invitations to be posted that afternoon. Mother had sent to Hely's stationers in Dublin for gilt-edged cards but since there was not enough time to have them engraved, my sister had been entrusted with this impor- tant work because of her beautiful handwriting. Mine was regarded as slapdash.

I had been consigned to the kitchen, to polish silver under the eyes of Mother and Nanny as they sorted tablecloths and linen napkins for laundering. I was uncomfortable, not only because of the strenuous, smelly work but because the room was so full of steam from the coppers boiling on the range. Strands of hair stuck to my cheeks and my clothes were sticky with perspiration. Even breathing was unpleasant.

Then Mother checked in the pantry and found we did not have enough starch. 'Roderick has already left for the shop.' She frowned. 'I do so want to get these done today. The drying is so good outside.' Whatever about tablecloths, napkins had to be crisp, with folds as sharp as knife blades.

I put down the fish slice on which I was working. 'I'll go to the village for you, Mother.'

'How would you get there?'

'I'll walk, of course.'

'No.' She was decisive. 'Knowing you, Violet, you'd dawdle and would take too much time about it. You're better employed at what you're doing.' She turned back to Nanny. 'We could wash anyway, Nanny, and when Roderick comes home this evening, I'll send him back for the starch. I can add it myself to another rinsing tonight. We'll just have to take our chances that tomorrow will be fine.'

'I could take Nanny's bicycle?' I would not give up.

Although she was approaching seventy, Nanny still travelled everywhere on what she called her High Nellie, a stern black upright with a curved fork, squarish chrome handlebars and a huge, silvery bell she kept so highly polished that even on dull days it flashed. She had taught me to ride this bicycle on our avenue. 'What do you think, Nanny?' Mother surveyed the pile of napkins in front of her on the table. 'I suppose we should take advantage of the sunshine today.'

'What harm? Let her go,' Nanny did not look up from where she was checking closely for stains on a damask cloth. 'If we need the starch, we need it. She'll be careful in the traffic, won't you, Violet?'

'I will, Nanny. Never fear.' Before they could change their minds I was taking off my hessian apron. 'And get some laundry blue too,' Mother added, as I folded it. 'We have enough, I think, but I wouldn't like to run out.'

'I will, Mother.' I was already at the back door. Nanny always propped her bicycle against the back wall, under the meat safe.

As I cycled round the side of the house, I knew that what I planned was brass-necked and risky, but if I was to catch Coley, even for a few minutes, I could think of no other option than to pay a visit to the creamery where, at this time of the morning, he would be working. Or should be: I had been so firmly confined to the house during the weekend I had not had a chance to go to our tree to see if he had left a note – and I did not want to waste precious time doing so now.

By the time I got to the end of the avenue, I had a story ready. It was a thin one – that since the creamery was on the way to the shop, I should extend our party invitation to Coley in person.

I pedalled so hard towards the village on Nanny's old bone-shaker that I was red-faced by the time I got within sight of the creamery, about two hundred yards from the first houses in the village. To give myself time to calm down and recover my breath – and to underpin that I 'just happened' to be passing on my way to our shop, I dismounted from the bicycle and set about picking a bunch of wild flowers in the overgrown verge.

I snatched indiscriminately at primroses and some flat, purplish blooms I could not name. That morning my senses were as overheated as my body, and even from my present perspective I can remember the distant, absurd bray of a donkey, the cracking as flower stalks broke, the subdued twittering in the fields and hedgerows. Then there were the smells: of earth and crushed grass and cow dung. Sounds and smells that before I met Coley Quinn I had never noticed.

I put my harvest into the basket strapped to the handlebars and, praying fervently that Coley would be in evidence, pushed the bicycle towards the village, trying to appear casual. My heart thumped, however, and not only at the prospect of seeing my lover. I had come here so boldly that it was possible Father would hear of it. This consideration, however, was outweighed by the reckless, overpowering feelings that went with being in love and I sincerely believed that my daring would go unpunished.

As I came level with the broad concrete forecourt of the creamery, I saw that among the congregation of local farmers chatting and smoking while they waited for their milk to be taken in, I knew two by name. They were customers of Rathlinney General Stores (as, probably, were most, if not all, of the others). 'Hello, Marcus, hello, Barney,' I called, and when, with a tip of their caps, they returned the salute, I slowed down and paused as if something had just occurred to me. 'Is Coley Quinn around? I'm on the way to the shop but if he's here, I have a message for him from Father and Mother. And isn't it a beautiful day?'

'It is, it is, thank God, Miss Shine,' the man named Barney called back. 'Coley's over there.' He pointed in the direction of the creamery shed. When I looked, I saw my lover deep in conversation with another man as they perused a receipt book.

All conversation and banter ceased while the men watched me push Nanny's bicycle, its whirring freewheel sounding excessively loud, towards the shed. Coley must have realised that something unusual was going on and turned before I got to him. His eyes widened, but only for a second, and, displaying a sangfroid I could only envy, he excused himself to the man to whom he had been talking and came towards me. 'Good morning, Miss Shine. What can we do for you?'

'Good morning, Coley.' I hoped his customer, watching me as keenly as all the other men, would attribute my burning cheeks to the effects of cycling in the sun. I spoke very loudly. 'Could we have a word? I have a message for you from Whitecliff.'

'Certainly. Let me take that for you.' He took the handlebars of Nanny's bicycle and wheeled it ahead of me and round the side of the building.

As soon as we were out of sight, he turned to me, eyes blazing. 'Violet.' He reached for me and would have taken me in his arms if I had not held him off.

'Ssh! Don't!' My bravery deserted me. For the two of us blatantly to vanish like this from the sight of all those farmers was madness and I could imagine the looks being exchanged on the forecourt. I had planned only to ask if he could manage to get away from the creamery for a few minutes.

'This was a mistake,' I babbled, 'but I do have a genuine message for you . . .' I told him quickly about his being invited to the party. 'And please bring one of your sisters along?' I backed away.

'Wait, Violet, wait! You want me and one of my sisters to come to a party in your house?' To say he sounded amazed would be an understatement.

'You'll be getting an invitation in the post.' I was too frightened to stay any longer. 'Listen, I'll try to leave a message under the tree.' I kissed him swiftly, straightened my shoulders, snatched the bicycle and wheeled it back round the corner of the shed.

He had the presence of mind to follow me immediately. 'Thank your parents, Miss Shine. What date will that be?' he called, as, in front of my fascinated audience, I mounted Nanny's High Nellie.

'Next – next Tuesday,' I faltered. 'They will be sending the letter to your house. Please give our best wishes to the rest of your family.' I went to place my feet on the pedals but missed one and grazed the inside of my leg against the chain, got up again and wobbled away with as much dignity as I could muster. The donkey brayed again, which, to add salt to my wounds, was followed by a volley of snorting and high-pitched male sniggering, only half suppressed.

I can only describe my short journey to our shop as a nightmare of self-recrimination and terror. If my heart had been over-active while I was approaching the creamery it was now pounding. I felt nauseous and dizzy. I even had a dreadful, sweetish taste in my mouth. Was it blood? Had I bitten my tongue?

'What's happened, love?' Sheila, the woman who had worked in our shop for as long as I could remember, looked up in alarm when the doorbell jingled and I rushed in.

'Nothing's happened,' I gasped. 'We've run out of starch, that's all. And we need laundry blue as well.'

Father, who had been slicing corned beef, wiped his hands on his butcher's apron. 'A starch emergency?' He grinned. He had obviously been infected by the general *joie de vivre* that had overtaken Whitecliff because he never made a joke.

At any other time I would have responded with delight to the novelty but not now. 'It is, Father, it is a bit. They're waiting for me to return with it!'

'Here, Violet.' Poor Sheila, reacting to my all-too-obvious panic, heaved her stout body to the corner of the store where the dry goods were kept on the shelves, took down the starch and the packet of blue, then virtually threw them at me. 'God, this is a great occasion, wha'?'

'It is, Sheila. Thank you.' I turned and ran back towards the door. Then, desperately, 'Oh, by the way, Father, I forgot to tell you. I passed the creamery on my way here and Coley Quinn was there. So I stopped to tell him we were inviting his sister and him to our party. I hope that was all right?'

## 15

# COUNTING CHICKENS

If I have news for Tommy, Tommy also has news for me. For a start, the house, he says, when I ring him the following morning, is not a listed building.

That could be good or bad, I think, depending on one's point of view. For Tommy it means Whitecliff can be demolished if he thinks it wouldn't be worth restoring. For me it means that if he thinks it is, I have to get my act together – before he starts working out what he could do with the place.

Contrary to instructions, I had waited until I was home from my jaunt before buzzing him last evening. Before I talked to him, I had wanted to be perfectly clear as to what course of action I would take on my own behalf.

I had delayed until I was sure he was safely ensconced at his *cumann* meeting, then, 'Talk to you tomorrow, Tom,' I chirped to his voicemail. 'Sorry I'm late getting back to you, but access into Whitecliff was tricky. I did get in eventually, though. It's going to need a bit of discussion. Talk in the morning – see ya!'

'Well? What's it like?' His excitement charges the telephone line. 'Did you get into the house? And were you spotted?'

'No, I wasn't spotted,' I lie. 'There's no way anyone could have seen me. Even going in through the entrance lane is like trekking through the Amazon jungle. I'll tell you, Tom, getting into that place is not easy, lucky for us so much of the wood is rotten.' Then, before he can ask any more questions, I go through what I think is salient: the decayed interior, the serious damp, the calamitous roof, yet I walk a fine line. I don't want him to settle on demolishing the house without even seeing it: when Tommy gets stuck on an idea, it's very hard to shift him, no matter what the evidence.

'The land?'

'A different matter entirely. Great possibilities, Tom.' I'm so enthusiastic I'm daytime TV. 'Good and dry, nicely undulating without being too hilly. It's covered with brambles and bracken and all kinds of growth—'

'Ach.' Tommy dismisses this, as I had known he would. While farmers burn brambles off their grazing land at intervals to fertilise the sward underneath with the ash, wilderness is never a problem to developers or builders who, like a US incursion force, simply ride in and uproot it with their monstrous machines. 'Did you get off that Greenparks stuff, by the way?'

'I did. And I'm coming to meet you. Be there in an hour. We need to talk.'

'Uh-oh. You're not handing in your notice, are you, Claudine?'

'No, I'm not quitting just yet, you chancer, but don't push your luck.' It's a running joke but there's a serious side to it. Tommy lives in fear of this and I know why. He would never get anyone new to put up with his chaotic [non-]filing systems, back-of-envelope notes and the way he fastens on to some deals to the exclusion of others. A kid, even one who graduated top of the class with a shiny diploma in property management, would be completely at sea. Over the years we've come to suit each other: I can anticipate what he's going to do; he's flexible about my hours.

Tommy never locks his door, and when I get into his house, I find him seated at the little table in his topsy-turvy kitchen where bulging file covers, a Rolodex and a prehistoric adding machine, the kind with a winding handle, fight for counter space with kettle, crockery, microwave, toaster and tinned food. Having designated the smallest bedroom in his house as an office, he dislikes it and prefers to do most of his work here. He doesn't hear me come in.

'Hiya, Tom! I see the wife's hard at work?'

'Wha'?' He looks up.

'The new wife.' I point to his audibly sloshing dishwasher, hooked up but standing in the middle of the kitchen because he has not yet pushed it into the space provided beside the sink. He glances at it. 'You were right to make me get that, Claudie. It's great. Take a pew.'

'At least you're using it.' I sit opposite him. 'What are they?' I can see he's been poring over a set of smudged and grainy photostats.

'Pulled a few strings yesterday. I've found out who owns the pile.'

'So?' I hold my breath.

'It's not a codger like I told you, it's some old dear called Collopy with an address in West Cork. But Directory Enquiries said the phone was ex-directory so I rang a contact of mine down there and apparently she cashed in her chips about eighteen months ago and it hasn't been re-registered yet – but you know how long that takes. There's a huge backlog. There's a sister. Pretty ancient, I gather. She probably inherited. Or it could be an executor's sale.'

'I see.' An executor's sale can be a very long-drawn-out affair – but the owner's sister would have the same information about my mother, surely.

He peers at the back of a crumpled receipt. 'Her address is somewhere way out in the Atlantic. My contact says you'd need a mule and then a canoe to get to it.' He giggles. 'Listen,' he says then, 'to be serious, you don't need a canoe but apparently it is the seaside.' Then, music to my ears, he suggests what I've been gearing up to suggest for myself: 'What about you go down there, Claudie? Pretend you're on your holliers. Nose around. See what's what. Even if it is an executor's sale, you never know what stroke we might be able to pull if you go to see yer one in person.'

I'm mentally in the car already but don't want to sound too eager. 'Listen, Tom, this is big – it could be the big one for us. Why don't you go yourself?'

'Ah, no.' He looks horrified, as I knew he would. To my boss, everything outside the Pale is Injun territory: he feels uncomfortable any place not within fifty miles of the south inner city, and came to live in the sticks, as he calls it, because even before they died, his parents' huckstering business was going into decline. There's also another factor. While of course he deals with them when he has to, he's even softer with old ladies than he is with first-time buyers, finds it difficult to drive a hard bargain with them, no matter how many times he might refer to them as dames, old dears or oul' wans. 'Ah, no,' he says, 'you go. I'd be useless down there, you know that. I can never understand a word those people say. Anyway, this is a case where you'd do much better than me. You know, woman to woman, Claudie, sympathy, that sort of thing.'

'Let me think about it.'

'And guess what,' he acts as if he hasn't heard me, 'I met Ferdy Macken last night at the *cumann*. He said if we can get some serious money to come in with us, he won't see us stuck.' Ferdy, a political pal of Tommy's, is the area manager for one of the larger banks. 'He says he'll introduce me to some people.'

'How did you hear about the place coming on the market? I don't want to go all the way down there on foot of just a rumour.' I don't tell him, yet, that to secure this house for myself, I'd swim to Alaska.

'It's not just a rumour – do you want a cuppa, Claudie?' He heaves himself to his feet and trots across to the counter beside the sink, extricates a flex that is tangled in two others, fills the kettle, plugs it in, then hunches intently over it as if by watching it he'll force it to boil faster.

'Not just a rumour. What is it, then?'

He hesitates, then turns to face me. 'The sister was seen going into the local solicitor's office.'

I sit back in my chair. 'That's it? That's your information? The elderly sister of the deceased was observed visiting her solicitor?'

His eyes won't engage with mine. 'The solicitor is a cousin of a chap I know down there. I did him a favour a while ago and we just happened to be chatting . . .' He's looking shifty.

'"Just happened", Tom?' Now, don't get me wrong, Tommy O'Hare is basically honest. But OHPC, being such a minnow, has to get business where it finds it: it runs on contacts and information gleaned in pubs and golf clubs, anywhere people meet, plus lucky guesses, of course. 'This chap you know,' I ask slowly, 'what does he do?'

'He's, er, he's an auctioneer.'

'Wait a second. You're alleging that this woman's solicitor rang his cousin, the auctioneer, who then paid you back a favour by tipping you off that she might bring her estate on to the market?'

'I'm not saying that at all.' He's making a good fist of sounding indignant. 'This is Ireland we're living in, Claudie. We're a small country, and you know how things work here. The woman lives in a spit of a place apparently. She could have said it to one of her pals in the local shop – she could have told anyone. She could have been talking on her mobile in the street and someone heard. You know how it goes . . .'

The kettle boils and clicks off. He turns and makes the tea.

'Remember I said there was something I wanted to talk to you about?' I address his back.

'Yeah . . .'

'Remember I told you how crap the house is – but how the location is terrific and the ground is good and dry and the view is to die for? This wouldn't be just first-time buyers, Tom. I could see this development being upmarket. Detached properties, a Millionaire's Row – you know?'

'Yeah?' He comes towards me with two mugs and looks piercingly at me. 'We know that. What are you gettin' at, Claudie?' He sits down.

'What I'm getting at is that, if we secure this deal, I want you to detach the house from the land. Break the property into two lots. I want the house with maybe one acre around it, enough for privacy. And I want it at cost. You talk about favours, Tommy, you owe me a few.'

'You want the house? Come off it, Claudie. What do you want it for? It's falling down, according to you.'

'I want to restore it. To live in it.'

'You must be joking!' He starts to laugh. But when I don't laugh with him, he stops. 'Holy-moly, you're serious about this.'

'Deadly serious.'

His eyes narrow. 'Are you telling me the truth about that place? Is it as bad as you've made out?'

'Believe me, it's bad.'

'Does your husband know about this mad notion?'

'I told him last night.'

'He thinks it's a good idea?'

'No,' I say honestly, 'but he'll come round.'

He gazes at me and I can almost hear the grinding in his brain. 'You go on down to West Cork,' he says slowly. 'See what you can do with the oul' wan. And if we get the deal, we'll talk. Fair enough?'

'Sorry. Not fair enough. We make our personal deal first and then I agree to go to West Cork.'

'I could go myself, you know.'

'You could.'

A staring match.

He grins wryly. 'You drive a hard bargain, Mrs Armstrong.'

'You taught me well, Mr O'Hare.' I jump up and give him a long, fervent hug. 'Hey, hey!' he protests. 'Not in front of the dishwasher!'

I stand back and grin idiotically at him. 'You won't be disappointed, Tom, I promise you. If that place is for sale, I'll get it for us. You can tell your pal Ferdy it's in the bag.'

'Let's not count our chickens. Here,' he shuffles the papers on the table, picks one and thrusts it at me, 'just came by courier. Your pals at Greenparks rejected this.'

'Fine, fine – I'll work on it.' Nothing can faze me. I've done enough for today. Now all I have to do, I tell myself, while I check out the dispiriting red circles and crossings-out over my carefully crafted eulogies on the delights of Cruskeen Lawns, is to get myself to West Cork. I'm not only excited about the house, I'm already far down the road of convincing myself that this old lady down there knew my mother, or if she didn't, she certainly knew someone who did.

# 16

## LANTERNS IN THE TREES

Johanna and I speculated for days about what we would wear for the party, and eventually I decided on something white to contrast with my colouring. We debated about our hair: whether she should pin hers up, whether I should let mine loose – loose for both us, we agreed. Then, while I tried to guess how much rouge and face powder I could wear without Mother sending me up to my room to wash it off, my sister worried about the welfare of her friend, Shirley. 'I know she's a teacher, Violet, but underneath she's quite shy, you know. I do hope she has a good time. She will be my personal guest so I do feel responsible for her.'

It was the day before the party and we were on our knees in the hall, washing the flagstones before buffing them. A local band had been engaged to play on the landing above us – it was hoped that guests would dance – so it was up to us to provide a suitable surface. Johanna wrung out her rinsing cloth. 'Is your friend Mary Kelly coming?'

'She's in Wexford, with her family. I told you that, Johanna.' I realised, too late, that I had snapped at her. Any mention of

149

the shortness of my invitation list alarmed me. 'The other Mary, Mary Quigley, is coming,' I amended.

'I forgot.' Johanna's expression was sombre. 'Sorry.'

'Oh, look – there's a patch we missed.' On the woollen mat I was using to cushion my knees, I propelled myself towards a corner of the floor beside the staircase. I did not want my sister to enquire further about my party guests. Convinced she would refuse, I had invited Mary Quigley for appearance's sake but, to my chagrin, an acceptance had come by return of post. I was devastated at the thought that I would be saddled with her for the entire evening but hoped I could convince one or both of the twins or, alternatively, Young Samuel, to take her under his wing and introduce her to friends. I had to be free to grasp any opportunity that presented itself for Coley and me.

Meanwhile, I had to remain wary. I thought it significant that Johanna had not brought up the subject of Coley Quinn. After all, she had heard me mention his name that evening at dinner when the idea for the party first came up. Yet she had not asked about him since, not once, although while we worked together, almost all of our chat and speculation concerned the opposite sex – whom had the twins invited? They had been sent four invitations each. How many young men would come down from Dublin with Young Samuel? What would these young men be like? Would they be un-attached or would they bring girls? Yet I continued to be uneasy about her possible glimpse of what I had been writing in my diary that evening when she had stood at my shoulder.

As for Mother and Father, they were seriously distracted by the extraordinary, almost chaotic state of preparation that had engulfed the household. For instance, when he, sent by her, had approached me with the invitation list and I had had to admit that my only three guests would be Mary Quigley, Coley Quinn 'and, of course, Florrie Quinn, one of his sisters,' he had not seemed to find this of note, except to make one rather jocular comment: 'I'm relieved, Violet. I'll be in the poorhouse after this and any reduction helps. But what happened to the whole army you were going to ask? Mother seems to think you planned to invite a battalion.'

Grateful that he was frowning at the list in his hand and not at me, I mumbled something about not having got round to any more invitations. Then I could not resist gilding the lily: 'I'm sorry now I asked anyone. It's not my party, after all. But I did ask those three and I cannot now unask them.'

'Yes, yes, good girl,' he said, over his shoulder, as he hurried off, leaving me limp.

When I deemed it safe, I returned to scrubbing beside Johanna and, to my relief, she steered the conversation to Marjorie.

Nobody knew whether or not our sister was coming alone. She had been mysterious, apparently, when speaking on the telephone to Father at the shop. 'She said she might or might not,' he had reported, 'but she did say we should have an extra bed ready just in case.'

'If she does bring a beau, he might have another friend, Johanna,' I teased now, arching my back to ease the ache. 'You, too, might find a suitor!'

'Stop it, Violet.'

I could see I had hit a nerve and dropped the subject. 'We'll never get through all this in time.'

'We will.' She did not let up. 'We have to.'

Although one would not have thought so on that day

151

before the party, the week-long build-up, although hectic, had been organised, thanks not only to our free labour but to Nanny's housekeeping skills and Mother's inherently level disposition – which, however, I was beginning to question. During the hard work and bustle I would have expected her to be irritable but the contrary was the case – despite her frequent protests that she was sorry she had ever mentioned the wretched word 'party', I detected a certain lightness of tone, even a sparkle in her eyes. She laughed a great deal more than usual and, although I could not swear to this, I believe I heard her hum once while she was ironing. Mother was enjoying herself!

Mealtimes went pleasurably askew during that period, and instead of insisting that we all sit at table at set times, Mother ate Nanny's sandwiches standing over the copper boilers, or while she and Nanny turned out cupboards. (Why? It was a mystery to Johanna and me why even the linen closet had to be spick and span. Were our guests invited to our house to embark on a tour of inspection?) She even ate her soup from a cup, rather than with a spoon from a bowl, and allowed Johanna and me to do the same.

Strange to say, it had never before struck me in any real way that my mother might once have been a lighthearted girl, but seeing her flashing gaily through her chores and joking with Nanny, I began to wonder if, day to day, she might feel as oppressed by life at Whitecliff as I did. I remembered our last family visit to the Theatre Royal in Dublin for the variety show, how startling it was to hear the deep-chested heartiness of her laugh. Given her impeccably ladylike demeanour, it was astonishing to hear it peal longer and louder in the packed theatre than almost anyone else's.

I hesitated to put two and two together. This was my mother, for goodness' sake, and her feelings, even a metamorphosis such as this, were not something on which I wished to dwell. I must not become soft or drop my guard, because that might lead to an unwitting betrayal of my secret. Anyhow, at Whitecliff we were not in the habit of discussing feelings, and where my mother and I were concerned, the phrase 'generation gap', although not yet in use, would have been apt.

Throughout this period, we girls did not complain. This was not only because there would have been no point in doing so but because, for once, the dreary tasks had a purpose: we were working on Whitecliff to show her old bones at their very best. For myself, although I resented my confinement to the house, I decided there was no point in being upset about it. I had to be patient, and contented myself with confiding my frustrations to my diary each evening.

On the day before the party, the house smelt like a field because of the armfuls of greenery and white hawthorn (hawthorn!) that Mother had arranged in tall vases everywhere. Having finished the hall, where the flags were now of such a high shine they might have been made of porcelain, we were sent to take care of the portico. And when we had finished that last major chore in the late evening, its twin pillars – scrubbed with warm water and washing soda, then dried with soft cloths – gleamed like marble and we could do no more. Final food preparations were being left to the last minute and, as far as we were concerned, the house was ready, inside and out.

We called Mother to inspect our work. Giving the right impression from the start, she had insisted, was important because of the tone it would set for the entire evening. We hung back as she moved around, scrutinising the pillars, the shining door brasses, the quarry tiles, so slick that the slanting evening sun could pick out not a single speck of dust; we had even combed the end-tassel of the bell-pull so it was as silky as a show-pony's tail and even Mother, with her almost impossibly high standards, had to admit that everything was as it should be. 'That's fine, girls,' she said, then looked up at the rapidly gilding sky. 'Let us hope this weather holds!'

Then, with a vehemence that astonished, almost shocked us: 'Oh, how I hate this damnable war! If this were a proper party, we would have lanterns in the trees and torches flaming along the avenue. The house should blaze with light from every window!'

My sister and I stared, slack-jawed. This was not the mother we knew. This woman was passionate. She swore. We could not believe it.

She could not believe it either: she shot us a glance, then concentrated on tucking a stray strand of hair into the chignon she always wore at the back of her head. 'I'm sorry.' She was again demure and would not meet our gaze. 'I did not mean to sound petulant – and please, girls, do not follow my bad example with the language I used. Of course it will be a proper party. Look – hasn't Martin done well too?'

Over the days, our workman had worked tirelessly on creating a good first impression for our visitors. There was not a weed to be seen in the velvety lawns on both sides of the driveway, and in front of the portico, he had spent hours painstakingly raking the gravel into a complex series of concentric whorls. Mother, no doubt ashamed of her outburst, now warned us in her most severe tone that we were to walk on this gravel at our peril. Until the party started the following afternoon, family, she decreed, must skirt it and use the back door.

I had recovered sufficiently at that stage to point out that Uncle Samuel, who was driving the twins from their training barracks outside Belfast, was due at any moment to arrive from the north. 'If he may not disturb the gravel, where shall he park his car?'

'He's family. He shall have to park on the avenue,' she said brusquely. 'Father, too, when he gets back. You stay in the hall to watch for them, Violet. Go out as each of them approaches and explain. I want this forecourt kept clear. And don't scuff that gravel when you intercept them! Go wide along the grass.'

I did not mind at all being asked to play sentry. In fact, I looked forward to it as an opportunity to get my thoughts together, because the next hour or so was to see an influx and none of us would have a minute to think: we were expecting not only Uncle Samuel and the twins, but Marjorie and Young Samuel too. They were travelling down together from Dublin, and Father had gone to meet them off the bus.

'Well,' Mother said, unpinning her apron, 'I must go inside. However, I must say that you two girls have been very helpful over the past week. You have worked splendidly together. Well done!'

'Oh, Mother, thank you!' She had never been given to praising us and, impulsively, I threw my arms round her neck to hug her.

'Gracious, Violet!' But as she disentangled herself, she was smiling. 'What on earth was that for?'

'Nothing,' I said, close to tears. I could not articulate my feelings. I was happy to receive such an unprecedented compliment, happy with her uncharacteristic outburst, happy to have seen her happy during the previous week, that our family would all be together again this weekend, that there was gaiety in my home, but mostly that I was in love and that I would see Coley Quinn the next day, no matter how nervous we both might be.

Mother looked closely at me. 'Are you going to cry, Violet?'

'No, Mother. Not at all. I think I may be quite tired.'

'Well,' she said, 'I think we are all tired. It has been worth it, I hope.' She glanced up again at the Titian-tinted sky. 'Time to draw the blackout curtains. And I must change out of these old clothes. We will all eat together when everyone has arrived. Nanny is laying the table in the dining room.' She smiled again at both of us, then touched my cheek. 'Good girl.'

I was undone. Our family is not emotionally effusive, as I have said, and this spontaneous gesture of affection did bring forth the tears.

'Dear me,' Mother said, peering towards Johanna for enlightenment, 'what have I done now?'

'Nothing. Nothing,' I snivelled. 'I told you, I'm very tired.' I rooted for the handkerchief in the pocket of my apron.

'You go on, Mother,' my sister said. 'I'll stay here with her.'

'There's no need.' I blew my nose. 'Sorry about this. I have no idea what came over me but I feel grand again now. It must be the lack of food as well as the tiredness. I'm quite hungry, aren't you? You don't need to stay, Johanna. I'm sure you'd like to change too, to wash. I shall not mind at all being by myself while I wait for the cars. It won't be for long, I'm sure.'

I was not being considerate. While it was never a burden

to be with Johanna, and I did not know how to express it without hurting her, I longed for a spell alone. She said again to Mother that she would stay with me and I was left with no choice. It was a small matter in any case.

So, after our mother had left, the two of us tiptoed across our clean hall into the drawing room and sat on one of the window-seats from which we would have a clear view of the avenue. I settled in with my back to one of the open shutters, drew my knees to my chest and hugged them. Above us, the windows were open to that stillness that sometimes comes with the setting sun. 'We'll hear them before they come anyway,' I said, admiring the rosy crowns of the beech trees. 'Look at that wonderful sky, Johanna! Red at night, shepherd's delight, for a fine day tomorrow. Don't you love this time of evening?'

'I do.' She sounded pensive.

I was content to sit in silence after that, but then became aware that my sister seemed uneasy. 'Is there something wrong?' I looked away from the sunset to see her sitting with hands folded in her lap. She had tied a scarf, gypsy-style, round her hair and in the soft light, she reminded me of one of those slightly melancholy figures you see in the Brueghel paintings of which the younger Miss Biggs was so fond – she frequently brought prints and postcards into the art-appreciation class to show us. 'There's nothing wrong, Violet,' Johanna said, 'but—'

'Yes?' I encouraged.

'I was going to mention it to you earlier, a few times, actually, but I couldn't find the courage. Anyhow, I know it is none of my business.' She fidgeted with a fold in her skirt.

I knew instantly what she meant, of course, but, strangely,

instead of trying to suppress it, my overwhelming desire now was to force it into the open. As she struggled for words I felt sorry for her but drove on nonetheless. 'Not your business? What's not your business?'

'I – I just think you should be careful tomorrow. That's all,' she stammered.

'Careful about what?'

'During the party.'

'Tell me what you mean, Johanna.' I swung my feet to the ground and straightened my back.

'You know what,' she cried.

'I don't, Johanna. I really don't.'

As we gazed at each other, I saw how I had distressed her and, contrite, reached out with one arm to hug her slim shoulders. 'I'm sorry, Johanna. Forgive me. I didn't mean to upset you like this. You're the best sister in the world, you really are. I do know what you mean. And I will be careful. I promise.'

'I don't mean just tomorrow either, Violet.'

'I know.' I was about to reassure her further when we heard the thunk-thunk of Father's engine – we knew it was his: in musical terms there was always a semi-quaver rest, a tiny beat between thunks. 'I'll go.' I slid off the window-seat. 'You get changed, Johanna. I don't care what Marjorie or Young Samuel thinks of me. In their minds I'm probably beyond redemption.'

She did not smile.

I hugged her again. So much for our family not being demonstrative, I thought. 'Listen, Jumie,' my childhood name for my sister when I could not pronounce her real name properly, 'please don't worry about me – and, again, I'm sorry.'

'I forgive you.' She wiped her eyes with the palm of her hand. 'Hurry, Violet, we need to get ready. The car is nearly here – we don't want Mother on the warpath . . .'

# 17

# RELAX, WEE VIOLET

Uncle Samuel, glass of whiskey in hand, stood in the drawing-room window, looking out at the lawns. 'Why don't you make a tennis court out there for the young people, Fly? Yous have plenty of space. That there side lawn's ideal.'

Every time Uncle Samuel came to visit and I heard him and my mother speak together, I realised once again how much of her northern twang she had lost. 'I've more to be doing than thinking of tennis courts.' She flicked an errant speck of dust off the mantelpiece. Although it was ten minutes to five, she was still tweaking and adjusting, plumping and arranging.

We had decided that since the party was to start so early, evening dress would not be appropriate but in a sheath dress of royal blue satin with sequins and padded shoulders, its belt fastened with a diamanté buckle, I thought Mother was *à la mode*. Goodness knows where she found such fabric in those hard-pressed times but she had somehow acquired enough of it — and the time — to make the dress and cover her shoes. They, too, sported diamanté buckles.

I had forgotten how good-looking she was, but that afternoon, her cheeks rouged and her hair fixed in a sausage-roll round her hairline, as was the fashion then, she looked as though she had stepped out of a magazine.

'You look marvellous, Mother.' I smiled up at her while she tightened the tieback on the curtains beside where I sat. 'You smell lovely too.' Mother's scent of choice was a concoction that smelt of lemons and vanilla. It was made up specially for her in an old-fashioned chemist's shop in Belfast and sent to her by post.

'Thank you, dear,' she said, looking across to the doorway into the hall, then clicking across to it. 'Roderick?' she called loudly, to make herself heard over the tuning of the band already *in situ* upstairs. 'Johanna? And you boys up there! Are you all nearly ready?' Even this was a novelty. Mother raising her voice!

'I am, Mother.' Young Samuel strolled past her into the room. 'Ready, willing and able. Afternoon, Sam.' He saluted our uncle on his way to the sideboard where he proceeded to mix himself a gin and It. The cocktail's name had always intrigued me until I had found out only that evening that the 'It' stood not for some secret and exotic ingredient but for Italian vermouth.

I had been ready since half past two but, fearful of being put to work again, had come down only in the last few minutes to perch in one of the window-seats from which I could keep an eye on the arrivals. So nervous I was sure it would show, I clasped my hands together so they would not tremble and prayed that Coley would not be the first to arrive. Then I changed my mind and prayed that Mary Quigley would not, then reverted to Coley. What devil had possessed me that I had asked Coley Quinn to come to my house?

161

Uncle Samuel sat down beside me and winked. 'Have you your eye on anyone these days, Violet? Any young upstarts I should put my own beady eye on?' I was so anxious that even this mild witticism made me jump while my face reddened.

'Oh dear!' Young Samuel called. 'You've touched a nerve there, Uncle!'

'Don't mind him.' Uncle Samuel patted my knee. 'You're a right bonny wee girl. I've never seen you look so good and my guess is you'll need a pitchfork to keep off thon boys the night.' I blushed harder, and tactfully, he turned round to look through the window. 'Weather's holding up anyhow. So, tell me, how did your studies go? Are you nearly finished up?'

'I am indeed, Uncle.'

Uncle Samuel's mantra had always been that no one could have too much education, even when I was about five years old and seated on his lap at some family gathering. 'And there'll come the day when little girls like Violet here will not be content with second best. I'm talking university, boys. There'll come a time when there'll be more of them in thon Dublin colleges than what there are lads,' he had said. At the time, all the adults in the room had smiled at such a crackpot notion.

Nanny, dressed for the occasion in black except for a white apron, came into the room. She was walking very slowly because she was carrying the silver punchbowl that was normally taken out only at Christmas. 'That was a lovely lunch, ma'am,' Uncle Samuel inclined his head towards her in courtly fashion, and Nanny was so obviously pleased I believe that, if she had not been afraid she might slop the punch, she would have curtsied. 'Thank you, sir, sorry it was so rushed. But for sure we'll have a proper Sunday luncheon tomorrow.' She placed the bowl in the centre of the drum table in front of the french windows and proceeded to marshal the little cups. 'Isn't it great to have all the young people around us again, even if it is for such a short time? But we'll make the most of it, I'm sure.'

Nanny had entered into the spirit of the occasion as much as any of us, more so in some respects because she had little to prove. Having worked like a Trojan all week, she was now content to act as senior waitress for the evening – hence the quasi-uniform – and had recruited a local girl to help her. 'Isn't it a bit early for spirits, dear?' She fixed her gaze on Young Samuel's drink.

'Oh, Nanny, don't be such a spoilsport.' He remained cheerful. 'I'm a grown-up now. And am I not the guest of honour?' Cheekily, he raised his glass to her and drank. She pursed her lips and muttered to herself.

Nanny's father, we gathered, had drunk himself into an early grave and while, professionally, she would never balk at serving alcohol to us, she had herself never touched a drop and proudly wore an emblem to indicate that she was a life-long member of an abstinence association. It was going to be interesting, I thought, to observe how she managed if any of our family or guests this evening became intoxicated and asked for more.

Marjorie burst into the room. 'Come on, before the mayhem, everyone outside for photographs. Posterity must be served. I bought this specially.' She brandished a camera. 'You too, Nanny – and winkle those boys down, will you?'

I have never liked having my photograph taken, my dislike doubled on this occasion. I was terrified that, in the process, I would be caught short, as it were, by the arrival of Coley and his sister. I did not know how I could handle that in full view of my family.

Outside the portico, we all posed in different groups, then together. Marjorie was a natural organiser and within ten minutes we were all back inside the house. I got to my station in the window as the doorbell clanged, and the band on the landing, taking it as their cue, burst into a lively Irish tune. I whirled to see the first arrivals. 'And they're off!' Uncle Samuel nudged me playfully, and I jumped for the second time that night.

The bell clanged again and Nanny threw up her hands. 'What a racket! People nowadays have no patience. Where the dickens is that girl?' She rushed out of the room to answer the summons.

'Relax, wee Violet.' Uncle Samuel patted my knee. 'This is going to be a great night. Enjoy yourself.'

Our guests were nothing if not punctual, and in the next few minutes, cars, bicycles and pony-carts came up the driveway almost nose to tail. A few, obviously hackneys, dropped their passengers and drove off again but most parked willy-nilly, ruining poor Martin's immaculate gravel. Although both front doors stood wide open now, the bell rang constantly, vying with the accordion and fiddles overhead; people obviously felt that, rather than walk straight in, they should announce their arrival.

The party was in full swing, with almost all of the guests present before half past five. There was still no sign of Coley. Or of Mary Quigley. I was beginning furtively to hope she had been struck down with a head cold, toothache or some other mild malady – I did not want to be mean – that would keep her at home for this one evening. Then the doorbell sounded yet again and there she was, tall and awkward in yellow taffeta with a hairband to match. Like an oversized daffodil, I thought nastily, then felt immediately guilty. 'You look lovely, Mary,' I said. 'Come on in. You're very welcome.'

She was busily looking around. 'What a lovely house,' she said, peering upwards in the hall, eyes wide, spectacles glinting in the sunlight streaming through the doorway. 'And so big! I'd heard you lived well, but I had no idea how well. How on earth did you stick our little school?' I had no doubt she had meant it tartly but somehow, instead of intimidating me, as I suspect she had intended, it steadied my nerves. 'Thank you very much, Mary,' I said sweetly. 'Would you like me to show you around? Let me take you up to my bedroom so you can freshen up. There will be plenty of room. As it happens, my bedroom is really huge.'

'That would be nice.' She did not react to the barb but continued to gawp up at the landing where the musicians showed through the banisters. 'Maybe later.' She handed me a package, wrapped in brown paper. 'My mother sent you this. It's a potion she makes from herbs and goat's milk. She says she saw you recently in the village and it occurred to her it could do your skin the world of good. You rub it in every night and every morning.'

'Do you use it yourself, Mary?' Whatever about the state of my own skin, which was, I fancied, quite good, due not only to all the fresh air I was getting in recent times but also to Mother's good, plain cooking, a clear complexion was not one of Mary Quigley's more attractive features. This time she recognised the insult. She frowned at me but had no chance to retort because I got in first and took her arm in comradely fashion. 'Thank your mother for me, won't you? Please tell her I shall use it with great pleasure. Now, come and have some fruit punch and let me introduce you to my family and some of my brothers' friends.'

'What are they like?' She forgot her displeasure as, like an eager puppy, she accompanied me towards the drawing room where all three of my brothers were in boisterous mood. 'They are very nice,' I said. 'Most of them, of course, are girls.' I let go of her arm and walked ahead of her. I could not believe how cruelly I was behaving towards the poor girl. After all, I had invited her. She was my honoured guest and, in the absence of Coley Quinn and his sister, maybe the only one.

That was the problem I had with her: she was not Coley Quinn. Yet my disappointment vied with relief. For sure I wanted desperately that he should be there, but I was delighted at some level that he was not. We would have other opportunities.

What I had said to Mary about girls outnumbering boys was not true. Three of the seven who had announced themselves as having been invited by James and Thomas were indeed girls, but four were boys I hazily remembered from national school. I did not forewarn Mary Quigley about their provenance, however: she had no doubt envisaged dashing men in uniform, not farmers' sons with strangling ties and hair so thickly brilliantined that the scent overpowered Mother's flowers.

As for Young Samuel's friends, three girls and two young men, they were so far ahead of Mary and me in age, I knew that even she would not see a chance of romance with them. Anyhow, they all, including, intriguingly, Young Samuel himself, seemed to be paired. His girl wore her hair short, almost like a boy's.

Meanwhile, after all the speculation, Marjorie, limber in a white lace dress that clung to her curves, had brought not a beau but a female friend. What was more, she was expecting another to come off the late bus and was meanwhile cajoling everyone to pose for photographs as near as possible to the gaslights. In truth, I saw few possibilities for Mary Quigley.

I decided it would be easiest to start the introductions with Marjorie and turned to take Mary's arm again but while I had thought she was right behind me, I saw she was dithering in the drawing-room doorway. She was clearly overawed.

No wonder, I thought. In the sunlight pouring through the bay windows, the room glittered with refracted light from the crystals on the two huge gasoliers, from the mirror reflecting the banks of tallow candles, already lit on the mantelpiece – and, I dare say, from the furniture and parquet floor buffed to a high shine by Johanna's and my hard labour! While upstairs, the poor musicians trilled for their own benefit, the drawing room, usually so quiet and sedate, rang with chat and laughter from groups of merchants, suppliers, neighbouring farmers – perhaps forty-five or fifty people – who quaffed drinks, clinked glasses to toast each other and munched dainty canapés from silver trays handed around by Nanny and the temporary maid.

At the bay-windowed end, Uncle Samuel was at the centre of Young Samuel's crowd, who seemed to find him fascinating; James and Thomas, together as usual, were horseplaying in front of the fireplace with the three girls they had invited while the farmers' sons looked on uncomfortably; near the french windows, Mother was handing out small glasses of port and sherry to a gathering of women, including our rector's wife, clustered on an arrangement of chairs and small sofas around two coffee-tables. For his part, Father was now deep in conversation with the rector and some of the husbands. I recognised the bank manager and the two local doctors, Ryan and Willis.

'What's the matter, Mary?' I went back to join her.

'Nothing. I'm just taking my time, taking it all in . . .'

'Come and meet people then.' Involuntarily, I clutched at her arm and it was not to lead her to introductions. Because, to my horror, I could see that one of the men talking to Father was the creamery manager. He must have arrived while I was distracted by Uncle Samuel. Suppose he told Father about my vanishing round the side of his building with Coley Quinn? 'You're hurting me, Violet!' Mary wrenched away her arm.

The doorbell rang. Both Mary and I, who were still standing just inside the drawing-room door, turned to look. Standing on the quarry tiles outside were Coley Quinn and one of his sisters.

# 18

# OUT OF THE BLUE

'Where the hell are we?' Irritably, Bob swings the car on to the wet, boggy verge, even though there's no safe place to stop on this corkscrew road, a bare two-car width where every short-order corner is blind. He had consulted some colleague who claimed to know this part of the country like the back of his hand and we had been following the route the guy had recommended. 'We should've done what I wanted to do in the first place and get the AA to give us a proper route.'

Heroically I desist from pointing out that this was something I had advised but that at the time he had pooh-poohed: 'Murph knows what he's talking about. He says his way will cut maybe half an hour off the trip. No towns and only one or two little villages. And he says there's very little traffic.'

I have also desisted from pointing out that twice, as we drove through the villages of Kilmichael and Coppeen, I had suggested we ask for directions in a pub. 'No no, it'll be fine,' he'd said the first time, and on the second, 'I don't want to stop – otherwise we'll never get there.'

All afternoon we'd been travelling through driving rain,

first on the long, fraught journey to Cork, where we spent most of the time, when we weren't watching out for speed traps, dodging muck and spray from sixteen-wheelers. Then, after a pit stop for bathroom and coffee, hours ago it now seemed, we had turned off the wide Cork–Killarney road on to this torture trail. We are now at the top of a mountain pass, not all that high, according to the Ordnance Survey map spread out on my lap under the map light. Beyond this pass there should be the Atlantic and our destination.

Right now, we can't see a thing other than a sludge of whitish-grey mist licking at our windows and reflecting back at us in the beam from our useless headlights. 'Maybe we should turn back.'

'Thank you for that, Cee! That's most helpful.' He grabs the map off my lap, consults it for a millisecond, then flings it any old how over his shoulder into the back seat. He snaps the car into gear. 'I must have been mad.'

The experiment in marital togetherness is not turning out all that well.

You might ask why Bob is with me on this trip into the wilds. I'm asking too. I must have had a rush of blood to the head to agree to it.

We had continued our Whitecliff discussion in bed, on the night I had broached it. It was quite friendly and, if you remember, while he was watching the football, I had managed to persuade him that we could at least try. I had spooned into his warm back: 'Nothing is written in stone, Bob. This owner, whoever he is, mightn't want to sell at all. He might have ideas about developing the place himself. He might even want to move back in.'

'I've said "all right".' He turned to put his arms round me.

'Provided you give me a kiss. Still no promises, mind. And, naturally, I'll have to see the bloody place.'

'No promises,' I'd agreed. 'All I'm asking is that you keep an open mind – and, of course, you'll have to see it. Some afternoon, maybe, when you're not too busy.' I'd felt giddy with excitement. Having moved him this far, I knew I could move him further, even all the way. So I had kissed him and the kissing, inevitably, had turned into making love.

When he was asleep, I ran happily over the events of the evening. Winning Bob over to the extent I had – and even without him bitching all that much – had proved to be far easier than I had expected. It had been almost too easy, I thought suddenly, then quashed that as unworthy.

I was more surprised the next evening when I announced at dinner that I was off to West Cork and he had immediately suggested coming with me. 'This is a bit out of the blue, isn't it? Aren't you busy?' I asked.

'I'm always busy. There's never a good time. But we haven't been away together, just the two of us, for ages, Cee, and this might be the perfect opportunity. Neither of us knows that part of the country. If the tourists can do it, why can't we?'

'But I want to go tomorrow.'

'So? I'm the bloody MD of the company, and what's the use of that if I can't take a couple of days off now and then to be with my wife? I'll delegate. Those management seminars I send everyone else on? They come back and tell me that the golden rule is delegation! All I'll need is an hour or two on the phone tomorrow morning and I'm clear.'

'This isn't holidays, though, Bob,' I was truly astonished, 'this is business. You'll be bored silly. What'll you do while I'm talking to this woman? She's ancient, apparently. She could even be deaf. I'll have to stay as long as it takes with her and we might be talking hours here – I can't be worrying about you getting in a snit because you're hanging around. That'd be too much pressure and I might screw up.'

But my husband had yet another surprise in store. 'I could help you talk her into it. Selling is my business. I'm a salesman.'

'Come off it! You sell cars—'

'So? If I can persuade some guy to buy a car worth a hundred K when his budget is only half that, surely I can persuade an old lady to become a multi-millionaire by selling a place she evidently hasn't seen for decades? Piece of cake, I'd say!'

'Hang on. We don't know yet what we can offer her. Tommy hasn't mentioned any millions. This is just to have a chat, to try to persuade her to give us an exclusive. Anyhow, the estate isn't zoned residential—'

'Yet! All the better. We get it at agricultural prices and have it zoned later.' On a scale of one to ten, Bob's cynicism is nearer twenty but in that he was spot-on. In the current climate where local authorities are disagreeing with their own planning experts in a frantic rush to provide housing, zoning is a trifle. Maybe he should come, I thought. Selling the old lady on the project would certainly secure his involvement – and he was also right about us not having been away without our 'gang', for years. Those tingles of dislike I've spoken about were undeserved; he was behaving terrifically about this whole thing.

Anyway it would be very interesting to see how we would get on. 'There's just one thing. What about Jeffrey? It's short notice for the kennels.'

'We'll take him with us. We'll find somewhere pet-friendly

to stay, and if we don't, he won't mind sleeping in the car. Jeffrey's a dog, Cee. He'll love Cork. All those foreign smells!' Clearly he was determined to come.

'All right. Why not?'

I'm seriously regretting that decision now because here we are, with him in a filthy humour, crawling along in a swirl of what looks like liquid cotton wool and getting nowhere fast. I retrieve the crumpled map from the back seat and look at it again. Things are not going to get much better: if I'm reading it correctly, at this pace we're still an hour, maybe a lot more, from anywhere we could stay or even eat, let alone our destination. 'Stop the car!' I say firmly.

'What?' But, reflexively, he slams on the brakes.

'A few miles back I saw a sign that said, "Bandon 10". We should turn back and head for there. Bandon is quite a big town, I think. We can get food and probably a hotel. We'd be there in twenty minutes. The fog wasn't too bad lower down.'

He's so scandalised you'd think I'd suggested informing the police his granny was a kleptomaniac. 'Go back?'

'Fine. You don't want to go back. You decide.' I attempt to fold the map, finding the original creases, smoothing them out. 'You want to keep going? Maybe end up crashed into a cow on the road or something? This is not only stupid, it's dangerous, Bob.'

He hangs his head in that way men do when they have been tested beyond endurance by the silliness of their wives. 'Right! You asked for this!' Roaring through the BMW's forgiving gears, he starts the three-point turn, on this narrow road a difficult manoeuvre for a big car at the best of times but in these conditions perilous beyond belief. For all we know there could be a ravine on both sides, or a juggernaut trundling towards us. The radio is on and we can't hear a thing from the outside world. But I suggested this. There's nothing I can do to help. So, I close my eyes and clutch at the sides of my seat.

Bob is a good and experienced driver, and he makes the turn without mishap. But it doesn't improve his mood. 'On your head be this, Cee,' he warns as, going as fast as he dares, he weaves us round the hairpins back the way we had come.

I'll give you just a flavour of how the rest of the evening goes. We find a B-and-B with a helpful landlady who will allow Jeffrey to occupy our room with us for an extra few bob, but she doesn't do evening meals. By the time we get back into Bandon proper, the only place still serving food is the local chipper. 'This country!' Bob grouses his way through his fish and chips. 'It's only three hundred and something long and a hundred and something wide – we've been on the road for how long? And we're not even close yet? When is this government going to get its act together and do something about the roads? It's a bloody disgrace! Third world, that's what it is. If this was Spain or France now—'

'Would you ever stop complaining?' Now I'm as ratty as he. 'May I remind you that it was your idea to come along on this trip? If I'd driven down alone, I'd be there by now because I'd have asked for directions.'

He challenges me on this, and our joint crankiness escalates into a full-scale row. I.e.: 'Do you ever listen to yourself, Claudine? You're always right, aren't you?'

'Who's the one who insisted on carrying on until we couldn't go any further? If you'd just for once have the humility to ask for directions . . .'

Et cetera.

That night, we lie as far as possible from each other in our standard-sized double bed, while Jeffrey, lucky dog, snores blissfully at the foot. It's at times like these that I miss a mother, someone to ring up and complain to about my husband. She'd let me go on and on and then, when I ran out of steam, she'd make soothing noises and tell me I signed up for the deal and would just have to take the good with the bad. She'd point out Bob's good points – of which I would have to admit he has many – and she'd make me see that I don't have it so bad after all.

I suppose it's because of the way Daddy pampered me that I cannot abide confrontation or rows. I don't hold grudges, *per se*, but each new spat can stir up the ones before, sloshing them all poisonously together until any relatively small incident can threaten to drown me. So while superficially I might appear 'feisty' – Bob has referred to me thus to his mates when I disagree with him in front of them – and I can hold my own when I believe in an issue, if someone is angry with me or even raises a voice, I fold. Inside only, of course: the person causing the grief would be the last to know I'm seriously upset. Tonight's quarrel was about a trivial matter, or that was how it started, but it has added to the toxic stew that, long after my husband is in dreamland, keeps me awake, hashing and rehashing the hurtful things we said to each other and composing the even more hurtful things I should have said.

I try to turn my concentration towards the business in hand, why we are here and how I'm going to handle the old lady. Will she ask many questions about the house? How much should I tell her? Will there be a balance to be struck between upsetting her about the condition of her home and letting her know that we're doing her a favour in taking it off her hands?

I think about the mysterious vandalism to the staircase up to the attics. Should I mention that? Does she know about it?

I'd asked the old man about it, naturally. 'What happened here?'

He had clumped towards me – still avoiding walking on the carpet runner with his muddy boots – to stand beside me, hands on hips. 'Well, doesn't that beat Banagher?'

I'd glanced sideways at him. His response had sounded too ready. And that expression on his face? Too puzzled. 'You never noticed this?'

'Never.'

'And you have no idea who could have done it?'

'No.' He'd taken a couple of steps towards the stairs, stuck his head through the doorway and peered upwards towards the attics.

'Or why anyone would chop off nine-tenths of a stair-case?'

He'd shrugged and, his voice half muffled in the door-ope, said, 'There's young fellas goin' these days and you'd never know what they'd be doin'.' He'd stepped back and closed the door with such finality I'd felt it might be advisable to let it go. Now, however, my fraught imagination grinds into overdrive. Maybe my self-vaunted ability to make judgements on people had let me down and this old guy was not as inno-cent as he had seemed. Maybe up in those attics there was the scene of a crime. Even a body.

Feverishly, I try to think back to his makeshift toolshed. He had certainly had the equipment to do it.

I tell myself not to be ridiculous, that the likelihood is that he was the culprit but there's probably nothing sinister about it. He'd probably needed firewood. Naturally he'd be evasive about that.

It is a long time before I get to sleep.

Next morning, weather-wise, we wake to an entirely different country – intensely blue sky, bright sunshine promising a hot day – and after Bob has walked Jeffrey, he puts him in the car and we eat our Full Irish on the patio behind our landlady's house. We seem to be the only clients, and in the absence of others on whom to eavesdrop, the silence between us is heavy. We still haven't spoken to each other in any real sense, other than 'Do you want to use the bathroom first?' and 'Will we have breakfast before we leave?'

The landlady, by contrast, is chatty. 'Isn't it gorgeous now, thank God?' she asks rhetorically in her up-and-down Cork singsong as she refills our coffee cups.

'It sure is.' Bob grins up at her. 'What's the forecast?'

''Tis good, 'tis good! I was watching last night and they said there's a high coming in from the Atlantic and that it'll settle for the next few days. We should all make the most of it now, while we have it. Are ye touring around?'

'We are,' I answered, for both of us. 'But there's someone we want to call in on. Maybe you could help us. It's our first time in the area.' I extract the Collopy address from my handbag and give it to her. When she goes off to consult her husband, I glare at Bob, expecting another round of the argument: 'Do you mind? I'm not going to spend another day driving and not getting anywhere.'

His expression is wry. 'Of all the stupid rows, last night's was the stupidest.'

'It sure was.' I relax – and resist the temptation to point out how it was All His Fault. Instead, I lean over and kiss his cheek. 'Let's take the woman at her word and make the most of the day. OK?' I swallow hard. 'Sorry for my part.'

'Me, too.'

After a few minutes, the landlady comes back with two sets of instructions written out on a piece of copy paper: '1½ Hrs' by one route, '2 Hrs' by another. 'That longer way's the scenic way. That'll take you across the Healy Pass. On a day like this, 'tis gorgeous. I'd envy you that now. I'd take off myself but I'm expecting a big party of fishermen from England.'

We thank her, pay the bill and set off. 'Scenic, I suppose?' Bob asks, when the engine is ticking over and we're belting ourselves in.

'Nah.' I shake my head. 'We've lost enough time already. Tommy'll be doing his nut.'

It turns out the landlady has sent us back on to the route Bob's colleague had recommended. He'd been right on the money about the dearth of traffic anyhow: we have met only one car since we turned on to it off the Bandon link, and twenty-five minutes later we again crest last night's mountain pass and I think that whatever about the landlady's scenic way, this scenery is quite good enough to do me, thank you very much.

Around us is the panorama we should have seen the previous evening. The gently folding hills in front and to each side of us are clothed in multiple greens, golds, browns and the rich mauves of heathers and, in the distance, serious mountains dream quietly to themselves in a purple haze. Presumably they sweep down to the Atlantic, not yet visible. 'Not bad, eh?' Bob smiles at me and briefly takes my hand. He seems desperately to want to make up to me for last night's row.

'Wonderful.' I smile back.

We stop in Glengarriff for coffee. It's impossible not to: to speed through this village, straggling along the edge of a beautiful lagoon, would be akin to vandalism. Bob and I are again on an even keel and, having decided not to go immediately into the hotel opposite the lagoon but first to take a stroll along the sea-front, we hold hands while we watch the tourist ferries trundling people out to a heavily treed island. 'This is the life, Cee?' He smiles again.

With Jeffrey panting happily at our feet, we sit on the low sea wall, angling ourselves so we can continue to watch the activity where, closest to us, a clutch of open boats is reflected in the water and a yachtsman tinkers with a piece of equipment on the deck of his two-master. 'You really want this deal, Cee, don't you?' Bob's voice is so low I can barely hear him.

'I do. You know I do. Oh, Bob, if we get it you won't be sorry.'

'I'm sure I won't. You're a great homemaker, Claudine. You're a great wife . . .'

We're still holding hands but, suddenly, his has stiffened. 'What is it?' I search his face for a clue. He has reddened a little. A good poker face is a tool of Bob's profession, so this is rare.

'What do you mean?'

'Look, Claudine,' his grip tightens, 'there's something I have to tell you.'

Sneaky little weevils of fear creep up my throat. He went for a medical check-up recently. He's had the results but he couldn't tell me. He's got prostate cancer – he's the right age. The radio is full of it, these days. And, come to think of it, he has been looking very tired lately and, as I've said, he has seemed to brood more than usual. 'Tell me.'

'Don't get upset—'

'Tell me—'

'Promise me you won't freak.'

'Bob, if you don't stop this, this instant . . .'

He looks down at the ground, then out into the lagoon. 'I've been rehearsing in my mind. I just don't know how to come right out with it.'

'Just say it. Whatever it is we'll deal with it together.' Whitecliff is off the agenda. And all that speculation I've been indulging in about why we were still married? Tosh. What is most important in my life is this man here, this marriage—

He grasps my hand so tightly my fingers throb. 'I slept with someone else.'

# 19

## THE SILVER LINING

It was just after seven thirty, the blackout curtains had been pulled and, to Mother's evident relief, many couples, mostly the younger ones, were now dancing. I had overheard her saying earlier to Nanny that she was afraid our guests were not enjoying themselves: 'People are not mingling as much as they should be. And, look, the rector has no one to talk to. Quickly, Nanny, offer him another port.'

It was true that, after the initial burst of hilarity, the party had quietened somewhat. Mother and Uncle Samuel begged Marjorie to sing a party piece for us – she was the most musically talented of our family – but she had stoutly rejected their entreaties. After the food had been served, however, after wine and other alcohol had loosened tongues and ties, the atmosphere livened again and a happy clamour rose in the pale yellow light, fuggy with cigarette smoke, from the massed candelabra and gasoliers. Even the band upstairs, now that their efforts seemed to have borne fruit, jigged a little faster and the event felt like a real, proper party, the kind I had read about and imagined.

Yet despite the general gaiety, and the good-humoured

teasing from the twins and their friends, who were by far the noisiest in the house, I was not enjoying myself. None of Young Samuel's friends had bothered with me. Anyway, I did not like them: they drank too much and laughed too loudly and one girl in particular, staring at the twins' group, had been highly uncomplimentary about the local lads, referring to them as 'culchies'.

It was not only that, however: I had two linked problems.

Every time I checked, poor Coley and his sister, Florrie, who was a very nice person but shy and quite fat, were lurking in a corner with only each other for company. At the earliest opportunity – when the canapés were still being handed round by Nanny and the helper with the assistance of Marjorie, Johanna and me – I had introduced them to Mother: 'You know Coley Quinn, Mother? This is his sister, Florrie.'

'How do you do, Florrie? And of course we know Coley – how are you, and your father and mother?' Mother's good manners did not desert her, but immediately after Coley's shy answers, she had click-clacked away to wait on the bank manager and his wife. Although I was relieved at her departure, I thought it quite peremptory. I introduced them to Johanna and Shirley, to some of the twins' crowd, to Marjorie also, but each time within minutes they had retreated again to their corner. I longed to speak to Coley alone, naturally, but this had not proved possible. I could see he was watching me all the time, and I was so frustrated I felt my brain would burst.

The associated problem, the kernel of the situation, was Mary Quigley. Since her arrival, she had stuck to me like a limpet. That was when she was not simpering at Coley.

It had started when Coley and Florrie arrived. 'Don't

abandon me, Violet Shine,' she hissed, when I went to greet them, so I was forced to take her with me to the front door. 'Good afternoon, Coley – how nice to see you,' I said, as if he were just any guest. After he had introduced his sister, I turned to Mary, who was hovering like a bee at my shoulder. 'Coley, Florrie, you don't know Mary Quigley, I presume?'

Mary instantly cosied up to my Coley. That is the only way to describe it. She behaved coyly and, in my opinion, disgracefully. I trusted Coley, of course – and we managed to exchange one or two significant glances – but as the evening wore on, the situation became intolerable.

As I was on hospitality duty with Johanna, Nanny and the temporary maid, my choices, when I had any respite, were to leave Mary with Coley or to haul her round the room with me in the hope that she might pick another target. She refused, however, to attach herself to anyone else.

It was Uncle Samuel who came to my rescue. 'And who's this lovely wee girl?' he asked me as, after supper, Mary and I yet again did a tour of the room to make sure the guests' glasses were fully charged. 'This is my friend, Mary Quigley, Uncle,' I said flatly.

'Come here to me now, young Mary, and tell me all about yourself.' Uncle Samuel winked at me while patting the seat beside him. 'I've been watching you two girls and you've been working flat out the night. I know young Mary here's been a great help but she and I are going to have a great conversation now and you, Violet, you take a little break for yourself. You go and ask one of thon young men to take you and those lovely dancing shoes of yours for a twirl.'

I gaped at him. He must know that girls did not take the initiative in such matters.

'I'll go too!' Mary made to line herself up beside me but he winked again.

'Oh, Mary, dear, you wouldn't leave an old man all on his own, now, would you? Sure I can talk to me niece any time. No. Sit you down here and let Violet do what her oul' uncle tells her.' Catching Mary's arm, he pulled her on to the seat beside him.

'Thank you, Uncle.' I smiled, assured the clearly annoyed Mary that I would not be long, and I left them.

Johanna was coming into the room with a fresh soda siphon and I went to her as fast as decorum would allow. 'I have not danced at all,' I implored, 'and my feet itch. The only young man I really know here, apart from our brothers, is Coley Quinn.' Using his name to her was rash, I knew, but I was desperate. 'My difficulty is that he cannot leave his sister. Please, Johanna, will you look after her while I have just this one dance? Then we can exchange places,' I added. 'I shall ask Coley to dance with you while I entertain his sister.' That, I thought, had been inspired.

Then, without giving Johanna any time to respond, I rushed to where Florrie and Coley were standing. 'Johanna wants to have a proper chat with you, Florrie – and as for you and me, Coley Quinn,' I announced archly and very loudly, hoping I sounded like someone carried away with the general jollity, 'we're going to dance!' Before either could react, I half dragged the astonished girl towards my sister. 'There now,' I said to Johanna. 'Here she is, like you wanted. I'll be back in two shakes.'

On my return to Coley, I saw that neither Uncle Samuel nor Mary Quigley had missed my performance and it occurred to me that I was in very dangerous water, but I was feeling so reckless, so driven to have Coley in my arms even for a few minutes, I cared little what either of them thought. At that moment I would have walked to Coley under Father's nose, over Mother's feet. I took him by the arm and led him into the throng of dancing couples as if it was the most ordinary event of the evening. Through the thick fabric of his suit, I could feel his arm trembling, a sensation that further inflamed me and by the time we reached the space where we could turn to each other it is not an exaggeration to say that every inch of my body burned.

Our musicians had temporarily abandoned their repertoire of Irish jigs, reels and old-time waltzes and were playing 'Moonlight Serenade', a tune I recognised from the wireless. All around Coley and me, couples were dancing cheek to cheek and, safely concealed among them, without hesitation, I laid my own cheek against my lover's.

I quickly discovered, though, that dancing was not Coley's forte. He moved rhythmically, but had no idea how to get his feet to do the foxtrot or the quickstep, while I, tutored by the other girls at the Misses Biggs's during breaks, was quite proficient. It mattered little. I knew by the expression in his eyes and the tension in his arms that he loved me. We were together, moving to the music and the urge to kiss him was overwhelming. This, though, would have been a step so unsafe as to be fatal. 'Oh, Coley,' I whispered into his ear instead, 'I love you, love you, love you.'

'You look wonderful, Violet,' he whispered back. 'Could we slip away, maybe?'

'Impossible.' I almost laughed. 'Not that I don't want to, of course,' I added hastily, in case he thought I was going off him.

'Can we meet at the tree?'

I glanced around but no one was watching us.

'When?'

'Tomorrow morning, very early. Could you get away then? People here will sleep late.'

I performed another quick survey to make sure we were not overheard – and encountered the cheerful gaze of the creamery manager, dancing with his wife a few feet away. I gave him my most dazzling smile and was rewarded with a friendly nod. I decided it was too dangerous to whisper to Coley, signalled as much to him with a widening of the eyes and, eschewing his pained lead, abandoned myself to the strict but sultry rhythms of the foxtrot, while thrilling to each 'accidental' touch of my breast against his arm, or of my hip against his.

Too soon, I knew, from the way the band was slowing the chords, that our dance was coming to an end. 'I'll try to get away,' I whispered urgently, without moving my lips and staring up at the musicians above. 'It will have to be very early, though. Six o'clock? I shall have to be back in my room before seven.' Whatever about the younger people, or even Uncle Samuel, Mother, Father and Nanny were not lie-a-beds.

Over the final drumroll and cymbal clash, I pushed him away and stood well apart from him while we applauded the band. Nearby, James was whirling his partner round and round, so strongly that she was actually off her feet, to the laughter and cheers of his companions. 'Thank you so much, Coley,' I said, waiting for the cheers to die down so I could be heard. 'That was very nice. Don't forget, you have to dance with Johanna now.'

'Well, hello there, Violet.' James steadied his partner on her feet. 'Didn't see you there. Hey there, Ginger,' he called, steering his dancing partner towards one of the farmers' sons, 'you take this one,' then turned back to me. 'I want to dance with little Sis here.' He smiled down at me. 'Come on, let's have a go.' So, while the band launched into 'Look For The Silver Lining' and while, over his shoulder, I saw Coley retreat towards the drawing room, my brother caught my waist.

I gave in gracefully. Who could fault me for dancing with my brother for a few minutes? Florrie would survive for the length of one dance, I thought. I had worked hard all evening in the service of the party and, as Uncle Samuel quite rightly said, I deserved a break.

James had always been light on his feet and, before I knew it, I was thoroughly enjoying myself, not only because in a few hours I would be with my lover but because I was caught up in the moment. It was wonderful to be young and in love; wonderful to be surrounded by exuberant, energetic young people; wonderful to have my whole family together in a house filled with music, good cheer and pleasure.

My blood danced as vigorously as my feet while James swung us skilfully around the periphery of the other dancers. He looked so handsome in a pale linen jacket over his white cricket trousers; the only jarring note was his severe haircut, identical to his twin's. Thomas was moving past us with his partner in a sedate quickstep. 'Having fun, Violet?' James smiled at me and, with a small shock of pleasure, I realised I was now almost as tall as he.

'It's wonderful. Everything is wonderful.'

'You look beautiful tonight. White suits you, Sis. Doesn't she look beautiful, Thomas?' he called, over the heads of the couples who separated us.

'Oh, she's all right!' Thomas called back, grinning. 'Great night, though! Good old Rod. Good old Fly. We'll remember this.' He was gone.

'That's the best you'll get out of him. But seriously, Violet, we'll have to lock you up to keep the boys away from you.'

'You try that, James, you just try!' I laughed joyfully. Then joined in with the singing, or rather shouting, of the words of the song, which threatened to drown the vocalist on the landing.

'Never forget this night, Sis,' he yelled into my ear. 'Promise?'

'Oh, yes, yes, yes!' I yelled back. 'You too?'

'Of course.' But he was looking over my shoulder and the expression in his eyes gave me pause. I stopped us both and followed the direction of his gaze in time to see a flash of royal blue glitter vanishing behind the drawing-room door. 'What is it, James?'

'Nothing. I'm worried about Mother, that's all. I've caught her watching us a few times tonight. Won't you look after her, Violet?'

'Of course I will, you goose!' I was blithe. The idea of me, at sixteen, looking after my self-contained, formidable mother was laughable. 'Come on, we're supposed to be dancing.' I held up my arms to him but his expression did not alter. 'Is it the war?' I meant it sincerely but at the same time selfishly did not want these darknesses intruding into such a happy occasion and fervently hoped he would say no.

'Not looking forward to it, I have to say – but you're right, Sis.' This time, albeit with an effort, he did brighten. 'Tonight's tonight. Don't let's waste a second of it – tomorrow can wait.'

'James?' I hesitated. I wanted to say something profound

and supportive. Instead, I heard myself reiterate the constant refrain of the district: 'You'll be home by Christmas. Everyone says it. And sure that's only – what? Seven, eight months from now?'

'Sure thing!'

'You will!'

'Of course I will. We both will.' Then James looked me in the eye. 'Ready?'

'Ready when you are, Gunga Din!'

We danced hard, tapping firmly on the unyielding flagstones until that brief look into the shadows had been firmly obliterated, certainly for me. I was now released again happily to wonder if Coley, too, thought I looked well in my dress, if he liked the pre-war silver sandals Mother had allowed me to borrow. If he thought my waist was trim and my breasts perky.

If he was imagining what I was imagining lay in store for us tomorrow.

I sang again at the top of my voice, sharing the words with my brother as we all once again: Looked For . . . the Silver Lining . . .

## 20

# ANOTHER LOVELY ADVENTURE

All that mulling and conjecturing about the state of our marriage. All that wondering about his moods . . . His unexpected desire for a trip away, 'just the two of us together' . . .

Jeffrey strains at his leash to follow me as I back away from my husband.

Bob has adroitly chosen his moment and his location: 250 miles from home, in the open, people all around . . . Unlike the dog, he doesn't try to follow me. He isn't even looking at me: he's staring at the ground.

Half blind with emotions I can't yet identify, my feet carry me across the road. Seemingly of their own accord they mount the steps into the hotel where, on finding myself in the lounge bar, I ask for a coffee.

'Surely!' The girl behind the bar turns to the machine. 'And would you like a scone?' Sing-songing over her shoulder: 'They're hot from the oven. We make them ourselves.'

'Thank you.'

'And would you like a drop of cream with it?' She turns round to smile conspiratorially at me. 'With jam too?'

Yesyesyes, Idon'tcarewhatIhavejustshutup. Instead of screaming at her, though, I agree I should have jam and cream with
my scone. I agree it is a magic day and that, if we're lucky,
we'll get a good few days out of it, that the omens, dolphins,
old forecasters from Dingle, prospecting bees, are good.

It is only when I sit down at a window table that I realise
I've no money. I've left my handbag in the car.

I can't think about what Bob has said, not just yet, so I
force myself to take in my surroundings: old-fashioned wallpaper, long mahogany bar, two middle-aged men ensconced
side by side on stools, both wearing tweed jackets and,
weirdly, trilby hats or fedoras or something. Who cares what
kind of hats they are? The pint glasses in front of them are
half full and although, having chosen to sit together at the
end of the otherwise empty counter, they must be friends,
they are content simply to sit peacefully together. Lucky,
lucky men.

Through the window, I can see Bob. He is still sitting in
the position in which I left him, staring at the ground. The
incongruity of his saying such an ugly thing in the midst of
such natural beauty and relaxed activity strikes me. All along
the sea-front the gentle water and warm sun have opened
people up as if they were flowers, influencing them to smile,
stranger to stranger, sending out couples to saunter arm in
arm, causing tourists of all nationalities to wave to one another
from adjacent ferries as though they are kindergarten kids on
a school outing.

But here we are, we two married people: him outside, me
here, registering irrelevancies while simultaneously trying to
keep submerged the slimy, inky thing that insists on bobbing
to the surface between us.

Deirdre Purcell

'Okey-dokey.' The girl places the coffee and scones – plural – on the table in front of me. 'Enjoy that now. And if there's anything else, just give us a shout.'

'I will. Thank you.' But out of the corner of my eye, I see that my husband is hauling a reluctant Jeffrey back to the car. Are they leaving? Cashless though I am, I actually don't care. Not right now. I'll deal with that when and if it arises. At least my mobile is in my pocket: habit, drilled into me by Tommy O'Hare, dies hard.

But no. Bob's not leaving, he's moving the car across the road into the hotel's car park. He's driving right past the window. He's searching for shade. He's going to leave the dog in the car with the windows open for air. He must be coming inside.

I hunt for some place to hide but, as I look around, catch the eye of the bar girl, who instantly smiles at me as if we are scheming together to enjoy forbidden fruit. I try to smile back.

I can hear Jeffrey's muffled bark. He hates being shut up in the car.

Now here's Bob. His expression is unreadable. What am I going to do? How am I going to handle this? I can't feel angry. I can't feel anything. All I feel is panic. It's paralysing me.

'May I sit down, Claudine?'

'Of course.'

He pulls out a chair and sits opposite me.

The girl approaches. 'Good morning! What can I get you?'

I wish she had some other clients. But there are only the two silent men and us. 'Just coffee, please.' Bob's voice is strained. Ridiculously, I feel sorry for him. This is transient.

'Just coffee? We can't tempt you to a scone or even a biscuit?'

'No, thanks. Just the coffee.'

'All right, so. Coming right up.' But she looks curiously from one to the other of us. Maybe we are not as good at hiding things as we think we are.

We both look through the window at Shangri-la outside.

'You staged this!' I say calmly, watching two youngsters, Scandinavians, I would say, kissing each other while they sit on the wall near to where my life had changed.

'What do you mean?' I can tell he's turned towards me.

'This. You couldn't land it on me at home? All that guff about going away together, the two of us? You planned it this way, Bob.' Now I do look at him. 'Salesman that you are, you planned it so I'd be trapped and you could talk me round. Well, I've news for you. I'm not trapped. I have a credit card. I can hire a car. I can buy a car, if need be. I can transfer enough money into that credit card to buy myself a Merc. We have a joint account, remember?'

I've shocked myself. When reading in the tabloids or magazines about women vowing to bankrupt their philandering husbands in the course of divorcing them, I had always thought, How pathetic! How undignified! Plus I had sancti-moniously opined a bunch of claptrap about each party being an individual with the same rights and nobody owning another person, and it shouldn't be about money et cetera—

'You have every right to be angry, Cee—'

Before he can say any more we're interrupted again, this time by the arrival of his coffee. But the girl leaves it without comment and goes back behind her bar. For which I am truly grateful. Blameless and charming as she is, I think I would have hit her if she had opened her mouth to say something. I am no longer paralysed and my husband is correct about my anger: the sight of Bob Armstrong sitting in front of me has caused my breath to come so fast and shallow I can barely keep up with it. I find I want to grind that handsome face into the floor beneath my feet, to stamp on the back of the head so that features are mangled and pulped—

Yet as before, habit dies hard, this time habit ingrained at a private school by the ladylike teachers who trained me well.

I could break up this lounge bar, glass by glass, but I can still hear those clipped school vowels: other than public humiliation, what would such undignified behaviour achieve in the long run?

'Are you all right?' Bob sounds worried now.

'Apart from realising I've been a blind idiot, do you mean? Poor Claudine Magennis. So easy to deceive, such a simple, trusting soul.'

'Claudine—'

'Who is she?' It cracks through.

I check to see that nobody else in the room has heard. The two men still sit like Toby jugs. The bar person is polishing glasses. Maybe she heard. If she has, she shows no sign. I don't really care.

Bob looks at me. Pleading. 'Who was she, you mean?'

'Oh? She's dead? Sorry for your trouble!'

'No, she's not dead.' He looks again at his incomparably interesting feet. 'In a way, that's the problem,' he says, so softly I can barely hear him.

I have heard him, though. 'Charming. You make love to a woman who's not your wife and then you wish her dead? What a gallant person you are, Bob.'

'It was a once-off,' he says, in a monotone. 'And it certainly wasn't making love. More a drunken – I don't even remember it.'

'Oh, spare me the details.' I raise both hands as if to ward off the evil eye. 'You still haven't answered my question. Who is she, Bob?'

'You don't know her.'

'At least that's some consolation. But do try me.'

'Just a woman I met in Galway.'

'At that sales conference?' I remember the drunken phone call on the Saturday night of that weekend, the riotous shouting and laughing in the background. I remember thinking, *Thank God I'm not there tonight.*

'Yes. That's when it happened. I'm not proud of myself, Cee. I'm the idiot. And before you say anything else, I know what a pathetic, stupid cliché that is – that the whole thing is.'

Something rises to the surface. Something cold and slithery. Why now? Do he and Miss Conference Congeniality have plans together? 'Would it be too much to ask why you are telling me this at this point?'

'Believe me, Claudine, if there was any way I could have avoided hurting you like this, if I had to cut off my finger—'

'That won't be necessary. Aside from the obvious, that you slept with the woman in the first place, why did you tell me?'

He stares at me and I remember more: the late nights in the past few weeks. The tiptoeing up the stairs, the huffing as he got undressed in the dark. The smell of drink when he got into the bed. 'It wasn't a once-off, was it, Bob?'

'I swear to God, there was just that one time. I was out of my skull: I'd been drinking since lunchtime. I hate the woman now, Claudine. But she . . .' feet again '. . . she's

195

reading more into it. I've been trying to talk sense into her—'

'I see. If you weren't going to tell me, she was?' My stomach might be churning but outwardly I was senior counsel, interrogating a tricky customer in a courtroom. I was calm. Reasonable at all costs. No bullying in front of the judge. 'But why, Bob? What's in it for her? If, as you say, this was a once-off from your point of view—'

'I'm telling you. She won't believe me that it was.' He's speaking to himself. He even has the nerve to sound aggrieved. 'Look, Claudine, the cards are on the table now. There's nothing I can do or say to make it more palatable for you. But if or when she does ring you, or turns up on the doorstep, as she has threatened to do, at least you'll know my side of the story.'

'You sound relieved. As if this is now the end of the story.'

'I might be an idiot, but I'm not thick. Of course I know it's not the end of the story. But you're right, I am relieved that it's out in the open and that I can ring her and tell her she no longer has any hold over me. It's been an awful burden.'

'Poor you.'

'Yeah. Poor me.' He smiles bitterly.

'Is that it?' I'm freezingly polite now. 'Perhaps there's more? She wouldn't be pregnant by any chance, this mistress of yours? This couldn't be the reason she's pursuing you? Let's see now, let's deal with the timings—'

'Stop it, Cee!' He puts out a hand to stem the flow and thinks better of it. 'She's not pregnant.'

'Oh, thank goodness. That's such a relief.'

He hesitates.

'Oh dear. There is more, isn't there? Spit it out.'

'I know how inadequate and awful this sounds. I know what

an absolute stupid fool I've made of myself. I know it won't help. But I'm truly, deeply sorry. And I know you won't believe me now, but something like this will never happen again.'

I have no idea in the world how to react to this. I have no experience. I have no one to ask. *If only Daddy were alive—* at the thought, loneliness, pure and cold, knifes through the centre of my body, head to toe. Bob is watching me, and when I offer no verbal response to what he has just said, he indicates my untouched coffee and scones. 'Are you finished?'

'Yes.'

'Then let's get out of here.'

As we go outside and get into the car, I realise I will never pass through this beautiful place without thinking of this. He has ruined the beauty for ever and everything seems tawdry, the kissing of the Scandinavians ostentatious rather than heart-warming; the sparkle on the surface of the water, pound-shop tat.

Bob turns to me before starting the engine. 'Where to? Do you want to go home?'

'Absolutely not.' That he has asked this has given me courage. Although he has killed the excitement, I'm on a serious mission, more than ever now.

'All right.' He turns the key. 'And I know what you think of me, Cee, but my offer to help with this deal still stands. Whatever you want.'

Whatever I want. I fondle the soft, smooth fur on Jeffrey's head, thrust between the two front seats. What I want is for this not to have happened.

Jeffrey gives me a little lick. To him, we're all of us, our little family of three, just setting off on another lovely adventure.

# 21

# RAFFIA

'How are you going to approach this, Claudine?'
'I haven't decided.'

Those are the first words spoken since we pulled out of Glengarriff forty minutes previously. We are coming into the village indicated by the Collopy woman's address. It consists of a single narrow street between terraces of small, two-storey houses interspersed with a couple of pubs and tiny shops. Although many doors are wide open, the visible population at present numbers two bristling collies squaring up to each other in the middle of the road.

Although I have found the silence between us oppressive, I could not have broken it for a millionaire's ransom. Somehow Bob's revelation has become unreal – as if this was happening in a movie, or to someone else, but for whatever reason, I am certainly no longer reeling. Actually, although I know I am very angry with my husband, I have simultaneously become numb, if that does not sound too contradictory. In this respect I am my father's daughter: 'When things get tough, chicken, count to ten before you collapse. And the slower you can do it the better because between nine and ten something will happen to give you strength. Nothing stays the same. That's the only thing you can depend on in this world.'

'You should have a plan, something in mind . . .' Obviously Bob is not put off by my tone. He even sounds as if he has been encouraged.

So, I make things absolutely clear. 'It no longer has anything to do with you. Stop here!'

After a brief, sideways glance, he obediently pulls the car to a halt in front of a shop–cum–post office. I need more directions. The woman's address indicates that she lives in a townland somewhere outside the village.

It's lunchtime and the post-office booth is shut but the girl behind the shop counter looks curiously at me. 'Mrs Collopy, is it? I'm afraid she's dead. Are you a relation?'

'No, not a relation. I did know she's dead, but I'd like to talk to her sister if that's possible. I understand she had a sister?'

'She had, she had, although I think you might be talking about a sister-in-law? There was only the two of them in it this long time, that's until the missus died, but I don't know if she's there, though. Today's Wednesday – she might be in town. She gets her hair done on a Wednesday. Wait till I ask Judy.' Before I can interject, she has opened a door and trotted into a back room, allowing the aroma of boiling potatoes to waft into the shop.

For a few seconds, I can hear a low murmur from inside, then she emerges with an older woman, who is wiping her hands on a tea-towel. 'You want the Collopys' house?' While the girl hangs back, this older woman goes into the post-office booth and picks up the phone. 'I'll ring it for you. That'd be the quickest way to find out if she's there or not. Who shall I say wants to know?'

'The name is Armstrong, Claudine Armstrong. But she won't know me. It's a business matter.'

'A business matter.' The woman laughs. 'Well, we'd better find her, so!' But she looks sharply at me and I realise I've made a mistake. Within hours – minutes, perhaps – everyone in the district will be agog.

'It's ringing anyway.' The woman is holding the receiver to her ear. 'She's slowed down a lot since the sister died, God love her. Ah, you'd feel sorry for her, the crathur. It's lonely for her down there. But very independent, she is, I'll say that for her. We love to see her coming in here for the few messages. She's a gentlewoman.'

I'm under no illusions but that I'm on notice. There is a subtext here, one I used to encounter in the small villages of North County Dublin before they were transformed into Commuterland. No flies on us and we take care of our own. Watch your step! Through the window, I can see Bob talking on his mobile phone. Briefly, I wonder if he's on to 'her', but catch myself on and smile at the two women in the post office as brilliantly as I can manage.

It turns out that Miss Collopy is at home. 'Hello, this is Judy in the post office.' The voice of the postmistress is deferential. 'There's a lady here who's asking about you. She says it's to do with business. Will I ask her what's it in connection with?'

She listens for a moment, then covers the mouthpiece with her free hand. 'She wants to know what's this business in connection with?'

'I wonder if it would be OK to talk to her myself?'

'Certainly.' She uncovers the mouthpiece. 'She'll talk to you herself, Miss Collopy. Hold on a minute there now.' She picks up the entire phone, takes it out of the booth and hands me the receiver.

'Hello – Miss Collopy?'

'Yes?' The voice is surprisingly strong.

'My name is Claudine Armstrong, but you already know that.'

'Yes.'

'Would you have a few moments to talk to me? It's about Whitecliff.'

At the other end of the line, there is silence.

'Miss Collopy, are you still there?'

'I'm here. Are you a friend of John Thorpe's?'

I take a punt: John Thorpe has to be either the solicitor or the auctioneer. I should have checked with Tommy before I left. 'A friend of a friend of his,' I say quickly. 'I don't know if you know Thomas O'Hare? He has a connection with Mr Thorpe. He has a business in North County Dublin near Whitecliff and asked me to call on you.'

Silence again. Then: 'Do you know where I live?' It's hard to place her accent. It's strangely old-fashioned, from *Brief Encounter* or one of those other movies you can catch on BBC2 on wet Sunday afternoons. 'I have your address, but I think Judy here,' I turn to beam at the women over my shoulder, 'will tell me how to get to you.'

'I shall expect you presently.' The line goes dead.

'Thank you so much,' I say to the postmistress, as I give her back her phone. 'How much do I owe you for the call?'

'Nonsense.' The woman puts it away. 'That's what we're here for. I'd better give you directions, so. Now it's a bit remote,' she adds. 'Would you like me to go with you? It'd be no trouble.'

'No, thank you. I've taken up enough of your time and your dinner is waiting.'

'Well, if you're sure.' She tears a brown-paper bag in half and writes. 'You have a mobile, I suppose?'

'I do.'

'Everyone has one of them. God be with the days when we were the only telephone in town. You're too young to remember.' She laughs as she gives me the paper. 'Now, if you get lost, be sure to give me a ring and we'll help you out. Oh, I'd better give you our number . . .' She takes the paper back and scribbles on it again. 'Tell Miss Collopy I've kept the duck eggs for her, but she'd need to come in soon. I forgot to mention it to her when I was talking to her there.'

'I will. You've been very kind. Thank you so much. I'm sorry I've interrupted your dinner,' and I escape, promising to ask for more help in the event we get lost.

Bob is still talking on the mobile phone when I get outside. At the sight of him, my numbness evaporates. One quick puff, and it's replaced with boiling anger and resentment. Hurt, I suppose, will come later. I wrench open the car door as quickly as I can in an attempt to hear his conversation only to find that he is either a lightning-fast dissembler or he is genuinely on to his office. 'Fine, Jack, fine,' he says, glancing at me. 'I'll keep the mobile on. The coverage is patchy but I'll keep checking and you can leave messages.' Jack is the supervisor of the service area at the garage.

'So much for togetherness, just the two of us.' I'm so venomous I hate myself. I'm almost disappointed he wasn't talking to *her*.

'You weren't here,' he points out.

'Are you sure it was Jack you were talking to?'

A beat. Then he realises what I mean. 'Yes,' he says quietly. He takes the phone out of its holder on the dashboard and holds it out to me. 'Check the dialled calls if you like.'

'That won't be necessary, thank you.'

'Look, I have to find a bathroom quickly. Do you mind if I take a few minutes to go into one of the pubs?'

'Yes, I do mind, actually. I want to get to this woman immediately. I'm afraid she might go off the boil.' Suffer, baby. Suffer.

'All right,' he says mildly. 'But I'll have to find a bush somewhere along the road.' He puts the car into gear and moves off, and while I give him instructions, we take the narrow, corkscrewing road leading from the far end of the straggling village. 'I know you're burning up, Cee,' he says, without looking at me, 'and you have every right to. I've been a prize ass.'

'Bull or rabbit, more like.'

'Whatever – although I think that was pretty cheap.' He slows to a crawl while a tractor towing a huge spiked contraption inches past us in the direction of the village, then resumes speed. 'I can't undo what's been done. I'm a human being. Flawed, yeah, and I'll accept anything you mete out, any sanction or punishment, with just one caveat. I won't allow myself to be humiliated. At least, not for ever.'

'I'll decide what course lies ahead from here on – not you.'

'It happens, Claudine,' he sounds weary. 'I'm not the first guy who—'

'Stuck it into the first piece of skirt that offered?'

He looks across at me, so astonished he nearly runs us into a ditch. I'm floored as well. I had no idea I could be so coarse. And I could be even coarser: right now, every piece of rotten language I've ever come across in books, in films and on TV seems, willy-nilly, to have flooded my vocabulary 'Turn left here,' I say shakily, 'at that signpost where it says, "Trá", and then after about fifty metres, you have to take a laneway going right. Apparently it's very narrow.'

He negotiates both turns and, even in my present state, as we bump along the laneway I find it impossible not to notice how breathtaking the scenery is here. With hedges of fuchsia in full red bloom brushing the paintwork of the car on both sides, we are going steadily downhill towards the sea, as blue as the Aegean, dotted with as many islands – although of a much greener hue – and with a wild and rocky coastline broken by a multitude of coves and inlets. 'How much further?' Bob is concentrating on his driving.

'As far as it takes.'

He purses his lips but doesn't respond.

Because he won't fight back, I'm beginning to be ashamed of my behaviour. But then I think, *What have I to be ashamed of?*

In novels, when you read about affairs and infidelity, it's sort of run-of-the-mill. Sometimes you're even rooting for the 'other' woman (or man), but let me state that in real life there is nothing run-of-the-mill about it when you're the one betrayed. It's hard and horrible. It's torture. It feels as though you're made of raffia and the hordes have descended to pull you apart, strand by fragile, brittle strand.

Hands shaking, I consult my brown-paper instructions. 'We should be coming up to it very soon. It'll be a farm gate, five-barred, painted green. There'll be a white postbox on it with the name Collopy.'

'There it is!' Bob brakes, then turns sheepishly to me. 'I

really do have to go, Cee. Look, you go on in. I'll take Jeffrey for a walk – he has to be as desperate as I am. We'll do our thing and then I'll join you. That's if you want me to.'

I look at him, my husband of more than two decades. I can't say our lives flashed before my eyes, but for that instant I see before me not Don Juan but an ordinary, essentially decent human being as flawed and wonderful as the institution of marriage itself. Certainly my marriage: a graph outlined in sand, on which the peaks and the troughs are equally at risk from the tides of outside events and should be daily redrawn. I'm not ready to redraw, though. 'I can't forgive you yet, Bob,' I say tonelessly. 'I'm not big enough simply to take what you say at face value. I'll need to hear the whole story.'

'Now?'

'No. Not now. When I'm ready. Which, I promise you, won't be long from now. Were you sleeping with the two of us at the same time? Coming from her bed into mine?' It seems my tongue has a life of its own and, without any conscious input from my brain, my left arm simultaneously raises itself, crosses my chest and the hand at the end of it slaps him across the face. Hard. Because of the angle it's more of a punch.

We're both stunned. He's holding a hand to his face, already marked. I'm cradling the sting of my left hand in the right.

'I thought you didn't want to talk about it.' Under the red, I can see through his fingers that he's pale.

'No, I don't.'

I get out of the car and slam the door. Then I unlatch the green farm gate and close it firmly behind me.

## 22

## WE'LL MEET AGAIN

There is a lovely magnolia outside my window here; each spring I wait impatiently for it to bloom and it never lets me down. I could watch it for hours and quite often do. I find it particularly beautiful at night when, through the darkness, the waxy, tulip-like blossoms seem to hover and flit through the bare branches, ghost-ballerinas for ever in mourning for lost lovers. I am sorry, now that it is too late, that there is only one: I would love to plant a forest of them – what a sight that would be in spring! At this stage of my life, however, I would not see them mature.

At my age, I suppose, everyone suffers many regrets, great and small. I am no exception.

Do not misunderstand me. I do not regret for one moment what defined my life: falling in love with Coley Quinn. I was no Miss Havisham, embalmed in the amber of what happened to me in the spring and summer of 1944, for the opposite was the case. Memories of that time sustained me through everything that occurred subsequently and, I believe, helped prevent a descent into bitter old spinsterhood. (Allow me to modify that. Those memories merely prevented me becoming bitter, not from becoming an old spinster.)

Regret, in my case, is more subtle, even surprising. In addition to 'big' items such as being upset that I gave up playing my violoncello, that I made no effort formally to study zoology or archaeology – except vicariously, through my ever-expanding collection of *National Geographic* magazines – or travelled anywhere off this island, there are others, seemingly insignificant yet of such life-draining properties that they are actually more telling.

For instance, I am sorry that for most of my life I followed the ingrained precepts of our house in keeping things for 'good'. At Whitecliff, even for our party, we used only second-best china: we never ate or drank from the 'good' sets, even at Christmas, in case one piece got broken, rendering the service incomplete. 'Good' cutlery remained shut away in baize-lined trays and the wonderful Irish linen sheets and tablecloths Mother inherited from her own mother and brought with her from Northern Ireland were permanently stored, wrapped in black tissue, to be taken out only for inspection and relaundering during the annual spring cleaning. Meanwhile, she spent long evenings darning and mending the cotton ones we actually used. When the sheets had worn so thin in the middle that they were almost transparent, she cut them in half, then rejoined the two pieces, top to tail.

Consciously or unconsciously, I followed this pattern for years. For instance, my godfather gave me many presents. I think I have mentioned the watch, which I used daily, but he also gave or sent me some beautiful, if modest pieces of jewellery, among them a fine neck chain of rose gold, a pretty silver bangle inlaid with lapis-lazuli, an enamelled brooch in the shape of two bluebirds, brought from a holiday in Italy, a locket he had had engraved on the inside with my name and the date of my birth. Along with a silver ring and pair of aquamarine earrings of Marjorie's, donated to me when she moved out of the house, all, as pristine as the day I received them, were kept in their leather presentation boxes in my bureau, in case wearing them might result in loss or damage.

Mother not only approved of this, it had been at her instigation that my gifts remained unworn. 'When you are twenty-one, Violet, and therefore more responsible than you are at present, you can bedeck yourself to your heart's content. Your uncle Samuel has been so good to you that we would not want to upset him with reports of your carelessness, should you lose any of those pieces.' This was during the week when the party approached and I had suggested I might wear at least some of my trove.

I had protested, of course: 'But this is a party, Mother. And Uncle Samuel will be there! He'll be expecting me to wear them.'

In response, she offered me a suite of her own: a necklace, earrings and bracelet of river pearls. 'None of your pieces matches any other, Violet, so you may borrow these little pearls. They are very suitable for a girl of your age and will nicely set off your dress. But please be careful with them. I expect them to be returned in the same condition.' Easily distracted as I was, I fingered the cool iridescent beads and promptly abandoned my own trinkets; at that point, I thought matching jewellery to be the height of sophistication.

When I think now about all that scrimping and eking, I am not only regretful but angry. Such waste! Why have beautiful things if you do not use them? Marjorie's limpid aquamarines sit incongruously on the lizardskin of my lobes, but I wear them permanently. I also wear all of Uncle Samuel's pieces all the time, when a pleated neck might be better served with drapes or scarves, liver-spotted hands by oversized cardigan sleeves.

Strangely, despite her shortcomings and all the distress she caused me, I regret, too, that in the short time allotted to me I did not work harder to become friends with my mother, or even to spend time talking to her so I could understand how she could be so closed-up and parsimonious on the one hand, yet so gay and outgoing during our sporadic outings to the theatre and most spectacularly so on the night of our party. That night she was transformed into a twinkling socialite, although once or twice I did see a deep flash of fear in her eyes when her gaze alighted on one or both of her twin sons. Perhaps all that gaiety had been forced, although if it was, Mother was a superb actress. I shall never know now.

This is in hindsight, of course, and at the time, consideration of my mother, her enjoyment or worries, was of little interest and I passed them off as having nothing to do with me.

I do think a great deal about that party sixty years ago, perhaps because it was the final social occasion of my life. When people look at me now they see a stick insect, a desiccated old woman. But, like my mother, I, too, was beautiful that evening and I knew it. I saw it in Coley Quinn's eyes, felt it in the trembling of his body as he held me to dance, heard it in the teasing, yet underlying sincerity of the compliments paid me by my brothers – and, of course, in the jealous gibes of poor Mary Quigley.

I have forgotten many particulars, like guests' names or what we ate, although I do have a mental image of cucumber slices so thin and transparent they seemed as deeply pink as the two enormous salmon they decorated, but not a single aspect of Coley Quinn's sojourn there has dimmed. The dancing I have already described but I can also remember precisely where Coley stood with his sister at every moment, the inclination of his head as he spoke to her, the intensity of his eyes as they swivelled to follow my progress round the drawing room with food or drinks.

If put to it, I could accurately mimic his slow, careful handling of Johanna while, after his dance with me, he piloted her gravely round the perimeter of the floor to the strains of yet another old-time waltz, of which the band seemed to have an unlimited repertoire. Under the pretext of placing her strategically ('Would you not like to dance, Florrie? How can anyone know you are available if they cannot see you?') I had manoeuvred his sister towards the doorway so we were in position to watch him. Unfortunately Mary Quigley joined us there. She was most unhappy. 'Your uncle is very nice, Violet, but I have to say I think it is very rude of you to abandon me.'

'I apologise, Mary, if that is what you think I have done. But you do know it is one of my duties to look after not only my personal guests but others too?'

'And I suppose it was also part of your duty to throw yourself like a wild thing around the dance floor with Coley Quinn?'

'Did no one ask you to dance, Mary?' Even at the time I knew this behaviour to be appalling, especially in front of Coley's poor sister, who, like a spectator at a horrific tennis match, gazed wide-eyed from one to the other of us as we sparred. I rationalised defiantly that Mary was behaving as obnoxiously as I – but, of course, she was quite justified in her complaints about my rudeness and it is another of my enduring, if useless regrets that I insulted her so. We brought out the very worst in each other and that night I permanently eradicated any possibility, even the vaguest, that we might become friends. I never saw her again but I do know she went on to become a renowned university professor of English and a literary critic of such severity that at one point her censorious style provoked a long controversy in the letters pages of the *Irish Times*. I enjoyed reading it.

The end of the party came quickly, on the stroke of midnight. One minute everyone was dancing, chattering, drinking; the next, the band on the landing had segued from a spirited quickstep into a slow rendition of Vera Lynn's 'We'll Meet Again' and everyone in the hall and in the drawing room, including those seated on the stairs, joined hands and sang along. While the younger people, in particular the group around Young Samuel, who obviously could not contemplate the possibility of not meeting again, swayed from side to side and sang raucously, the older folk, including Mother and Father, were more circumspect.

Caught between the rector and Nanny, who for those few moments had abandoned her waiting role, I could not reach Coley to take his hand and was marooned in the more sedate side of the gathering. I could not even see my lover, although I twisted my head this way and that – and caught sight of Mother. She was in tears and appeared to be making little effort to control them. Mortified, I turned away and pretended I had noticed nothing.

Then, over the next quarter-hour, while Father and Mother
– composed again – took their places at either side of the
front door to see everyone off, the musicians packed up and
the air filled with goodbyes, thank-yous and assurances that
this was the best party the guests had ever known. Johanna,
the temporary maid and I were charged with reuniting
everyone with their belongings and steering them towards
the correct cars and hackneys.

When I saw that Coley and his sister were among the
leave-takers queuing to pay their respects to Mother and
Father, I joined my parents. 'It was very nice to have you
both,' I said, shaking hands first with Florrie, who, no doubt,
could not have enjoyed herself very much, poor girl, and then
with my lover. 'Please give our best to your father and mother,
Coley, and I hope we shall meet again very soon.' Because
Mary Quigley was next in line, I did not dare look at him
in any telling way, but hoped I had conveyed my message.

Father was engaged in some last-minute discussions with a
fellow-merchant so Mother, too, shook hands with Coley and
his sister then and, although I did listen for signals – had she
noticed anything? Was her tone different with Coley from how
it had been with any of the other guests? – I discerned nothing
except, perhaps, the slightest hint of detachment. This was not
significant. Although she was always perfectly pleasant and polite
to them and to others like them in the village, Nanny was the
only one from outside our circle with whom she was relaxed.

Having safely seen off the Quinns, I turned to my third
guest then and, doing my best to sound earnest, friendly, even
apologetic, shook her hand too: 'I hope you get home safely,
Mary. I hope you did enjoy yourself. Thank you very much
for coming.'

Thank goodness Mother rowed in then. 'You were so kind to come, Mary,' she said, smiling at my so-called friend. 'Now that you know where we are, please come again. It would be very nice for Violet. Have you a lift?'

'Thank you, Mrs Shine.' Mary responded after only the briefest of hesitations. 'My father is outside – I can see him. It was a lovely party. It was lovely to be here.' Her manners put me to shame, and although it was too late to make amends for my outrageous neglect of her, when Mother turned away to the next set of people, I did try. 'Sorry I was so busy that we did not get much opportunity to talk. We shall see each other after the holidays.'

'Perhaps.' She drew her coat round her and stepped out of my life, leaving me to deal with my guilt while I rushed off to find a mislaid clutch bag for one of the farmers' wives.

On the subject of guilt and regrets, as I said, I do not regret a single second of my relationship with Coley Quinn, not that we became lovers, not the consequences. I regret only that we were not clever enough to manage them.

As I have described, the view from that tower room was of parched, sandy headland on the cliff over the sea. Yet I did have a partial view, sadly not of a magnolia but of a specimen beech tree at the corner of the house – either some ancestor had planted it at the same time as its confrères on the colonnade along the avenue or it had been a wayward seedling – and if I balanced on tiptoe with my chair at a certain angle, body tightly twisted into a corner of the window, cheek pressed against the glass, I could see approximately a third of its wide canopy.

One year, around mid-May, I think, I was granted the privilege of watching it come into leaf. Believe it or not, that tree greened in one day, if you take a day as twenty-four hours; it was almost like watching it happen in slow motion on a TV nature programme.

On the first morning, the tree was still brown and bare, although when the sun came up and lit it from the sea, I could see that, all over it, twigs had sprouted spigots of whitish buds. By early afternoon, they had produced a tracery of green among the branches; that evening, at sunset, brown and green were in equilibrium but next morning, when the sun again came up, tens of thousands of lime-coloured leaves fluttered from their brown scaffold, tiny prayer flags in the dawn breeze. It seemed to me like a miracle.

I am uncertain as to why I am relating such a detail at this juncture, unless it is as a reminder that, contrary to what might be believed by well-meaning people concerned on my behalf, once I had come to accept it, my incarceration was not without its compensations. It would not have been my chosen way of life, but while my view of the outside world was limited to a pie-shaped slice, unhurried contemplation of it rewarded me well. In addition, within certain constraints I could choose how to spend every second of my life. This, I find in retrospect, was a privilege. How many people leading ordinary 'free' lives these days have time to watch buds open?

The legacy of that time is that, more than most people, I appreciate the freedom to walk in forests, to bathe in the sea; I remember that shortly after my release early in 1979 I pricked my finger on a furze bush, relishing the unexpected sting and the trickle of my own bright blood; and even during my first visit to a dentist in thirty-five years (necessary, but I had never indulged in sugary foods and all of us in the family had been blessed with strong teeth) I quite enjoyed the discomfort of his poking and prodding. It was as if all my senses had been hibernating and had re-emerged in celebratory mood.

Sometimes in this hurry-hurry era I actually miss the days, weeks, months and even years that must seem so empty to an outsider. What is not so odd, I think, is that I had lost all sense of fear of the future, of fear *per se*. I wonder if that marvellous beech is still standing. I saw the phenomenon only once.

I have confided none of this to a soul. No one has enquired. I am sure that people around here consider me eccentric and I am happy that the theory be maintained. I am the last of my family. The secret is safe.

Was I lonely during those tower years?

I did not miss socialising with friends because, as I have explained, I had none, so socialising had never been part of my life to begin with – but, yes, of course I was lonely. I missed my family, especially Johanna. Talking to her through the hatch was not really very satisfactory, although I did look forward to it. I even missed sitting with Mother in the evenings, playing havoc with my eyesight while we worked on the dreaded Shine Quilt.

Loneliness cannot accurately be described – at least, not by me. The experience of the condition is unique to each individual, I think, and in my case it was as active as a baby in the womb and just as physical, kicking when least expected. It left tastes in my mouth. It constricted my throat. It ached in my belly and legs, in the hollow between nose and eyes.

It was most profound when I saw something through my window that fascinated me, or gained an insight I wanted to share, but had to wait, sometimes for hours, until someone came to the hatch. If it turned out to be Johanna, that was good – although by the time she came, the excitement of discovery had frequently worn off and my relating of the incident or thought felt flat and inconsequential. In many cases I could see from her puzzled reaction that what I was telling her seemed trivial.

If it was Mother who came, I stifled the impulse to communicate any discovery. In any event, she usually kept her eyes averted as she handed me my food, or laundry or whatever else I needed. As for Father, he came so seldom it counted as a major occurrence and when he did he seemed deeply uncomfortable. He spoke only to ask if I was all right and if I needed anything other than what he was delivering and in all the years I was imprisoned, I do not think I ever initiated a conversation with him.

As time went by, however, I became concerned about him. Probably because I saw him so infrequently, each time he came it struck me that, in the intervening period, he had become thinner; he had certainly shrunk a little.

I began to worry about his health and resolved to say something to Mother about it. I bided my time. All I needed was an opening.

It was she, however, who died first – in 1977 at the age of seventy-seven, just a year older than I am now; beneath her apparent poor health, she proved robust enough in the end. And I need not have worried unduly about Father, who lived into his eighty-first year. If it had not been for the war, we might have been known as a long-lived family.

# 23

# A TATHARARA

The morning after the party dawned clear. I had not slept. At the last minute, Young Samuel's Dublin friends had had to stay the night because their hackney had not turned up and we could find no other mode of transport to take them back to the city: Father's petrol tank was almost empty. So in the reallocation of bedrooms, Johanna and Marjorie had had to come into mine.

This would have been uncomfortable in any case: while they shared my bed, I had to sleep on the floor on an old mattress taken down from the attic. Because of my assignation with Coley, however, it was more than uncomfortable: it was a dreadful development. How was I going to get out without waking them? I could not even make any preparations for a stealthy exit, such as organising clothing, without arousing suspicion.

When I could see it was becoming light outside, and while my sisters snored in quiet dissonance, I slid off the mattress inch by inch and, taking up the party outfit I had discarded on the floor beside me, crept backwards towards the door, one step at a time. If either woke and challenged me, I was going to say, truthfully, that I hadn't been able to sleep and was going downstairs. It might have been simpler to say I was going to the bathroom, but would it have been credible that I had a party dress with me?

It took perhaps five minutes but I managed to leave the room without incident. I stopped for a few moments on the landing to release the breath pent-up in my chest. With every bedroom full to capacity, however, chances were high that someone might emerge from one at any time so I did not linger but hurried quietly down the staircase – thanking the unknown architect who had decreed it be constructed of stone – and flitted into the kitchen to get dressed.

It was strange to be here at this hour of the morning when the room, normally a hive of ordered activity, was so still and silent. Only the tin alarm clock on the mantel above the stove made its presence felt with its wheezy ticking. There would be some work needed in here later on, I thought, as I surveyed the piles of ware and ranks of glasses as yet unwashed. The sight of them increased the urgency of my present mission: it was unlikely that either Mother or Nanny would allow this chaos to persist. They would be down here early. The blackout blinds on the big window behind the sink had been raised, which was normal. Mother raised them each night after lights out because she liked the geraniums on the sill to get the benefit of the early-morning sun and, indeed, through the window, on the horizon I could see a thin red glow between sea and sky on the horizon. I had to hurry.

I went into the pantry. It had no window so I had to leave the door open and stay alert in case I should hear anyone approach. Quickly, I stripped off my nightdress, folded it haphazardly and bundled it under an upside-down colander

218

at the back of a shelf, on the premise that, should I not get back in time to retrieve it before the kitchen exploded with activity, this was one utensil unlikely to be used in the preparation of breakfast.

Then I dressed. My frock, so smart and grand last night, was now as crumpled as a dishrag but Coley would not mind. As for Mother's silver sandals, I was taking a huge risk in wearing them outdoors but I would have plenty of time to clean them, I hoped.

What I had forgotten, as I let myself out through the back door, was that a pink and gold dawn in late spring, while enchanting to see, was cold and that a linen dress, bare legs and open sandals were entirely inadequate for the conditions. My shivering, though, was only partly due to the temperature: I was nervous, excited, terrified and thrilled all at once. What would we do this time? Would we do 'it' naked? Would we do 'it' at all?

There had been a touch of ground-frost overnight, and as I hurried across the fields, Mother's sandals crunched on crystallised grass that flashed and winked in the rays of the rising sun. I, however, was blind to beauty as, arms folded tightly across my chest in an effort to keep warm, I hurried along: according to my watch, it was not yet six o'clock. Would Coley be already there? Would he be late? Suppose he did not turn up at all?

Suppose we were caught?

I saw him before he saw me. Sensibly huddled into a peajacket, he was watching something out at sea. Too late, I realised I had come out without even combing my hair and half-heartedly dragged my fingers through it, no doubt making it worse. At least, I thought, there was no wind.

He turned and saw me, resulting in one of those moments I shall remember on my deathbed, at least I hope I shall, for I forgot about the cold, about my disgracefully crumpled dress and Mother's sandals, about my hair, as disordered and wild as a burned bush. His eyes and the hollows under his prominent cheekbones were in deep shadow and, in that instant, the pleasure of seeing him was so intense I actually thought I might die of it.

Within seconds he had cleared the short distance between us and we were kissing in each other's arms. 'You're shivering,' he whispered, tightening his grip, 'poor little thing.' Then, 'You'll catch your death – here, put this on.' He took off the jacket, placed it round my shoulders and buttoned it up so my arms were imprisoned. 'You silly girl,' he scolded, as if he were an uncle rather than a lover, 'why didn't you wear a coat or something?'

I might have gone into tiresome detail about why this had not been possible but, instead, stood on tiptoe and kissed him on the mouth.

Underneath the jacket he was wearing a cotton workshirt and, revelling in the roughness of the fabric, I laid my cheek against it. He put his arms round me again and leaned his head on mine. 'Violet,' he murmured, into the nest of my hair. 'Violet . . . Violet . . .'

Entwined like this, we rocked gently in slow, sumptuous parody of last night's dance. It felt adult, even profound, and as for previous speculation about doing 'it', nakedly or otherwise, this was sufficient. I have no idea how long we stood there, a full five minutes, perhaps, but then he detached. 'Why don't you come away with me, Violet? I know we're sealed up from the outside world in this country but there's ways around it. We could go up to the north and I guarantee you I'd find a way for us to skip across to Scotland.'

'Like Deirdre and the Sons of Uisneach!' I thrilled to the notion. This pre-Christian Gaelic saga, learned first in national school, had been one of Miss Lucy Biggs's favourites. It is a story of royalty, bloody war and betrayal but, above all, it is the story of the deep and enduring love between an upright hero and a beautiful maiden. (I found it convenient to ignore the tragic ending where the hero and his brothers are poisoned by the jealous king so he can marry the maiden, an ambition thwarted when she – presumably no longer a maiden, having lived in Scottish exile with her lover for years – throws herself into his grave. Or under the hoofs of the horses bearing her lover's remains, whichever version one believes.) 'But what would we do in Scotland? How would we live?' The questions were rhetorical: I would have gladly allowed my hero to carry me off to the Arctic Circle but, in the meantime, I thought I should show him how mature I was. 'I have no money of my own, Coley.'

'I'm strong and healthy.' His expression was ardent yet very serious. 'I'm quick with figures and I can work with my hands too. I'm sure the creamery would give me a good reference if I sent for it once we were there. I could support us.'

'It sounds so romantic.' I hesitated for a moment then took the plunge. 'I don't want to appear forward, but does this mean you're asking me to marry you?'

He dropped to one knee. 'Violet Shine, will you marry me?'

No need for hesitation now. 'Oh, yes! Yes! Yes!' I was dizzy with joy. So was he. He jumped to his feet again and kissed me so enthusiastically that without the use of my arms as ballast, I was in danger of toppling over like one of those jolly, limbless toys with a weighted, curved base.

But my happiness began to disperse when I realised there might be a hitch in this plan. A big one. I knew from Nanny that 'mixed marriages' were notoriously difficult: Coley would have to get what they called a 'dispensation' from the Pope (or maybe just a bishop, I forgot which), a process that would take years and years and would cost a fortune. That was not the end of it either. Nanny had a stock of lurid stories about 'dispensations' denied, but assuming we were lucky and got one, we were still not out of the woods. I would then have to swear on the Holy Bible that our children would be brought up as Catholics. I would have to swear that I would take them to Mass every week. We would all have to eat fish on Fridays and deny ourselves all kinds of treats while fasting during Lent.

I put my hands on Coley's chest to stop the kissing. 'But you're a Roman Catholic.'

He had an answer for that: 'Only if I want to get married in a Catholic church.'

'But surely—'

'Violet!' He put a finger on my lips. 'Do you really think I would let religion stand in the way of our being together?'

I was half scandalised, half elated. He, a Roman Catholic, would give up his religion for me? That was unheard-of. It had to work the other way round: that was the impression I had got from Nanny over the years. 'But would they let us? If they knew we were of different religions, I mean.'

'I hardly think it would matter in Scotland. It's not a Catholic country. Anyway, have you never heard of Gretna Green?'

'Not really.' I stood mummified in Coley Quinn's pea-jacket, redolent of cigarette smoke, food and what I thought of fondly as 'honest' sweat, while he disposed of piffling obstacles to our being together and educated me about star-crossed couples, elopements and the famous forge. I was paying attention, of course, but not fully. My excitement was fuelling visions of (discreet) bridal outfits set against spectacular and windy Scottish Highlands. I was also watching the way the corner of my fiancé's mouth curved into a little dimple on certain words, and admiring the straight lines of his eyebrows.

It occurred to me then that, while we thought we were alone up there, it was possible we were the first Irish couple in history whose engagement had been witnessed through the periscope of a U-boat: rumours were rife that they were prowling up and down the Irish Sea and in my present state of euphoria the concept appeared terribly funny. Were all those German sailors crowding round the base of the periscope to have a look? Taking turns to see the mad Irishman who was proposing to a mummy? *Achtung*, Friedrich! *Lookenzie hier* at *der* lunatic *Irischer*! I giggled.

'What did I say?' Coley was taken aback.

'Nothing, darling!' Oh, how wonderful it felt to say that word. 'Nothing, darling, nothing, nothing, you said nothing! Please, Coley, will you unbutton this jacket? I want to hold you properly.'

As he did so, his fingers shook. We both knew what came next – U-boat or no U-boat – but while he spread the pea-jacket on the ground as I had in Loughshinny, I worried fleetingly about the risks – of staining, or of ruining the dress completely; of him doing something to me that would leave a telltale mark, or of the two of us getting so carried away I forgot about time and went home fatally late. All such considerations popped off when he took me into his arms and tumbled me to the ground. Then all I cared about was the sensation of our bodies grinding together hungrily as if to ingest each other's souls. We were not just responding to physical desire and attraction this time: as two betrothed we were making lifelong pledges to one another and, this time, not only did the act itself not feel violent, it felt wholly right, a physical celebration of what it was to be alive, in love, belonging together for ever.

'Mother will kill me when she sees the state of this dress!' Ruefully, I looked down at the dishrag, as spent, hand in hand, we lay alongside each other looking up at the sky, a pre-dawn blue and so infinitely clear I felt as if I were floating in it. I certainly felt weightless – and, for some reason, no longer cold.

'Does she have to see it?' Coley smoothed the linen over the swell of my stomach.

'Maybe not – maybe I can wash it myself. The key will be if I can get it into the washing water without her seeing it.'

'Very soon you won't have to worry about what your mother, or anyone, thinks about you. You'll have only me to answer to – and I won't be a hard taskmaster!' Playfully, he tickled my tummy with both hands, causing my whole body to contract. 'Stop it, Coley, stop it!' But he tickled harder until both of us were rolling over, off his jacket and into the drenched grass. He would have instigated lovemaking again but the wretched dress, bunched up and wet under me, had become a matter of serious concern. What also struck me was the passing of time. Sober now, over Coley's shoulder I checked my watch. To my horror it was almost seven fifteen. 'No, Coley, please.' I pushed him off me and scrambled to my feet. 'I have to dash.'

'I'll come with you.' He, too, stood up.

'No. No!' I backed away. The thought of being discovered in his company at this hour of the morning terrified me.

'But we have to talk, we have to make plans, and there's no one about yet. It's still very early—'

'Please, Coley. Don't come. We will make plans, I promise. We'll meet again very soon – maybe tonight? I definitely won't be able to get away to leave a note here, so say we meet at about eleven o'clock? Please don't be disappointed if I don't turn up. I'll do my best.' Swiftly, I kissed Coley and ran for my life. Any plans, even for elopement – even if that was to take place as early as next week – could wait: the more immediate situation was extremely perilous. I had thought seven o'clock to be the outside time at which I could hope to get back undetected into Whitecliff; all I could do now was to run hard – and although I was not known for either the frequency or efficacy of my prayers, to pray.

When I arrived within fifty yards of the house, I stopped briefly to calm down and catch my breath. There was no sign of life but that was not surprising since all I could see was the gable end. Unless I did a complete circuit there was no way of knowing, for instance, if blinds had been raised or curtains pulled back at any of the windows.

Rather than approach the back door directly, I moved cautiously to the fence along the clifftop and stopped to take another survey: it proved as ineffective as the first. Top to bottom, all the windows acted like mirrors reflecting the sun so it was impossible to see behind their dazzle. I would just

Deirdre Purcell

have to take my chances, I thought, and formulated a plan, whose beauty was that it was mostly truthful. Should I encounter anyone I would simply say that since I had not been able to sleep, largely because of the overcrowding in my bedroom, I had gone out for a walk. To add realism, I plucked a handful of the tiny blue and yellow pansy-like wild flowers that grew in clusters along the base of the fence. Then, briskly, hoping I looked wind-tossed rather than wanton, I walked from the fence to the back door and pushed it open on a nightmare made flesh.

Three people, Mother, Nanny and Uncle Samuel, turned their communal, startled gaze on me as I came into a kitchen full of steam from the coppers on the range. Nanny and Mother were standing at the sink washing dishes. Seated at the table, Uncle Samuel was nursing a cup of tea. He had brought his own ration with him from the north.

It was he who reacted first. 'Fair play to ye.' He stood up, crossed the kitchen and refilled his cup from the teapot stewing beside the coppers. 'Most of them are just turning over for the second sleep. Lazy lumps.'

'Where were you? And just look at the state of that dress! Are those grass stains?' As if he had not spoken Mother dried her hands on her apron, then reached out to take hold of the linen.

'I fell,' I blurted, and moved out of her reach. I was suddenly aware of how I might smell and I did not want her coming too close. I joined Uncle Samuel at the stove. 'Is there any more tea in that pot?' I lifted the lid and saw it was empty. Then, conversationally, to the room at large: 'I didn't realise it would be so slippery out there. Or so cold. There's a heavy dew this morning.' I turned to Uncle Samuel. 'I had goosebumps all over me. I even saw patches of ice crystals. Would you believe that?' I knew that ground frost persisted in these parts into early summer but I was babbling.

'Aye.' His expression was inscrutable and, out of the corner of my eye, I saw Mother and Nanny exchange a glance. I was about to do something silly, like burst into tears, but Uncle Samuel thrust his cup at me: 'Put a wee drop of cold water from the tap in that, dear, would you?' He winked. 'It's burning the mouth off me.' I smiled gratefully at him as I took his cup and went to the sink.

'Just look at my lovely sandals.' Mother was not finished. 'And is that grass in your hair?' Again she moved towards me but again I evaded her by going back to the range with the cooled tea. 'I told you,' I said over my shoulder, 'I slipped and fell.'

'Ach, Fly, leave the child alone.' Uncle Samuel leaned his ample behind against the brass bar of the range. 'It's early. What a tatharara for this hour of the morning.'

Mother again ignored him. 'You have failed to answer my question, Violet. What were you doing?'

'How many times do I have to tell you?' Defiantly, because at least I had Uncle Samuel in my corner, or so I hoped, I looked at the three of them. 'I could not sleep. The others were snoring their heads off. I could not stick it any more. You should hear the two of them – one on her own would have been bad enough but the two together was intolerable.' I was in my stride, working up a grievance, convincing even myself. 'It wasn't fair to put them in my room like that, Mother. And, before you ask,' I added loftily, 'I had no choice but to wear again what I wore last night. I didn't want to wake Marjorie or Johanna by rooting through my wardrobe.

I'm sorry I made such a mess of the dress when I fell, and of course I shall clean your shoes. I shall go upstairs now and change. They can wake up if they like or if they don't like.'

'We've work to do here.' Nanny took up the running by picking up two plates and drying them one after the other. 'Bring back down that dress, Violet,' she said quietly. 'We'll need to give it a good washing and airing.'

'Of course, Nanny. I'd be changed now if it hadn't been for all of this. Here!' With a flourish, I put the handful of already wilted flowers on the table as I passed it. 'I picked these for you, Mother. I thought you'd like them. Maybe you don't want them, maybe you do. I don't care.'

As I flounced out of the kitchen, I could hear Mother's flummoxed question to Nanny: 'What do you make of that?'

I did not wait to hear the reply. As I climbed the stairs, I was shaky with relief. It had been quite a performance. I had got away with it, it seemed.

# 24

# BEYOND DREAMING

Coley and I did meet again that evening at our fairy tree. Uncle Samuel was still with us – he was staying until the twins left – but with the departure of Young Samuel and his guests, the twins billeted in their old room and Marjorie and Johanna each in theirs, mine had been returned to me so it had been quite easy to escape. Everyone in the house, professing tiredness, had gone to bed early, which was exactly what I had hoped when I suggested the assignation. Sleep-deprived as I was, I should have felt tired too, but during that period, I seemed to have had an inexhaustible supply of energy when it suited me.

Strangely, after an initial kiss and hug, we were shy with each other. I supposed that the enormity of the step we proposed to take together had dawned on us during the day; it certainly had on me. He had brought a blanket and we sat on it with his arm round my shoulder, yet there was no urgent physical desire this time, and for quite a while neither of us spoke but sat staring out to sea. On my part, I was trying to decide how best to broach the subject of our elopement and I guessed it was the same for him.

The night was dry, cold and quite dark because the moon rode behind tattered cloud, filmy as muslin, that nevertheless dimmed its light. Rain was forecast for the following day; it was almost possible to taste it in the air and I shivered. 'Are you cold?' He hugged me closer.

'Not at all. I'm grand.' The shiver had been transient. I was far better prepared for the outdoors than I had been that morning, with a heavy woollen jumper over my school skirt, socks and sensible shoes, I was comfortable and snug.

'How did you get on when you got home this morning?' he asked eventually.

I told him, leaving nothing out.

'Are you sure they didn't suspect anything?'

'Fairly sure. I did get a few sidelong looks from Mother during the day, and she was not really speaking to me but that was understandable. You should have seen the state of me when I walked into that kitchen. And, probably, her bad humour had a lot to do with the muck on her precious sandals. I managed to clean them like new, though, and I worked really hard around the house for the whole day. I gave them no cause for complaint whatsoever. I'm sure everything will be back to normal tomorrow.'

'You're a little treasure, aren't you?' He kissed my cheek. 'You'll make a great housewife.'

I looked to see if he was teasing me but it was too dark to decipher the expression in his eyes. 'Now that the subject is out in the open,' I said soberly, 'I have to make one thing clear. I trust you to take care of us, Coley, but women nowadays don't just stay at home cleaning and cooking for their husbands. The war has changed all that. I intend to work too. I'm as healthy and strong as you are.'

'Of course you are!' He attempted to kiss me again.

'No, Coley.' I pushed him away. 'I mean it. I am a modern woman.'

'Of course you are.'

'Are you taking me seriously, Coley?' I was becoming annoyed. 'I don't like the way you're treating this.'

'What?' He was astonished. 'But I said it was all right for you to work.'

'That's exactly what I meant,' I cried. 'I will not need your permission. This is the middle of the twentieth century, not the nineteenth! Women all over Britain are working in factories. Women in America are running their own companies, for goodness' sake—'

'I know that. I'm not arguing with you. Do you hear me arguing?'

We stopped, shocked that we seemed to be having a row.

'This is important to me,' I said more quietly.

'Anything you want! Don't let's fight. It's not something that I've thought about much.'

'We haven't thought much about anything, really, have we?'

With the reverberations of the argument all about us, we gazed at each other. 'So what?' He shrugged them off. 'We're at the beginning of a lifelong journey. An adventure! Half the fun will be finding out all about each other. And we've just had our very first argument.' He reached out and cupped one of my breasts in his hand, squeezing it gently through the thick jumper. 'You do know what's the best part of having a row, Violet Shine?'

I longed for him to take the other breast too, and he did. I leaned in to him, arching my back. 'What is it, Coley Quinn?'

'It's the making up,' he said softly. 'Now I wonder how we

could do that?' The moonlight, weak as it was, glinted on his grin, and within seconds we were tearing at one another.

'Is this normal?' I asked him afterwards, when we had read-justed our clothes and were lying on his rug, my head on his chest, his chin resting in my hair and his arms round me. I felt secure, like a bird must feel in a safely hidden nest.

'Is what normal?' He sounded drowsy.

'That we should be doing it so often? This is the second time in the same day.'

'Sure I don't know what's normal any more than you do. Will we be doing it when we're seventy? I can't imagine old folk doing it at all, can you?' He laughed.

'No.' I laughed too. 'But you do think this is normal for people our age, then?'

'It feels right, doesn't it?'

'Yes.'

'Then I'm sure it is.'

'But it is a sin—'

'Yeah.'

'Do you care about it being a sin, Coley? Aren't Catholics very strict?'

'Am I behaving like a strict Catholic?'

'No.'

'Well, then. And anyway, aren't you Proddies strict too?'

'I don't know, really. We learned about Original Sin and so on in Sunday school, but in church our rector doesn't talk much about sins. It's more like everyone should try to be good and so on.'

'Well,' Coley said, with an air of finality, 'I don't see anything wrong with it at all. I certainly don't feel like a sinner.'

'Neither do I. We'd feel it, surely, if it was wrong? Isn't that what consciences are all about? For instance, I felt awful when I was lying to Mother this morning, I always feel awful when I lie, but I don't feel in the least awful about our lovemaking. Especially now that we're promised to each other for ever.' Feeling far from awful, I kissed him giddily. 'So, should we have another go?'

'Hey! Steady! Give a man a chance to get his strength back!' But he snuggled in.

'I want to see you naked, Coley,' I whispered, when I felt brave enough.

'Only if I can see you too.' He grinned again, and my blood roared and heated up so I could barely breathe.

We each took care of our own undressing. Coley's opinion was that since this was the first time we would see each other properly we should take our time because it was important to remember every second. Although it had been my idea, I was still glad I had some cover from the darkness: despite our passion and what we had just done together I am not sure I would have had the courage to do it in full daylight.

'Now, let's both stand up and face each other. All right?' His voice sounded as if someone was constricting his throat.

I stood. Looking at the rug, I saw his two bare feet and the lower halves of his muscular legs. I closed my eyes. 'Oh, Violet,' he breathed, 'you're so beautiful, the finest, most beautiful woman in the world. You're far more beautiful and finer than I even imagined.' He stroked my hair and although I still could not bring myself to look at him, I angled my head, trapping his hand between it and my shoulder. 'Do you know that when I used to come to your house with my father to pay the land rent,' he continued, 'it was because of you. Each time, I prayed you would be there.' He dropped to his knees

Deirdre Purcell

and wound his arms round my waist, pillowing his head against my breasts. 'I fell in love with you when you were only nine,' he said, his voice vibrating against my skin. 'I want you to know that. I was eleven and you were nine and when I saw you, like a fairy or Alice in Wonderland, with your big blue sash on your white dress and your smile, like – like the sun coming up, I knew as surely as I knew my own name that I could not live without you.'

Now I could open my eyes. Against the dimness, his long back, the mounds of his calves, the side of his face – what I could see of it – were pale. 'I never knew.'

'How could you know?' He looked up at me. 'All you ever saw was a clodhopper with muck on his boots and a dirty face. We were your tenants, Violet. Of course you never saw me. What you thought of me was that I was a local peasant, a tongue-tied ragamuffin that you had to be polite to because that's the way you were brought up. You were polite to everyone. I knew I hadn't a hope in hell with you. For instance, that afternoon when you came down here and saw me on the other side of that fence there? You had no idea who I was, even.'

'But you were so – so . . .' I searched for the proper word '. . . so prickly. I thought you were conceited.'

'I was dying inside. I didn't know what to say or how to behave. It was beyond dreaming that I would be alone with you and having a real talk.' His voice broke then and I clutched him tighter to me, crushing his head between my breasts, rocking him a little. He grabbed on to my buttocks and we rocked together. I thought he might even be crying and tears sprang into my own eyes in response.

I was thrilled, moved, experiencing emotions I had not

234

known were possible. Nothing else existed; nothing mattered except the enchanted circle we had created. 'Hush, darling, hush. I'm here. I'm sorry if you felt I hurt you or ignored you or insulted you in any way. I'll make it up to you for the rest of our lives. You don't have to worry. We'll be together always.'

He was clutching at me so fiercely I was in danger of over-balancing. 'Careful, darling.' I took a small step backwards and, as I did, out of the corner of my eye, I thought I saw something move and turned to look.

Father was standing five feet away.

## 25

# A BLOCK OF YEW

In an effort to vent my anger with my husband, I power-walk up the short, overgrown driveway to the old lady's house, but stop at the base of a tree to calm down and formulate how I am going to handle this.

First things first: before I can think properly, I have to consign Bob and his antics to a remote corner of my brain. Compartmentalise, Claudine, compartmentalise . . . Hate the word, love the concept.

Since this is essentially Tommy's mission, I have to negotiate for him but before I say even hello to this woman, I have to decide for definite if I want to go ahead with my part of the project, given that my life has been turned upside-down by one five-word sentence from Bob. Is my passion for Whitecliff still as strong? I know I'm too angry to be rational about my husband and right now never want to see him again – but that's knee-jerk: it could change, most likely will with time. Suppose it doesn't, though, and we separate? In that case, would I want to live alone at Whitecliff?

I lean against the bole of the tree to think, but am distracted by a whir of wings as a bird lands in the tree canopy above my head. The tree, healthy-looking, seems to be a magnolia, one of my favourites; it must be lovely when it's in bloom. Beyond it, the whitewashed house is in good condition. Big and solid, it is a nice example of a traditional Irish farmhouse but otherwise unremarkable. Like the driveway, it could do with a little TLC, but that's not surprising, considering that the old lady apparently lives alone; she probably has to pay someone even to change a lightbulb. Everything points to the fact that she is one of the increasing band of elderly people in Ireland, particularly women, who are, to use the current jargon, 'asset-rich but cash poor'.

The answer to the question about Whitecliff, I tell myself, is yes: with or without Bob, I want Whitecliff.

It's something I can't really explain: it has nothing to do with size, monetary value or even beauty. It has to do with atmosphere and the sense that the house wants me.

I think.

Oh, God almighty, I'm making no sense here . . . For the first time since I decided to go for it, I feel the stirrings of doubt. It's just as well Whitecliff's not yet on the market and I don't have to commit myself. Dammit, I think, Bob's confession has shaken up even my capacity for making decisions. I don't know what I want now.

I check my appearance in the little mirror I always carry in my handbag. Not too much makeup but enough to show I've made an effort. Hair all right too, and no sign of recent upsets. I seem to be calm now, or calmer: I think I'm the kind of person who gets through a crisis, then collapses afterwards when the curtain has come down on the drama.

My preconception of the old lady is blown away when she answers the door. Far from being a flittering, pitiable old thing with a dowager's hump, dressed in bombazine with cracked trainers and wrinkled socks on her feet, this woman is as tall as I am and with better posture. She is dressed conservatively but elegantly, cream silk blouse – to which a pair of rimless spectacles is held by a gold butterfly pin – tucked into straight brown skirt, stockings, and good shoes with a small heel. She is lean rather than thin and her eyes are bright and alert. Interestingly, the expression in them switches instantly from polite anticipation to something approaching fright, followed just as quickly by appraisal. It's almost as if she had expected someone else.

'Ms Collopy?'

She doesn't respond.

Her continued scrutiny is unnerving me. 'I think I have some identification here.'

I reach for the clasp of my bag but she waves away the gesture. 'That will not be necessary.'

She holds out her hand then and we shake. Her grip is strong and she seems to hold on just a fraction longer than necessary. Is she lonely, perhaps? 'Thank you for seeing me.' I do my best to project what I hope is an air of gentle professionalism. 'Especially at such short notice.'

'You are welcome. Come in, please.' She turns and walks into the house, leaving me to follow or not as I please.

I close the door behind me and walk after her into a large living room, and again my expectations are proved wrong. Bright and pleasantly proportioned, painted white with a caramel-coloured carpet covering a lot of empty floor space, the room is neither chintzy nor stuffed with old-lady gewgaws and memorabilia. In fact, there are no ornaments at all, even on the mantelpiece; it is modern and neutral, even minimalist.

With a coffee-table between them, two small couches upholstered in serviceable navy stand at right angles to the fireplace while a pair of matched bookcases occupy the alcoves flanking the chimney-breast.

The only other piece of furniture is one the like of which I have never seen before. Taking up the wall-space between the two windows, highly polished but unadorned, it is a crescent-shaped bench seat hewn from a single piece of wood so dark it is almost black. Viewed from the side, it has been carved to the shape of a large, opened-up S, the seat curving sinuously into a low, rolled back-rest, the only straight line in the piece. It is timeless and probably priceless. 'This is beautiful, Ms Collopy.' I go over to touch its lustrous surface. 'How old is it?'

'Not so old.'

I look across at her. She is standing by the fireplace and that gaze is now even more disconcerting through the spectacles she must have put on while my back was turned. 'Seventy years or so,' she adds quietly.

I turn to the piece again. 'It certainly looks very valuable.' Then I remember the crescent shape I saw outlined on the wallpaper in the hallway at Whitecliff. 'It's a family piece, of course. It could be French or Italian. Where does it come from, if you don't mind my asking?'

'I do not mind. It is neither French nor Italian and I doubt it is valuable. Father made it from a block of yew. My sister and I brought it here from Whitecliff when I came to live here. Along with some china and linen Johanna took with her when she got married, it is one of the few things we have retained.'

Once again I notice the marked speech pattern. 'Your father must have been a wonderful craftsman.'

239

'He was. Shall we sit down? Would you like some tea, perhaps?' The message is clear. No small-talk.

'Thank you. That would be lovely.'

She leaves the room and I take the opportunity to check out the volumes in the bookcases, usually a good indicator of their owner's personality. These seem predominantly to be about nature and archaeology, with just a small number of art books and classic novels – Austen, Thomas Hardy, Thackeray, the most modern of which are *A Farewell to Arms* and *For Whom The Bell Tolls* by Hemingway, and *Herzog* by Bellow. Although her taste seems to have run into time buffers, this woman is no lightweight. Of course, I am assuming the books are hers and not her deceased sister's.

There is one oddity: tucked away in a corner at floor level there are several editions, hardback and paperback, of *Wuthering Heights*; one or other of the women must at some stage have indicated she liked this novel, which had resulted in people giving it to her as a present. Years ago I made the mistake of starting a collection of ceramic turtles. People, even Bob, seized on this and now I am overrun with them and don't know what to do with them all. When people visit, they expect to see their own donations to the zoo included in the displays. In Bob's opinion—

I mustn't think about Bob. As I continue on to the next bookshelf, to drown thoughts of him, I hum to myself: Somewhere – dum-dum-dee rainbow – du-umm – du-umm – fly—

'Are you a reader, Mrs Armstrong?' Behind me, the old woman's tone is as neutral as her room. I turn away from the perusal of her library to find her bearing a tray: cups and saucers, a teapot covered with a cosy, lump sugar with silver tongs. And on a cake plate probably a whole packet's worth of fig rolls. 'Can I help you with that?' My own tone bright, I take a step forward but she turns away, bending towards the coffee-table.

'I can manage, thank you.'

'Yes, I do read.' I seat myself on one of the couches. 'Not, unfortunately, as much as I would like, these days. I've fallen out of the habit, which is a shame. My degree is in English.'

'Most of our books are upstairs in one of the unused bedrooms. I have been meaning to sort them but so far have not done so.'

'You do have some very nice books. Is it you that likes *Wuthering Heights*?'

'I studied it at school.'

She is pouring the tea but again I'm warned off by her manner. 'I did too. I think everyone did. What a lovely tea-set, Ms Collopy.'

'Thank you. Do you take sugar and milk?' Something strikes me about the china: those gilded teacups – the lilies-of-the-valley. Pat's – or Colman's – inappropriate teapot. Definite proof of his connection with the house – done out of a job when the family moved out, yet loyalty undiminished? Not for mention right now, though. 'One lump, please, and just a little milk. I have to say, Ms Collopy, that the countryside around here is extraordinarily beautiful.'

'I think so too. The Béara Peninsula, I think, is one of the last unspoiled places in Ireland, although that is changing. There is a great deal of construction going on here now, as there is everywhere else, I hear. Tell me, Mrs Armstrong,' daintily, she employs the sugar tongs over her own cup, 'are you from Dublin?'

'Indeed I am.' I find I have picked up her rhythms. I hope she doesn't think I'm mimicking her.

'From the city?'

'Originally, yes.' I deliberately flatten my tone. 'From the southside, Glenageary and then Sandycove. I live in North County Dublin now, however, quite near Whitecliff as it happens.'

Would now be a good time to introduce the photograph of my mother, shouting at me from the wallet in my handbag? I reckon it's too soon.

When I have my tea and a cake plate holding three fig rolls in front of me, she settles back into her seat. Her expression is unreadable but as she seems in no hurry to get down to business I decide that, for the moment, she should dictate the pace. 'This is very kind of you. You can't beat the old-style biscuits. Although I do remember that when I was a child they were much bigger.' I nibble at one of the fig rolls. 'How long have you been living here?'

'Oh, quite a long time, since 1979. This house belonged to my sister and her husband, but it was big enough comfortably to absorb me. We rubbed along together well and, of course, there were just the two of us after he died in 1985. Obviously it was a tragedy for Johanna but for me, too, because he was a beautiful man in every sense. As the years passed, however, and we got over the shock, in many ways it was as though we were children again. It was nice . . .' She trails off. She is no longer staring at me but at her cup.

I am moved by her obvious sadness. 'It must have been awful for you when she died.'

'I confess I am still a little lost without her,' she says, after a pause. Then her voice strengthens: 'I suppose, however, that in life, each age brings strengths appropriate to deal with whatever is thrown at one. I manage well enough and I have very kind neighbours.' She lets silence develop again.

I relax into the sofa while, covertly, between sips, I study her. She is old, for sure – above the blouse, her neck, round which she wears some delicate jewellery, betrays her age – but it is impossible to guess exactly how old. She could be anywhere between sixty-five and eighty. I had been correct in picturing the whiteness of her hair but certainly not the texture, which is luxuriant; left to its own devices it is probably curly, even unruly. Cut in very short layers right now, it frames her heart-shaped face and emphasises wide-set, blue-black eyes that, faded now, must once have been almost as navy as her sofa.

'Do I pass muster?' With this first smile, her face lifts and it's evident that, while she is still a good-looking woman, she must once have been spectacularly so. 'I'm sorry.' I can feel the blush starting at my toes. 'I didn't mean to be rude.'

Now? Photographs now? No – professional business first. 'Look, Ms Collopy,' I put my cup down, 'I'm sure you've guessed why I'm here.'

'I have a good idea.' She nods. 'John Thorpe told you, or your friend in North County Dublin, that I am thinking of disposing of the property there. I must warn you that I have not fully decided. I have not made up my mind.'

I need to find out about this John Thorpe, but before I can frame a suitably non-committal question, we are interrupted by a knock on the door and my heart lurches in my chest. I have compartmentalised so successfully that I had forgotten about Bob. 'That will be my husband,' I explain. 'He was walking our dog. I didn't think it was such a good idea that we should invade your house *en masse*. He'd be happy to wait in the car—'

'Of course he should join us.' She leaves the room, and I hear the door opening in the hall and Bob introducing himself.

They come into the room. 'You'll have some tea, Mr Armstrong?' She pauses at the door. 'Shall I fetch another cup?'

'That's very kind, but no, thank you, not for the present.' Then, while she returns to her seat, he looks around and says genially: 'What a lovely bright room!'

He has struck exactly the right, light note: cordial, inviting confidence and – important with an elderly lady – unthreatening. At sight of him, the bile had risen in my throat, but I am reminded that while I know I can handle this myself, I'm in such a fragile state, especially with him beside me and acting as if nothing had happened, that it's almost a relief to have back-up. I can deal with our personal lives later.

'Are you sure I'm not interrupting?' Before he sits, he looks from the old lady to me and back again. 'I'll be glad to wait outside, ladies, if negotiations are at a critical stage.'

'We haven't started.' I don't look at him while I slide along the small sofa as far as I can to make space for him. I know the real reason he is there – to start making amends to me – but right now I couldn't bear for even our sleeves to touch.

'But Miss Collopy knows what's at stake?' As he sits beside me, he smiles at her.

'She does.' I move further along until I'm squeezed tightly into the armrest. 'She knows we might be interested in talking to her about Whitecliff.'

'How long is it since you've seen the place, Miss Collopy?' Earnestly, he leans forward.

'I have not been there for many years.'

'Then you won't know that it's semi-derelict?' I am conscious he has glanced at me for approval but I won't give him the satisfaction of granting it and concentrate my attention on the old lady.

'I am sure that the state of the house, even the house itself, is immaterial to developers.' She smiles that smile again and this time it is mischievous. 'I read my newspapers, Mr Armstrong, and I listen to the wireless. I also watch news on the TV, and even if I did not, I have agents. I am therefore fully aware of the property boom in that corner of the county. Whitecliff offers nineteen acres of prime development land in a very desirable area.'

'Indeed it does.' Bob gives her the benefit of the Armstrong charm. Again he glances at me and again I ignore him. 'But what we are proposing, Miss Collopy,' he continues, 'if it is not too presumptuous, of course, is that we enter negotiations with you on an outline but exclusive basis before you put the estate on the open market.' He opens both hands and reaches out as if offering a large parcel. 'The advantages to you must be obvious. I hope you don't mind my saying so, but at this point, you should be enjoying the fruits of your long life and not worrying about setting hounds against one another, if you get my meaning. Because, believe me, as soon as you signal your intent, even the merest hint, that you are planning to sell those nineteen acres, never mind the house itself, you will be besieged by all sorts. And not all of them savoury.'

'I am well aware of that.' Her smile widens. 'But I think

you will agree that, unlike the hounds, as you call them, I am at present safely ensconced in my lair. I hold all the cards, do I not?' To my amazement, she seems to be enjoying the joust.

'You certainly do. You certainly do.' Bob leans even further forward to engage her as fully as possible but we are interrupted by a volley of furious barking, unmistakably Jeffrey's. 'I'm so sorry.' He shoots to his feet and backs towards the door. 'I must have left the car window open too wide and he's got out. I'll sort him out – excuse me. But do hold that thought.'

'I will.' Still smiling, she watches him leave but as soon as we are alone, her attitude changes. 'What is your personal interest in Whitecliff, Mrs Armstrong?'

I am so startled at the sudden change I can only stutter something inconsequential about the house being a fine property and a fascinating refurbishment possibility.

She brushes this aside by standing up and walking to the window, then turns to face me. 'Forgive me if I am being intrusive but may I ask you a personal question?' With the light behind her, her expression is difficult to interpret.

'Yes, of course.' I feel wrong-footed, as if she is the teacher and I am the pupil caught cheating.

'Armstrong is your married name, of course?'

'Yes.' I am wary. This is self-evident; she's met Bob. Is it possible she's trying to make connections too?

'And, if I may ask further, what was your maiden name?'

She is. Obviously she is! Because when I tell her, instead of telling me her family bought a car from Daddy, instead of saying anything at all, she turns her back to me to look through the window. Her shoulders are rigid.

'Why do you ask, Ms Collopy?' I'm on tenterhooks.

Instead of replying directly, she asks another question. I know it is a question because I can hear the inflection but she has spoken without turning round, and so softly I haven't caught the gist. 'I beg your pardon?'

She turns back to me and, shadowed though it is, I can see her face has become very pale. 'Was your mother's name Marjorie?'

# 26

# LAMB TO THE SLAUGHTER

'Excuse me for a moment, Mrs Armstrong.' I stood up. 'I have just remembered that something needs my attention in the kitchen. And we could do with some more tea, of course. I shall be back presently.' Then I walked out of the room, leaving my niece alone.

My reaction to such a meaningful discovery might appear bizarre but it is an accurate account of what happened. My feet took me away and I found myself in the kitchen of the house I had shared with Johanna.

Once there, however, I felt lightheaded and had to sit on one of the chairs, Johanna's, as it turns out. I had not moved it or plumped her back cushion since the night she died; I am the last of my family, or so I had thought, and I had been holding on to the shards of my beloved sister's presence for as long as possible. Now, I think, as I try to calm my racing heart, by sitting down so thoughtlessly, I have destroyed her imprint for ever.

To me, Marjorie's child was always an editor's footnote on the drama of Whitecliff, forever a baby with no relevance to day-to-day life in my tower: my world having shrunk to the size of one room, I had become self-absorbed. But there is no doubt about who Claudine Armstrong is. Increasingly, as she spoke, I heard echoes of my second sister's voice and then, when I came in with the tea-things, I heard her singing . . .

We had known, of course, that Marjorie had married a car-dealer, apparently a florid but kind type, who was some years older than she. For whatever reason, whether from disapproval or dislike of him, or because Mother was still bound into her extended mourning for the twins, none of the immediate family attended their wedding when it took place in Paris. And after my sister died giving birth to the woman I have left standing in my sitting room, I cannot remember who did or did not go to her funeral. I find that while individual episodes and my reactions to them are as clear as ever, more and more frequently, memory lets me down with regard to chronology. In some cases time seems to have contracted so that past events pile in on top of one another and prove impossible to disentangle, while in others, they seem to have stretched over decades when logic dictates otherwise. You must remember that, in my tower, I was receiving news only sporadically and always filtered through the impressions of the giver; in that context, from the day Marjorie died, I knew that Mother had got it firmly into her head that the car-dealer was somehow to blame for her death and, as far as I knew, we had broken off contact with him and his baby daughter.

It was from Young Samuel I learned about the dealer's death some years later. He came only rarely because he was living in the north of Ireland, running the public house he had inherited from my godfather; I can still see his swollen, sputtering face as he confided through my hatch that when he had seen the death in the newspaper he had considered going to pay his respects but on the day had not been well enough. Over the years my poor brother had become his own best customer, but that day I was not to know that his own demise, alone in his bed 'over the shop', was only months away. As it turned out, I never saw him again. It is just as well we cannot see into the future.

Until today, Marjorie's dear face had almost completely faded from my consciousness; lately I had found that I had even been confusing hers with Johanna's in my mental cinema until this afternoon when I had opened the door to find Marjorie's reincarnation standing on my threshold. She looks to be in her late thirties or even early forties. It is difficult to tell nowadays, cosmetics being what they are.

This could not be, I thought at first, and dismissed the woman's appearance as a coincidence of nature. With each individual given a finite number of physical characteristics, it is only the excessively vain who could believe that, out of the billions on our planet, a double does not exist.

Yet even as I led her into the sitting room, the newly sharpened image of Marjorie herself rose to haunt me: more specifically, the expression on her face when Father and I entered the kitchen through the back door on the night he found us, Coley and me, locked in naked embrace.

She had gone to bed early but unable to sleep and, barefoot in her night attire, was heating milk in the kitchen when we came in. 'What's going on?' she blurted, looking from one to the other of us as, dumb, too scared even to weep, I shuffled in ahead of him and waited while he closed the door behind us. (I can only imagine how I seemed to her with my hair wild, my skirt creased and my jumper worn back to front in my hurry to replace it.)

'Father?' Marjorie appealed again, but then the milk boiled over, filling the kitchen with hiss and scorch and smell while she wheeled, too late, to pull the pan off the hotplate.

'Go to bed, Marjorie,' Father said gruffly.

'But – but what about this mess? I should clean it up.' She stared at me, questions crowding her eyes, but I was too frightened to signal any answers.

'Go to bed!' Our father used the tone we knew would brook no argument and, after a final, fearful glance at me, my sister put down the milk pan and left the room.

Lamb to the slaughter, head bowed, I awaited my fate. It did not come right away.

'As for you,' Father said, disgust dripping from every vowel, 'get up to your room. I'll deal with you tomorrow.'

Next morning, I was too terrified to leave my room. I had not slept, and when I heard the normal household sounds of early morning, cringed further under the bedclothes. Let them come for me, I thought, with a bravado I did not feel.

It was actually ten o'clock before I heard Nanny's heavy tread on the landing outside my door. She came in without knocking, her ruined face set in lines so lugubrious I immediately started to cry. 'Oh, Nanny!' I jumped out of bed and flew to her, flinging my arms round her thick, soft waist. 'I'm so scared!'

'There, there!' She patted my back. 'They only want to talk to you for the moment.'

'What do you mean, "for the moment"?' Twice as fearful, I pushed back and searched her expression for clues. 'Who's there?'

'Your mother and father, Johanna, Marjorie and your uncle. Not the boys, though—' Her composure cracked. 'What in God's name were you thinking of, girleen?'

251

'What am I going to do?' I wailed.

'Hush,' she said. 'Stop making a show of yourself like this. You're a big girl now. What you're going to do is dry your eyes and brush your hair and put on some nice clothes. You're going to look respectable, that's what you're going to do.'

'I'm in dreadful trouble, Nanny.'

'I won't deny it. Where's your hairbrush?' Averting her gaze, she walked across to my bureau and picked it up. 'Dress yourself now,' she added, over her shoulder, 'as quick as you can, and I'll do your hair for you.'

'What are they going to do with me?' I made no move but stood looking at her broad back. 'Do you know?'

'It's not up to me to say.' Her voice trembled, sending me into further paroxysms.

'But you know, don't you?' I cried. 'Tell me, Nanny! Tell me! I've a right to know. If you don't tell me what's going to happen, I won't go down there. I'll – I'll kill myself!'

This brought her round. 'Don't talk *ráiméis*, Violet!' She was angry now. 'You'll do no such thing. You brought this on yourself with your disgraceful carry-on and you'll face the music, like I've always taught you. This is where you show what you're made of. Now, get dressed this instant or I'll go down there without you and it'll be the worse for you.'

Ten minutes later, neatly and modestly dressed with my hair confined to its braid, I stood outside the closed double doors of the drawing room. Despite my entreaties that she should come with me, Nanny had accompanied me only that far and had then withdrawn, not before giving me a quick hug. 'No, I can't come in, Violet. This is family-only business.' And, with a final squeeze and a muttered 'Good luck!' she opened one of the doors and all but pushed me inside.

'Come in, Violet, come in.' The invitation was issued by Uncle Samuel, seated beside Mother, pinch-faced, on one of the sofas. Father stood with his back to me at the fireplace; Johanna, who with downcast eyes looked as frightened as I felt, sat in a high-backed chair. Only Marjorie's eyes met mine. I could see she was trying to send me encouraging signals. This served only to increase my terror.

It was raining outside and my footsteps on the wooden floor, set against the gurgling of the gutters, sounded feeble. 'Sit down, dear.' Uncle Samuel pointed to the chair nearest Marjorie's. His tone was calm and my heart leaped. Maybe this was not going to be as bad as I had thought.

'Your mam and dad have asked me to do the talking, Violet,' my godfather said then, glancing at Father's rigid back.

'Because we don't trust ourselves,' interjected Mother, so beside herself with fury that she half rose from the sofa and might have lunged at me, if Uncle Samuel had not caught her by the arm.

'Sit yourself down, Fly.' He pulled her back to her seat. 'There's no future in raised voices and everyone getting in a pother. What's done is done and we all have to mind what we do next. All right? Agreed?' He held her arm tightly and looked again towards Father's unflinching back.

'Agreed,' Mother muttered, after a second or two, but not until she had shot at me a look so venomous I thought I might wither. She shook off her brother and crossed her arms in front of her, burying her hands in her armpits as if to make sure they would not assault me of their own volition.

Father still had not moved a muscle.

'Now, Violet,' Uncle Samuel addressed me gravely, 'you must listen very carefully.'

Here it was. In my chest, I felt a swelling as if my heart might rise to choke me. 'I will,' I whispered, because my uncle seemed to want a response.

'We are your family,' he said then, giving the word 'family' special emphasis, 'and we have to decide what's to be done with you. We've had a discussion between ourselves and there's a bit of a difference of opinion. Your mam and dad think you should be sent away from Whitecliff. There are a couple of places in the north that they asked me to investigate—'

'No!' I cried. 'Please. No − I won't go, Uncle. Please don't make me!' All I could think of was separation from Coley.

But Uncle Samuel held up his hand. 'You are not being consulted, dear. It's not your decision. But hear me out before you react. You must know that your mam and dad, all of us, have only your best interests at heart. And I don't agree that sending you away is the best option. I've told them that it is my belief you would run away.' He smiled wanly, then clamped his pipe between his teeth and set to lighting it with a match.

I waited. We all waited. The rain squalled hard against the windows and, in the draught, my uncle's match went out. He struck another.

I felt as if the soles of my feet were balanced on two cut-throat razors. I looked to Johanna and Marjorie for support; both, however, were staring at the floor.

When he was happy that the tobacco was lit and he could draw on it, Uncle Samuel spoke again. 'I've convinced your mam and dad that you wouldn't be safe, Violet, and that to send you away from Whitecliff would only make a bad situation worse. So we have all agreed that if you give your word, your solemn oath, on the Bible, that you will never see this boy again, that you will never leave this house without someone accompanying you . . .'

He stopped, waiting again, I supposed, for my response.

For the first time, I noticed that our family Bible, an ornate, leatherbound volume that had been with us for many generations, had been placed on a nearby console. I don't know what I had actually expected. To be publicly – or even privately – flogged? Imprisoned? Dragged to the police station? Placed in stocks? All they wanted was a promise. Relief, a high, warm wave, almost drowned me and I knew what it was to be given a reprieve on the eve of execution. Of course I would promise. I would swear to anything right now. After a while the pressure would ease, my crime would become a past crime and I would somehow manoeuvre it that I could be trusted again to go out. This promise not to see Coley was a temporary inconvenience. I thanked God. I felt like kissing Uncle Samuel's hands. Coley and I would find a way. God would understand. He was the God of Love and, after all, the two of us were engaged to be married. I would inform my family of this after a respectable period had elapsed and then everything would be all right. Every family liked to marry off their daughters, especially the troublesome ones . . . I was so happy I almost ran to pick up the Bible so I could swear what they wanted me to swear.

'We're waiting. What do you say, Violet?'

In my joy, I had forgotten that some response was required. 'I'm so sorry, Uncle Samuel,' I said, as humbly as I could. 'And yes,' I cast around at the whole group, 'I shall swear on the Holy Bible. But what about school?'

'No more school,' Uncle Samuel replied evenly. 'The Misses Biggs will be informed in due course. But if we do this,' he continued, 'I hope you're mindful, Violet, of the effect your escapades have had on your poor mother, especially at this time when James and Thomas are going off to war—'

'She couldn't care a fig about them. Or about me.' Again, Mother could not contain herself.

'I do care! I care about you all!' I cried passionately, including Father in my declaration. He, however, remained impervious. 'I care! You must know that, Mother – you have to believe me!'

'Then why didn't you think about us last night when you dragged our family through the mud with your sluttishness?'

The rain, as it does in Ireland, had stopped abruptly and in the quickened silence, the hateful words seemed to bounce from wall to wall. 'I'm sorry, Mother,' I whispered. 'I'm sorry,' and could say no more.

In the awful hush, Uncle Samuel got heavily to his feet, fetched the Bible and placed it on a low table in front of me. Obediently, I placed both hands on the worn leather cover and waited for instructions.

It was then that my father turned round and looked at me with eyes so full of condemnation, disappointment and even hatred that my skin crawled. Johanna must have noticed too, because she sobbed aloud and then so did I, so bitterly that I barely managed to repeat the promises intoned by my uncle.

Why am I upsetting myself like this, after all these years? Probably because of the appearance of this niece.

Save for me, all the players in the Whitecliff theatre are dead – or, in the case of Coley Quinn, presumed dead. I was devastated to hear the news of my godfather's death in a hunting accident: I loved him dearly, and deep in my heart, despite knowing that he, too, had been told I had been sent abroad, I had always felt that somehow he would find me and talk Mother and Father into releasing me. I had no such hopes of my poor brother: although he did his best to cheer me up during his infrequent visits, it was obvious alcohol was taking its toll until no shadow remained of the gay young blade he had been at that party. As Young Samuel got older and sicker, he became more, not less nervous in the presence of Mother and Father.

As for Marjorie and Johanna, neither would have had any influence over my parents; even Marjorie who, married and with her city ways, should not have been in awe of them, would not have dared bring our family name into disrepute by going to the police or some outside agency. In this era of 'openness and transparency' in Ireland I know this must be difficult to accept. The only explanation I can offer is that that was the way we were brought up, and as long as our parents were alive, none of us would have crossed them or damaged their reputation in any way. It was something we all accepted – which was why my flagrancy would have been so shocking to them.

In the backwaters of my life I have found peace and, during whatever years are left to me, I want only to be quiet, but here comes this niece, whose existence I had virtually forgotten but who will now wish me to rehearse all of this – and who, in addition, wishes to acquire Whitecliff! How strange life is!

The house itself is apparently nothing now but a mere shell. I shall never set foot in it again and care not a whit what happens to it. Johanna and I had discussed what we should do with the place and our only interest was that it should furnish us with enough money to 'see us out', to borrow Uncle Samuel's phrase. Neither of us could have borne the thought of becoming a burden on the Irish state.

I should go back into the sitting room. I have been unconscionably discourteous. After all, the woman, my niece, is as taken aback as I – oh, how I wish my darling Johanna was here to assist me.

I miss her dreadfully, even more than I did after her departure from Whitecliff, which was a severe blow. She knew it would be and almost gave up her chance of happiness for my sake. 'What will you do, Violet?' she wept, on the day after she had received her proposal of marriage. 'How will you manage without me?'

I could not bear her distress. I reached through my hatch and, although my own heart was breaking at the prospect of being without her, I tried to comfort her as best I could by stroking her bent head. 'Hush, Jumie, hush!' I begged. 'This is a wonderful day for you and I'm so pleased and happy on your behalf. Please don't cry.'

By all accounts Anthony Collopy, a cabinet-maker she had met when he and his employer came to Whitecliff to replace a set of kitchen cupboards, was a kind and loving man. Having been her confidante during his tender, but somewhat diffident courtship, I had dreaded this day, but was mentally and emotionally prepared for it. I knew that if she accepted him, they would move far away after their marriage, since Anthony had inherited his uncle's house, this house, and had refurbished it with a view to living there and setting up his own carpentry business in the district. 'I love him dearly,' Johanna cried, 'but I love you too and cannot bear to abandon you.'

'For goodness' sake, Johanna,' I said, as jovially as I could, 'you're not abandoning me. I have made peace with my situation. Mother and Father will not let me starve, will they? I will not hear any more of this. And you will write to me care of them. We can become great letter-writers. I look forward to that. And there are trains, these days, are there not? You will come to see us here at Whitecliff from time to time, I am sure. Go and be happy, Johanna, be happy for both of us.' I withdrew my hand then and, under the pretence that I needed to visit the bathroom, vanished from her view so I could get my emotions under control.

They are not under control at present: this new development has brought everything back as freshly as if it had happened yesterday, although at my age, one comes to terms with loss. Agitation, not death, is now the enemy. It will be my turn next to die, and although I do not welcome the prospect, I do not fear it.

There goes the doorbell again. It is probably my niece's husband, whose Christian name I have already forgotten. I cannot hide in here any longer.

# 27

# MOONWALKING

We're all to meet again tomorrow. She told us she was tired and virtually asked us to leave. Not rudely, of course. Although it was clear how shattered she was, her manners remained exquisite.

Actually, to be accurate it'll be today, won't it? It's now nearly two o'clock in the morning and Bob, having anaesthetised himself with Guinness, is out for the count. Lucky Bob. I'm so far from sleep I'm considering taking Jeffrey for a moonlight walk. We're in a B-and-B in some village whose name I can't pronounce, about ten miles from my aunt's house. It was the nearest pet-friendly establishment we could find.

Speaking of pets, somewhere out there a dog is barking. It sounds miles away and there's even a little echo. I thought the countryside where we live in North County Dublin was quiet but – barking excepted – the singing silence around this house makes our place sound like Dublin airport.

My aunt invited us to stay, 'We have four bedrooms upstairs, you are welcome to one,' but I could see the invitation was for form's sake and, anyway, I was as dubious about staying under her roof as she was about having me. She and I were both seriously in shock. After she had left me in that sitting room, I sat there with the words 'My God! My God! My God!' trundling continuously around a circuit in my brain, robotic toy trains overcoming all thought. I wasn't elated – not yet anyhow – I wasn't anything. I was devoid of feeling.

I can't get used to thinking of a stranger as my aunt. Although I'm hardly an expert, never having had one, she doesn't feel like an aunt. Maybe she will in time.

Right up to when Bob and I left, my new aunt and I continued to be very careful with each other. Although we spoke for nearly an hour, it was a conversation of the stop-and-start type; it certainly couldn't be characterised as a happy gush of reminiscence. I think we were both too dazed for that. When you read about these reunions – 'SEPARATED AT BIRTH: After sixty-nine years, twins Molly and Josh meet for the First Time!' – the headlines are always accompanied by photos of the joyfully tearful protagonists, who hug each other and swear never to be parted again . . . Well, I sure didn't feel joyfully tearful. In fact, even as the revelation was beginning to sink in, I wasn't sure how I felt. 'Stupefied' about sums it up. And I'm willing to bet that while I was sitting, statue-like, on her sofa, she, in her kitchen on the pretext of making more tea, was feeling the same.

She's not Collopy, of course. She's Shine. If I'd had the wit to ask, I might have made the family connection, especially when you add the fireplace picture – because, of course, I knew that my mother's maiden name was Shine, and although it's not unusual, it's uncommon in North County Dublin. But it wouldn't have occurred to me to question the name Collopy. Why would it?

It was Bob who asked her directly why she was known

by that name around this area in West Cork. 'My sister's married name was Collopy and when I arrived here to live, her husband, Anthony, being protective of my privacy, told anyone who asked that I was his sister. Now, of course, it matters little what anyone thinks and when I registered for a state pension in my real name no one passed any remarks. Yet the name has stuck. Everyone round here still calls me Collopy'. She picked up her teapot. 'Would you like some more tea?'

'No, thank you, ma'am. You must find it lonely here sometimes.' Bob was drawing her out. (Funny how I'm not thinking of him as The Rat at the moment. That'll probably come back tomorrow when I'm in the whole of my senses again. Obviously I can focus on only one trauma at a time.)

There's that bloody dog barking again and it's setting off all the others. Thank goodness Jeffrey isn't the kind of mutt that responds. Normally I wouldn't hear a thing: I'm not afflicted with insomnia. Except tonight. Maybe I should throw in the towel and go outside. You could read by that moon, it's so bright – 'Slowly, silently, now the moon, Walks the night in her silver shoon . . .' That's one of the few lines of poetry I can remember from my schooldays.

When my aunt's doorbell rang again yesterday I made no move to answer it. Yet on one level, while I was certainly in no rush to readmit Bob, on another I couldn't wait to share the news. There was a hiatus before they came in and I could hear her murmuring: she was telling him.

Sure enough, when he entered the room, he came towards me. 'Are you all right, Claudine?'

'Mmm,' is what I think I said, and for the next while didn't seem capable of stringing two coherent words together, never mind of making a contribution to the conversation that ensued between my husband and my aunt.

I must keep saying that. My aunt. It does roll well off the tongue. And so many people take it for granted, don't they? By way of chit-chat, I told her she probably wouldn't recognise Rathlinney: 'It's nearly a town now.'

'And the stores?'

'Oh, yes, that was your family business, wasn't it? Well, it's a large, bustling supermarket.'

'I see,' she said, but I got the impression that she was merely being polite and couldn't care less about Rathlinney or anything in it. I was stuck. I couldn't think of anything more to contribute from my side. I couldn't even think of any sensible questions because I didn't know what I wanted to know. Does that make sense? My mind felt like it had been whited-out.

Bob quizzed her gently about Whitecliff and the estate, and how it had come to such a sorry pass.

'I'm afraid I cannot help you,' she said to him. 'I haven't been there for a long time. I suppose it just happens with empty, neglected houses.' Then she stood up and, addressing me, 'Perhaps you would like to see some photographs.'

'That would be great!' I glanced at Bob and found him smiling at me as if I deserved a gold star for effort.

'Claudine—' he tried, after she left the room, but I snapped back at him.

'Please, Bob! Just shut up, will you?'

'We have to talk.'

'Now?' I looked disbelievingly at him.

'I suppose not.' And we sat in crackling silence while I tried to compose myself for my aunt's return.

When she did come back it was with a shoebox. She heeled the contents on to the coffee-table between the two sofas. I knew I was expected to ooh and aah over them but, all over the shop as I was, the little pyramid of sepia – you know the kind, small Box Brownie squares, curled edges – was somehow dangerous. Too much too soon, a sudden vista of unexpected relatives that was too foreign to take in at one sitting. Nevertheless, there were a few licks and nibbles of excitement in the pit of my stomach as I picked one off the top.

Two youngish men and a woman in summer outfits, maybe from the thirties or early forties; they were sitting in deckchairs on a lawn with a tall herbaceous border filling the background. One of the men was smoking a pipe, the other was leaning towards the woman with an arm round her shoulders, but the posture seemed uncomfortable. Individual features on the faces were hard to make out but all three were squinting into the sun. I turned it over to read the faded pencil lettering on the back: 'Mother and Father with Uncle Samuel, Dundonald 1939'.

'Who are these?' Although it wasn't hard to figure out, I wanted her to tell me. I held it out to her.

'They are ...' she hesitated '... your grandfather and grandmother and your grandmother's brother, Samuel. Mother was from the North of Ireland.'

She selected other images of my grandfather and grandmother, my twin uncles and another uncle (three little brown figures clutching the collars of their overcoats to their chins on a windswept strand), then one of these small boys alone, in knickerbockers, standing beside a cow. 'And this is Matthew. He died when he was only six.'

It turns out I'd had six uncles and aunts, including a pair

of twins, although three of the uncles had died before I was born. All these things I didn't know – and Daddy hadn't told me, dammit . . .

I picked up a snap of my mother and her two sisters. The three were standing in front of the entrance to what was unmistakably Whitecliff in its heyday. 'That was the last photo ever taken of me,' said this aunt, her tone matter-of-fact. 'We were having a big party that evening. Johanna and I had slaved over the preparations and the cleaning and had changed into our party frocks. Marjorie had just arrived from Dublin with a friend. She had a new camera and the friend took that photo with it. That's Marjorie in the middle. I'm the one on the left.'

I remember what's in my wallet. 'As a matter of fact, I think I have one from that night. Maybe you could tell me if it is, Violet.' I winkle out the fireplace photo.

'Yes,' she says softly, holding it. 'That's Marjorie, all right – and that's Young Samuel with a couple of his friends in the background.'

'I've had that photo for years and years but it wasn't until I went into Whitecliff and saw your mantelpiece—' I'm dismayed. 'Oh, Violet, we've wasted so much time.'

'Time is never wasted, dear. We always fill it as we will.'

The most intimate thing Daddy ever said about my mother, one of the few mental pictures I have held of her, is the image he projected of the day he fell in love with her when she came on to the forecourt of his garage to ask about the purchase of a small cheap car for herself. 'She knew about our place because the father of one of her pals dealt with us at the time. She was so beautiful, chicken. She was wearing one of those knitted-beret things. It was down over one eye,

265

and her hair, just like yours, was shiny and soft and wavy. And legs that went all the way to the North Pole. I would have given her a Roller for sixpence!' Instead, on the spot, he offered her a job. 'I asked her straight out if she would consider working for me and said I needed a secretary-receptionist – I didn't know whether the girl could even type. I didn't care. Lucky she turned out to have done a secretarial course, eh?'

I brought Violet's snap of the three sisters closer to my face to study it. The girl in the middle of this photograph had dark, bobbed hair. She was wearing a full-length, figure-hugging sleeveless dress in white or a pale colour, and her arms were round her sisters' shoulders; she was laughing and, of the three, looked by far the most carefree. The girl on the left, whom I now knew to be my aunt Violet, was clearly the youngest. Also in white or cream, with a cloud of dark hair round her face and half-way down her back, she was looking off-camera, almost pulling away, as if distracted and tense. The girl on the right, Johanna, whose hair was straight, even lank, looked serious, even dowdy, by comparison with the other two.

Something my aunt had just said struck me belatedly. 'How could that snap be the last one ever taken of you? You were only a young girl then.'

'I was sixteen.'

'I can see that. And you were very beautiful.'

'Thank you.' Then, uncannily re-creating the pose in the photograph, she looked off into the distance as if seeing something over my shoulder. 'When you are sixteen, no matter who tells you that, you do not believe it.'

'Well, you were,' I said firmly. 'You still are.'

She smiled at me then, a smile that reached all the way

into her eyes and changed my mind about what was the most striking thing about her. That smile lifted not only her face but also her whole body so it was possible to see that she was, indeed, the gorgeous young girl of the snap. 'You flatter me,' she said. 'At my age, looks matter not at all.'

'But – forgive me if I'm pestering you – you haven't answered my question. How come there were no other pictures of you?'

The smile vanished, and for the first time since Bob and I had crashed into her life, the woman visibly lost her composure. That was when she said she was tired and suggested we continue the conversation some time tomorrow 'at a time that is convenient for you both'.

## 28

# AND THEN SHE
# STARTED TO TELL US

I've told you that for quite a while, unknown to me, this aunt of mine was living five miles, maybe less as the crow flies, from my house. On our second visit to her, what she tells us about the circumstances of that existence is so incredible that I'm afraid at first I think she must be fantasising.

And yet, by the end of her story, she had brought us so thoroughly into her world, with so much detail yet so little bitterness that neither Bob nor I had the slightest doubt but that she was telling us the truth.

And as soon as her Coley Quinn came into the picture, I had realised there was a good chance that my 'Pat', who had told me his real name was Colman, was him; I was peppering to tell her, but the recounting was clearly taking a lot out of her, and rather than pile on yet another shock, even what I hoped would be a pleasant one, I managed to hold my tongue. Although I doubted it, there might have been two Colmans of that age in Rathlinney – but what were the odds that any other Colman would set up camp in the grounds of Whitecliff? Mind you, nothing would surprise me after the experiences of the last couple of days and I needed to make sure I had the right one before I got her hopes up.

I'm not sure she had intended to go as far as she did because she started that second day – after the obligatory tea – not by telling us about her love affair, but by filling me in on my mother, painting such a lovely portrait of her that it took all my self-control not to cry. By Violet's account, Marjorie Shine had been a lively, lovely person, independent, intelligent, musical – and very kind.

The cracks showed in Violet's own demeanour when I, in all innocence, babbled at her about my parents' wedding: 'I know it was very small and in Paris and you weren't there, Violet, but I'm sure you have the photos from it, like I have? They're black and white, though, and I think you'll agree it's impossible to tell whether her dress was ivory or pure white and Daddy was hopeless about things like that so it would be nice—'

Alarmed, I stopped in mid-sentence. There was something wrong with her. Her breath was coming in gasps. Was she taking what is euphemistically termed 'a turn'?

'What's the matter, Violet?' We were back on our original perches in her sitting room and Bob, who had established the first-name relationship from the moment we stepped again across her threshold, was up and across the floor to her in an instant.

'Nothing, nothing.' She waved him away. 'I'm sorry. Please—'

But it was obvious that she was far from all right. 'Should I fetch you a drink of water, Aunt Violet? Would you like to rest a little?' I, too, went over and sat beside her.

'I promised myself I wouldn't get upset,' she whispered.

'Look,' Bob said, taking charge, 'Claudine's right. Why don't you rest for an hour or so? This must be quite an ordeal for you and I'm afraid we're crowding you. We can come back later. Or even tomorrow.' He glanced at me for confirmation.

'Of course we can.' I nodded vigorously. It occurred to me, briefly, that Tommy O'Hare, who had been leaving increasingly impatient messages on my mobile, might have an opinion on this but I brushed it aside and, with Bob, gazed encouragingly at her. I even stood up.

But I was in for – yet another – surprise. 'No,' she said strongly, looking up at me. 'I have something to tell you. A secret that has been in our family for many years. I warn you, it is not a pretty story but I have wrestled with my conscience and my courage and, on balance, I think you deserve to know.' If she had been having a turn, it was well over, for she was now sitting up straight, her mouth in a determined line. 'I didn't mean to distress you,' she said calmly. 'Please. Both of you. Sit down.' And then she started to tell us.

# 29

# SECRETS

After the party the house gradually emptied. Of the group that had remained, Marjorie was the first to leave, in the early afternoon following the morning of my Bible oath. That was a difficult goodbye and at first I did not want to see her because she had been witness not only to my ritual humiliation but also to the reason for it – or, at least, its immediate aftermath. I was huddling under the bedclothes in my room when she knocked quietly and came in. 'Are you all right, Violet?' she asked, as she sat beside me. 'I missed you at luncheon.'

'I'm fine. Go away.' I did not want her to see my swollen, puffy face. I was also resentful that neither she nor Johanna had spoken a word on my behalf.

'Come on, little one.' She pulled hard at the counterpane, uncovering my head.

'Go away!' I attempted to draw it back over myself but she was too quick for me. 'You're just as horrible as they are,' I cried. 'None of you understands.'

'I know it was awful down there in that drawing room, Violet.' She remained calm. 'You must remember that Mother and Father are of a different generation. Naturally they're shocked at what you've done.'

'Are you?' I lifted my head from the pillow and challenged her directly.

'I'm upset.' Her gaze was steady. 'I'm sure you don't want me to lie. I'm upset for you and for them. For all of us. But they'll thaw out. All you have to do is to lie low for a couple of months. You'll see.'

To me, of course, 'a couple of months' was an eternity. 'It's all right for you, you're in Dublin. You don't know what it's like here. It's awful with just Johanna and me and them. It's like being in gaol.'

'I can imagine,' she said, 'but it's temporary. Don't forget, they're on edge. Your timing is terrible, Violet, because it's not easy to send your sons to this terrible war and you must make allowances for them. Try to put yourself in their shoes, what it must be like to be a mother and a father in these circumstances.'

Her evenness was having more of an effect than if she had harangued me and, despite myself, I could see glimmerings of my parents' point of view. That, though, could not be entertained. I covered my face with my hands. 'I can't not see him. I can't, Marjorie! Anyway, they've no right.'

'They may not be the most demonstrative people in the world, but if you could see that they care about you . . .'

I uncovered my face and glared defiantly at her. 'Well, they don't know the whole truth. He's my fiancé. We're engaged to be married.'

'Violet!' She was appalled. 'You're *sixteen.*'

'That's a legal age for marriage,' I was sullen now, 'and there is nothing anyone can do about it.'

'Oh, darling.' It seemed as though she might hug me, then thought better of it, probably because she was worried that to do so might encourage me. 'They do have a right. It might be legal, but until you're twenty-one you have to have their consent and they have every right to prevent you doing what they believe would not be in your best interests.' She hesitated. 'You must not provoke them, dearest. Will you promise? And don't worry, I don't have a Bible in my pocket!'

I scorned her attempt at humour. It was not worthy of reply. I flung myself back on my pillows and closed my eyes.

'After the boys leave tomorrow,' she remained relentlessly pleasant and reasonable, 'I'm sure things will improve. And, by the way, don't forget that Father's your best bet, all right? Appearances to the contrary, he's the softer of the two. And he's so fond of you—'

'Huh!' I treated this with derision. 'He has a funny way of showing it.'

'Think, Violet Shine! Use that smart head of yours. Think of what you did. What he saw. How it looked to him. How disappointed he must be in his baby daughter.'

'I know that. Do you think I don't? But, Marjorie, how would you feel if you weren't allowed outside the door of this place? And you've never been in love like I am—'

'You're just starting out in life.' She refused to argue. 'What's a few weeks or months here or there?'

'Months? I'll die!'

'You won't die. And there'll be other boys,' she added, 'plenty of them,' cementing my suspicion that she, too, thought of me as a baby. She had not the least idea what had happened to me. None of them had. How could there ever be another boy in my life?

Then I had a brilliant idea. 'Can I come and visit you in Dublin?' I sat up in bed: I could get a message to Coley somehow – they couldn't watch me twenty-four hours a day. They'd have to sleep some time. I knew Coley would be checking for messages under the tree. Distraught as he must be, our love was so strong he would find a way. I trusted him absolutely.

I seized my sister's hand. 'They'd let me come to see you, surely – you could tell them you'd keep an eye on me.'

'As if I hadn't enough to do.' She rolled her eyes. 'Listen, Violet, can you keep a secret?'

'Of course I can.'

'I'm starting a job as a secretary and receptionist next Monday.'

'That's wonderful, Marjorie! But why is it a secret?'

'I haven't told them here yet,' she warned. 'The truth is I'm half afraid to – I think they'd want something fancier for me than what I've been offered. It's in a car showroom. So don't you say anything yet, all right? I'll have to pick my time.'

'I promise!' I was thrilled for her. A secretary in a car show-room! It sounded glamorous to me.

'So, let things settle for a couple of weeks,' she continued, 'and then we'll see about you coming up for maybe a weekend. In the meantime, you be good now. All right?'

'Oh, Marjorie!' I threw my arms round her and hugged her tightly. For someone born into an undemonstrative family, I had become quite the opposite in recent days.

She did not pull away as I'd half expected, but put her arms round me. 'I've met someone too,' she breathed, after a second or two, 'but that's another secret between you and me. All right?'

I pulled back and looked at her glowing face. 'How marvellous. I'm so happy for you. Just think, we're both in love! Who is he? Now we only have to find someone for Johanna and everything will be perfect!'

'Don't forget what I've been saying for the last ten minutes!' She laughed, but then her expression darkened. She caught my arm and gave it a little shake. 'This isn't about me. Violet, listen to me. I'm serious about not provoking them. You've a lot to thank Uncle Samuel for. I know. I was there while they were all talking about you. Apparently, as well as last night's andramartins, you went to see this boy at the creamery, brazenly, in front of the whole world.'

I was aghast. Especially when I had thought I had got away with that. Marjorie was watching me closely. 'Are you listening to me, Violet? Will you promise to stay away from this boy?'

'Why didn't you bring your boyfriend to the party?'

'Because I don't know how Mother and Father will react . . .' she looked off into the distance, then, reflectively, '. . . more than ever now. Anyhow, we've known each other only for a short while and it would have been a bit early to introduce him as a boyfriend but, oh, Violet, I do think this is it!'

'Why won't they like him? Who is he?'

'I can't tell you, not yet.' Then she recollected her purpose. 'Violet! Stop changing the subject. Concentrate! Promise me you won't do anything foolish with this boy. Mother and Father are at the end of their tether right now and God knows how they'd react if you defy them.'

I agreed. 'All right, I promise, I promise,' but with my fingers crossed. I did not want to upset her but I had every intention of moving whatever mountains my parents built between Coley Quinn and me. 'Come on, Marjorie. Tell me all about him and I'll tell you about Coley . . .'

No matter how I worked on her, however, she would neither divulge the name of her beau – who, of course, turned out to be Chris Magennis – nor listen to anything I might say about Coley. But at least she left me with a chink of hope: I couldn't wait for my trip to Dublin.

Nanny was gone by teatime on the same day – not before creeping into my room with further admonishments – and Uncle Samuel left early the following morning. For the second night in succession, I had hardly slept and, just after sunrise, heard his car start and crunch off down the driveway. He did not come to say goodbye. I was sad about that, but guiltily relieved that I would not have to face a further barrage of exhortations to behave myself: physically and emotionally exhausted, I was wrung dry. I was also hungry and thirsty since, for the first full day and night of my disgrace, I had kept to my room.

Uncle Samuel's departure left only the twins as visitors to Whitecliff. I knew they were due to leave mid-morning: Father was to drive them to Drogheda to catch the Belfast train. I was so hungry that at about eight when I smelt and heard the sizzle of bacon in the kitchen, I decided to brave the breakfast table, hoping that one or other of them would be up to deflect attention from me.

When I entered the dining room Mother, who had been drinking tea, immediately put down her cup and left the room, passing me with averted eyes. I glanced at Johanna, imploring her for support, but it was obvious from her demeanour that she could be of no help.

'Good morning, Father,' I said quietly, taking my usual place beside my sister, but the twins came in then, saving him the chore of choosing how or whether to answer me.

James and Thomas, both in uniform, were oiled, buffed and pressed to perfection – except for a shaving cut high on James's cheekbone. He stopped in the doorway, gazing after Mother. 'What's wrong with her?'

'Nothing.' Father got up from the table, went to the sideboard with his plate and helped himself to eggs, bacon and puddings from the chafing dish. 'Come along and eat this while it's hot.'

I decided to include myself in the invitation and queued up behind my brothers. 'It'll be a long time before you see this kind of food again,' Father joked, bending towards the boys to cut me out. 'Not to mention ourselves! Because of that party, we owe favours to everyone in the district. It's bread and water for us for the next two months, always provided we can get the flour.' Only Thomas reacted to the witticism and the silence that followed was unnerving.

Before returning to his place, Father turned on the wireless to hear the morning news.

'What's happened in this house?' Thomas whispered to me, under cover of the announcer's recitation of the latest circumstances of war. 'Everyone was so gay the night of the party and now they're in a dreadful mood. Tiptoeing around. Is it because of us leaving?'

'You haven't heard?' I whispered back and, while James piled enough rashers of bacon on his plate to feed three men, 'are you sure no one has been talking to you about me?' I could not believe that, unlike everyone else in the house, these two had not been recruited to my firing squad.

Thomas shook his head.

'It has not to do with you two,' I murmured, then remembered what they faced, 'at least, not totally. I am a black sheep at the moment and have been sent to Coventry by everyone.' I hoped I had hit the right note. Confidential but insouciant.

'What did you do?'

Involuntarily, I turned to check if Father was watching us. He was.

'I'll tell you later. Or ask Johanna.' Then, loudly, 'If you don't mind, Father, I shall take breakfast in my room.'

As if I had not spoken, he continued to shake salt over his scrambled egg. In a way this was good because it enabled me to feel legitimately aggrieved as I piled my plate and left with my head held high.

The twins came together to say goodbye to me. 'Well, well, well!' James was grinning as they came in. 'Johanna's told us. Our little sis. Who'd have thought?'

'But she has to buckle down, James.' Thomas, ever the worrier, pushed him out of the way, moved my unwashed breakfast plate and sat on the bed where I was again ensconced. 'We're not going to judge you, Violet.'

'Thank you for that. And I don't want to talk about it.'

'We have to talk about it.' He looked pained.

'No, we don't!' I'd had enough concern to last me for the rest of my life. I pushed him off the bed and tumbled on to the floor. 'If you came here to talk only about my crimes—'

'No, we didn't!' James interjected. 'Leave her alone, Tom. She has enough people on her back. And you can calm down, Violet. We're off in a few minutes. We came to say goodbye. We don't want to leave in a pet.'

'Thank you.' I sulked. 'Goodbye.'

'No good-luck kiss?' he teased.

'Good luck,' I pecked his cheek, then repeated the gesture with Thomas.

The door of my room was still ajar and, in the gap, Johanna appeared. 'They're ready. Father has the car at the front of the house.' I saw the tears in her eyes and, too late, realised what was happening. 'James! Thomas!' I grasped both.

'Nobody's to worry about us,' James said, disentangling himself. 'It's going to be tough, we know that, but it's a great adventure too. And think of the stories we'll have to tell when we come home. Bye-bye now,' and, on the pretext of hugging me, he whispered into my ear, 'And you love who you like. Just be clever about it.'

'Thank you, James, I will,' I whispered back and, buoyed up again, was even able to wave as they left the room with my sister.

I let a few days pass – in my memory they have melded together in a haze of silent recrimination from others and white-hot frustration within myself. Generally I kept to my room – which was unfair to Johanna, who had to bear the brunt of the housework with Mother – except at mealtimes, which were excruciating. Not that either of my parents was explicitly rude or angry. It was worse than that: both were frigidly polite to me when I asked for the salt or a spoonful of potatoes, but otherwise my chair might have been empty for all the attention they paid me.

I did try to do as Marjorie had asked. I tried to make allowances for them, but it was hard. I was becoming more and more restless and now, increasingly, from the height of my sixteen years, resentful as well. Nobody had died, after all. We were all born naked, were we not, so what, I asked myself, indignation growing, was intrinsically criminal about being unclothed in later life? For that matter, what was wrong with making love? Would God have made the sexes attractive to each other if they had not been meant to act on it?

Only James, I thought, had shown with his parting words that, of them all, he was the only one who had any idea about the real — i.e. modern — world, as opposed to the world of the Whitecliff Museum.

The only distraction during those days was the arrival of our party-line telephone, and we were now the proud proprietors of Rathlinney 9. By pulling strings, Father had leaped over the five-year installation queue. Naturally he did not communicate this feat to me and I relied greatly on Johanna to report or interpret what was going on under our roof, where the silence was, if possible, even more intense than ever and not relieved by Rathlinney 9 — it uttered not a peep for the entire period, not even from the stores. Father had decreed that the line should not be tied up but was to be left free for a call from the twins. 'Suppose they're trying to get through, Fly, and you're babbling away to Marjorie in Dublin?'

'Surely they'd ring back,' Mother had suggested, not unreasonably.

'Suppose they can't?'

There was no answer to that. This conversation occurred in my hearing at the breakfast table.

To add to my misery, my purdah coincided with a period when, outside, the sun shone brightly from dawn until spectacular sunset.

On the Monday night of the second week after the twins left, I could no longer stand the confinement and sense of being under permanent threat of further punishment. I had been good. I had been quiet and obedient. I had stitched the Shine Quilt without a murmur of protest even though, as far as Mother was concerned, my labour was welcome but I was not. I had even helped Johanna scrub the hall flagstones again because the party had not been kind to them. Yet it all served to thaw not a splinter of the ice in which I had been encased.

I decided to make my move.

I waited until everyone had retired for the night and then, with only the sound of mice skittering behind the skirting-boards to alarm me, crept out of my room and down the stair-case, once again thanking God it was made of stone. I managed to get outside without incident and, checking once again to make sure my note to Coley was in my pocket, set off across the headlands towards our tree. After the confinement indoors, the keen sea air against my cheeks was exhilarating.

When I reached the corner of the sea field, I was momen-tarily disoriented. Our tree was not there.

Thinking I'd made a mistake and was in the wrong place, I stood for a moment to take bearings – but there was no mistake. This was the corner: the tree should have been where it always was. I walked right up to where it should be to find only a large hole in the ground. The tree, roots and all, had been neatly and thoroughly removed.

Not only that: I could see no debris, no sawdust, no leaves, no severed roots. I crouched and felt through the rough grass with my fingers. Not even a twig.

Stunned, I sat on the ground. There was only one person who could have done this: Roderick Shine had had the means and motive. It was also his tree on his land. He could do what he liked with it. His intention was to wipe Coley Quinn off the face of this earth.

Fury, a purple, sulphurous rage, boiled under my breastbone, and before I had considered what I was doing, I was racing helter-skelter, with no thought as to concealment, across the fields away from the sea and towards the main road. Father could not get away with this. I would not let him. I took the straightest route, heedless of the occasional bramble, thistle or even nettle that bit at my bare legs. By the time I had climbed over the stone boundary wall and dropped on to the public road, these stings and scrapes were a consideration. I paused briefly to search for dock leaves but could not find any.

Around me the countryside was calm and luminously grey under the moon, riding high between cloudbanks, but although the headlong run had calmed me physically, I had neither time nor inclination to admire it. If anything, I was more determined than ever to find Coley Quinn so that we could be together and, more importantly, discuss how to stay together.

From where I had come across the wall it was just over a mile to Rathlinney and I set off with no concrete plan except to find Coley's house. I knew vaguely where it was – he had described a row of cottages on the far side of the village: 'You couldn't miss us. We're the one with the cabbages and carrots in the front garden.' When I got to it, if nothing more subtle presented itself, I would simply knock on the front door and take it from there.

Having found it relatively easily – and having encountered no one of any consequence on the way – that was what I did. I rapped on the bottom half-door – the top was open to the evening. From where I stood, I could see inside only as far as the wall of a tiny whitewashed lobby, festooned with hanging pots of geraniums and nasturtiums round a centre-piece picture of what I knew to be the Sacred Heart of Jesus Christ.

It was Florrie who answered my knock, coming into the lobby from behind the Heart. 'Miss Shine!' Her hands flew to her head, festooned with curling rags. 'Look at the state of me. I was just for bed—' Then she clapped a hand across her mouth, removed it and, in a deep whisper, said, 'You're taking an awful risk, Miss Shine. You'd better go before me da sees you. He's fit to be tied.'

'Is Coley in? I'd like a word with him if he's around.' I was having difficulty maintaining my confidence, which was ebbing by the second. In fact, I was realising that what I had done was not only rash, it was madness.

'He's beyond in Birmingham,' she hissed. She looked furtively over her shoulder, then back at me. 'Did you not know?'

'No.' I was fighting nausea. 'What's he doing there?'

Again, she looked over her shoulder and unlatched the door to come outside. 'Did your da not tell you? He came to see my da and said if Coley was to stay in Rathlinney we could whistle for our conacre and we could also take our grocery business elsewhere. I'm sorry, Miss Shine, but what could we do? We're poor people.'

'Who's at the door, Flor?' A middle-aged woman came into the lobby and peered at me. Although it was night she was still wearing her criss-cross flowered pinafore. 'Oh, God!' She, too, took fright as her husband, Coley's father, came out to see what was going on.

'Thank you.' Face burning, I backed away. 'Thank you, Florrie, Mrs Quinn. I'm sorry I bothered you. Good night.'

Feeling three sets of eyes boring like hot lamps into my back, I fled back through the village.

My first instinct was to seek refuge with Nanny but then I realised I didn't know where she lived. I could hardly go knocking on doors at dead of night asking people did anyone know where my nanny lived – I knew how that would play locally – so I fled to what I knew, the stores. I let myself through a wicket used by the deliverymen and stood in the semi-darkness by the wall of the building to consider what to do next.

I had left Whitecliff with nothing except the note for Coley. I was not even wearing a coat over my dress and the temperature was falling. I had to go home.

I got back in without incident and, safely in bed, cried myself into an exhausted sleep and knew nothing until it was well into next morning and I could hear the telephone ringing downstairs. It was probably the shrillness that had woken me, or I might have slept all day.

I found that day very difficult but, after the disaster of the previous night, was grateful that no one was seeking my company and that, therefore, I had time to lick my wounds. Even Johanna, who was at sixes and sevens – not wanting to cross Mother and Father while at the same time wanting to show me that she was sympathetic to my plight – seemed to avoid me. I kept to my room and again retired early.

I knew no more until I woke to the sound of urgent knocking on my door. 'Mother and Father want to know if you're coming down to breakfast.' It was Johanna's voice.

'They do?' I could not understand. It was early morning again and, groggily, I called to her: 'Are you sure, Johanna?

'They sent me up to get you. Your place is laid.'

Under my punishment regime, nobody had seemed to care whether or not I ate. Perhaps it was to be eased.

# 30

## TENSILE STRENGTH

Half-way through breakfast Mother, who, flouting her own standards of table etiquette, had been leafing through a women's magazine, spoke civilly to me, although she did not look up from turning her pages. 'Eat your toast, Violet. Flour is precious.'

I glanced at Johanna, who shrugged.

I was definitely not imagining it. The atmosphere at the table seemed to have changed for the better and, furious with Father though I was, I decided to be clever, as advised by both James and Marjorie. I had not yet figured out a way to air my grievance or to get back at him but, right now, I'd risk an apology to see what would happen. 'I'm so sorry, Mother, Father,' I said cautiously, watching them both. 'I'm sorry I have created such unpleasantness.'

Mother continued to sip tea and flip through her magazine for a second or two, then looked meaningfully at Father who, instead of acknowledging my contrition, said something unexpected: 'We'd like you to help us with a project, Violet.'

'Oh?' I was taken aback. 'What kind of project?'

He put down his knife and fork and steepled his fingers.

I listened in astonishment as he outlined the plan. 'We are planning to refurbish this old place. It has not been touched for years. I think we all enjoyed having guests in the house but it became clear that when the family is all here, and we need to accommodate servants as well, we don't have enough bedrooms. The attics offer us an opportunity to remedy that and we thought we would start there. I, of course, shall oversee any reconstruction or repairs necessary. I shall send a message to Jack Montgomery as soon as I get into the shop. Business is slow enough for him right now so I'm sure he could help us out.'

This added to the novelty. Montgomery and Sons were local builders. In the past, they had done some repair work on our roof but Father had complained that they were robbers.

'What we'd like you to do, Violet,' he continued, 'is to help your mother pick out some colours for the walls, the type of fabrics and rugs and knick-knacks and so forth.'

'I'd be glad to, Father.' Flummoxed, I looked again towards Johanna, whose expression indicated that this was the first she, too, had heard of it.

'May I help, too, Father?' she asked. 'I'd like that.'

'Of course you may. Your mother will this morning order fabric swatches and colour cards from Arnott's. Now, if that's settled, I must get to work.' He got up from the table and left the room.

I shall not bore you with the detail of the next weeks. In the early days of the project, I decided that there was nothing for it but to hide my sorrow and anger, and in seeming to throw myself into the project, to lead everyone, even Johanna, to believe that I was recovering from the madness concerning Coley Quinn.

287

Meanwhile I was hatching a plan, one I was sure would work. I no longer trusted anyone to post a letter for me without opening it to read the contents, but now that we had a telephone, I would find an opportunity to ring Uncle Samuel. I would ask him for money instead of a present for both my birthday and Christmas – and I was sure I could persuade him to advance it to me. If he asked why, I would tell him that I was secretly saving to go to university to be just as good as Young Samuel. 'If Mother and Father see that I'm serious enough about it to use my own money, they must agree to let me go.' He, the man who set such store by education, would find it impossible to refuse me.

Then, with the unwitting Johanna – or Marjorie, or even both – to chaperone me, I would go to Dublin on the pretext of looking at different colleges and courses. At a certain point, I would give them the slip and – *voilà!* – would find my way to Birmingham.

The plan involved bribing Florrie to give me Coley's address and to keep her mouth shut. I was sure she would welcome a few pounds.

The only aspect of which I could not be certain was how Coley would react when he saw me but my faith that our love was strong enough to survive this temporary separation was rock hard. Even if he was initially worried on my behalf that Father would come after us, or would wreak revenge on his family back home, he would work out a way to deal with it. Once we were married at Gretna Green and our union was legal, it would have to be accepted by all.

The building work was completed with amazing speed: Jack Montgomery seemed not only to work flat out but also to have many more helpers than I remembered.

We worked, too, on the more aesthetic side of the project – the telephone was a real blessing here – so by the time the builders left, a new bed, a dressing-table, the rugs and curtains, sewn from the fabric I had been allowed personally to choose, had already been delivered from Arnott's in Dublin and, neatly assembled on the landing, shrouded in wrappings, awaited their final placing.

When the plaster was dry, the new plumbing tested, the floors fitted and sanded, Johanna and I worked alongside two decorators. While they painted the ceiling and pasted paper to the walls, we painted the skirting-boards and doorframes white, the doors themselves pale lemon.

When the floors had been varnished to Mother's satisfaction, Jack Montgomery and two of his men came back to lift the furniture up the new, but quite narrow stairs they had fitted, then left Johanna and me to dress the room to our hearts' content. It was late one evening when we finished and everything was in place, even linen. 'All that bed needs now is the Shine Quilt and everything would be perfect!' Tired but relatively happy, I stood beside my sister in the centre of the room while we admired our handiwork. I was quite sorry that the project was completed because, during the days at least, my troubles had receded for long periods. 'We should help with all the other refurbishments too, Johanna, and perhaps you and I even could start our own decorating business. We certainly have the right name for it, don't we? The Shine Sisters has a good ring, don't you think?' It was said in jest but, as I spoke, it occurred to me that after we were married, Coley, too, could be involved. He could do the heavy work, like stripping old wallpaper.

'Don't be silly, Violet.' Johanna smiled. 'We're girls! But I agree that we have made a lovely room for any guest. It's just a pity that the window is so high. And I wish we didn't have to have those ugly bars.' When I had queried them – 'Everything else is so pretty!' – Father had explained that the original builders must have felt them to be necessary: something to do with 'tensile strengthening' of the window-frame so close to the roof.

Reluctant to leave the room, we tweaked and primped some more, then tidied the small landing outside the door. Father, who was usually so meticulous about his tools, had forgotten them. 'Should we take them down to him?' Johanna frowned.

'Maybe not. You know how fussy he is about them. He wouldn't want us to touch them: he might want them for some last-minute adjustments.' I closed the toolbox and placed it neatly against the wall. Then, after a last look round, we congratulated each other on a job well done and went downstairs.

## 31

# A NEAT HINGED OPENING

Given my knowledge of Colman – I'm more than ever convinced that my tramp was him – I'm fascinated by Violet's story (she called him Coley, but this was the normal derivative) and it is both amusing and touching to visualise him as the magical youth she seems to see. Every time she mentions his name, her face softens and those dark eyes seem somehow to enlarge and liquefy. Yet although I continue to listen intently, at a certain point in my aunt's narrative I begin to think, So far, so sad, but not all that unusual – and I can see from the polite expression on Bob's face that he is thinking the same. She wasn't the first girl from a Big House to fall in love with an unsuitable boy or even the first whose parents did everything in their power to keep their daughter away from him. She had been young and it was a very different era.

Like many old people with time on their hands, my aunt is a good, if over-detailed storyteller, probably because this had all been building up for so long during her isolation. If I'm right, we're the first audience she's had outside her immediate family. Yet, while I've been moved by some passages – I could barely see while she was talking about Marjorie, my mother – I glazed over a little during the decorating of Whitecliff's attic. I was tempted to tell her it was at present inaccessible and probably rain-damaged beyond repair, but she seemed so proud of her handiwork I didn't have the heart to interject.

But she has been talking for almost half an hour and, like Bob, I'm listening now more out of politeness than because I am riveted.

That's until we come to the bit where she was tricked into that attic room and kept there for half a lifetime, an event she related in the same matter-of-fact way she had told us about decorating it. The woman seemed to harbour an astonishing lack of resentment about her life being ruined.

'How did it happen?' This newest twist is so startling I am literally breathless.

'That morning, the morning after Johanna and I had finished the refurbishment, I was aware at breakfast that Mother had something on her mind. It was a Saturday when, customarily, Father let Sheila unlock the stores and went in rather later than usual, so the atmosphere was leisurely. A glance passed between the two of them. "I think, Roderick," she said, "I shall go in to Dublin today. Now that we have completed the attic room, I should like to start work on one of the bedrooms. I shall take Johanna with me to help with any parcels."

'I could see by Johanna's expression that she was pleased about this and had to subdue my own envy. Then I realised I would have Whitecliff to myself for the day – a hope dashed when Father announced that he was taking the morning off to catch up on his accounts. "Sheila knows," he told Mother. "I arranged it with her yesterday."

'Mother and Johanna left in a hackney for the railway station, leaving me to do the dishes in the kitchen. I was about half-way through this task when I realised that Father was standing behind me. "There's something I need to show you in the attic, Violet," he said. "Would you come up with me, please?" I dried my hands and, glad of the distraction, preceded him up the stairs and then to the attic. "You left your tools here yesterday, Father." I smiled at him. "Johanna and I decided to leave them be."

'"Thank you," he said, rather oddly, but I thought little of it right then.

'As I went into the room, I heard the door click behind me. Thinking it had accidentally blown shut, I went over to open it again but as I grasped the doorknob, I heard the key turn in the lock. I was puzzled. I thought that perhaps Father was adjusting something and called out to him but he didn't answer. Then I thought he couldn't hear me. I knocked hard on the wood and called again. But, again, there was no answer.'

I shift on her navy blue sofa. My imagination is so stretched with horror I'm afraid it might snap. 'He locked you in?'

'Unfortunately, yes. I was kept there until 1979.'

I look at Bob. I can see that he is as disbelieving as I am but we know she is telling the truth. It has something to do with the calmness of her tone. He's the first to recover. 'When did you realise it was permanent?'

'When I saw my diary, open at a damning, unambiguous passage, in the middle of my bed.' She remains composed. 'When I saw my laundered nightdress folded on the pillow, the one I had left under the colander that morning after the party – and had forgotten about. When I opened a drawer in the dressing-table and saw a new jar of Pond's Cold Cream and a brand-new hairbrush. When I saw soap, toothpaste, two toothbrushes, mine and a new one, new soap, face flannels and fresh towels in the bathroom. They had thought of most things.'

She takes a sip from her cup. I shudder as my screen goes blank. A young girl shut up in a velvet prison? With the instruments of her betrayal as silent accusers on her bed? This is the stuff of myth and legend.

'I believe now,' she puts her cup back in its saucer with great care, 'that in allowing me to choose the colours and so forth they thought they were being kind. At the time, however, I thought it the cruellest blow of all. It felt to me as if I had been forced to dig my own grave.'

'1979, Violet? That's . . .' mentally Bob does the sums '. . . that's thirty-five years. How did you get out? And where's Coley now?'

'I do not know.' She remains matter-of-fact. But then the expression in her eyes, which up to now has been candid, closes over. 'He – he came back from England once, as far as I know, but that was all. If he's still alive,' she adds softly, 'he would be near to eighty now although, believe it or not, I cannot remember how much older he was than me, two or three years. Old age is sad. There was a time I could have given a master class on every physical aspect of Coley Quinn . . .' Then, perhaps realising that this is too much information, she hurries on: 'As for getting out, after Mother died, with only Father and me left in the house, Johanna came to see him and begged him to release me. She pointed out that thirty-five years of such punishment was long enough and that she and her husband would take me down here to West Cork to live with them, out of our vicinity altogether. She promised Father that my identity would be protected and my removal would be discreet so there would be no scandal or awkward questions in the district, and therefore no repercussions for him or for the family name. He agreed to that. I think he was tired by then – he was only eighteen months away from his own death.

'Marjorie – your mother, Claudine – was right, you know. Of the two, he was the softer one. I had plenty of time to think, as you can believe, and quite early on it became clear to me that my incarceration was Mother's idea.'

Softer, my foot! I want to know whether that monster, my grandfather, had ever expressed regret, contrition, anything human; I also want to know whether my mother and Daddy, my adored daddy, left this girl to her fate – or did they, too, come to beg for her release? Did they even visit her?

It strikes me now how thoroughly she was abandoned not just by her family but by all of society, by the populations of Rathlinney, its surrounding villages and townlands – thousands of people, many of whom dealt in Rathlinney General Stores. Yet despite Violet's sudden disappearance, despite all the ghost stories and rumours even I had heard decades later, at the time no one had either cared enough or had the courage to penetrate the mystique that hung around the Big House. 'People in the locality must have known something was going on, even asked questions. Everyone knew everyone else's business back then.'

'Very early on Mother and Father came to see me, one of the few times they came together. They told me through my hatch—'

'Hatch? What hatch?'

'Father was a good craftsman, as you know.' She nods in

the direction of the yew bench. 'Some time later that first morning, he came back to the attic and cut a neat, hinged opening through the centre of my door. This was the purpose of the tools on the landing. There was already a lock in the door proper, but he fitted another, a padlock, to the outside.'

'What did you say to him? When he cut this hole out of the door he must have been visible to you?'

'I'm afraid I'll leave that for you to work out. I was already exhausted from weeping but, yes, I did beg and howl and demand to know how long I was to be locked in. Eventually I wore myself out and could make no more sounds.'

'And all the time he was just sawing and hammering away?'

'Yes. But I think now,' she adds, her gaze sliding away from me to the window, 'that what he was doing was as hard on him as it was on me.'

Bob's fist reaches out and grabs the air. 'Why didn't you reach through that hole to punch him? I would have.'

She seems astonished. 'Dear me, no. He was my father. I couldn't have done that.'

I manage to contain myself. 'Go on, Violet.'

'When the hatch was fitted and finished to his satisfaction, Father told me what my regime would be. I would be fed as part of the family; my laundry would be done. Anything I asked for within reason would be provided. He told me that the only thing of which I was to be deprived was liberty.

'And then he told me why. One reason was that on the morning after my visit to Coley Quinn's house, Coley's father had gone to the post office and had telephoned Rathlinney nine to inform my parents.'

'That's nearly the worst of it all — I can't bear it.'

'I no longer blame the man,' she says quietly. 'I did at first, of course. In fact, I blamed the entire world for my plight. But time passes, you know, and as Florrie said to me that night, the Quinns were poor people. Their livelihood was at stake and, conacre being scarce in our district at the time, what he did was understandable. It was also unnecessary because they would have locked me up in any case.' Her face lifts a little with the merest shadow of a smile. 'You see, that diary was full of a young girl's excitable ramblings – except that in it I was unfortunately quite explicit about what exactly Coley and I had been up to in a physical sense, where and how often. I left nothing out.

'That night I raced to Coley's house, I had not been as clever as I had imagined because Mother, who did not sleep soundly, thought she had heard me leave. She went to my room to check, found my empty bed – but also spotted my diary on the dressing-table where I had been filling it in earlier that evening. Normally I kept it hidden but during that period I was so . . .' She trails off, and it's not hard to imagine what she's seeing in her mind's eye. 'I got careless,' she amends what she had been going to say.

Bob and I remain silent. We have nothing to contribute.

After a few seconds, my aunt resumes her story. 'Naturally, Mother read the diary. She took it to Father. He read it too. They decided together that night what they would do. Although, of course, I was ignorant of it, by the time I slipped back into the house the decision had been made and the diary was back exactly as Mother had found it so as not to arouse my suspicions. Mr Quinn's telephone call was *de trop*, as the French say.'

'What they did, getting you to believe things were improving, getting you to decorate that room was so – so—'

I'm stuck for the right word. 'It was so calculating,' I offer feebly.

'Perhaps it seems so from this perspective,' her gaze is steady, 'but I have had many years to think things over and, looking at it from their point of view, they believed I was bound on self-destruction.'

'You shouldn't have to look at it from their point of view! You were sixteen! And why did it go on for so long? They could have let you out, for instance, when you turned twenty-one.'

'How could they have done that? How could they have trusted me not to go to the authorities? Our whole family would have faced public opprobrium, Claudine.'

'Would you have? Gone to the authorities?'

'Probably not. They, however, could never be sure. I know it's hard to take in, but you must remember the context and the era. We all got caught in a maze with no exit. I am sure they suffered too.'

Yet again we were all silent for a few moments. Her forbearance was driving me mad. I don't know what Bob was thinking but, caught in the scenario she had painted, I was bottling tears of rage. Afraid I would make a show of myself, I prompted her again: 'So, to go back a bit, you were telling us about your mother and father coming together that one time to the hatch your father cut into your door. What did they say?'

'It was she who spoke. She told me that no one but the immediate family knew or would ever know that I was confined for my own safety. That was what she said. For my own safety. She told me that, since everyone in the district knew why Coley Quinn had gone so suddenly to England, they would readily believe it when they heard that I, too, had been sent abroad, to relatives in America.'

'But it was wartime. Wouldn't people have questioned that? There were travel restrictions.' This is Bob.

'I am not aware of how Coley got to England, but where I was concerned, you must remember that our family was the leading family in the area at that time. Also, remember Mother was from the north, with Uncle Samuel still living there. For people in our district, the North of Ireland was a foreign place and northerners were different – and when you add in the assumption that people such as we lived by different rules or had the personal contacts that would enable us to get round the rules . . .

'Anyhow, whether people guessed, I don't know. No knight in armour, shining or otherwise, rode to my rescue. However it appears now, I think that by their lights they meant it when they said they had incarcerated me for my own safety. You must remember I was single-minded when I was young, and self-willed—'

'I don't know how you can be so calm about it.' I'm almost foaming. 'I'd have taken the world and his mother to court!'

'How? What access did I have to anyone? The only person I ever saw outside my immediate family was the doctor, who was trusted enough to keep the secret.'

'But what about your sisters?' My opinion of my mother lurches towards the negative. 'Your brothers? That godfather uncle?'

'Easy there, Claudine. You're upsetting your aunt.' Bob pulls me back into my seat from which, in frustration, I was about to leap. He's right to do so, because now that he has brought it to my attention, I can see that two bright red stains have appeared high on my aunt's cheeks. Family loyalty is a deep, mysterious enigma and I'm putting it under severe strain. And of course two of her three remaining brothers were somewhere on a battlefield.

'In this age,' again she is looking towards the window, 'I agree it is hard to accept how something like this could happen.' She shrugs. 'It may be different now, although human nature does not change much, but people in those days had family secrets. I don't expect you to understand.'

'But I'm trying to understand. I really am.'

She reaches out and touches one of my hands, clenched in front of me on the coffee-table. 'You must not think harshly of your dear mother,' she says perceptively. 'Marjorie was kind and good and wise. She did visit me frequently, even in later years when she was pregnant with you, Claudine . . .' She flinches, as though remembering something painful.

'Please, Violet, don't distress yourself.' I hate myself for putting her through this; at the same time, avid for even the smallest scrap of information about my mother, I don't want her to stop.

'I have broad shoulders, Claudine.' Her tone is resolute again. 'How your dear mother was looking forward to your birth! On her last visit, when she was about to go into hospital, she was bubbling with joy. She had insisted on coming to Whitecliff even though she had been warned by her doctors not to travel because of the bumpy roads we had then. She suffered from some kind of anaemia and, on the following day, was to go into hospital where she would have to stay in bed with her feet elevated for the last month of her pregnancy. "I don't care if I have to stay in hospital for the rest of my life," she said to me that day, "but, of course, that won't happen. I still can't believe it, Violet. At my age! We've waited so long – I'd almost given up hope! Next time I come I'll bring the baby. I can pass him in to you and you can hold him. Won't that be terrif?" Marjorie always had the latest slang from Dublin. She was convinced, by the way, that you were going to be a boy. Of course, neither of us could have known that this visit would be her last. She always hoped that next time she came things would be back to normal. "I'm a hundred per cent sure that this year will be your last up here, Violet," she said each time. And as for my poor Johanna, she had to live with Mother and Father – that was, of course, until Anthony came along.'

Violet's cool, calm room seems suddenly stuffy and claustrophobic. Daddy was no storyteller and the picture I have of my mother now is so much more vivid and poignant than the one he had attempted to convey. I'm terrified of forgetting the most minor detail.

'Did my father know about your circumstances?' I hardly dare ask the question but have to anyway: if he had known, it might explain the puzzling outburst at the breakfast table that time when Pamela mentioned Whitecliff. Guilt that he hadn't acted?

'No. She did not tell him. She felt that if he knew, and decided to take action, some worse fate might befall the entire family, like prosecution. Definitely scandal – and, as you may have gathered by now, my parents were terrified of scandal and we were imbued with this. Marjorie was very disturbed about it, and while I tried to reassure her, I perfectly understood her dilemma.'

'But here's another thing, Violet. He told me my grandparents were dead. Why would he lie to me about that?' I

Deirdre Purcell

am getting upset. Maybe Daddy's pedestal needs to be a little lower than the one I had erected for him.

She hesitates. 'I can't answer that. You must understand that, with Marjorie dead and no contact . . .' She looks at the floor. 'This is difficult for me . . .'

'I'm sorry, Violet. If you don't want to say any more . . .' Have I been badgering her?

'Is it possible he was trying to protect you from them? Perhaps it was as simple as him not wanting you to come under their influence, Claudine.' She looks up. 'The atmosphere at Whitecliff—' she stops again, thinking. 'I do know that when he and Marjorie came to tell Mother and Father about the engagement, they were not very welcoming. It was Johanna who told me that, not Marjorie, whose loyalties were obviously divided. And Johanna, who thought the best of everyone and never wanted conflict, was no doubt glossing the matter. It is possible that, far from being "not welcoming", they were hostile. For whatever reason, he never, as far as I know, came again.'

'Why would they behave like that to him? He was lovely! And did you ask her about this – my mother, I mean?'

'I am afraid the "why" question is one I cannot adequately answer.' She shrugs. 'I did ask Marjorie why he never came, and although I could see I had upset her, she confirmed they did not like him. She also said – I hope this won't upset you, Claudine – that he was very stubborn when he made up his mind about something and she had found that if she persisted with something about which he had dug his heels in, he could be irritable. She did not like to cross him. I did not pursue it. I did not want our precious time together to be spoilt by agitating her. So, I don't think we shall ever know the precise reason for our parents' disliking him. Perhaps it was to do with him being older than she was, or even his religion. He was a Catholic, was he not?'

'Non-practising, and he brought me up as Church of Ireland.' I jump instantly to his defence. 'He said it was in deference to my mother – not that we went to church often.'

'All of this does sound unthinkable now,' my aunt says slowly, 'especially how, for such a long time, it could be managed that no one outside the inner family knew what had happened to me. And before you ask, your mother was deeply saddened, not only about my seclusion but that she could not tell her husband about it. "I hate keeping secrets from him, Violet. It's not right," she used to say. To maintain the fiction with her husband that I was abroad, she was even forced to employ certain ruses – for instance, sending Christmas and birthday cards to a fictitious address in America, deliberately not giving a return address.'

'How did she explain she never got any back from you?'

'I don't think he noticed.' Her smile is wry. 'He was always about his business.'

She waits a moment as if to let it all sink in. Then, 'Where I am concerned, you must not feel sorry for me, my dear. I am not to be absolved of culpability, after all, and until I met Coley Quinn, I had had a very privileged childhood. "Golden", I think, is the apt term. And I have long ago come to terms with everything.'

'How could you? How could you "come to terms" with such monstrosity?'

'Believe me, I have. Within the confines of my tower, I was treated generously. The most difficult part of it was loneliness, of course, but one gets used to solitary living, you know.

And I developed the reading habit. They never stinted me on books.' Her lips twitch again. 'I've often wondered how, in the early days, Father explained his sudden liking for romantic fiction to our local librarian.

'So that is what happened.' She sits back. 'In raking over my life in such detail, I am being self-indulgent, perhaps, but I do think you have a right to know your family history.'

'Can you honestly say you have forgiven them for this? Truly?' I remain incandescent.

'Oh, yes! Long ago. Mother and Father are no longer alive to know of my displeasure, so what is the point of being angry?' She laughs. I don't join in. All of this is so over-whelming, I need to go somewhere now to be alone, to sort out what I feel.

Bob, though, is still on the practical side: 'And did you have relations in America? Do you still?'

He can't have bargained on what she tells us next.

'American relatives? I don't know.' She looks us both in the eye. 'We did have relatives, distant ones, who communi-cated with us and we with them, only at Christmas time. I think they might have lived in New York or New Jersey but I'm sure they are all dead now.

'However, there is one possibility. Something that may give you a little more perspective on what Mother and Father had to deal with. I had a baby. A daughter.'

## 32

# TWO IN THE MORNING

I gave birth to Coley's child at two in the morning with only our family doctor present; he could be trusted not to betray the secret and, in fact, became part of it. Because as soon as the baby was born, he wrapped her up and took her away immediately. I begged to hold her even for a few minutes, but he wouldn't hear of it. 'It would only distress you, make things harder. You must forget about this night, Violet. Let your mind heal along with your body or you will spend the rest of your life in regret and resentment.'

Although I can remember every detail of my labour and birth pangs, I can barely remember him telling me some months earlier that I was pregnant. The announcement, made in his dry, flat voice, seemed so preposterous that by the time I had understood his words he was already packing his bag, and of what he had said in the interim, I have no memory at all.

This man had been our family doctor for many years. He was of our parish and, in wartime, although he would have been entitled to a petrol ration for his car, preferred to use his horse and buggy. He had courtly manners and a reputation for being upright and reliable – and, crucially in our case, keeping his own counsel. His views about women were old-fashioned, even for that era, and while he was never didactic, he always let it be known, even to me as a child, that he did not, for instance, approve of women going out to work.

I had been feeling rather poorly for days, was off my food but, even so, was vomiting and eventually, my parents had sent him in to examine me.

Mother came with him into my attic. She left the door open behind her and, for a moment or two, it crossed my mind to bolt, but I knew I would not get far.

'Lie there on the bed for me, Violet,' he said and then, looking around, 'What a charming bedroom.'

'Yes.' Mother's tone was agreeable. 'Violet and her sister chose the colours: they chose well.'

He listened to my chest and did the usual things, then asked me to get undressed. 'You may get in under the bedclothes if you wish, my dear,' he said kindly.

I had never been examined internally and was shocked when he did things to me – by feel, to give him his due – that I could not have imagined. All the time, I was supremely conscious that Mother was sitting across the room from us in my armchair.

'Yes, Fiona, I'm afraid it is true,' he said to her, when he had finished. 'She is definitely pregnant.' There followed a conversation in hushed tones between them, but sitting up under my bedcover, clutching it to my chin, I was so embarrassed and humiliated by the insult to the part of my body where only Coley Quinn had been that I did not take in the implications of what he had just said. It was when he had put away his stethoscope and I noticed that, as she talked with him, my mother's eyes were glowing with anger that I grasped the horror. Pregnant?

There is little point in belabouring the emotions of the next days, weeks and even months: there are only so many words in the English language to encompass wretchedness and despair. Having been left in no doubt about what would happen to my baby – it was to be given to an American couple by prior arrangement with an orphanage, quite a common practice at the time – throughout most of my pregnancy I refused to think of it as anything other than a blob that, like a malign sponge, had invaded me. I had tried to convince myself that my only wish was for the whole mess to be done with as speedily as possible.

Yet, as the time of my confinement neared, my baby had become far from a blob in my thoughts, and as it kicked and squirmed, I visualised it as a miniature Coley. I sang to it at dead of night and told it stories about the love between its father and mother; I described my dear Coley to it in great detail and apologised for his absence. 'If he knew about you,' I crooned, 'no mountain would be too high or sea too deep to keep him away.' I begged it over and over again not to forget me.

The labour was arduous; for most of it, Mother and Father, assuming correctly that I would make no attempt to escape, allowed Johanna to sit with me. She, of course, had no experience of either nursing or childbirth but she did her best, holding my hand and encouraging me through the worst of the pain.

Dr Willis arrived at about midnight and took over. Both my sister and I were exhausted and he sent her to her room for a rest. 'I'll stay with her, dear. I'll call you in about an hour.'

He did not call her, and when he delivered my daughter, I was too spent to remind him.

My thoughts are still haunted by my little girl's first cry, the terrified, choking scream of a small animal caught in a snare, but she was quiet as he ministered to her and to me, and as he carried her out of my room. 'I'll wake your sister, Violet, to tell her the news,' he said, just before he closed the door behind him. 'And, of course, your mother and father are waiting downstairs.'

'And what about Coley Quinn?' I wanted to cry, but of course did not.

'You rest now,' he continued. 'You can be assured she'll have a good life. I've arranged for her to be given to a God-fearing family.' Dr Willis was a Roman Catholic and I doubt if by 'God-fearing' he had meant people of our faith. 'Console yourself that she will grow up as a happy little American, with every creature comfort a little girl could want,' was the last thing he said that night – or morning.

She cried again as he was taking her down, but then he closed the entry door at the foot of the stairs and I could no longer hear her as she set out on her travels.

# 33

# TV CAN BE EDUCATIONAL

S haken, Bob and I arrive back at our pet-friendly B-and-B to pick at the fish and chips we had purchased on the way.

She didn't know the name of the orphanage, she didn't know which county it was in ('They did not tell me') and, of course, her revelation explained the hiccup in her telling the story of my mother's visits to her: after what happened to her, it must have been torture for her to see and hear her sister's happiness at being pregnant.

No wonder she was hazy even about the date of her daughter's birth: 'You must understand that dates meant little to me and, at my age, time has telescoped and glazed over. It was definitely close to Christmas Day, though – before-hand, because I remember Mother saying something about how typical it was of me to discommode everyone at such a time.'

There was no suitable opportunity for me to tell her about the man I thought was Coley Quinn, which was perhaps just as well. I deemed it best to hold off on delivering this news to her until I was sure of my facts. You can imagine how I'm feeling now that I have discovered not only a new aunt but, somewhere on this planet, a cousin too. As for what had happened to Violet, the concept was too large to take in in one gulp. For the time being, it has been relatively easy to park Bob's infidelity.

Before we left Violet's house, I had asked her if she had any idea where her child was. 'No.' She had shaken her head. 'America is such a huge place, and I don't even know her name.'

'If that child was born at Christmas 1944, as Violet believes,' I say now to Bob as we toy with our meal, 'she would be fifty-nine. The way Violet tells it, though, she's still a baby.'

'In her mind, yes. That's understandable. It's so sad.'

It's not like him to be emotional and I glance sharply at him, but I can see he's sincere. 'Listen, Bob, do you think we should offer to help her find her daughter?'

'That's up to her, surely?'

'We-ell.' I consider this. 'She's suffered such a horrific wrong. Isn't it up to someone like me to help her? I'm her niece, after all. And wouldn't a reunion with her daughter be wonderful at the end stage of her life?'

'Make sure she wants the help first, Cee. Don't go barging in. I think your sudden appearance might be enough for one week, or even a month, don't you? I got the impression she was settling into a peaceful old age and while she wanted to co-operate – and may indeed count you as a blessing eventually – she wasn't exactly ecstatic. She's been out in the world for a long time now. If she'd wanted to follow up on this she'd have done it.'

'Maybe she didn't know where to start.'

'She was institutionalised for a long time, granted, but she doesn't strike me as the helpless type.' He pushes away the remains of his food.

We're eating or, rather, playing with our meal in the over-decorated residents' dining room of our B-and-B. It's a bungalow, and the crashing and banging of crockery and pots from the kitchen at the other end of the corridor from where we're sitting is reassurance that the landlady is not within eavesdropping distance. Bob's right to warn me: my instinct is always to jump in and try to fix things for people. Especially at times like this, when activity can be used temporarily to bury emotional trauma. Immediately after Daddy died, for instance (and before I'd discovered what was in his will), from having had no interest whatsoever in horticulture, I had insisted that Pamela let the gardener go and, for a time, frequently starting at first light, mowed, trimmed, weeded and hoed the garden in Sandycove all day, barely stopping to eat or even for a cup of tea until I collapsed into bed at sunset.

Unless I can do something, anything, now, I might blow up. 'Yes, but as you say, she was institutionalised and did nothing for herself for decades. Wouldn't that kill anyone's initiative? Anyway, this is my first cousin we're talking about here. I'd like to find her.'

'I'll just say one more thing and then I'll shut up.' Bob toys with his takeaway fork. 'Suppose you do find this woman, and Violet gets her hopes up and then you discover that the daughter doesn't want anything to do with your aunt? That does occur in these cases, you know. There aren't that many fairytale happy endings in this world. And if Violet gets to know that you've found her long-lost daughter but you've failed to convince the woman to make contact, wouldn't it make things far worse for her than they are right now? She's just discovered you. Let her get used to that at least. Take a bit of time for the two of you to get to know each other.'

'There's an easy way to protect her from disappointment. We simply won't tell Violet we're searching. We'll let it be a surprise.'

'More secrets?'

'Pleasant ones.'

'Can you guarantee that? Here's another problem: suppose the daughter agrees to meet, then turns out to be a gold-digger? Your aunt is due to come into a not inconsiderable few bob with the sale of Whitecliff. And when she pops her clogs, that house down the road there won't be sold for less than a million, I'd reckon.'

'Suppose the daughter turns out to be the nicest person in the world? Suppose she's been looking for her mother for forty years?'

At my feet, Jeffrey lumbers up on to all four paws, then whumps back down in a different position. I pull his ears and he gives my hand a little lick.

'Look,' Bob says then, 'if you really want to go down this road—'

'I do. But I'll tell you what – I'll ask her first. And if she gets upset I'll back off.'

'I'll help as much as I can if she goes for it.' He pauses. 'Am I forgiven?'

'That's not fair.' I stare at him. 'You're manipulating this situation.'

'Of course I am. Wouldn't you do the same if the situation were reversed?'

His honesty is disarming. I shouldn't let him off the hook, that's for sure, but it has been good to have him here. 'Lookit,

Bob, for obvious reasons I can't get into this now. But I'm warning you that you can expect a lot of talking about it when I'm ready.'

'Of course. So, in the meantime you'll forgive me? Or try to?'

I don't like being railroaded. 'All right. But it's only a truce. That's if I can believe you that it's not this great big giant affair—'

'Believe me!' He makes a sound, probably a laugh, but so rueful it's more like a snort and, funnily enough, I do believe him because his eyes had swivelled to the right. I watch *CSI, Crime Scene Investigation*: I know that during questioning, when the suspect – or, as in Bob's case, the perp – looks to the right, he's remembering the story. When he looks left he's creating one. TV can be educational.

My mobile rings. I look at its glowing, bouncing screen: Tommy O'Hare's number. Again. 'I'd better take this. I'm probably fired by now. Hello, Tom?'

I wait, not reacting against the salvo of effing and blinding and where-have-you-beening that pours into my right ear. Then, when he winds down a bit: 'You'll understand when I tell you what's happened down here, Tommy.'

'This'd better be good.'

'It is. For me.' When I've finished telling him, as succinctly as possible and leaving out the more gruesome bits, his reaction is predictable. 'I'm glad for you, Claudie, of course I am. But where does that leave the deal on the house? Did you mention it to her?'

'That's why I'm here in the first place, isn't it? You were right about the probate. She doesn't own it yet. But she will.'

'And will she sell it to us?'

313

'We're both a bit shaken up by what's happened. Do you think it was the right time to go pushing her? And, by the way, it was pretty emotional for me too, you know.'

'Is nothing simple these days? Keep on it anyhow, will you? And – er, congratulations, if that's appropriate.' Knowing Tommy so well, I can see his little screwed-up face as he attempts not to betray his exasperation. 'Keep me posted.'

'I will.' I click off, consigning OHPC and real-estate concerns to the back-burner and take up where Bob and I left off. 'I'm very hurt and angry, Bob. It's going to take time for me to come to terms with what you've done. So, when we get home you move into one of the spare rooms.'

'We slept together last night,' he points out, not unreasonably.

'You slept. I didn't. Anyhow, last night is not what we're talking about. It's when we get home that counts.'

'I don't see the logic, but I suppose it's fair enough.'

I've made my point, no profit in going on at him. 'So, I agree we should ask Violet first before we go searching for her daughter. If she does, what do you think should be our first step?'

'The Register of Births, Marriages and Deaths,' he answers promptly. 'The child would have been registered – she would have needed a birth certificate to get a passport.'

'She could have been put on the passport of one of those Americans as if she was theirs. You can do that with infants.'

'She'd still have to have a birth certificate for that to happen.'

'They could have forged one.'

'Forging, Claudine? Will you try to curb that overheated imagination of yours and stay on track here? Have you a better idea?'

I haven't, of course. But I'm still itching for action. Anything to save me from thinking too deeply, particularly if I have to re-examine a few things about Daddy: the phrases 'very stubborn' and 'irritable' keep rising to the surface, like an oil spill on the sea. I had known about those traits but, in my sanctification of him, had preferred to overlook them. 'Look, I think I'll call Violet to ask her if she'd like us to do something. No time like the present, OK?' And then, when I see Bob's answering frown, 'Don't worry, I'll be careful.'

'Remember what I said, Cee. Meddlers and do-gooders sometimes get their comeuppance. She mightn't react in the way you expect.'

'I'll be careful.' I punch in my aunt's number. She sounds sleepy when she answers. 'I'm very sorry, did I wake you, Violet? It's Claudine here.'

'Don't worry.'

I do worry. She must have gone for a nap as soon as we left. In the flesh she had seemed taut, elegant and energetic. Now, in that girlish voice, I can hear every year of her seventy-six. Bob is right. She needs time to adjust. 'I'm sorry, Aunt Violet,' I say quickly. 'I just wanted to say to you again before we leave that we'll stay in touch and we'll see each other again soon. And if you ever need anything, you have only to ask.'

## 34

# A USED TEA-BAG

'Greenparks liked your blurb for Cruskeen Lawns, Claudie.' Tommy flings it to me across his kitchen table before I've had a chance to put down my handbag. I pick up the paper, still heavily illuminated with red-circled crossings-out, but with additional suggestions and exclamation marks now marching like exotic beetles up and down the margins. 'Well done!' He picks up the telephone and spins his Rolodex to find a number. 'Just do us up a couple of clean copies there and the job's oxo.' He's behaving as if I've come in to work at a normal time instead of at two o'clock in the afternoon.

I had spent the morning alternately cleaning like a dervish and sitting stock still on a couch or a chair, staring into space while I tried to put some order on my thoughts and feelings. I knew one thing for sure: Greenparks and Cruskeen Lawns were so uninteresting to me now – as was the rest of the work I had scheduled – that I had to have some time off to sort myself out. I had been expecting a row about my extended absence but Tommy, who is shrewd, has my measure. He knows when to push and when to back off. The initiative is up to me. 'We have to talk, Tom.'

c

'Hate tha'!' He grins, and is already turned away and dialling.

Two hours later, having dealt with the Greenparks' paper-work and set up three viewings for the following day, I'm on my way to Whitecliff to renew acquaintance with Pat/Colman. This is not, I assure myself, to interfere or be bossy: this is simply a fact-finding mission. All I want to do is to identify that we have the right man here.

At first, Tommy had objected: 'I have to say, Claudine, that you're like the feckin' Scarlet Pimpernel these days. What are you going up there again for at this stage?'

'You want this deal, don't you? The woman is my aunt, remember? She trusts me,' I add, while wondering if it has sunk into his brain that my interest in the estate is now more than ever personal.

He gives no indication that it has. 'All right,' he says reluc-tantly. 'But don't go AWOL on me again now, d'ye hear? Keep your mobile on.'

I assure him I will.

I have butterflies in my tummy as, this time taking the narrow coastal road out of Rathlinney, I approach the house from the north. As I catch sight of the boundary wall ahead, my nerve almost fails me. I have accepted that things should be taken slowly (not: 'Remember me? Well, I know who you really are and guess what? Violet Shine is alive and well and living in West Cork') and have no intention of doing other-wise. So, what's to be nervous about? My set of survival mechanisms seems not to be working: I've lost confidence, dammit.

I stop the car to think but the more I bat things around and try to anticipate Coley's reaction to my news about Violet and that he has a daughter, the more I wonder if I'm doing the right thing. I'm on the verge of turning the car to go home, then give myself a swift kick for being a frightful ninny. My motives are good, and if I'm careful and gentle, I won't cause any problems for anyone.

I'm here anyway. I might as well go and talk to the man. I'll play it by ear. If he is Coley, I'll take it from there. If not, no harm done. There's no rush, anyhow – and it's best that I don't reveal too much today. I'll let him lead the conversation and see what happens.

I drive to the approximate spot where I first met him, park the car and, taking a golf umbrella with me, hop over the collapsed wall. Bingo! Sure enough, when I use the umbrella as I had seen him use the slash hook, the brambles part as they had before, exposing the pathway. I make cautious progress until I get to the clearing where we had our strange tea party. It is as I remember it. There isn't a sign of Coley Quinn or of Coley Quinn's belongings.

At first I think I must have made a mistake and taken the wrong pathway, but then I see the blackened area where the fire was, and the patch of compacted earth where his storage shed had stood.

I remember his insistence that he travels as light as a sparrow and that he could, in an instant, vanish without trace, but although I bend low to search the ground, I cannot find as much as a used tea-bag.

## 35

## SMALL TENDER THINGS

They were horrified, I could see that. Once I started to talk, however, I could not restrain myself and revealed far more than I had intended. Perhaps the reason I was so indiscreet is because I had never told anyone all of this before but I find it difficult to believe that, after a lifetime of reticence, I poured out my life's story so easily to virtual strangers, and in such a self-centred, sustained and vulgar manner. Within just an hour or so of meeting them for the first time, there I was, splurging as though I were a young girl.

I also fear that in failing to emphasise sufficiently how different everything was sixty years ago, especially in the way parents treated children, I have demonised Mother and Father. I should not have done that. My niece deserved a better introduction to her family, and I should have included the small, tender things that happened to me during my incarceration.

For instance, during one particularly cold winter, Mother sent up the latest Shine Quilt – reminding me ironically of what I had said to Johanna: that to complete our work on that room, it was the only item lacking. She sent with it a message that she had finished making them and this was the last one. I recognised how significant that was: we all knew how much she valued her reputation at the fête – and therefore her public image within the parish. I am convinced that the gesture was her equivalent of offering an olive branch, maybe even a plea for forgiveness. Her health, I knew, was beginning to fail.

I took that last quilt with me here to Johanna's house; it covers my bed and sometimes, on warm nights, I get from it the faint scent of lemons or vanilla, the overriding notes of Mother's preferred perfume, and when I do, I am inconsolable, far more so, I believe, than if we had enjoyed a loving bond while she was living.

I could have told them, too, of the occasion when Father came to my hatch, opened it and, having handed in my food, instead of saying a few polite words and then relocking as he always did, he simply stood there, framed in the opening and making no move. 'What is it, Father?' I was alarmed. By that time I had accepted my situation, had come to regard it as normal, and any change in the usual pattern worried me.

'Violet . . .' He hesitated, then reached out and gripped my forearm so violently I dropped my plate.

'Father, what's the matter?' I cried. 'You're hurting my arm.'

'I'm sorry.' He let go. 'I didn't meant to hurt you.'

'Is something wrong?'

'Nothing's wrong, Violet,' he said quietly, but I noticed that his jaw was working in the way it always did when he was deeply affected. 'Nothing and everything,' he added. Then, very quickly, he closed and locked the hatch but I knew instantly that something profound had happened between us.

You will appreciate, however, how difficult it can be to convey the emotional nuances of such outwardly unimportant and fleeting incidents; how, as I stared at the wood of my hatch and listened to his heavy footsteps descending the stairs, I felt both distraught and elated – elated that he had been trying to communicate something to me and simultaneously distraught on his behalf. On that occasion his anguish was almost palpable and, I believe, scythed through my heart more painfully than it had through his. For many years afterwards, that one seemingly tiny moment caused me to cry bitter adult tears. Speech is inadequate to describe why: one would probably need cinema.

So, you see, Mother and Father were not heartless, and to balance the picture I undoubtedly presented to my niece and her husband, I could easily have mentioned these small episodes and more besides.

I wonder if Claudine and I shall become friends. She, I can see already, wants to develop a relationship between us but I am so unaccustomed to new people that I shall find this difficult.

My God, I even told them obliquely how I had entered details of our lovemaking in my diary—

I burned that diary. After a flurry of entries in the immediate aftermath of my being locked in, I gradually stopped writing it. *Pace* Anne Frank, there are only so many ways one can describe frustration and misery and, without outside stimulus, I had already bored myself silly by the time I had made peace with my circumstances. When I came here with Johanna, I did not want to leave it behind, perhaps for others to pick over, but at the first opportunity, I threw it into her fireplace and was glad to watch it curl up and blacken. As I let my past waft up the chimney, I did fancy I felt physically lighter.

Now that past has come back to haunt me, waking and sleeping. I dozed only fitfully last night, starting awake with fragments of dreams already evaporating. I can remember only a few wisps – the coffin of my little dead brother, the imagined face of my baby, Mother's blue sheath dress, Father poring over invoices and paperwork, Coley and I lying in a hayfield above the shoreline at Loughshinny. I have been very quiet since Johanna died but the sediment under my settled existence has been stirred up and such upheaval and excitement is unnerving and stressful; when I made the appointment with this Mrs Armstrong to talk about Whitecliff, little did I know what lay ahead. I was worn out by the time they left – and why on earth did I further complicate matters by mentioning my daughter?

I should better have explained why, after my release, I never instituted any searches for her: that having been cut out of the world for so long, I felt like an automaton and I had to learn again to do the simplest things, to post a letter, to make a decision about whether to have white or brown bread. In addition, I had convinced myself that to threaten the stability of her life by materialising at this very late stage would be selfish.

Up to this point, I have managed my feelings about her quite well, I think. She exists in the red memory of my belly, in my ears that heard our shared screams, and in my imaginings of the good, structured life she has lived in America. I truly believe she should be left to that life, safe from the stories I should feel compelled to tell her.

Or should she? Might she be yearning for me as I do for her in my most private, self-centred moments?

My niece's materialisation has caused me to question

whether I have been all along rationalising and, in cowardly fashion, opting for a quiet life.

Claudine's professional interest in Whitecliff is a complicating factor. I will shortly need quite a lot of money and the estate will have to be my source one way or another. Until recently this has not been an issue. The Irish state has been good to me: I live modestly and my Old Age pension is adequate for my needs with a welcome bonus at Christmas time; I have a free television licence, free travel, and I also receive a contribution towards my fuel and electricity bills. Since I don't drink or smoke, do not run a car, entertain or socialise, I manage quite well.

Yet this house of Johanna and Anthony's is old and draughty and, to judge by the thunder over my head when a gale blows from the south-west, will soon need reslating. The wooden sash windows, graceful and appropriate to the house as they are, also need to be replaced: the winters here are mild but very wet, frequently stormy, and the salt-laden wind wreaks havoc on even the sturdiest mahogany, such as ours. The garden and outbuildings need a thorough overhaul. Finally, there is the question of warmth. I am hardy, but with advancing age comes the desire for proper central heating. I closed off the rooms upstairs during the winter last year after Johanna died, but the boiler is barely adequate to cope even with the few rooms I do use. At my age one sees the future in terms of declining health and even dependency. I may need all the financial resources I can lay my hands on in order to guarantee a comfortable dotage.

But with all of that, I cannot deny that it is thrilling to have found some family. I must not get carried away, though: I am seventy-six, so am I really open to upheaval and change of such radical nature? I have to admit that the prospect fills me with excitement and dread in roughly equal parts but at least, with someone like Claudine around, life will never again be dull.

Was it not extraordinary that, although it was clear she had no idea of our family connection, my niece made a beeline for Father's yew bench? But how it came to be here in this sitting room is another story I shall never be able to tell her and illustrates perfectly what I was trying to say about the poverty of words.

When I was leaving Whitecliff with Johanna to come here, her dear Anthony was driving us. Having kept the secret of my incarceration from him for years, as Marjorie had from her husband, she had finally told him of my existence, having made him promise he wouldn't do anything about it after I was safely here.

Believing I might have some belongings, even furniture or linen with me, he had come in his carpenter's van and was waiting outside on the gravel while Johanna helped me gather up the bits and pieces I wished to take, of which there were few. I was disinclined to take any but the most personal items – although at the last minute I did bundle up the Shine Quilt, as I have already outlined.

There was a small and unexpected difficulty as I walked through the newly opened door (the wood had swollen and both Father and Anthony had had to work on it) to face the downward chute of the staircase to the landing below. It may sound unlikely, but I had not used stairs for so long that I became disoriented, then quite fearful. Looking down, I had the sensation of falling, even found myself swaying a little, and if Johanna had not caught me from behind, I might have stumbled. She had then to squeeze in beside me to link me down. Then, safely in the entrance hall, while I held the Shine Quilt in my arms, she carried the rest of my possessions, which filled just two valises, through the front door and out to the van.

I hesitated before following her. Father was sitting in the drawing room, illuminated by only a single electric table lamp; through the open door I could see his outline in one of the armchairs by the fireplace but could not discern his features. I did not know whether to go in to him and instead, called, 'I'm off now, Father.'

I thought I saw him move in the chair, and waited for him to respond, but when he did not, unexpectedly grief-stricken, I followed my sister outside. It was raining, I remember, and I had to hurry across the gravel towards the van.

'Got everything, Violet?' As I clambered in, Anthony leaned across Johanna, beside him on the bench seat. I had met him for the first time that evening and, in every way, heartily endorsed my sister's high opinion of him.

'Thank you, Anthony.' Glad of the rain to cover my tears, I kept my face averted as I settled the quilt and myself beside Johanna and closed the door. It was very strange to feel rain-drops clog my eyelashes and, in the cab of Anthony's van, to smell something other than my room.

'We're all set, so.' He started the engine.

We were pulling away from the house when we all became aware of a commotion at the rear of the van. Anthony applied the brakes and opened his door to look behind him. 'It's your da,' he said, in astonishment.

I froze. Even at this late stage, was Father trying to prevent my leaving? I got out and, because the rain was heavy now, used the quilt to cover my head as I ran to the back of the van where I found him struggling to open the doors, repeatedly and frantically depressing the outside handles. He was wearing only a shirt, already transparent at the shoulders while rain streamed off his hair. 'I want you to have this,' he said, still scrabbling at the doors, 'but they seem to be locked.'

It was only then that I noticed, at his feet, his beautiful yew bench. 'Oh, Father,' I cried – and, without thinking, threw myself at him. The Shine Quilt fell off my head to lie disregarded on the ground as, for the first and last time in my life, I hugged my father. After a second, his arms came slowly round me in response and he held me to him for a fierce moment before Anthony came round to unlock the doors.

As we finally drove away with the damp quilt and the yew bench safely in the back of the van, I looked back through the downpour to see him: a stooped, lone figure, standing in the shadow of Whitecliff's portico, lit from the side by dim yellow light from the uncurtained bay. Although I cannot be sure, I think one hand was half raised in tentative farewell.

## 36

# THE PATIENT

When I woke on the morning after my abortive excursion to Whitecliff, my brain kicked in immediately, perking with ideas and plans for Whitecliff and reunions: Violet and her daughter, Coley and Violet, restoring the house . . .

Rather than indulge it as usual, however, I reined it in, sternly ordering it to lie down. Bob was right. The solid floor of my life might have developed a wobble, I told it, but that did not justify my rushing in unbidden to set other people's floors in motion.

At the same time, after a lifetime of such behaviour, the notion that I would do nothing was too radical. So, after my shower, with Bob safely gone to work, I allowed myself to hit the phone. In a search for Colman Quinn, I left my name and home number (home only – that was part of the compromise) with hospitals, gárda stations and health centres. Finally, I rang Rathlinney post office to ask if he had been in to collect his pension and, correctly, was told politely that this was none of my business.

I hadn't much hope that any of this would yield a result

but I had satisfied my instincts and also my conscience: there was a possibility – I hoped it was an outside one – that he had done a runner as a result of my visit to the estate.

After that last call, I replaced the wall phone in my sunny kitchen and stood quietly for a moment, savouring the silence. Jeffrey padded over and sat at my feet. As I leaned down to pat him I decided I had reached the limit of what I would actively do. I made a vow to initiate no further phone calls, but to let Fate decide what was to happen next. From this day forth, that was the brand new me.

On the way to work, the new me rang Violet, not to delve, just to chat. 'Good morning, Claudine.' She sounded chirpy when I announced myself. 'Are you well? Obviously you got home safely.'

'We did, Aunt Violet.' It was novel, nicely novel, to be making a social call to my own aunt. Up to now I had been able to make them only to Bob's aunt Louise. 'And I'm very well, thank you. It's a beautiful day here.'

'Here too. I'm going into the garden later to have lunch.'

We chatted inconsequentially for a few minutes, so inconsequentially, in fact, it became obvious that we were both avoiding undercurrents of previous conversations but I must admit – nature will out! – that I was hard pressed not to revert to type and start asking questions. Instead, as we finished up the conversation, I invited her to come up to stay with us 'some time'.

'I'd be delighted, Claudine,' she said, and, promising to stay in touch, we hung up.

It's lunchtime now and I have come back to the house, partly because I have no clients to meet this afternoon so I can work from home, and partly because I can't wait to change out of a pair of new shoes that have skinned the back of my heels during a viewing this morning. They are hurting so much that I kick them off even before I insert my key into the lock of the front door; I don't bother to pick them up but leave them outside to repent their sins. As I dump my files on the hall table, I see that the message light on the phone is flashing. I try to ignore it. It might be a cold call trying to sell me a cheap phone service or telling me I've won a Caribbean cruise . . .

But as I go into the kitchen to plug in the kettle, I can no longer resist.

Two minutes after I've listened to the message, I'm gazing at the phone, debating the right thing to do against what I want to do. It's a titanic struggle. New me says wait until this evening and consult Bob. Old me says, 'Pick up that phone right now.' One of the health centres has returned my call about Colman Quinn. The public–health nurse would like to talk to me and has left her mobile number. The caller used that name, Colman Quinn. So my tramp is definitely Violet's Coley.

Crunch time.

I decide to have lunch and think about it.

I'm only half-way through when I get up to make the call. 'Oh, good,' the nurse says immediately, when I make myself known. 'Are you a relative of Colman's?'

'No.' I don't think it's appropriate to go into speculation involving a long-lost cousin and our mutual connection to her.

'What, then? What's your involvement?' This woman, who is from the north to judge by her accent, is the no–nonsense type.

'I hardly know him. My knowledge of him is through Whitecliff, the house where he was – er – camping. I was a little concerned that he seemed to have gone.'

'Ah, yes. That. Well, what has happened there is providential. We've had all his pucks and traps removed. It's safely in storage until he decides what he wants to keep and what can be thrown out. And that should be most of it, if you want my opinion . . .'

It turns out that Coley is in hospital but is fit for release. She tells me he was climbing over a gap in the boundary wall during a heavy shower and slipped on the wet moss, fell heavily and, although he managed to haul himself into a sitting position, was unable to get up any further. 'Luckily,' she adds, in her brisk, clipped way, 'he fell out on to the road and not back below the wall or he might not have been found until much later and the dickens only knows what might have happened to him.'

'Did he break a leg or get a heart-attack or something? And who found him?'

'He was found quite quickly, a man walking his dog. Nothing broken. But he has a bad sprain in his right ankle so his mobility is compromised for the moment. He's a tough old chap, though, and we expect a full recovery and fairly quickly too. Once we had him, we took the opportunity to keep him in for a couple of days to give him a thorough check-up. He's actually in very good shape for a man his age.'

'Who dismantled his campsite, though? Surely—'

'We can't be doing with it,' she cuts me off, then gives me a quick rundown on the authorities' plan. A unit has become vacant in sheltered housing. 'I've managed to get him in there. There'll be a bit of adjustment involved after so much independence and living rough for so long, but we want to have him settled before the winter.'

'And did he agree to this?' I remember the old man's insistence that he wanted to live out his days alone on the land at Whitecliff. I'm also aware of the irony of my question. Until my recent reformation, I Was That Nurse. 'When I met him he was adamant that he wanted to live out his days there.'

'It took a little persuasion,' she says, 'but now to more pressing matters. The maisonette will need to be refurbished before we can move him in, but what to do with him in the interim? As you probably know, there is huge pressure on step-down facilities and nursing-homes and I haven't been able to find any suitable vacancy. He's in an acute bed, and we do need to move him on. He says he has no living relatives who might be able to take him.'

'True enough,' I remember the old man's graphic image of relatives buried all over the world.

'Oh dear. Well, that's a bit of a conundrum. Friends? Anyone who'd take him in — it would be only for a couple of weeks?'

I remember Coley's threat to up sticks and go to his remaining friends 'over' but doubt if that was anything more than bravado. 'I don't think so.'

The nurse sighs. I can hear pages turning and, in a tone that indicates she is talking to herself, 'This bloody system . . . It's only a sprain . . . It wouldn't be ideal but I suppose we could get him into emergency accommodation.'

'He can come to our house for a few days.' The words are out before I can stop them. The image of this fiercely independent old man, whose roof for so many years was an infinite sky, thrust into some overcrowded B-and-B in the inner city cheek by jowl with hordes of screaming kids, homeless drug addicts and bewildered asylum seekers is too upsetting to contemplate.

'Wonderful,' the nurse says. Then, probably afraid that, given half a chance, I'll retract the offer, 'Just a moment, Claudine. It is Claudine, isn't it? I'll put you on hold for a wee second while I check what the situation is in the ward. He'll be entitled to transport, of course, and we'll send someone with him so no need to bother yourself by coming in to the hospital. I'll call in myself to check on him. And I'll try to arrange for the loan of a wheelchair. They're like gold dust right now.' She clicks off.

Wheelchair? Me and my big mouth. What have I done? At the same time, the poor guy has to go somewhere . . .

'Sorry, Claudine, having a little difficulty getting through to the person I need, be with you shortly . . .' The nurse is back. 'Just a little longer, all right?'

'All right.'

She clicks off again.

I'll need time off to look after the poor old guy. I wonder how Bob will react.

Bob. The thought of him brings disquiet tumbling over my head. Yet I find that, for the present at least, I'm not agonising over my husband's infidelity. New me sneaks in to have a word: 'Could it be, Claudine Armstrong, that somewhere deep down you admit even partial liability?'

I think back to the debate I had with myself that night his aunt Louise came to dinner. If I remember, I buried my questions about our marriage by pouring all my energies into conniving to get the house. Now, although I would hate to admit it, those questions have come back, Lazarus-like, to haunt me.

I put myself in his shoes: maybe his inamorata was one of those adoring, sitting-at-his-feet types, flattering him and making him feel big? When did I last make him feel big? And while I wouldn't want anyone's marriage bounced on to the radar in the shocking way mine has been, maybe this event, awful as it is, was timely. I have to consider that I probably did take him for granted. When was the last time we had a serious discussion about 'us'? When did I last ask him about his feelings?

'Claudine? We're all set . . .' The nurse is back to explain to me what's to happen and I quail. However, I offered and can't back out – and, strangely, both new me and old me agree that, whatever about subconscious motives, I have performed a decent, charitable act.

It's not going to be easy. I've never had much to do with old people, except as clients, and I've certainly never had to nurse one – I've never had to nurse anyone, as a matter of fact, and while I hear complaints all the time about how difficult life is for carers and am always sympathetic, my sympathy up to now has been theoretical.

It's only when a taxi arrives and I see Coley's white head in the back seat and, crucially, the rope tying the half-open boot of the car over the handles of a wheelchair, that I realise, complaints to the contrary, what a hassle-free life I've led.

Thanking Providence that this is only temporary – the public-health nurse has assured me that, because of the unusual circumstances, he will be moved into his new accommodation 'as a top priority, Claudine' – I rush forward and pull open the door of the cab to shake my house guest's hand. 'How are you?'

'I'm fine, thank you.' His voice is weak. An old man's voice.

This is not the Pat I met, strong, agile and obstinately awkward. In the time since I last saw him, he seems to have aged, even shrunk. His eyes are filmy and dull, his colour ashen, possibly a reflection of the truly awful threadbare dressing-gown he wears: once this was white terry but now it's as limp and grey as an old floorcloth. It bears the faded legend, stencilled in blue, 'St Mary's'. His veined legs are bare, the right ankle tightly strapped. He also displays a livid bruise on the right side of his face. His hair is neatly combed and this, more than anything, seems to demonstrate how much of the stuffing has been knocked out of the poor man.

'Good afternoon!' The nurse's aide introduces herself cheerily, and while the taxi-man unties the rope and excavates the wheelchair and I, as useful as a spare thumb, stand watching, she helps the patient swing his bony legs sideways so he's sitting with his back to the open door. 'This great strong man. That right, pet?' She addresses this directly into his ear, raising her voice as though he's a baby, or deaf. 'You get plenty rest now in house of your friend and you be OK real soon.' Then she and the taxi-man, who has clearly done this before, make the transfer into the wheelchair with some assistance from Coley.

I watch in dismay. He's accepted this handling without a murmur. By contrast with the bolshy creature who swung that slash hook with such strength and confidence, he's as passive as a rag doll. How am I going to handle him on my own?

The aide anticipates this. 'He sleepy now. Lots of pills for pain.' She mimes throwing them into her mouth. 'He probably sleep for the rest of day. But he actually real good.

'His prescriptions.' She gives me two, and a white-paper

bag with bottles of pills. 'Instructions on there. Next dose at six, seven o'clock this evening, yes? And his stuff.' She reaches into the front of the car and takes out another, bigger, paper bag. She gives the lot to me and stands expectantly. 'OK?' She looks puzzled. 'We go inside?'

'How long can you stay?' I look fearfully towards the taxi-man, who is already getting into the driving seat, then back at the old man listing in the wheelchair, eyelids drooping in his lolling head.

'No worries.' The aide remains cheery. 'I stay fifteen minutes. Plenty of time.' She glances along the façade of the house. 'Nice place!' Again she bends to Coley's ear and semi-shouts, 'You lucky man!' She seizes the handles of the wheel-chair, pushes it towards the open front door and navigates the shallow step in front of it without difficulty.

The public-health nurse had warned me that my guest was not yet in a position to negotiate stairs and, once inside, I direct her along the corridor towards the downstairs bedroom I have set up. I had rushed to put fresh linen on the bed, had scoured the *en-suite* and then had opened the windows to air it. Just before we reach the door, the telephone rings. 'Sorry, I have to take this.'

'No worries, dear.' The aide carries on towards the bedroom.

The caller is a client, put on to me by Tommy. It's a marriage separation and, God love her, she's looking for something near Skerries for under two hundred K. I grab my list and see that there is one property on our books at €193,000; it's about a mile from the town and is in awful condition but could be tarted up. I make an appointment to show it to her tomorrow. But as I talk to the woman, I'm watching Coley being manoeuvred slowly through the door of his quarters. How would my aunt, that elegant woman, react to this frail, flaccid old man?

I'm in over my head. I should not only have listened to Bob's warnings about meddling in other people's business; I should have acted on them.

# 37

# REVISIONISM

The décor in the bedroom I've given Coley Quinn is wildly unsuitable for a man. Most of our house is done up in modern, broadly neutral colours, but after Bob and I once spent a weekend in one of those lovely Hidden Ireland hotels, I'd had a rush of blood to the head and papered this one's walls in a pattern of green leaves and spring blossoms. The bedcover and matching curtains are flowery too, in toning colours, there are lots of cushions and the carpet is a deep rose: it's lovely, if the English-country-garden look is your bag. I'd had a sentimental notion that it could be Louise's room, if she ever came to live with us, and put in a TV, also one of those high-backed, high-seated armchairs, upholstered in soft pink velvet, of the type you see beside hospital beds. But despite the feminine ambience, in another important respect it's by far the best room in the house for its present tenant: the previous owners had a disabled son and the doors to the bedroom and the *en-suite* are wide enough for a wheel-chair.

I spent an uneasy afternoon trying to concentrate on my work for OHPC while listening for signs that my patient was awake. When the aide ('Great room – nice sheets! Wow!') and I had got him into bed, I'd given him a little china hand bell, urging him to use it if he needed anything. He was so dozy he fell asleep right away, and I don't know whether he registered what I'd said. So, because I was listening out for tinkling, and tiptoeing into his room every half-hour to check on him, I couldn't concentrate and had to read paragraphs over and over again because I hadn't taken in their gist. Tommy, I have to say, had been decent when I explained that, once again, I'd need a bit of time off. 'Fine, fine,' he said. 'Just keep the mobile on.' Summer is a slack time of year in the property business so I didn't feel that bad.

It's six o'clock now and, with Bob due home in an hour, I feel I should wake the patient and bring him something to eat. Anyhow, according to the nurse's aide, he's due his tablets.

He's lying on his back, snoring lightly, mouth open. He must have been too warm because he has pushed off the bedclothes, exposing the upper half of his body in the navy pyjama jacket that the aide had produced from the brown-paper bag. He didn't even wake up when, with a glass of water and two painkillers, I placed a little tray with tea and toast on his night table – I had assumed that tea-and-toast was what elderly invalids required.

I look down at him now, at the prominent cheekbones rising from the weathered, seamed landscape of his face. There's hardship written on it and, at least in sleep, deep vulnerability; but as I could see in Violet how she must have looked at sixteen, I can see that he, too, must have been a beautiful young man. Their child must have grown up to be a stunning woman – maybe still is, even if she is approaching sixty.

Suppose my aunt rings? Should I put the old man on to her? Oh, God.

Bob isn't the only one who has given out to me about my impulsiveness: Daddy had always warned me that some day it would land me in real trouble. Well, here, in front of me, is trouble. Now I find myself asking automatically, as I usually do in tough times, How would he handle this?

With a shock, I realise I don't know. All my life, this type of question has been answered immediately – Daddy's gruff voice has been a constant in my head, but I can't hear him this time. The voice is gone. Instinctively, too, I know it's gone for good. I am on my own. I'm the grown-up. Perspiration gathers across my forehead, and I think I might suffocate.

This room is at the front of the house and the evening sun is streaming in. I walk over to the windows and throw them open, breathing deeply and compelling myself to concentrate on the silky sheen of the grass outside, the riotous flowerbed display of busy lizzies – Pamela hated them. Maybe that's why I've planted them year after year.

Why did she, of all people, pop into my head then?

Even more surprising, I find I'm standing outside my usual, judgemental self where she's concerned: I am considering, for the first time ever, how difficult it must have been for her to live beyond the ramparts Daddy and I had constructed around ourselves. After all, she had made efforts, always rejected, to mother me: in the early days of her occupancy, she used to come into my room to read me a bedtime story, but as soon as I saw her I would turn out the light. She persisted for a while, then gave up.

Fast forward to my twenty-first, on which she had given me a little diamond and aquamarine brooch that had been her grandmother's. 'It'll look lovely on your party dress, Claudine.' I didn't wear it and drew attention to that fact by wearing instead a cheap diamanté horse given to me by one of my friends. And two days later, having to sit beside her for form's sake at the meal after Daddy's funeral, I took my rage and sorrow out on her, virtually cutting her dead at a time when she, too, must have been grieving – which, in my selfishness, I did not consider. These images of my younger self, never fully confronted before, are truly awful. How did the woman put up with me? She was the one, after all, who had caught him in her arms as he had his heart-attack, less than a minute after he had led her on to the dancefloor. What must that have been like?

The old me shoots to her feet and demands a hearing. 'What about the legacy débâcle?'

You can't work in the property area without gaining first-hand knowledge of how wills and legacies are a notorious breeding-ground for discord within the nicest, sanest families, and relentless new me now points out that my father was a shrewd businessman. He had been round the block when he met Pamela: he would have recognised a gold-digger, wouldn't he? He was so protective of me and my interests that he wouldn't have compromised them? A sneaky thought occurs: maybe, as with Bob's infidelity, there were two sides to the story of the disposition of Daddy's estate.

And now a strange thing happens. With Daddy's voice absent, one flash of this line of thinking has been enough to clear at least some of the bitterness, as thick as the brambles around Whitecliff, that I have so assiduously cultivated around memories of my stepmother. After all, Pamela had lived with my father and had had to put up with the fact that I, not she, ruled her household for seventeen years. She deserved her dues. She might have been more reasonable, even generous, if I hadn't been so hell bent on court action from the start.

As for Daddy, hard though it is, I may have to accept he wasn't altogether the flawless saint I have created. He might have made things easier for his wife but he didn't: he always took my side against her and indulged me. Again, I remember Violet's mention of his stubborn streak and, reluctantly, have to acknowledge that this rings true. For my sake, despite my grandparents' coldness towards him, he could have swallowed his pride and made an effort to keep me in touch with my mother's family, but he didn't.

And in the years since he died, I have conveniently ignored, or quashed, a few other not so saintly traits: Violet's mention of his low flashpoint, for instance, when irritation over a small matter might flare without warning into a full-blown temper tantrum, had to be acknowledged too. I never had to bear the brunt of this – and if I witnessed it, I smugly blamed Pamela, telling myself she must have provoked him.

Revision of passionate (if skewed) beliefs is difficult for anyone, and the destabilisation of the image and memory of the person who has underpinned, even defined, my entire life is excruciating. It's too much for now. I'll think about it some other time. I promise I will. Right now I have things to do. I check my watch. I must wake Coley Quinn. He's been asleep for more than four and a half hours.

But shouldn't I let him continue? Sleep is the best doctor—

Stop it, Claudine. You're procrastinating because you don't want to deal with it.

I deal with it. His tea will be getting cold anyhow. I go back and shake his shoulder gently.

He opens his eyes but I can see from his puzzled expression

that at first he has no idea where he is or who I am. 'Hello, Colman. I'm Claudine. Remember? You came here from the hospital to stay for a few days.'

Recognition dawns and he tries to sit up but, evidently having put pressure on his sore ankle, winces and falls back. 'Take your time. Here, let me help you.' I perform my first solo act of nursing, placing my arm under his shoulders and heaving, while at the same time inserting extra pillows behind him so he is semi-upright. 'It's time for your tablets.' I hear myself ape the loud, cheery tone of the nurse's aide. 'And I've made you some tea and toast. Are you hungry?'

'Thank you.' He's been asleep long enough for the mists to clear, because his voice is the one I remember from our encounter at Whitecliff. 'I won't be taking any more of the tablets.' He hooshes himself higher. 'And thank you for the bed too. I'm sorry you've been put to this trouble. But I'll not be stopping. I'll stay the one night, if you don't mind, but I'll be out of your hair tomorrow.'

'Please don't be in any hurry. Your maisonette won't be ready for ten days, they said.'

'Hmmph!' Derisively. 'There'll be no maisonette.'

The transformation from weak, half-there invalid is extraordinary. Except that he's in pain and probably won't be able to walk, he's back to his old, narky self and there's little need for me to tread on eggshells around him.

'I need the toilet.' He looks away towards the door. 'Where is it, please?'

'It's right over there – through that white door.' I point towards the *en-suite*. 'Let me get the wheelchair.'

'No wheelchair.' He heaves himself off the bed and, using it as support, hops towards the bathroom.

342

As he closes the door behind him, I realise it's time I rang Bob. He's probably on his way home but he has a hands-free kit in the car.

I make the call from the hall and can hear he's in a good mood so, without preamble, I launch straight in. 'Hi, it's me. I have to keep my voice down. Now, I know you think I'm a terrible meddler—'

'Well, good evening to you too, Cee.'

'But it wasn't my fault—'

'What wasn't your fault?'

'Well, there's a bit of a situation here at home, but I didn't ask for this, Bob, it just sort of happened . . .'

## 38

# LORD OF THE ROADS

In fairness, when he gets home, Bob seems to have had enough time to come to terms with our unexpected guest and, beyond a few rueful shakes of the head, is relatively equable about it.

After he has flipped through his mail, he goes into Coley's room to introduce himself and have a chat. I leave them to it, figuring that my presence would mess things up. But I'm hovering in the corridor near the bedroom when he comes out, carrying the tea-tray. 'Well? How'd you find him?'

'You were right about him being independent.' He closes the door. 'He insists he's leaving tomorrow, but that's daft. I didn't push it – it wasn't the time. He did admit he's hungry, though, so I said you'd bring him in a rasher sandwich or something and, in the meantime, I turned on the TV for him. Apparently he hasn't seen TV for donkey's years and I had to show him how to use a remote control. He's sitting up there now in the bed, flicking away.'

'Thanks, Bob.' I go to hug him but just in time remember why I shouldn't. So I turn it into a touch on his arm. 'I know it's a lot to land on you like this. You're being very good about it.'

'Sure I'm a saint!' Then he grins. 'Don't answer that.'

Half an hour later, having given my patient his rasher sandwich, I'm standing beside his bed, with the despised pills in one hand, water in the other. 'You must be in pain, Colman, and you'll need to sleep.'

'I've had worse.' His eyes are already straying again towards his television where the occupants of the Big Brother house are sitting around the floodlit pool. 'And I've had enough sleep.'

'Well, if you're comfortable enough, see you in the morning, then?' He doesn't answer and when I bid him goodnight, he doesn't hear.

Next morning is stormy, the kind of morning when the inclination is to snuggle down under the bedclothes and wish the day away. But when I take breakfast in to my invalid, I find him sitting up, fully alert with remote in hand. On screen, the Big Brother cameras are switching between the kitchen – where two of the housemates are arguing over what's left of a sliced pan – and the dim, foggy-looking bedrooms, where the rest of them are still asleep. 'Good morning, Coley, did you have a good night?'

He drags himself away from the programme. 'Yes, thank you.'

I place his breakfast tray on his lap. 'I remember from the time we met that you like cornflakes. But I've taken the liberty of giving you a bit of scrambled egg on toast as well. OK?'

'Thanks.' He picks up the remote again and I fear he's going to turn up the sound to drown me out. Instead, he switches the TV off and looks up at me with eyes restored to the clarity I remember from the hour I'd spent with him at Whitecliff. 'I know who you are.'

'What?'

'The minute you turned up at that wall, I knew you from somewhere but it wasn't until you mentioned your da was Chris Magennis that I realised.'

'But you said nothing?'

'You put on a good act yourself. Why'd you take me into your house?'

I explain that I'd gone up to Whitecliff again only to find him missing. 'I was worried about you. I just made a few enquiries, that's all. It seems they had nowhere to put you. It's no big deal, really – I couldn't have them turfing you out on to the side of the road, now, could I? Anyone would have done the same, and Bob and I are rattling around in this big house, just the two of us.'

I pour tea into the cup on the tray. 'You may or may not believe me, Colman, but I didn't know until a few days ago that I was connected to that family. That bit of a conversation we had about the rumours and legends concerning Whitecliff that day we met? I was only repeating stories I'd heard over the years.'

'So how did you find out, then?' His expression is as sceptical as any I've ever seen.

I pull the upright granny-chair into a position facing him so he can see me without strain. What I'm thinking is that if the old bastard had said something, anything, about recognising me that afternoon I might have been a bit more emotionally prepared to meet my aunt. But I suppose we'd had opposing priorities that day: mine was to acquire the house, his to protect his own bailiwick. 'How did I find out? Easy. I learned the Whitecliff family name was Shine, that this is the name on the deeds of the house. My mother's name. It's been an extraordinary few days, learning about my mother's family.' I'm quite proud of myself. No lies, not the whole story but, as far as it goes, incontrovertible. 'At the time, you thought I was coming to suss out the house because I wanted it for myself.'

'Of course. After I recognised who you were. How come you didn't know until now?'

'That's a good question. My mother died having me, as I think I told you already, and my father seems to have had his own reasons not to tell me too much about her family. Is that why you let me into the house, by the way? Because you recognised who I was?'

'Why wouldn't I? You'd every right.'

'I was telling the truth when I said my employer had sent me there. Do you remember I said I worked for a real-estate company?'

'I remember.' He's staring at me.

'Something wrong, Colman?'

'Nothing wrong.'

Although I'm dying to seize him by the arm and tell him my aunt is alive and well and I can take him to her this morning, new me is in the ascendant and I remain careful. 'Something on your mind, then?'

'Me and Violet Shine were together when we were young. She was the youngest. She was—' He changes his mind. 'It didn't work out.'

'I see.' I try to keep my tone noncommittal. 'Is that why you decided to move on to that land?'

'About ten years ago I got this mad notion that she might come back some time to look at the house, like, but she never did.'

'Do you know where she is she now?'

'Dunno,' he says bleakly. 'Dunno whether she's alive or dead.'

I wait.

'I came back from over for my mother's funeral,' he says then. 'She died in 1970. My sister Florrie and me used to write to each other, d'you see, and years back it was her told me that there'd been no sign of Violet Shine and that the story around the place was that her people had packed her off to America. But it was only at that funeral Florrie told me that the sister, Johanna, had moved out of the Big House a good few years ago and was living in West Cork.'

'How did she know that?'

He raises his eyebrows. 'Why wouldn't she? Everyone in Rathlinney knew about Johanna Shine gettin' married and going down there. Rathlinney's a small place and it was news at the time. Florrie even had the name of the townland she went to. It never occurred to me to ask how.' He stops and it's obvious he wants to tell me something significant. I feel I know what it is. 'You went down there, didn't you?'

'I did,' he says immediately. 'I did. Just the once. I thought it might be a bit of a chance. I couldn't exactly march up the driveway to the Big House in Maghcolla to have a tea-party with the mother and father and demand to know where Violet was these days, could I?' He smiles wanly.

'And what did Johanna tell you?'

'She told me what she knew.' His stare intensifies, and I figure we're playing a complex game: that just as I'm trying to suss out how much he knows, he's fishing for the same

348

with me. I feel my loyalty is to my aunt so I can't show my hand. Not yet. 'What was that?'

'She told me there was a child, a little girl she was. And that she was adopted by Americans.' He has difficulty with this and I feel desperately sorry for him. The urge to spill what I know is almost overwhelming. But I can't, I can't.

'I got no change out of Johanna about what happened to Violet after the baby.' His eyes swivel towards the bed covers. He's remembering. 'Except,' he pauses, 'except that she said that's why Violet was sent to America after.'

'Oh?' I hold my breath. 'Did you ask for her address?'

'She seemed frightened to tell me any more. Don't forget, the mother and father were still alive. It was Johanna's husband jumped in then. He said it was true. He said,' he lowers his head further, 'that she was gettin' married over there.'

Oh, God, oh, God, more secrets, I think, praying that I can keep a rein on my tongue while at the same time vowing, new me or not, that I won't keep this poor man in the dark for long.

'They knew who I was, d'you see,' he continues, head still bowed, 'and why I was asking. I suppose he thought I was going to upset the applecart for his wife and was protecting her, like. The two of them probably thought I'd rush away after Violet and cause problems for the whole family. They were all afraid of the parents, and Johanna was always a gentle little thing. Not like Violet,' he adds softly. 'Chalk and cheese they were, them two.'

'What did you say when you got that news?'

'What could I say? It was all over then, wasn't it?' He shrugs, but I can't see his expression. 'I went back over. Nothing for me here, was there?'

'What about your daughter?' I'm trying to be as gentle as I can. 'Were you not anxious to find out what happened to her? This was what? 1970? She would have been in her twenties by then—'

This triggers anger. 'Not want to find out? What do you think? Johanna Shine told me Willis had taken the child away for Americans to adopt. And as far as I could make out, that's what Violet was told too. But at least I knew from what she'd said that one more person outside that family knew about me daughter because he was there that night and I decided to go ask the horse's mouth for some information. Horse's arse, more like.' He breathes this last to himself.

'I beg your pardon?'

'That doctor! I went to see that gobshite doctor!' And just as Violet had got caught up in her story, he is caught up now in his and I'm not sure if my presence is even relevant. 'I'd heard, bad cess to him, that the man was on the way out but I didn't give a shit. His wife didn't want to let me into the house but I went in anyways.

'There he was in the bed, lovely and soft and comfortable it looked, and him shrunk to a small little wisp of a thing in it. He used to trot round in a horse and cart, you know, lord of the roads, he thought he was. Well, he was no lord now. He got a right land when he saw me. "I've no money up here," he bleats, like a frightened sheep. He thought I was an intruder, d'you see, coming in to rob him blind, and when I told him my name,' he smiles a thin, sour smile, 'he got even more frightened. Well, I might have been in a bit of a temper that day and I might even have had a bit of drink taken. I don't touch it now but in them days I was fond of the few jars.'

The smile hardens. 'I sat down on the side of his bed anyways, nearly on top of him I was, and I told him straight out that I wouldn't leave his house until he told me what he did with my child that night. I wanted names and addresses.'

He's breathing hard in an effort to calm down. 'Willis was a convert, you know, and I suppose converts worry about sin more than the rest of us do, and he knew he was dying – and maybe that's why he told me what really happened, his conscience, d'you see—' He stops. During the five minutes we had been having this conversation, whatever colour had been in his cheeks has drained away. He looks exhausted.

'If this is too hard for you, Colman – and by the way your eggs must be stone cold by now—'

'Hard?' He's contemptuous. 'Lady, you don't know hard. Do you know what that holy Catholic doctor did with her? With that little child?'

I hold my tongue. I couldn't have got a word in anyhow.

'There was no American adoption. That flea-bitten shite-hawk whined at me that "under instructions" he wrapped up my child, and at four o'clock that same morning, he left her outside an orphanage with a note attached to her. Then he rang the outside bell and ran away.'

# 39

# TEMPERING INTEMPERANCE

Oh, how I wish Johanna was here. She was such a wise soul and she would have known if we were doing the right thing. It would also have been exciting to travel together. I knew things were different nowadays, but had no idea quite how different. We do not have any rail service within ninety miles of Johanna's house and I have not taken a train since the 1940s when my carriage was pulled by a belching steam engine and when a window was let down on its strap, one was engulfed in gusty warm air, pungent with smuts.

Trains, these days, seem more comfortable, certainly more colourful, but the individual seats are very close together, giving one quite a feeling of claustrophobia; I miss that lovely chug-chugging sensation underfoot. Somehow, with this breathtaking but silent speed, with rucksacks and cheap canvas sports bags piled everywhere higgledy-piggledy – instead of brown-paper parcels, picnic baskets and smart leather suitcases on cats' cradles overhead – I believe that perhaps something nice has been lost. Perhaps it is different in first class, but one cannot even open a window and I dearly wish I could; the smell of the cheese and onion potato crisps being crunched by my seat companion is overpowering.

I do not mean to sound retrograde, I am all for progress, and this is certainly an adventure, which, given different circumstances, I might thoroughly enjoy. People along the way were very helpful too, pointing me in the right direction and showing me what to do – it is one of the advantages of being elderly. Right now, however, I am so nervous I am considering alighting from this train at the next stop and taking the next one home. After all, no one would be any the wiser and it would cost me nothing except a dent in my self-esteem.

My decision to make this journey had seemed perfectly logical in the darkness of last night. Now, however, the nearer we get to the city, the more anxious I become. I am constantly changing my mind: while my stomach churns with the excitement of possibility (and in wonder at my own audacity), my mind informs me I have been rash.

Claudine is not aware that I am on my way to Dublin: it was a very quick decision, and when I tried to telephone her this morning to advise her, her house number was engaged for the half-hour I tried it and her mobile number did not ring at all but went straight to her voice, which asked me to leave a message. I did not leave one: I felt that if I waited until she rang me back, I might lose courage in the interim. I would also have missed this train.

I have no idea how she will react, but she is a modern woman and is probably accustomed to her friends dropping in. She invited me to stay, and although initially I thought I would accept her hospitality, I have changed my mind and shall not impose this time. My plan is to book in somewhere small but pleasant in a back-street.

I believe we both need to consider what has happened to us before we meet again. Until a few days ago, my niece had lived for more than forty years in blithe ignorance of my existence, while I cared not enough to try to find her. Now that we have surfaced in each other's world – and only time will tell whether or not this has been a good thing – there is no going back. Over the period we spoke together in Johanna's house, and even more since she left, my life, which I had thought settled, has been in a state of constant eruption and flux. While I was unable to sleep last night in the silence of the countryside, I realised that because so much of a fundamental nature has changed it is now impossible for me to revert to my isolated but serene way of life – and if I am confused, Claudine must be doubly so. My revelations must have struck her as painfully as a bolt of lightning. I have a duty, have I not, to help her? I must fill in some gaps in her knowledge of her dear mother, even though my ability to help in this regard is limited.

I have asked myself if I am using Claudine's upset as an excuse to justify this journey. In all truth, the answer is no. I am here because the agitation and bother caused by my niece's visit has brought dreams of my daughter and of Coley Quinn to fever pitch. The yearning to meet my daughter before I die has never been absent from my life since the night she was born. Having intensified, if that is possible, in recent years, it has in the past few days become so strong it takes my breath away.

As for Coley, since we were so summarily parted, there has not been a full day when I have not thought about him, or loved him freshly, but in that regard there is a running sore in my heart: a short time before she died, Johanna confessed to me that, in search of me, he had come to visit her and Anthony many years before, she could not remember exactly when. Fearing what action he might take, she had been afraid to tell him the truth, and Anthony had backed her up in her story that I was in America, adding the detail, devastating for Coley, that I was engaged to be married. They never saw him again.

In telling me, she was inconsolable and there was never a moment when I felt anything for her but compassion as she sobbed in my arms. While she could not grant forgiveness to herself, she said, she begged for mine, which I gave immediately and with a full heart. 'The account is more than paid, Johanna,' I told her, broken-hearted to see her grieve so. 'You and your Anthony rescued me. You are my dearest darling sister and friend, please don't distress yourself.'

In private, however, I cannot tell you what a blow that news was to me and for many days I, too, was distraught: it seemed like the final act in the melodrama of my life, an extinction of hope. I could not let her see how badly it had affected me, however, because among our family, I believe that Johanna was the only one of deep faith and as she got ready to meet her Maker, as she saw it, she had to be reassured that all was well.

In latter years, I have tried to temper my intemperate thoughts of Coley with the knowledge that, at my age, this urgent desire to revisit a long-ago love might well be absurd. The Coley I loved could not be the Coley he is now, any more than the Violet I have become (so changed in personality and appearance) could be the girl who was snatched from him and whom if he still lives he probably pictures. And so, inexperienced in these matters as I may be, in my more rational moments I accept that my continuing love for Coley Quinn is an impostor: that love in the absence of the beloved is probably best left to poets. What is more, I am fearful that an actual meeting could be catastrophic and Coley and I would be much better off with the purity and bitter-sweetness of our memories left intact.

Anyhow, there is practically no possibility we will ever meet again so the longing to do so is redundant; nevertheless, I ache with it.

Since Claudine Armstrong arrived at my doorstep I have found hope to be a resilient warrior, determined to winkle me away from passive hiding in the hinterland of Western Europe. In fact, my niece's visit, her reaction to my story, has thrown a glaring light on how passive I have been for most of my life. I could make many excuses for it, and have, but no longer. It may be too late to achieve any result, but I am determined I will no longer behave like a sloth and, as long as my energy holds out, will from now on exert every ounce of it in pursuit of goals I should have pursued many years ago.

If I ask them, I have no doubt that she and her husband, both of whom seem very efficient, will help me. Even with their assistance, it is possible that the search either for my daughter or for news of Coley may not bear fruit, but at least I can go to my grave in the knowledge that I have tried.

I am sure Claudine and her husband find it incomprehensible that, whatever about Coley, I have not until now made an effort to find my daughter. Part of the reason why must be self-evident to the most casual observer: when I was released, I believe I was but half formed as a person, intellectually capable but emotionally stunted. Rightly or wrongly, as I told my niece, I came to the conclusion that I would be acting to fulfil my own needs and it would be selfish of me to cause upheaval in what I hoped was a good life with good parents whom she believed were hers. Perhaps a psychologist would tell me that this was post-rationalisation, or fear of rejection – it matters little now. My longing for my daughter will no longer be denied.

In my heart, she remains an infant but while I lay awake last night, I came to terms with the reality that wherever she is, she is nearly sixty now.

Of course I had always known her chronological age to within a few days and every Christmas had marked her birthday. What happened last night was more profound than that, however: it was the realisation that, whatever the popular misconception that chronological youth can last until death – where one reads that 'forty is the new thirty', for instance, or 'sixty is the new fifty' and so on – sixty is, in fact, a highly significant milestone. At that age, with a few exceptions, most people have less than a third of their lives left before them.

My daughter and I are both running out of time: 'some day' has become now and since she is incontrovertibly a grown woman, whatever way her life has gone it is probably set. It is, therefore, unlikely that my appearance in it, even if it shocks her at first, will cause irreparable upheaval.

So, the overriding force that will keep me from turning round to board that train home is the conviction that the best chance I have of finding news of my daughter or of Coley Quinn is in a city stuffed with resources and with an obviously kind couple on hand to help. To sit alone in Johanna and Anthony's house in the countryside of Béara offers me none.

# 40

# A POSSIBLE TRACE

'There was no American couple?' In the background I can hear the echoing whine, clash and clang of machinery: Bob has taken my call in the workshop of his dealership. 'But as soon as he found out, why didn't he do something about it?'

'I did ask him, when he'd calmed down. But his answer was logical. He had no money, and not the faintest clue how to go about it. I think, too, reading between the lines, that in the past he might have hit the bottle a bit. But Bob, why do you think my grandparents ordered that to be done to a little baby? The way she tells it I can almost understand why they locked her up, dreadful though that was, but why do you think they lied to her about the American adoption? That was appalling!'

'Who knows? People have very mixed motives. My guess is that it was a sort of inverted kindness. They wanted her to believe that her baby was going to a good life. They wanted her to be able to let go.'

'Then why not arrange an actual adoption?'

'That's easier to figure out, horrible as it is. From what she told us, it sounded like public image was everything in that family. I suppose they were afraid the kid might learn who they were and come back to haunt them, create a scandal.'

'Inverted kindness': I roll the phrase round in my head. It's something to hang on to, I suppose.

The doorbell rings. 'I have to go, Bob. Will you give me a shout back when you get a chance?' He promises he will and I make for the door.

'Hope I'm not too early.' The caller dripping on my front doorstep is my phone buddy, the public-health nurse. I know who she is because I recognise her voice, although she looks nothing like the large, overpowering person I had imagined from her bossy phone manner: this woman is a little choux pastry, plump and fair and about five feet tall. 'I thought I'd catch you on my way to work.' She shakes out her umbrella, then looks up at me. 'It's only a short bit out of my way. I live in The Naul, don't you know.'

'Great! Please come in. You're not early at all.' I hold the door wide for her. 'We're well aired.'

After exchanging pleasantries about the foul weather and all the housing and road development ruining the character of where we live, we have a short conversation in the hall outside Coley's door where I tell her about Coley's refusal to take any more tablets, and his stated intention to leave today.

'Fine.' She takes it all in her stride. 'We'll see what's what.' She gives me a handwritten business card with her name (Rosemary something, beginning with C – her handwriting is execrable) and a mobile number, should I need to contact her. Then I show her into Coley's room and retreat to the kitchen to wait for developments, instructions or whatever.

'He's physically grand.' She breezes into the kitchen about a quarter of an hour later. 'As tough as an old boot, actually. And I hope I've not been presumptuous but I think I've persuaded him to stay for another day or two here, if that's all right with you?'

'It's fine. He's no trouble, actually. We hardly know he's here.'

'You're a wee saint, Claudine. We'll organise a bit of physio for that ankle and don't you worry about it. You go about your own business. He'll be collected and delivered, would you trust him with a temporary key?'

I don't hesitate for a second. Whatever else he might have been, I have not a scintilla of doubt about Coley Quinn's honesty. 'With a heart and a half.'

'Brilliant. I'll do my best to gee up the work on the maisonette – I've prioritised his case because of his age and homelessness. We'll have him out of your hair as quickly as possible. There's just one thing. While he's good physically, I did think he was a wee bit agitated. "Something personal," he says, but I'm wondering if we shouldn't consider getting a doc to come in and look at him. He might need a mild tranquilliser. It happens with the elderly – they can get anxious about even small things.'

Now I hesitate. Should I tell her? While new me urges continued discretion, old me screams that this woman could be helpful with the big issue. She's in the general area of health and social work, after all, and she'd be used to dealing with all sorts. 'Look, Rosemary, I do know he has something very real and very big to be bothered about but it's highly confidential and I'm wondering if it's my place to tell you. Sometimes I'm inclined to go bald-headed into things and make a real mess. My motives are good, though,' I add quickly, in case I'm giving the impression I'm a basket case.

'Don't tell me if you don't want to.'

'I'm not sure – oh, feckit, do you have time for a cup of tea or coffee?'

'Always welcome. Coffee, please. And anything you tell me stays in this room. Lord knows, my poor little brain holds enough secrets to stock the vaults of MI5.' She takes off her coat and settles herself into one of the kitchen chairs.

She doesn't bat an eyelid during the telling of the story. I am brief, omitting the tower bit: it would be too much to take in and isn't germane. I tell her simply that in an era where pregnancy out of wedlock was the number-one scandal in the prevailing ethos of Ireland, Violet had become some-what of a recluse after she'd had her baby.

'I can see where you're coming from,' the nurse says briskly, at the end of it. 'It's an old story, isn't it? Very sad. Thank the Lord we've a more enlightened attitude now, but I can under-stand very well why your poor aunt would have elected at the time not to go into a mother-and-baby home. The things we're hearing about some of them these days!' She rolls her eyes. 'No wonder poor Colman's a bit edgy. Are you hinting he and your aunt might be interested in tracing the child at this late stage? And don't worry. I understand the softly-softly angle with the complications of them not knowing of each other's existence at the moment.'

'I think they'd be interested all right – but,' I add virtu-ously, 'I wouldn't want the process to get legs and run away without their involvement.'

'But you yourself would like to find this person, wouldn't you?' She grins.

Deirdre Purcell

'You can tell?'

'Sticking out a mile, my dear! No harm in making initial enquiries.' She stands up and plucks her coat from the back of her chair. 'I wouldn't be involved myself, but there are pretty good systems now – and you know there's new legislation and all that?'

'I know absolutely nothing, to be frank. Less than a week ago I knew nothing about any of this.'

She gulps the rest of her coffee. 'Can't promise anything. I'm not a social worker but I think the drill is that the impetus will have to come either from the parents or the child herself. I'm fairly sure that as a cousin you wouldn't qualify without the permission of the birth mother.'

'Of course. I understand. But it would be fantastic if you could mention it to one of your work colleagues. Just so we could get a steer—' I realise suddenly that the old me is about to take flight and so, rein her in. 'Best not to get their hopes up. Could it be our secret for the present?'

'Surely, Claudine. I'll be in touch soon. You have my numbers,' and she leaves.

When Bob rings again, some hours later, the lunchtime news is burbling in the background so I can tell he's relaxed and in his own office.

I give him a brief rundown on the nurse's visit and mention the tracing as something he had himself suggested: 'So we might talk to Violet about it if she brings it up.'

'Sure thing.' He pauses and I can almost hear him thinking. 'There's always the private-detective route, you know. We have a guy on our books, actually. He leases from us.'

'Sounds a bit drastic – but maybe if tracing doesn't work?

'And what about newspaper archives? I'll bet you anything

362

you like – I'll bet you a new car, Cee – that this would have been front-page news some time over that Christmas period in 1944. An abandoned baby? Any time it happens, the story is picked up by the newspapers, other media too. It's on TV and talk shows these days, people lap it up. I bet they did then too in the printed press. And this one's at Christmas? A wartime Christmas when everyone's starving for something other than war news and here's a little newborn baby in swaddling clothes? That kind of story is manna for newspapers. If I was an editor I'd have put the kid in a manger, with donkeys and goats and cows and little lambs – the whole shebang. Imagine the picture!'

'Gross!'

'A new car, Cee? Are we on?'

'What do I have to give you if I lose?'

'We'll think of something.' I can tell he's grinning.

'Oh, for pity's sake, get back to work and stop being such a bloody hero, willya?'

As I replace the telephone I think that, given opportunity, we do work well together, although we haven't done much of that lately. The way things are going right now, I might be on the verge of forgiving him. Unnoticed until now, forgiveness may even have crept up on me and is already blowing into my ear with vanilla-scented breath.

# 41

# A NICE PLACE TO STAY

I am bamboozled. My plan was to find a nice place to stay in a back-street but, as far as I can see, each street in the city is worse than the last, roaring with buses and cars and buzzing motorbikes and careless hordes of people rushing about. My last visit here was to the Theatre Royal: I am aware that it was demolished long ago but I am so disoriented I cannot even find the site so I can get my bearings. The noise is indescribable. Even O'Connell Street, where I am standing, is no longer recognisable but is buried under hoardings, cranes and heavy machinery. It seems to be all ripped apart.

Then I remember that Father used to speak highly of the Gresham Hotel and, dimly, it occurs to me that it is on this street.

I am standing near a bus stop, where there is a long queue of people. 'Excuse me?' I approach a middle-aged woman, laden with parcels.

'Yes, love?' She cups her ear against the racket of a pneumatic drill nearby.

'Could you tell me where the Gresham Hotel is, please?' I'm having to speak as loudly as I can.

'It's at the far end,' she yells in response, pointing. 'And it's on this side. You can't miss it. Just keep walkin', but listen, love, you mind yourself now, and take your time. With all these bloomin' roadworks, you'd never know where there'd be holes. There's new ones every day. Breedin' they are.'

I thank her and set off, keeping as close as possible to the inside of the footpath to avoid being jostled. Luckily, I have brought with me just one small overnight bag but even that is proving quite heavy.

It is a relief to reach the hotel but once inside, as I drop my bag on to the polished marble floor, I see that it will be too expensive for my limited means. Yet right now I am exhausted from lack of sleep, compounded by the exigencies of the journey, and cannot face going back outside where, I notice through the revolving doors, it has now started to rain.

As I stand, locked in indecision, a small man in a uniform comes towards me. 'Are you all right there, ma'am? Can I do anything for you?'

'I should like a cup of tea,' I draw on every last shred of self-confidence, 'but I'm afraid it's my first time here and I don't know where to go.'

'No problem.' He picks up my bag. 'Come on with me, and I'll get someone to look after you. This way.' He leads me into a plush lounge bar, furnished with easy chairs and sofas and with what look to be genuine artworks on the walls. There are large windows at one end, through which there are views directly on to the street. Although many of the tables are occupied, the atmosphere is peaceful. He installs me in a corner beside a window. 'Relax there now, love, I'll send someone over straight away,' he says, and bustles off.

Dublin people can be very nice, I think, settling gratefully against the cushions.

I spend the next hour sipping tea and nibbling at a very expensive but tasty smoked-salmon sandwich, while I watch what appears to be the whole of Dublin's population passing by my window. At this end of the street, the construction work is minimal, the rain had been just a shower, the sun is shining and it is a delight to see young women exhibiting firm, tanned skin as they push their babies in buggies. The young men, I find, with the exception of those in business suits, are less fashion-conscious, tending to favour T-shirts and denim jeans in all shapes, from glove-tight to baggy. No one has pressured me to hurry or move out of this pleasant seat and I find I am thoroughly enjoying myself, a true novelty, yet the enjoyment is tinged with regret: I have led such a quiet, solitary life, I think, it is a pity that it is only now, when it is coming to a close, that I am allowed a glimpse of what might have been.

I shake this off immediately. Why complicate such a simple treat?

I am fascinated by the young couple on the seat in the other corner of the room. I find it difficult to judge young people's ages, but they must be at least eighteen because they have been drinking champagne and have just now ordered two more snipes. They, too, might have been enjoying the passing parade through their window but they are so enthralled with one another's company that they look nowhere except into each other's eyes, lovebirds in a glass cage. They have not noticed that I have been staring at them for at least fifteen minutes.

In no sense could I say that they remind me of Coley and me at that age: they differ from us as yellow does from black, not only in their glossy good looks and the careless sophistication of their clothes, but most specifically in that they take no pains to conceal their sexual hunger for each other but stroke and pat, giggle and whisper, showing no embarrassment whatsoever. What are they celebrating? Their engagement? Or could they be on honeymoon? Neither wears a ring so it is probably not the latter.

As I continue to watch, the girl stands up, gathers up her handbag, kisses her young man, and says, loudly enough for me to hear, that he shouldn't go away, that she'll be back in a jiffy. Then, blowing him another kiss, she trips gaily away from him, searching high along the walls – obviously for signs directing her to a bathroom – and I am utterly shocked to see she is pregnant, which I had not before noticed under the fringed silk shawl she wears over her low-cut black dress.

Enjoyment haemorrhages from the afternoon and, for a moment, the world seems to turn black and white – not from my disapproval, you understand, but from eviscerating pain: could the contrast between the estate of this vibrant young couple and that occupied by Coley and me sixty years ago be more stark?

Now I notice that there are eviscerations everywhere in that room. That svelte American girl – she is wearing a jacket with PROUD TO BE A DEMOCRAT written across the back – who is sitting alone making notes from a heavy hardback book: a student? Is this what my daughter might have looked like forty years ago while at college in America? What does she look like now? I do not even know her name.

That older woman drinking wine happily in the company of two younger ones, all three laughing uproariously at some joke: mother and daughters?

The couple sitting beside each other, he with a pen in his hand, both in quiet contemplation of a crossword clue. Coley and I in middle age?

This is what life offers. It is what life did not offer me. For the very first time in many, many years, anger, hot and wild as bushfire, rampages through my body.

I pick up my overnight bag, my coat, my handbag and my umbrella and go to the reception desk of the Gresham Hotel to book in. I need immediate privacy.

I ascertain the room rate and, although it is savagely expensive for someone of my means, request one for a night. I am asked for a credit card.

'I'm sorry, I do not have one. I shall be paying cash.'

The young woman behind the desk is nonplussed and excuses herself for a moment. She comes back with a man, who asks if I have any identification. I am becoming angrier by the moment, but I give him the pass that entitles me to free travel.

'Is that the only identification you have, madam?'

'It is. Is there something wrong with it?' I am aware my voice has risen.

'Not at all, madam.' He looks around to see who has noticed. Clearly he does not want an altercation and he has seen that I am on the very precipice of giving him one. He hands me back the pass with a deprecatory smile. 'I apologise, madam.'

He has been perfectly amiable throughout, as has the young woman. They are blameless, and I have behaved badly. My anger subsides as he hands me a piece of paper and shows me where to sign. Then he asks me for the cash in advance. I pay it, aware as I count it out that I will now have less than twenty euros left in my purse. 'Thank you, madam. Have a good evening. Breakfast is from six thirty. Will you be wanting a morning newspaper?'

'No, thank you.'

'Your key? Room 227 on the second floor.' He hands me a little card in a notebook. I do not blink. I will certainly not betray my ignorance of how this flat rectangle of plastic could work as a key. He shows me where the lift is.

I thank him and, eschewing the help of a porter (I am thinking of my depleted store of cash; my need to conserve it overrides entitlements to gratuities), aware that he and the young woman are looking after me, keep my back ultra-straight as I sweep towards it. At least I know how a lift works: there is one in Mr Thorpe's office building.

I find my way to room 227. Luckily, the little card folder displays instructions and, after only one false start, I am inside. I barely notice my surroundings: anger has now drained away, taking with it the last vestiges of energy. I am done in.

In her last weeks of life, Johanna had great difficulty sleeping and was prescribed tablets, some of which have remained in our bathroom cabinet. I have swallowed one now and then, during periods of persistent insomnia, and have found them therapeutic. Having slept so badly for the last two nights, I had taken the precaution of packing the little phial. I wash one of the pills down with the bottled water kindly supplied by the Gresham Hotel. I do not care that it is only six in the evening.

I pull the heavy curtains to block out the light, and by the time I have undressed and am in bed, the drug is taking effect. My last waking image on the first night I have ever spent in Dublin is not of my daughter or of Coley but, puzzlingly, of my mother. She is wearing the robes of the guardian angel in Nanny's picture and is floating free above my tower at Whitecliff.

The next morning, for several minutes after I wake, the afterglow of sleep persists and I feel delicious, featherlight, adrift in a calm sky. It is a feeling I want to prolong and, stretching to my full length, I luxuriate in the warmth and smoothness of sheets and soft pillows in the immensity of this unfamiliar bed.

Gradually, like unfolding origami, I remember where I am and why. I check the numerals glowing red on the bedside clock. Although I can hear the muffled sound of traffic outside, it is still only 6.15 a.m., but I have slept for more than twelve hours.

I snuggle against the pillows to allow my brain, refreshed but barely ticking over, lazily to scan the possibilities of the coming day. As consciousness returns, so does the urge to start my searches. Should I telephone Claudine as soon as the hour is respectable enough? Then I remember the pleasures rather than the pain of yesterday afternoon and wonder if, rather than involve her straight away and plunging us both into renewed intensity, I should take advantage of this unprecedented freedom to have a little holiday. No one on earth knows where I am at present.

With so little money in my purse, the options are limited, but with my travel pass, I could spend the day riding the buses – and I am aware that the museums and National Art Gallery have free entrance. I have until five thirty this evening, the time of my train. Eleven whole hours – the prospect is attractive.

Everything seems so much brighter this morning as I lie

in this huge, wonderful bed – no wonder they charge so much in this hotel: the laundry bills for linens of this size must be astronomical. I am aware that I am hungry – also an unusual sensation for me of late. The young man at Reception had said that breakfast is at six thirty: I shall be one of the first customers, and I shall eat so much I will not need to eat again for the rest of the day.

Perhaps it is the effects of Johanna's drug, but the anger and distress of yesterday afternoon seem melodramatic now, their intensity a distant memory. I indulged in bitter, unworthy thoughts in that lounge bar, and now I ask myself, Of what benefit was it to me? Of what benefit is bitterness to anyone, except to keep the blood unpleasantly on the boil?

I get out of bed to run my bath: I shall take advantage of everything this hotel has to offer. I shall use every drop in the little bottles of shampoo and conditioner and shall dry my hair with the convenient hair-dryer on the wall; I shall fill my bathwater with scented bubbles and employ all four towels on the rack. By the time I have finished and am dressed, it will be time for breakfast, when I shall eat and drink as much as I can from everything on the menu.

Then I shall go out into the Dublin morning. I shall choose between a trip to Howth or Dalkey – those mythical places of which I have read so much in newspaper columns – to see for myself 'how the other half lives', as they say. Or I might go to a bookshop and indulge in the free pursuit of browsing or even, for a time, sit in a café where no one will watch me or make judgements about me, good or bad. The benefits of anonymity!

The bath should be drawn by now, I think, but here I see in this leather folder on my dressing-table that I do not have

Deirdre Purcell

to check out of this hotel until noon. Perhaps this morning I shall do nothing except lounge around in luxury, enjoying this magnificent room.

What wonderful choices, I think, as I step into the bath. What a beautiful day!

The giddiness ebbs more than a little when I get out again because I see through the steam a mirror image not of the carefree sprite I had somehow made of myself but a pink, silly old lady with dripping hair, wrapped in a white bath-towel. This old lady is here on a mission, not a jaunt – and with that thought, sanity prevails. Almost. Because while I stare at myself, I realise wistfully that I had never before in my life had the prospect of such a carefree day.

The thrill and intensity of the encounters between Coley Quinn and myself were in a different category from what I had envisaged for today – a taste of what most people take for granted. It is difficult to let the idea go.

I decide to compromise. While I shall start my searches when offices open, the rest of the morning will be spent enjoying my freedom. I shall telephone Claudine at lunchtime and see what that brings.

## 42

## SALT CELLARS

Early next morning, after Coley was collected for his physio, I get ready to head into Dublin. I planned to visit both the Register of Births, Marriages and Deaths and the National Library, where they keep the newspaper archives I'd need to peruse if I'm to follow the second of Bob's two suggestions. Not mine, you'll notice! No bull-in-a-china-shop rampage envisaged: just a calm browse. No harm, I reckon, in making a few enquiries, so that if Violet ever does bring it up, I will have at least some information for her.

My gut instinct is that she won't be long in asking. If I have been so piquantly aroused by the notion of looking for a mere cousin, how much more potent must be a mother's urge to look for the child to whom she gave birth? Being childless myself, the depth and strength of such a drive is difficult for me to understand but I should imagine it is physical as well as emotional; I'm convinced that although she hasn't searched before it doesn't mean she won't now, especially since, with my two big feet, I have cracked open her shell.

As well as being excited about what I might find, I'm

nervous about the nuts and bolts: I hadn't been inside the National Library, and although the lady who'd told me on the phone about the access procedures had been charming, I'd never before encountered the word 'microfiche' and didn't want to make an eejit of myself in what I presumed would be profoundly scholarly – and technologically competent – company.

On the way into town, however, my mobile goes off. It's Tommy O'Hare. He has double-booked himself and is in a stew. Greenparks, who are paying most of OHPC's bills right now, are having a board meeting and, at the last minute, the company wants him to attend for a couple of the agenda items so he has to hop to it. But he'd arranged to meet an English client, who is flying in specially for a viewing. 'I had to pull out all the stops to get him over. I know it's a big favour, Claudie, but I really need you to do this for me.'

I can hardly refuse. 'What time is he arriving?'

'You're a topper.' Tommy's relief dances across the air. 'Thanks a million, Claudie. I owe you one. I'm relying on you to snag him. Do anything, sleep with him if you have to.'

'Oh, very droll!'

Then he asks me if I've made any progress on the Whitecliff deal. 'I'll ring her the minute I hang up from you, Tom. I'll let you know as soon as there's anything.' I'm a little guilty anyway that I haven't been in touch with my aunt since that keeping-in-touch phone call the day before.

Whatever about (temporarily) keeping Coley's where-abouts to myself – he has rights too – she should know what really happened to her daughter. But when I ring her house, there's no answer. I have no idea whether that's odd or not because I don't know what her routines are: she's probably just out at the shops.

The viewing with the English client goes well, and having left him back to the airport, I report as much on my way home in the early afternoon.

The message machine is blinking at me when I let myself in but I hear the television blaring from Coley's room and go down to him first.

He's sitting in the chair beside his bed watching *Judge Judy*. 'Good afternoon, Colman. What's that?' I point to a glassful of pink gloopy stuff on the table beside him. 'It's a strawberry drink.' He glares at it. 'They said at the hospital that I'm not the right weight for my height.'

'Everything go OK there?'

'I've to go back in three days. They gave me a crutch!' He sounds agitated.

'Mind if I turn this down?' I'm finding it tough to compete with Judge Judy's stern telling-off of a fat, middle-aged woman whose hair is in blonde plaits, and pick up the remote. 'There, that's better. I'm sure you're ready for a cup of tea. Are you hungry?'

'No, thanks. They gave me a dinner voucher for the canteen in the hospital.'

'Well, it's not far off teatime now. I'll bring you in something later.'

'Don't be bothering yourself.' He's avoiding my gaze as if he's guilty – or something's worrying him. I wait, but when nothing's forthcoming, I leave him with the exhortation that he's to ring his little bell if he wants me. 'Or,' I stop in the doorway, 'maybe you'd like to come out into the kitchen. Change of scene, Colman?'

'Not at all, not at all. I'm grand here where I am. Couldn't be better.'

'Well, if you change your mind . . .' I leave him to it.

The message on the answering-machine is from Violet – thank goodness Coley's TV is again at top volume: it's hard to hear her, there's a great deal of noise and babble in the background – she's obviously on a public phone. 'This is Violet Shine speaking,' she says, in that awkward postcard style adopted by those who are uncomfortable with technology. 'Sorry you're not in, Claudine. I'll telephone again later. Thank you. Goodbye.'

The call is timed from ninety minutes previously. I ring back straight away but there's still no answer from her house. She couldn't have been out at the shops since mid-morning? I'm getting concerned. Was the call from a hospital, perhaps?

Don't be silly, Claudine. If she were in hospital she wouldn't be ringing you on a public phone. And anyway, it wouldn't be her, but someone in authority – a nurse or a doctor.

I should buy her a mobile phone.

And with that thought I notice I'm already thinking of her in the way I've heard others talk about the elderly rela- tives for whom they've taken responsibility. It's a rush. I like it. It gives me a feeling of belonging to something bigger than myself.

With that, the phone rings. This is probably her ringing back. I pick it up and utter a cheery hello. It's not Violet, it's Rosemary C, the nurse. She doesn't have much to tell me except to pass on the name and number of a social worker. 'I spoke to her briefly about that other matter, Claudine, and she'll be expecting your call. She's busy this afternoon, and she says you can ring her after six on her mobile, but if I

376

were you I'd wait until the morning. We oblige people but we all hate being disturbed at home. How's the patient?'

'Thanks for the steer, Rosemary – I'll wait until tomorrow. And Colman's fine! Becoming a telly addict, I think.'

'He could be addicted to a lot worse. The good news is I've moved heaven and earth to get his place sorted for him. Waiting for a call about it, actually.'

'Grand.'

'Gotta run. Good luck with your search.'

I thank her again and we break the connection.

While I'm unstacking the dishwasher fifteen minutes later, I hear a sound behind me and straighten up. It's Coley, minus his crutch, hanging on to the doorframe and holding his injured foot off the floor. 'Colman! Is anything the matter? Anything you need?'

'Nothing, nothing. If you're busy I'll come back – but you did say—'

'Come in, come in, I'm not busy at all.'

'Thanks. Do you mind if I sit down a spell?'

'Of course not.' I pull out one of the kitchen chairs for him and, using the wall as support, he hops across, lowers himself into it. 'Here.' I carry over the little stool I use to reach into the back of cupboards. 'Put your poor foot up on this.'

'Thank you very much, Claudine. And listen, I'm afraid I forgot me manners. I should've thanked you for your hospitality. I don't think I ever said it out straight. But I won't be bothering you much longer. I don't like being a charity case, d'you know?'

My heart melts as I look at him, old lion brought to heel. 'Of course I know that, Colman, but you're not a charity case, far from it, put that right out of your mind. We've enjoyed having you – sure we've hardly seen you at all. You're welcome to stay as long as you like.' I mean it.

'Well, anyways, they told me down at the hospital that the new house should be ready in a few days.'

'That's marvellous.' I stop myself. He doesn't seem to think it's marvellous. He's fidgety. He looks haunted, actually. 'Are you not happy about it, Colman?' I sit in the chair kitty corner to him. 'But you do know that, no matter what, you can no longer live in the open like you're used to? You were lucky with your ankle, that it was just a sprain, but suppose something serious happened to you and no one could see you in the middle of all those brambles and stuff?'

'I'll have to make the best of it but I don't like the idea of people tellin' me what to do. I'm not going to pretend it'll be easy. But, anyways, that's not it . . .' He trails off.

'Oh? Anything I can help with?'

'As a matter of fact, I just want to ask your opinion about something, Claudine.'

'Fire away.'

'Remember we were talking about my daughter, yesterday?'

'I certainly do.'

'Well, I was thinking . . .' He begins to play with a salt-cellar in front of him on the table, twirling it within its own axis.

'Take your time, Colman.' To give it to him, I get up and pretend to check that I've pressed the off button on the dish-washer.

When I get back, he seems more composed, although when he speaks again, he is addressing the salt, not me. 'I'm getting on now, d'you see,' he mutters. 'Everyone keeps telling me that and it's driving me crazy, but they don't have to point it out. I know it. This –' he raises his injured foot a couple of inches '– is the holy proof of it.' He places the salt precisely within a corner of the table. 'It would be nice just to meet her, to see what she's like.' He looks up at last. 'Just the one time, now. I wouldn't want to impose or anything like that. Just to see her the once.'

'And you want my opinion as to whether it's possible?'

'Yeah.' He beams in relief. 'And how I'd go about it, like.'

'Well, look, she's my cousin too, you know. My aunt's child – I wouldn't mind meeting her myself.'

'Begod, that's right!' His smile widens, then he erupts with that bark-like laugh. 'Of course!'

'There's an official way to trace people in these circumstances, you know. As a matter of fact I was asking the public-health nurse about it earlier when she was here. She's putting me in touch with – with someone who could help if we wanted it.' Given what I've seen of his attitude to 'the social', best not to mention social workers yet.

'I knew you'd have ideas, Claudine!' Unexpectedly, his eyes fill with tears. 'Sorry. I'm sorry.' He tries to wipe them away.

This time, feeling more and more like a Judas in that I have not told him yet about Violet, I pretend to see a rogue crumb on the floor. As I bend to pick it up, however, I remind myself once again that I have to respect her entitlements. I just do.

I straighten up again. I can't bear to see the hope in his eyes; couldn't cope if it were to be dashed. 'There are no guarantees, Coley,' I say quietly. 'As a matter of fact there are all kinds of risks. If we do manage to find her, she might be reluctant to co-operate. You can never predict how people will behave.'

'I'm sure she wouldn't be reluctant at all. Why would she? We could tell her in advance we won't bother her. We can tell her it's just the once we want to see her, Claudine!'

In his mind the poor guy is already walking towards her. I had been so occupied with Violet's pain and loss I hadn't really considered the depth of his. My mistake. Time to put the hope back – and to make sure there's a basis for it. 'I was also thinking we might try to rustle up a birth certificate for her. And I'm willing to bet that there was something in the papers at the time about her being abandoned. It would have been a great Christmas story at the time, I'll bet there were even photographs.' (Thank you, Bob!) 'What do you think, Colman?'

'Actually—' He stops. He is bright, bright red. 'Maybe if we went to the American embassy, they could help us find out what happened to Violet?'

## 43

# WHISKEY AND PIE

'I have to tell him, Bob!' I'm making this call from our bedroom so Coley can't possibly hear. 'She's rung here once already and left a message on the answering-machine. She'll ring again and he might hear her. He'd never forgive me – more importantly, she wouldn't – and now that he's brought it up, you can't accuse me of being bossy or of sticking my nose in to organise other people's lives!'

'Calm down, Cee. You're right. We have to tell them – both of them. At the time we discussed this we had no idea he'd turn up in our spare bedroom, did we? And before you say anything,' he speeds up as I draw breath, 'I know how it happened, and I probably would have offered, the same as you did. You'd want to have a heart of stone to let the poor man be shoved around from pillar to post just because he's unlucky enough to have no one to take care of him. But take this one handy, won't you?'

'I will. Tell you what, I'll hold off until you come home. You'd never know how he'd react. Underneath all that macho stuff he's very emotional. The problem is, though, she's the one should be told first and I can't get any answer from her house. Anyway, this isn't something that should be told to her on the phone. I'll have to go back down there—'

'One step at a time. For better or worse, he's the one living with us. We tell him. See what he wants to do. He's old but he's an adult with all his faculties.'

'What a mess – and if you say, "I told you so," I'll kill you!'

'I won't. But I did.'

'I've been really good and I've held off, you've no idea how much.'

'I do know. I know you very well, Cee. But, listen, it could be a lot worse. What you're worrying about now is detail. Keep your eye on the big picture. When she was talking to us did you notice how her face changed every time she mentioned his name? And from what you tell me about him, each wants as badly as the other to meet again. A little glitch about timing or who knew about the other first won't matter a damn in the long run. If this works, they'll be grateful to us for the rest of their lives.'

'But suppose it doesn't? They could blame us, Bob – Violet might blame me!'

'Hey! That's my line. Talk about a reversal of roles!'

'See you later.' I smile as I hang up, but the smile doesn't last long and for the next half-hour I attack the wardrobe in my bedroom, filling charity bags, even including garments that are still ready to give service.

For the first time, Coley accepts my invitation to join us for our evening meal in the kitchen. He demurs at first, but then allows himself to be persuaded. Over the course of it, he tells us, haltingly, having to be drawn out, a little about the hardships of working 'over' in an era when the money was a pittance and being hired was at the whim of venal foremen. From his perspective, the Irish labouring man was despised by landlords of tenement houses and by British society as a whole because of his reputation for drunkenness and fighting. 'There was a lot of it in certain quarters and I'll admit that I wasn't innocent meself. There's many a Sunday morning I woke up with me face a mess and no memory as to how it got that way. Don't get me wrong now, I was big and strong and I could hold me own, but it just seemed to happen. It could happen over the name of a greyhound.'

Bob and I don't normally have pudding but in our guest's honour I had taken a lemon meringue pie out of the freezer and after we'd finished the lasagne, I bring this to the table and put it down with a flourish. 'Hope you like sweet things, Colman!'

'I do. Thank you. It looks lovely.' He's as relaxed as he'll ever be, I think, flashing a glance at Bob, who nods to give me the go-ahead.

'Listen, Coley, Bob and I have something to tell you.' I have deliberately used the diminutive and I can see he has noted it: surprise competes with alarm across his face. 'What?'

'Don't worry! It's nothing bad,' I sit well into my chair so as not to crowd him. 'This may come as a shock, but I hope it'll be a nice one. You were talking earlier of searching for your daughter – and then you mentioned that you might like to look for Violet too.'

'Yes?' He glances at Bob, then back at me and I hesitate, searching for the right words. I can find no easy way into this, however, except to say it straight. 'In the case of Violet, we have good news for you. We met her in West Cork when we went down to talk about Whitecliff. She's living in Johanna's house.'

In the course of a few seconds, he reddens from the base of his neck to the roots of his hair. 'But she can't – how—' Then he pales to a chalky white. 'Why didn't you tell me when I talked to you about her?' I reach over to take his leathery hand but he rebuffs the gesture. 'I'm just an old fool, is that it?'

'I'm really sorry I didn't tell you before now, Colman,' I say quietly. 'I didn't think it was my place. Not until I was sure who you were.' Despite his reaction, I'm relaxing a little, relieved the situation is now in the open. 'You'll have to believe me when I tell you – again – that my connection with Whitecliff came as a complete shock to me, as did the fact that I had any living relatives from my mother's side of the family. And, by the way, it was Violet, not me, who realised it: she clocked the fact I resembled Marjorie.'

He's blinking rapidly. It's sinking in.

'So, I know you're probably pissed off at me right now,' I plough on, 'but think about it, Coley. This is fantastic news for you.'

'So why didn't you tell me?' he repeats, but less antago-nistically: his mind is working.

'I couldn't be sure at the time you were the Coley she talked about. You'd mentioned your first name to me that day but there could have been any number of Colmans and it was only when the nurse called you Colman Quinn – oh, never mind! I've told you now.'

'Hmmph!' But, like the glow of a faraway fire, I can see excitement kindle behind his eyes. 'So what's changed?'

'Your accident. That's what changed things. I did jump in then, rather than have you go somewhere horrible, but that made it complicated. I didn't know what to do or who to tell first. And I guess I just stumbled on blindly for a couple of days, kind of hoping something else would happen that would sort things out and I wouldn't make a complete mess of everything for one or both of you.'

'I suppose—' he says, and I can see the fire take hold. Then he looks down at his workman's hands, knuckles of ham on his knees. 'Did she get married?' very quietly.

'No. I can tell you that for absolute definite, Coley.'

'Did she mention me?' so low he's barely audible.

'She certainly did.' This comes from Bob, silent up to now. The old man's head snaps back up. 'What did she say?'

'I got the impression that, from her side, your love affair was of biblical proportions, Colman.' Bob grins, man-to-man, but the head has dropped again.

'Are you all right, Coley?' Remembering how he reacted the last time when I went to touch him, I hold off. 'It's a lot to take in, I know . . .'

He doesn't answer. Bob and I exchange a glance as we let the silence develop. I busy myself cutting slices of pie. Then I notice that the backs of the old man's hands, still tightly fisted on his knees, are wet. He is weeping.

Although he averts his head as far away from me as possible, he doesn't shuck me off when I leap to put my arms round him. There is no sound coming from him but his breath is intermittent and he's shuddering. 'Don't cry . . .' I'm close to tears myself. 'Please don't cry, Coley. This is really good news, isn't it? After all these years?'

'She won't want anything to do with me when she hears—'

'Of course she will.' I hate to see him upset like this. 'She wouldn't blame you for what happened to her—'

'You don't know what you're talkin' about!' Now he does swat me away, then seems to recollect himself. 'I'm sorry.'

'Don't be sorry.' Desperately, I look towards Bob.

'Colman, did you hear what I said?' Bob rises to the occasion. 'In my opinion, she has never stopped loving you. I was there, remember? I heard the way she talked about you.'

'But she's a beautiful woman, she's a lady – and look at me. Who'd have me?' His despairing gesture encompasses his hurt foot, his old clothes, the entire kitchen.

'Yes, she's still beautiful, but she's seventy-six, Colman. Time has moved on for her too, you know.' Bob stands up. 'Now, I think we could all do with a drink.' He makes for the cupboard where we keep the spirits. 'How about stiff whiskeys all round?'

He must have forgotten what I told him about the old man's self-confessed propensity towards alcoholism. I glance at Coley, whose posture is stiffening. None of my business, I think. He's an adult. But when Bob brings the whiskeys, he is confronted by a polite but firm, 'No, thank you.'

'Sorry.'

'That's a good friend and a worse enemy.' The old man pushes his glass to the side.

'Dead right! I could certainly do with a drop, though. How about you, Cee?' Without missing a beat, Bob puts down the other two glasses and retrieves Coley's. 'Tea for you so, Coley?' He goes to the sink, pours the contents of the third glass away, then clicks on the kettle.

'I've embarrassed you.' Coley raises his elbow and buries his eyes in the fabric of his jacket, then shakes his head as though to clear it. 'It won't happen again.'

I gulp the whiskey; it doesn't combine well with the

mouthful of lemon meringue pie I'd had to cover the previous silence. The second mouthful is better, I find. 'I think you should take a chance and meet Violet. What do you have to lose? I'd be happy to drive you down there any time you like.'

Coley consults the ceiling. Then: 'Thank you for the offer, Claudine, but no thank you. I'll go meself if you don't mind.' He's suddenly full of resolve. 'The two of us have a lot to talk about.'

'You sure do!' I can barely imagine how that conversation might start. 'In the meantime, Coley, what do we do if she rings? She's due to ring, you know. She left a message earlier.'

'We'll cross that bridge when we come to it.'

'OK. You're the boss. We'll just have to play it by ear.' I finish my whiskey with one burning swallow and then, emboldened: 'There's just one thing I'm curious about. Stop me if you want to, Coley, but you're worried she might blame you. For what exactly?'

He doesn't respond. He's very still.

'For what happened to her? It was you cut down that staircase to the attic, wasn't it?' I'm careful that he shouldn't think I'm accusing him.

'It kept me warm many the winter's night out on the land,' he's a little belligerent, 'but if you or anybody else want it rebuilt . . .'

'Of course not. It's nothing to do with me – not yet anyway. I keep telling you. So, it was just because you needed fire-wood?'

He stares at me for a long time before answering. 'It's a long story, Claudine.'

'Don't tell us if you don't want to.' Bob is busy with tea-bags at the sink.

'Ye've been good to me, fair play to ye. I don't mind telling.'

'Are you sure?' I mean it. 'I don't want you to upset your-self again.'

'When I finally came back from over,' he pays no heed to me, 'I had nowhere to stay. I went up to Whitecliff because I knew that, by then, there was no one left living in it. I broke in. I was plannin' maybe to set up camp in some room. After all, here was this mansion going to rack and ruin so who'd give a damn if I just occupied one little part of it? I wouldn't be botherin' no one. I was careful, mind, getting in,' he adds stiffly. 'I didn't cause hardly no damage. The wood on the back door was rotten and I fixed it after.'

'Go on.'

'I went into every room.' His speech slows and I can see he's reliving it. 'My father and me was always kept in the kitchen when we paid the rent and this was only the second time I ever saw anywhere else in the real house. She invited me to a party once, d'you see, where there was dancing . . .' It becomes too much for him and his voice seeps away.

'Don't upset yourself again like this, Colman. Leave it for the moment, Claudine, eh?' Bob flashes a warning signal at me, but again the old man carries on as though no one had spoken.

'The drawing room was grand that night, with lights and flowers and lovely dresses and the boys in uniform – you know that two of them were killed in the war, Claudine?' Abruptly, he veers from his train of thought.

'I do.'

'Lord rest them.' He's reflective. 'All the finery and food that night and as much drink that'd float a battleship, and what for? Them two gone less than a year later, and now here

388

look at it, all empty and grey and cobwebs to beat the band. As big as wedding veils them cobwebs were, all over the mantelpiece and the windows and piled up round the gaslights. I cleared them away as best I could and I did that every so often afterwards, by the way.' He glances sideways at me.

'Go on, Coley.'

'And the kitchen! When I went into it from the back door the first thing I saw was lots of things left there, milk cans and buckets and bastibles on the range, things like that, and I tidied them away into the larder – I don't know why I did that now. But I did anyways, and I kept some of the things aside that maybe I'd need, like saucepans and the cans – nobody was using 'em.'

Bob puts the tea in front of him but he doesn't react. 'I went around everywhere, up, down and everywhere, thinkin' maybe to choose one little corner for myself, and I was picking up stray bits of ribbon or a button and wondering if it was one of Violet's or a little bit of thick fluff here and there, and listening to the mice. They sound always very loud in an empty house. I found a good warm blanket in one of the bedrooms and I thought that might do for me, and I hung it over the banisters but then I went up to that attic—'

He seems to notice the tea in front of him and picks it up, but then puts it down again without raising it to his lips. 'That attic room was just as she must have left it. I saw her things, her bed, all tidy it was, her little picture with the angel . . .'

I remember the picture I'd seen in his lean-to sleeping quarters in the grounds.

'Then I saw that cut-out in the door,' he says, 'and the size of the padlock hangin' off the outside latch. It wasn't hard to put two and two together – and I knew then there was no being packed off to anywhere for Violet Shine.'

'What did you do?'

'What d'you think?' His eyes burn with reconstituted rage. 'I bought a fucking hatchet. I wouldn't touch her place, because that wouldn't be right, but I took it to them stairs. I made a terrible mess. I swung it around as if I was knocking down the whole world. I think I was even shouting and roaring. Anyways,' he looks challengingly at me, 'when I went back the next day I saw I'd damaged the walls a bit but there was nothing I could do about that. But I made a proper job of the stairs and as I say, I cut them up and hauled them to my own fire and burned them bit by bit, and with every curl of smoke and every ember I cursed seed, breed and generation of them Shines. Sorry, Claudine.' He remembers where he is and with whom. 'I think I was a bit off me head at the time.'

I'm transfixed, not only at the depth of his rage but because, remembering Violet's vivid description of her tower, I'm seeing what he must have seen on entering it, that *Mary-Celeste*-like room: sewing-box half open, a forgotten pencil, the chair cocked under the barred window – she had used it as a look-out to watch the sun and the sea – but bed neatly made, because that was how she and Johanna had been brought up. 'Her stuff must still be up there.'

'I guess,' Coley Quinn says. 'I took one thing.'

'The picture of the angel.'

He doesn't seem surprised that I know.

'So that's why you think she blames you, Coley? She blames you for her being locked up?'

He looks at me as if the question is beneath contempt. 'What do you think, Claudine?'

'I think she doesn't. I don't think the idea has crossed her mind. Where did you think she went after she got out?'

'Dunno.' He shrugs.

'You didn't want to go after her? Maybe go down to Johanna's again, because she would have known where Violet'd got to? She was still alive at the time and you had gone down there once.' What a surprise he would have had, I think – but he's gazing at me with sad eyes.

'You don't understand,' he says. 'Things was different. I had work that first time, bad an' all as it was. But I had nothing at all when I broke into that house. Our own house in Rathlinney was sold and all my family was scattered and gone. I was too old to go back over. England was finished for me, I needed a clean break from it and from the company I was keeping. People who'd lived like me in places like Camden was burned out. My life got very bad after that first time when I came back and found out what that family had done to Violet's child, and it wasn't until I got back here for good and sorted out a few things for meself that I got back me health, if you take my meaning. And that took a bit of time.'

'I see.' What else could I say? His life got very bad? In those few words dwelt an entire world of self-destruction and chaos. 'Thank goodness you came back so, Coley.'

'Mm. So when I did, I guess I just kept putting off doing something about Violet. Oh, I had all kinds of fancies. I sorted me health out first, and when I was in a bit better shape, I went looking for a start on the sites. I thought that maybe some local builder would take me on, but this was a time when there wasn't the kind of construction there is now and, anyways, I was in me sixties. So even if she'd'a' had me, what could I offer a person like Violet? No job? No money? No house? So, as I say, I kept putting things off and before I knew it I got old and it was too late to offer her anything.'

'You decided you wouldn't live in the house after all?'

'That house? After what they did to her in it? But . . .' He looks towards Bob – who, sipping his whiskey, has been quiet all this time – and, as if appealing to him: 'Living outside on the land was different, d'you see? If it wasn't exactly neutral, they'd always just owned it and didn't work it, just rented it out. My father and his father before him had grazed that place. So I felt sort of entitled. But the real reason was, as I told Claudine before: I always hoped that, wherever she was, she'd come back some time to visit the old homestead, like people often do. Looking back, that was a barmy notion, I know. She wouldn't come back here, probably, to save her life. Not after what that crowd done to her. Just the same way I know it's pie in the sky to want anything more than to meet her again. I'll want nothing more than just that one chance. Sorry for going on.' He picks up his cup and drinks deeply, then, carefully, replaces it in front of him.

I remain stunned. I suppose that, with the best of intentions, we're inclined to forget that a person's nature burns on, even through old age. We infantilise and patronise elderly people, particularly when they're infirm, and in that context, to my shame, I've heard myself use the high, bright tone with Coley, the same as the nurse's aide used.

'Thank you, Bob and Claudine,' he says quietly, looking from one to the other of us, and while we murmur concerted tritenesses about having done 'nothing, nothing at all' he is not paying attention. He is staring at something beyond the two of us and this kitchen, and I see not a grizzled old man but the passionate boy my aunt had described to us.

## 44

## MARY OR EVE

It is just after seven in the evening now, and although there is a late train to Cork, I'm not going to take it but have booked in for a second night at the Gresham Hotel. As soon as I made the decision this afternoon, I telephoned Mr Thorpe to explain where I was and what I wanted to do, but then confessed to him that I had very little money; he very kindly arranged with the hotel that he would pay for me with his credit card. He also offered to wire me some cash, but I assured him it would not be necessary – the tremendous breakfasts they serve in this hotel are so sustaining. He will put the charge on the bill he will send me eventually when everything is settled, he said, then wished me luck and offered his help 'in any way I can, Miss Shine'. Mr Thorpe has been wonderfully helpful to both Johanna and me. He is unmarried and I sometimes think that he fills the lonely places in his life by taking such an interest in his clients' affairs.

By this afternoon I had only eleven euro and some cents, having made the telephone call to him and to Claudine – I was unfairly charged the full amount although I had spoken for less than thirty seconds – indulged in an ice-cream cone in Howth and rewarded myself for my sense of adventure with a cup of coffee and a scone in Clery's department store when I got back into the city.

I had a productive day. Fully expecting to take the five thirty train as planned, I left my overnight bag with the concierge at the hotel and, on leaving it, discovered a tourist office very close by that offered maps of the city. The young man behind the counter marked on one of them the locations of the Dart stations and the Register of Births, Marriages and Deaths – the latter to be my first port of call.

While discussing the provisions of Johanna's will with Mr Thorpe some months ago, I made a short will of my own, naming him as my executor and therefore having to confide in him the existence of my daughter, who was to be my heir and would, depending on the length of my life, inherit a considerable sum of money. Although I had been steeling myself for days to make this revelation, he did not turn a hair and promised that, in the event of my death ('and may that be a long time hence, Miss Shine!'), assuming I had not already done so, he would initiate a search for her. It was he who had suggested that for any official documentation, such as a driving licence or a passport, she would have needed a birth certificate. 'Should you wish to search for her yourself at any time in the future, Miss Shine, you should go first to the Register of Births, Marriages and Deaths.'

Although I had butterflies in my tummy, getting there proved a pleasant walk, partly along the Liffey Quays, which were unrecognisable from my days visiting the Theatre Royal: they are now lined with wonderful glass buildings that dazzle the eyes in the morning sunshine. It was rush-hour, of course, and one takes one's life in one's hands crossing those huge bridges.

The process of getting a birth certificate, even with incomplete information such as I have, proved to be surprisingly easy. With the help of the efficient and co-operative staff, I quickly located the folios containing the births that took place around Christmas 1944 in the county of Dublin, but unhappily no mention of Maghcolla, of Rathlinney or of myself – even of Father – despite my going back as far as 1 December, a date I know is too early, and forward to the end of January 1945. This extension was at the suggestion of one of the clerks – 'Sometimes there are mistakes made in the actual dates, especially if a birth takes place at home, is registered late and by someone not in the family.' With her assistance, I searched again. We were now looking, within that span of dates, for female entries where both father and mother had been listed as 'unknown'. We found two Marys and an Eve Mary. One of the Marys was registered in Co. Longford and so was ruled out, the other and the Eve Mary had been registered in Dublin at the beginning of January with the dates of birth given as 20 December for the Mary and the twenty-fourth for the Eve. The floor seemed to fall out of my stomach as I realised that one was mine.

I learned that each certificate had to be paid for but this would have decimated my small store so, trying not to betray how I felt, I noted down, with her permission, the names and addresses of the people who were the 'informants' of these two births – in Mary's case, a gárda from Fitzgibbon Street station, in Eve's, a Sister Benedict, who gave her qualification as a matron, with an address in Newtown, Dublin. There was such a tremor in my hand, however, that my handwriting was well-nigh illegible. 'Are you OK?' the clerk asked. 'Would you like a glass of water? Or I could bring you a cup of tea?'

'No, thank you. You are very kind.' All I wanted to do was get away to consider the momentous thing I had learned. I took a fresh piece of paper and noted the information again, printing it this time while, like a little drumbeat, the two names thumped in my chest: Eve, Mary, Mary, Eve – which was mine?

I thanked the girl and left.

My first instinct when I emerged into the sunshine was to telephone Claudine, but somehow I felt I needed to take in this information privately. It was I who had carried my baby and I wanted to hug her to myself for a little while. I would call my niece later. I would need help with decoding the names and addresses of the 'informants' and certainly with finding them or someone who knew about them.

I was overwhelmed by what I had done – and found. Although I had had butterflies beforehand, I had not expected such quick success. Now the quest had become real, and rather frightening in many ways. Be careful what you wish for – is that not an apt saying? In addition, a little voice deep in my soul was urging against premature celebration ('These are just names on birth certificates. You have a long way to go . . .'), but I managed to ignore it. If I was not going to telephone Claudine right away, I should carry on with my plans for the day, I thought.

So Mary, Eve and I walked the short distance to the Dart station to board my train for Howth.

I shall not bore you with descriptions of the rest of today's travels: I am aware that for me, caught in excitement and self-congratulation at my daring, my day was the equivalent of a trek to base camp in the Himalayas, while for everyone else it would have been merely a tiny sup of the life known to every city-dweller. Yet I did experience something unique: each step was accompanied by that little drumbeat close to my heart. I would see something that interested me – a huge monkfish on the deck of a trawler in Howth, say – and for a few seconds the volume would diminish, but then it would rise again as I moved off.

I made the decision to stay a second night while I was in St Mary's Pro-Cathedral, round the corner from my hotel, a place that I came upon by chance and entered purely out of curiosity but also, I believe, because I was influenced by its name: I might have a daughter named Mary.

I had never been inside a Roman Catholic church. It sounds absurd, I know, but during my childhood, although we and our Catholic neighbours in Maghcolla were perfectly civil to each other, it was not done to attend each other's religious ceremonies, even for funerals. This church was vast, lightsome and redolent of what I took to be incense; footsteps clopped and echoed on the tiles in the main aisle to compete with the silvery sounds of a choir rehearsing in the loft.

I sat into a pew near the back to listen and found myself beside an old man, who was snoring lightly. Although it was a warm day outside, his head lolled against the lapels of his thick brown winter coat, belted with a piece of rough string.

Looking around, I saw we were two of a shifting population of perhaps twenty in the body of the church where believers bent the knee as they passed the high altar, pushed buttons to illuminate votive lights stacked at the feet of pretty pastel statues, knelt briefly to pray, then hurried away. They seemed to be as impervious to the singers as my seat companion, and I believe that I, and a pair of youngsters – tourists to judge by their dark complexions and backpacks festooned with water bottles – were the only people who were listening as the choir master put his subjects through their paces.

This was early music and, on risking a glance upwards, I could see that the choir included a number of young boys who were to the fore. They soared and swooped, were stopped by the master, did it again. Then, finally, they sang in thrilling, effulgent unison, pouring forth a twisting cord of pure sound in which individual voices blended indivisibly.

Suddenly I was in tears. Not for myself, or my daughter – although, given the shocks of the previous days, that might have been part of it: the reason was complex. I wept because, of itself, the world is so beautiful.

My seat companion snored on, oblivious, as I asked myself how many more years I might have in which to enjoy the beauty of the world. And when I went before God on His throne, would He not ask me how well I had partaken of what He had provided?

Not well, so far, I thought, blowing my nose. I had been born into a large family but had spent the major part of my life in seclusion; I had borne a child but had lived childless.

Well, if there was one thing this small holiday had taught me it was that something had to change. That was when I decided to stay in Dublin for one more night.

I was tired in all senses, physically, mentally and emotionally, when I got back to the Gresham Hotel to collect my overnight bag and check in again. This time, of course, there was no difficulty about credit cards: Mr Thorpe had worked his magic. 'Everything's taken care of, Miss Shine,' said the same young man behind the counter, 'and we've put you in a very nice room. I hope you like it. Enjoy your stay with us.'

This time the room was not only 'nice', it was magnificent, with a sitting area as well as the bedroom – and not only that: there was a basket filled with fruit on a low table. Mr Thorpe's magic was powerful, I thought, as I unlaced my shoes, then lay on the bed to take a short nap.

I did not wake up until five minutes ago, at just before seven.

Still set about with tendrils of sleep, I made my way into the bathroom to splash cold water on my face. (Two soft white bathrobes hung on the back of the door!) I sensed that something had happened, but could not remember what it was. Then the drumbeat recommenced. Mary or Eve.

I am back in my room now, sitting at a huge desk affair with a lighted mirror above it. I am staring at the telephone because I must order my thoughts before I use it to talk to Claudine.

When I am fairly sure I know what I should say, I lift the receiver.

The call is answered on the third ring. 'Hello, is that Claudine? This is Violet here.' I try to sound calm and casual, a difficult combination. 'I tried to ring you before. I left a message.'

'Gosh, yes.'

She sounds a little fraught, I think, and I offer immediately to ring her back. 'This sounds like a bad time, Claudine.'

'Oh, no. Don't do that. I got your message. I'm delighted you rang, actually. I've tried your house several times but there was never any answer. Was there something wrong with the line?'

'I'm in Dublin, actually. I'm here since yesterday.'

'In Dublin? What a lovely surprise!' She certainly does sound surprised – even a little alarmed? 'And since yesterday?' she continues. 'Where are you? Should I come and pick you up?'

'Oh, no, not at all. Please don't put yourself out in the least. I know you very kindly invited me to stay with you, Claudine, and I truly appreciate it, but I am very comfortable here. I am in the Gresham Hotel. It is a little holiday for me, you see, and Mr Thorpe has taken care of everything. But next time I will stay with you and Bob, I promise. There is something I need to tell you, however.'

She listens as I tell her about Mary or Eve and finish by saying I shall need her help. 'That is, if you don't mind.'

'With a heart and a half,' she says brightly. 'How exciting! Bob will be delighted – well done! To tell you the truth, we had thought of going down that road ourselves – with your permission, of course – but you beat us to it. You must be thrilled.'

Despite the words and breezy tone, there is an undercurrent of tension in her voice I cannot fathom. In the background, I think I can hear two men talking. 'Are you sure this is not inconvenient? Should I not ring back some other time, Claudine?'

'Aunt Violet, listen—' She stops then, and I know from the sudden muffling of sound that she has covered the mouthpiece. Her voice had changed too: it had become lower and far more serious. That tension, if anything, had increased. There is definitely something up. I have always hated communicating by telephone: it is so difficult to discern what people are really saying. If I cannot speak to someone face to face, I much prefer letters.

'I hope you won't be upset, Violet,' she is back, 'but we have some news for you too.'

'Oh? What kind of news?' In their nests beneath my breastbone, Mary and Eve lurch. 'I hope it's not something bad?'

'It depends. Listen – as a matter of fact, Aunt Violet, we have someone here who would like to have a word with you.'

There is another pause and I hear a sort of scuffling noise and then a bang, as though the receiver had been dropped. 'I'm sorry about this, Violet, but could you hold on just a second longer?' Then I hear her urgent whisper: 'Go on, go on! She's waiting. Hurry up or she'll hang up on us!'

'Hello?' It's a man's voice. 'Is that you, Violet? This is Coley. Coley Quinn.'

In my beautiful room in the Gresham Hotel the muscles in my legs will no longer hold me. I am not the fainting type but I find I cannot stand.

## 45

# AN INCLINATION OF THE HEAD

I had taken Violet's call in the kitchen, but as soon as I handed her over to Coley, Bob and I had retreated to the television room to give them privacy.

We're on edge, I more than he: while I don't want to know what Coley is saying and am truly trying to concentrate on the TV, one ear is cocked in an effort to catch the tone in which he is speaking to her. I can hear nothing at all, however, leaving all too wide a space for my imagination to work overtime.

To see it benignly first: they're reminiscing. At the other end of the scale: he's making a case for himself and she's rejecting him. He's going to be devastated? She's going to be devastated? They both are?

After ten minutes or so, the wait becomes unendurable. 'What's happening?'

'Leave them, Claudine. They've a lot to catch up on.' Bob uses the remote to raise the volume even further and I have to have patience.

It is five more endless minutes before Coley appears in the doorway. His hair is wildly untidy as though he's been raking it with his fingers and he is desperately agitated. 'She wants to see me. She wants to know if I can go into Dublin tonight to see her.'

'Is she still on the line, Coley?' I spring to my feet.

He is holding on to the doorjamb but with his free hand, makes a gesture towards the kitchen. 'Hurry, Claudine, please—'

I race, and on picking up the phone, can hear even in her 'Hello?' that she is as disturbed as he is: she sounds out of breath. How am I going to handle this? 'You want to see Coley tonight, Violet?'

'Is that possible?'

'We could come in and collect you—'

'Would it be at all possible that you could drive him here, Claudine?' She cuts across me. 'I think we would prefer that.'

'Of course, of course. But how would he get back here?'

'This is very awkward and I apologise for it, but I am afraid I have been rather impulsive where cash is concerned and have very little. I do not have a credit card, so if you could give Coley enough money for a taxi, I should be so thankful and of course I will reimburse you at the earliest opportunity.'

'That will be no problem at all. It will be our pleasure, Violet.'

'Thank you.' She sounds immediately calmer but I'm conscious of a flood of protectiveness towards her. 'Is everything OK, Violet? Are you sure you want to see him tonight? We can easily get him in to Dublin tomorrow morning. You must have had quite a shock.'

'Yes,' she says wryly, after a hiatus. 'He has explained how it came about that he is in your house and why up until now

– oh, never mind! We have been speaking now and that is the main thing. He seems very fond of you both. He is terribly grateful. I am too,' she adds softly. 'You have a big heart, Claudine.'

'Are you sure you don't think I'm just a nosy-parker?' I can feel, once again, a sting behind my eyes.

'Neighbours around here have been found decomposing on their kitchen floors because people were afraid to interfere. If you had not done so, my dear, I would not be sitting here in this lovely hotel room waiting for Coley Quinn. In fact, I doubt I would be sitting here with or without that wonderful expectation. Whether you realise it or not, in the few days I have known you, you have had a profound influence on my life. If it does not sound too schoolgirlish, you may have dug me out of a premature grave.'

Profound? This is too much for me – certainly for this conversation, particularly with Coley perhaps within earshot. 'I did very little, Violet, only what anyone would do.' Then, to turn the spotlight away from me: 'Did Coley tell you anything about his life up to now?' I want her to be prepared.

'A little. He says he will fill me in when he sees me.'

'Are you nervous?'

'I don't think I have ever before been so nervous. Well,' she laughs a little, 'maybe that is not accurate. I think I have forgotten how to distinguish between nervousness and excitement – age and experience tend to blunt the sharper edges. I am not unruffled, put it that way – yet why should I be in any kind of state? We are merely two old friends who have a lot in common, getting together after a long separation.'

We contemplate that sentence.

'Perhaps it is not that simple, after all.' Her chuckle is richer, gayer, higher in pitch than the last, and just as I fancied I saw the young Coley's passion in the old man's rage, I believe now I hear the echo of a young girl's excited giggle. 'We'll drive him in to you right away, Violet. All the luck in the world, and I hope the two of you have a great evening.'

'Thank you.'

'Well?' Coley is hovering just outside the doorway of the kitchen. 'Am I going in or not?' He has reverted to the peremptory speech I remember from Whitecliff.

'Of course you are. Are you ready to leave right now?'

He looks down at his worn trousers. 'I can't go in to her looking like this.' He sounds angry, but the look on his face is of despair.

'Would you like me to see if there's anything of Bob's that would fit you? You're about the same height, but you're a lot thinner – there's nothing we can do about that, unfortunately. Just let me check with him.'

Twenty minutes later, I'm helping Coley into the back of the BMW. Bob's charcoal-grey suit is falling off his shoulders a little and the pearl grey shirt is far too big round the neck – I had decided against white as it accented the old man's general pallor – but the pale, iridescent blue of the silk tie picks up the colour of his eyes. He has stubbornly refused to bring his crutch – instead, after much persuasion, he agreed to take one of the walking-sticks we keep for Louise – yet despite this flare-up it's difficult to equate this nervy person with the wildly obstinate yet confident creature I'd first encountered in the grounds of Whitecliff. When he is safely inside, I lean in impulsively and kiss his newly shaved cheek. 'You look terrific, Coley Quinn. If I wasn't a married woman I'd run away with you myself.' Then, so as not to embarrass him, I close the door and go round to the front to get in beside Bob.

We are all three silent on the way in to town. It has been a showery day, and, as soon as we get on to the main road, the tyres swish. I glance over my shoulder once at Coley, but his head is turned at a right angle as he gazes out at the grass verge whizzing by.

The Gresham has a drop-off point at the front, and when we pull in, Bob puts on the flashers and both of us get out to help Coley from the back seat.

Coley, however, has other ideas. He waves us away impatiently. I suspect he might believe Violet is watching him from a window because, on the pavement, he straightens up to his full height and, with only minimal use of the stick, makes his way up the shallow steps to the hotel's entrance and through the revolving glass doors.

We stop just inside the entrance to get our bearings. Coley is standing beside me and, despite his erect posture, out of the corner of my eye I can see that the sleeve of Bob's suit is quivering a little on his wrist.

'Will we ask for her at the desk?' Bob walks away from us, but I have seen her. She is sitting in a winged easy chair at the back of the lobby, near the restaurant entrance. Her hands are folded in her lap over a closed book. She is sitting straight-backed, knees, ankles and feet perfectly aligned. She is wearing a silver-grey cardigan over a pale pink blouse and darker grey skirt, and the light is catching the modest jewellery at her neck: she looks like a distinguished actress waiting attentively for her cue. Although I have no doubt but that she's seen us, she doesn't move.

'Bob,' I call softly. He hears me and turns away from the

desk where he's been waiting in line behind a gaggle of Japanese girls. 'She's here,' I tell Coley.

'Where?' Wildly, he looks right and left. 'I don't see her.' Then he does.

She sees he's spotted her and stands up.

His limp is hardly noticeable as he walks towards her. He is using the stick almost as a theatrical prop and is holding his shoulders back as a soldier would.

Bob goes to move after him, but I link him and hold him back. 'No, let them. We should leave.'

Outside, the evening sun has overcome the clouds and O'Connell Street, roadworks included, is bathed in light. I look back through the glass doors before I descend the steps to get back into the car. They are both standing in front of her chair. She is holding her book to her chest with both hands, his are by his sides, Louise's stick trailing behind him on the floor. Although they are not touching, there are only inches between them and his head is inclined over her upturned face.

# 46

# A TENANT FARMER'S SON

No matter what my mind dictated, in my heart Coley Quinn was a vigorous boy.

Father's grip on my arm had been so tight that last night it left bruises yet, terrified as I was, I continued to look back at my darling. Ever since, my dreams have been haunted by the image as, too shocked to rise, he had continued to kneel beside our hawthorn tree, his nakedness pale as a clamshell in the treacherous, intermittent moonlight. My very last glimpse had been of him falling on all fours and lowering his head to the ground, a palomino horse, mortally wounded.

In light of that, as he stands with me now, the civilised greeting I had hurriedly planned for this moment, old person to old person, is of no consequence.

It is he who breaks the silence, but not memorably. 'Hello, Violet,' he says, and, after that, seems to have as little to say as I. We stand, each taking in the changes and sameness in the other's face, until I fear we will attract attention. 'Shall we go into the lounge bar, Coley?' I feel no strangeness in his company – I certainly feel no need to be polite or to adopt a heartiness foreign to my nature.

'I don't drink any longer, Violet, but I'll have a mineral.'

'In that case, why don't we go to my room? It is splendid, with a couch and a chair and even a desk. There is a kettle and some tea, coffee, fruit and biscuits.'

'Are you sure you won't mind that people might talk about you?'

This is so funny that I laugh. 'All they will see are two old folk doddering along.'

'I don't feel old right now.' He seems shy. I do not remember Coley Quinn being shy. I smile up at him. 'Neither do I, Coley.'

We have the lift to ourselves and do not speak until I let us into my room. He stops just inside the door. 'You weren't joking, Violet. This is some room.'

I close the door behind us. 'Are you really Coley Quinn?' It is rhetorical, of course, uttered just to hear his name out loud.

'After all these years . . .' His shyness had been fleeting and there is wonder in his voice. 'I recognised you straight away. You couldn't be anyone else, Violet Shine. You are still so beautiful.' He reaches out and touches my cheek, and although it is a butterfly touch I can feel the calluses on his fingers and know that my face must feel to them like parchment. I close my eyes nevertheless and commit to memory this sensation of skin to skin. Aside from handshakes, with Mr Thorpe, with people to whom the women at the post office introduce me from time to time, I have not been touched for years. Old people are not touched, I believe, unless by a doctor, or have the means to pay a masseur. He takes his hand away and the spell is broken.

We are still near to the door. 'Let me make you a cup of tea. Or I have bottled water?'

410

'Water would be grand.'

I walk towards my table but do not reach it. Instead I turn back to face him. 'Oh, Coley, I don't know how to start, or where!'

'Me neither. Will I sit down, Violet?'

'Anywhere.'

He sits on the chair by the writing desk, I give him his water, pull up the armchair to be near him, and we embark on a strange, halting conversation that, as the light fades outside, becomes easier until, after almost an hour, we are meshing with each other in telling our individual stories.

He relates his own experiences in such an everyday manner that it is difficult for me properly to imagine the hardships visited on him while he worked in England: the shared, squalid digs and squats, the hostels, the cruelty of the lump system on the sites, the flippancy of the foremen at whose whims men and boys like Coley ate or starved. So different from my own story: while I lived in comparative comfort, albeit with no choice in the matter, he, a tenant farmer's son from a small Irish village, was forced to follow the labouring market up and down the concrete length and breadth of England and its cities. 'It's hard to explain what I missed about Ireland – apart from you, of course!' He grins, easy now.

'I'm sure you missed Rathlinney in particular. And your mother.'

'I missed the grass and birds and the trees,' he says slowly. 'I missed the sea, too, and the wind. And even the rain of Ireland. Ach, you'll think me daft, saying that.'

'Of course I won't, Coley. So. Then you came back?'

'I did, I did . . .' And when he tells me, I find it more difficult still to comprehend that his most recent years had been spent living rough on the land around Whitecliff. 'But why, Coley?'

'I dunno, really. I just wanted to, I guess.' He is being evasive. I feel I know why, but I am hesitant to probe: it would be too prematurely intimate, even presumptuous. We are relaxed now in each other's company but, as we had during that initial phone call, we are concentrating on the events of our lives while skirting round the essence. It is raining again and the streetlight outside the window shines through the streams on the glass so that Coley's face and part of the wall beside it are patterned with tumbling lace. 'Should I put on a lamp, Coley?'

'This is nice, don't you think?'

'If you're sure?'

'I like the darkness. You can be anyone you want in the darkness, Violet.' There is a new undercurrent to his tone. The former ease has evaporated.

We lapse into silence. Perhaps, I think, I can help him with his struggle, if I have interpreted it correctly. 'Did Claudine tell you that you and I had a daughter, Coley?' I broach it cautiously.

'She didn't need to. I already knew.' Then, equally careful, he tells me how he knew and seems to think I should condemn Dr Willis.

'It's all too long ago, Coley. Everyone was acting under different rules.'

He considers this. Then: 'You never tried to find her?'

'By the time I got out of Whitecliff, I felt it was too late and would have been unfair to her. Did you?'

'So she could boast to her friends that her father lived in a field? She wouldn't want to know me, Violet – but—'

I have misinterpreted. His struggle is something else, I can see and feel it. I decide he should make the running. 'What is it, Coley?' I reach out to touch his knee and he traps my hand in his.

'We'll talk about our daughter again,' he says. 'Now's the time to do something about her, and Claudine and Bob are the people to help us. But there's something you have to know about me before we talk about that.' His grip on my hand intensifies until its bones are grinding together. He realises this and releases it, carrying it to my lap as if it is a ladybird he is placing on a leaf. 'The reason I want the darkness, Violet,' he says quietly, 'is that I don't want any secrets between us and you mightn't want to know me after this, either for yourself or as a father for our daughter, but I have to tell you. And it'll be easier for me if you can't see me properly.'

'Nothing you could tell me, Coley—'

'*Listen*, Violet!'

'I'm listening.'

'I didn't tell you the full truth of it when I was talking about my life over.' He runs his hands through his hair, and behind him, the hands of his shadow, enlarged and distorted by the angle of the streetlight, peck like a flock of birds at a mound. I am suddenly afraid that his fear might be justified: that what he will say next might be truly terrible and I will have to suffer it alongside him or, worse, be forced by its depravity to cast him from me. Having found him again, I could not bear that. 'I don't need to know the details – whatever it is, I accept it and will not judge you. Please, Coley—'

'I have to tell you. Make a clean breast of it, Violet, otherwise I'll not be able to look you in the eye, or meself either.

You can decide whether or not you want to know me after, or whether I'm a fit person to be a father to our child.'

I sit, mute.

'I went to the bad, Violet.' He's speaking strongly and clearly. 'Do you understand what I mean by that? It's why I came home in the end. It's why I camped out on your daddy's land. I hoped that if I went through enough hardship, whenever I saw you again I'd be clean. Do you understand?'

'I understand.' I am moved that he had thought so much of me for so long, and having read between the lines of his account of life in England, I am also much relieved that this is all he's concerned about. Like everyone else, I have seen documentaries about Irish navvies and lump workers. 'Drink, Coley? Carousing? Fighting?'

'Aye, and more.'

I hold still. I cannot see his eyes: there is too much shadow. The rain has stopped – it was merely a shower – and, although his face is still patterned, the pattern is no longer moving. 'More?'

'You weren't there, Violet,' he cries. 'I thought at the time you were in America, that you were married. I thought you were gone from me for ever! I didn't care what I did back then—'

'You mean you went with women?'

'None of 'em meant a thing to me. I was always drunk. I couldn't tell you the name of a single bloody one. You were my forever, my clean, lovely Violet – and you were gone. I'm sorry, maybe I shouldn't have told you, but I had to. I'll go now.' He tries to get to his feet but stumbles, almost falls, rights himself by clutching at the corner of the desk. 'Shite! Where's that bloody stick?'

I stand up slowly and switch on the nearest lamp, a standard, beside the window. I am conscious that my drumbeat, which has been quiet so far this evening, has started up again. Coley is looking at the lamp: he seems dazed. He has found his stick and is leaning heavily on it.

'You are a goose, Coley Quinn.' I move away from the standard lamp and advance on him slowly. 'Such a song and a dance – I thought you were going to tell me you are a murderer or something worse.' I feel taller than I am. I feel invincible, my own army, a queen in my realm.

'What murderer?' He is puzzled.

'If you went with a thousand women a night, there was never a love like ours. I don't care if it was a million women, a million, million women a million times over.'

His expression is almost comical. My reaction is probably the exact opposite of what he had imagined when framing his confession, but I am not behaving like this for drama or effect, because I want to comfort him, or because I do not want him to rush away: it is truthfully how I feel. I do not care if he has been with every female creature in our galaxy.

Perhaps my attitude would provide a rich field of study for a psychologist; perhaps it is merely another advantage of age, when it becomes easier to accept the world as it is without trying to shape it to one's own desires, but mostly, I think, it has developed from a lifetime spent thinking in solitude. For whatever reason, I have come to believe that true love, immune to outside forces, does exist. If a person is lucky to find it in this life, nothing can shake it and it will survive separations, outside events and misguided attempts by the two people involved to subvert or subdue it.

It will even survive death. I may never have met Coley

415

Quinn again on this earth, but I would have loved him without deviation, and I had never lost faith that he felt the same and that, somewhere, our spirits would finally mingle.

As I got older, I may have experienced a moment or two of doubt when I realised how others might see this, that such a conviction might be inappropriate for a woman of seventy-six years old, but that does not mean I doubted it. My true love has returned to me and now I care not a whit what anyone thinks. In any case, who has been given the right – or who has conferred it – to dictate what is emotionally fitting for someone else of any age, young or old? In any context, old people are not to be tidied away like so many files in an archive.

'You don't mind?' He is still looking at me as though I am mad.

'It's that I don't care. And you don't have to tell me those women meant nothing. I know they meant nothing. They never would have. They mean nothing to me either. You are mine and mine alone, and you will never be anyone else's.' I pull his head down and I kiss him on the lips.

# 47

# HUMAN LOVE, IN OTHER WORDS

Later that evening, in the *en-suites* of our separate bedrooms, Bob and I are getting ready for bed.

On the way home, we'd gone for a drink in the Coachman's Inn, near the airport; it was packed as usual with airport workers and commuters stopping in for food and it was so noisy we didn't really have much of a chance to talk – although he had brought up the subject of Whitecliff: 'Still in a tizz about us buying the place?'

'Has to be on hold for the moment,' I'd told him honestly. 'I think it's safe to say that events have overtaken us.'

'Well, you will let me know how your thinking's going?' He's wry. 'I wouldn't want you any other way, Cee, but it's hard to keep up with you sometimes.'

We left after only one drink, and in the car on the way home he suggested we should take a multi-track approach to finding Violet's daughter. 'As well as everything else. Remember I told you we have a private detective in our customer database? I looked him up – seems to have all the credentials. What have we to lose?'

'I thought you felt we should stand back?'

'Of course we should, and we have, but that was when you were getting so carried away, Claudine. There was a danger you wouldn't give your aunt a chance to keep pace. But, as you say, events have overtaken us. So, no harm in sussing out the chap? Anyhow, the sooner we find this woman, the sooner things will settle down around here. It's been like living in a play – at least, I think it has.' He sounded rueful and I realised I hadn't sufficiently taken his reactions and feelings into account. 'So what do you think?' he continued. 'We can suggest it to the two lovebirds.'

'Ah, Bob, don't be snide!'

'I'm not!' He was genuinely taken aback. 'It was meant affectionately. For God's sake, I'm as caught up in this whole thing now as you are.'

It was true, I thought, looking at his profile. He had been more than accommodating and helpful. This is how marriage works, I suppose: at the beginning you think that The Other will fulfil all needs, and as this ridiculous expectation breaks down, the disappointment turns to resentment, blinding you to what you saw in your partner in the first place. 'Thank you, Bob.'

'For what?' He was wary, glancing across at me. He wears specially tinted spectacles for night – or dusk – driving and I couldn't see his eyes.

'Oh, I don't know. For being an all round good egg.'

He didn't answer, but turned back to concentrate on the road, leaving me vaguely embarrassed, probably because what I'd just said didn't sit comfortably with some of the other things I'd said to him recently or with slapping his face. This was not to exonerate him, but perhaps, I thought, I was picking up some of Violet's attitudes. 'I wonder what's happening back there between the two of them.'

'We'll never know. And some things we shouldn't need to know.'

'You're right.' But as we sped home, past the rapidly darkening fields on either side of us, I couldn't help getting all mushy. While I didn't envisage them running towards each other in slow motion through a meadowful of daisies, I really hoped Violet and Coley would get together in some fashion. They certainly deserved it.

I'm brushing my teeth and still thinking about them when there's a knock on the door of the *en-suite*. 'Can we talk, Claudine?'

Bob is in his dressing-gown, which I'd bought him last Christmas. I know by the tone – and his expression – that this is something grave. 'Can it wait? I'm really tired.' This is genuine: my legs and back ache. 'Is this more about forgiveness?'

'Partly, but there's something I've been wanting to say to you for a long time. I suppose it can wait, but there is never a good time, is there? Remember you asked me to give you five minutes about Whitecliff that night? Could you give me five minutes now?'

'Come on in.' I rinse my mouth and turn off the tap. I'm apprehensive.

In the bedroom, I get into the bed and he takes the armchair I sometimes use for reading. The light is mellow in our room, perhaps because the dominant colour is a very pale cream. At night, lit with the bedside lamps, a standard in one of the corners, and my makeup lights on the mirror at my dressing-table, the atmosphere is restful and cocoon-like. Bob is fiddling with one of the upholstery studs in his armrest. 'Here's the thing,' he says and then, quietly: 'I know

I can never measure up to your dad, Claudine, I've always known it.'

'What?' This is so unexpected I'm dumbfounded.

'You heard me. Whether you knew it or not, all through our marriage you've been judging me by his lights, and those lights are too brilliant for anyone to match.'

My automatic defence mechanisms kick in. 'I never said anything you could possibly construe that way.'

'You didn't need to. Your father's presence has coloured our entire relationship. I know you think I should be like him, provide for you like he did. I'm sorry I haven't reached the heights he did. But unless something really unusual happens, for instance if I win the Lotto,' he smiles, 'I think I've probably reached the peak of my achievement and earning power, and if it's not enough, Cee, I'll understand.'

'What are you saying, you'll "understand"? Understand what?'

'I'll understand if you want to call it a day. Particularly after my being unfaithful. I know I've been crawling a bit, all the forgiveness business – but I'll understand if you can't. Really. You deserve the best, and maybe I'm not it.'

'That – that business is finished with, Bob. I love you,' I cried, and find I mean it. I'm reeling from his revelation of what he has been harbouring all these years about Daddy – particularly in light of the holes that have been so recently punched in my own estimation of my father. This is so sad. 'Look,' I get out from under the bedclothes and sit on the side of the bed to be nearer to him, 'there's nothing certain or scientific about any marriage. We're all just muddling through. Maybe I lost sight of who you really are, Bob, and I'm sorry. And I'm sorry you believe I was comparing you to Daddy all the time. Maybe I was, and I'll have to think about that, but it's what you feel that's important. As for owning the company, believe me, I'm not, repeat *not*, disappointed that you don't own the company. I thought you were.'

He absorbs this. 'I was disappointed because I thought you were.'

'Guess we'll have to hone our communication skills.'

'Guess we will.' He grins. 'Did you mean it when you said you loved me?'

'Yes, I did.' I get off the bed and walk across to my dressing-table to give me time to think. Then, leaning against it, I turn to face him again. 'I do love you. And I've already realised I had placed Daddy on an impossibly high pedestal.' This is painful for me but I carry on: 'I was spoiled, Bob. He shouldn't have let me ride all over Pamela like he did. She was his wife. And he shouldn't have let me believe that my grandparents and all my mother's family were dead: he should have kept me in touch with them after she'd died. If he had, who knows? Things might have been better for Violet – and they'd certainly have been better for me. Any family, even that one, is probably better than no family. I'll never know for sure why he did it.'

'You've decided he was human after all?'

'I wouldn't go that far.' My turn to grin. Then, carefully, 'I have forgiven you about that other thing and I'll try not to think about it any more. As best I can. I haven't, much, anyhow, because I've had so much else on my plate. You were blessed with your timing.'

'Sure I'm as lucky as a little black cat,' he says, but it seems automatic. Then: 'I wasn't going to mention it at all, but – I spoke to her, Claudine. I told her that you know. You won't be hearing from her.'

'How do you feel about it now?' I can't bring myself to use the word 'her'.

'Nothing,' he says quietly. 'Well, that's not true, I suppose – if you really want to know?'

'I do.' I might be a masochist, I think, but I do.

'I'm relieved to be rid of the problem. I suppose I mean her,' he says, his gaze inward. 'I'm sad that I gave you grief, upset that I was such a chump.' He shrugs. 'That's most of it. I'm also determined I'll never get myself into that kind of a situation again. I may not say it often, Claudine, but you're everything to me. That tawdry little event served as a wake-up call. I could see that I might lose you, with all your quirks and flailings, and I was devastated.'

'What quirks and flailings?' I'm not serious and he knows it.

'Here's an idea. Want to marry me all over again? The last one wasn't all that much to write home about.'

'You never said you didn't enjoy our wedding, Bob.'

'Did you enjoy it?'

'Well . . .' I had a brief flash of a quick march down the aisle of a sparsely populated church, on my own, fatherless and motherless, even stepmotherless, with a girl I didn't particularly like preceding me in a flouncy blue dress and Bob's skinny, tuxedoed shoulders in the top right-hand pew. 'Give me a break, Bob. I was still in mourning for Daddy, and the court case and all that didn't help.'

'Exactly. It was a long mourning. And a fraught engagement.'

I examine his expression. 'Are you serious about this?'

'If you are. It doesn't have to be a big one.'

'It's a mad idea . . .' But I was turning it over in my head. 'Let's think about it a bit, eh?' But I come back towards the bed and kiss his cheek.

He grabs my shoulders. 'Thank you, Claudine.'

'You're welcome.' Then neither of us seems to know what to say next.

'Might as well go for broke, I suppose,' he says eventually.

'Oh, God, not something else? Haven't we covered enough for one night?' I sit down on the bed again.

'This won't take long. You mentioned Pamela earlier.'

'What about her?' Reflexively, I stiffen.

'I liked her, you know. And now that so much time has passed – hang on a second.'

He gets up from the armchair, walks out of the room and I hear him hurrying down towards the room in which he's been sleeping. When he comes back, he's carrying his ancient wallet, in which money is almost an incidental extra. It's one of those huge affairs with multiple pockets, stuffed with business cards, expenses receipts, scraps of paper with scrawled telephone numbers; he's put it on the bed and is rummaging around in it, scattering the contents all over the duvet cover. 'I've been waiting for years to show you this – where the hell is it? I know I put it here . . .'

I'm mystified. 'What? What are you looking for?'

'Here it is!' Triumphantly, he winkles out a piece of notepaper folded in four. It is so old the creases have browned. 'Remember this?' He unfolds it and hands it to me.

It's Pamela's note, the one she'd sent us with the five thousand dollars. 'You've kept it?' I'm flummoxed all over again.

'I figured that some day you might want her address.'

I sit down on the bed. 'You think I should contact her. She mightn't even be there.'

'She might have left a forwarding address if she isn't.'

'She might be dead.'

'She might indeed. I'm not suggesting anything, Cee. I'm just giving it to you. It's out of my hands now. As I said, I thought you might like to have it. Some day.'

'You're some tulip! I mean that in the nicest possible way, Bob.'

'You're not so bad yourself.' He surveys the wreckage he has made of his wallet's contents. 'Here, let me get this.' He starts to gather it up. 'By the way,' his tone is casual, 'remember our bet? The new car?'

'That bet's still running, I guess. I haven't had time to go to the National Library.'

'Forget the bet. I ordered the car yesterday. Win, lose or draw, Cee, you deserve it. And I ordered it even before I knew whether you'd kick me out.'

'Oh, Bob! That was never going to happen – never! Hey – it's not a bribe, is it?' I'm bantering, but he isn't.

'No, it's not. Call it a gift.' He takes my hand. 'It's to show you, and say to you – and this will be for the very last time because I can't be doing with this any more – how sorry I am for what I did. You're a gift in my life, Claudine. Thank you.'

Bob doesn't do flowery. And in all the years I've known him this is the most flowery I've ever heard him. He starts again to gather up his bits and pieces. 'Leave it.' I reach up and pull his head down to my level. I kiss him, on the mouth this time.

Somehow, the kiss grows and we make love, quietly but

properly, in our own bed. Two people on an equal footing, conveying fallibility, good intentions and, most importantly, forgiveness and absolution to each other. Human love, in other words.

# 48

# DECIDING BELIEFS

The taste of Coley's mouth differed, naturally, from the taste I had so assiduously stored in my sense memory, and although he kissed me back – when he had recovered from his astonishment – we acted chastely. We were no longer children, in whom sexual desire is all consuming and yet, speaking for myself, it was not absent.

We stood back to survey one another. 'What do we do now, Coley Quinn?'

'What do you want to do?' He was shaken. 'Did you mean what you said about not caring about them other women?'

'I meant it, Coley. We may have very little time – who knows? Why waste it? The past is dead but we're not.'

'You're some woman yourself, Violet Shine.' He stepped forward and took me fully into his arms. He was trembling, I found, and I hugged him hard.

After such an auspicious start, we became physically shy with each other, as shy about nakedness as we had been that night at the hawthorn tree – and with better cause. So, by tacit agreement, we got into my magnificent bed only partially unclothed. We kissed and cuddled and talked until the early hours but we did not make love. I do not think this was solely due to age: I think we were both afraid that, whatever about our love, physical passion for each other might, after all, prove to be fools' gold. We had found each other again and for the moment that was sufficient.

We had so much to talk about in any case, and the talk came easily as we lay side by side, his old hand in mine, his heavy head on my shoulder, or mine on his. We drank tea until the little store of tea-bags ran out. (We did discuss the possibility of telephoning Room Service to ask for more – and some food – but collapsed into helpless laughter at the prospect of the shock occasioned to the poor waiter when he knocked on the door and saw the cut of us.) We had fun, playing and planning as if we were the children we used to be.

It was almost three in the morning when the fun ended, with him falling asleep. Long afterwards, I lay awake, churning in my head what he had revealed to me about our daughter.

I had initiated it by telling him excitedly about Mary and Eve. 'It will definitely be one of them, Coley. Isn't that wonderful news?'

Having been so playful and relaxed until then, he became agitated – which was not the reaction I had been expecting. 'What is it? Tell me.'

He sat up to face me and grasped me by the shoulders. 'I'm real sorry I have to be the one to tell you this. It's great that you have them names and we'll find her now, don't you worry. But there was no American couple, Violet.' He tells me then what really happened.

'She wasn't . . . I don't understand.' I could no longer feel his fingers digging into my shoulders. But, unfortunately, I understood all too well. I stared at Coley, whose eyes were only inches from mine. 'You mean she could have been in Ireland all the time?'

'She could. Or anywhere.' He threw himself on to his back and gathered me into him, rocking me. 'I know what this means to you, Violet. And now you know why I wanted to kill that bugger, Willis. If I could have done anything I would've. I should've. I let you down.'

'You didn't let anyone down.' My voice was lost against his chest.

'I did, I did, but I didn't know where you were.' He clutched me so tightly I couldn't breathe. I extricated myself. I wasn't thinking about Dr Willis. I was trying to come to terms with the fact that Mother and Father had lied to me so comprehensively and on such a fundamental matter; the depth of their mendacity seemed too bizarre to fit the upright personalities I knew.

I gathered my thoughts, however, and did my best to convince Coley of what I had said earlier in the context of his past 'badness': that looking backwards served no purpose – 'She has lived whatever life she has lived by now, Coley, and I have her birth details. We go forward.' In essence, I told him, this revelation made no difference to our current situation.

It is virtually impossible, however, to upend a lifetime's belief – or illusion – in one motion.

I had spent the greater part of my life picturing my daughter as a healthy, happy American, who was perhaps now eminent in whatever field she had chosen for herself – a compensation for my own shrivelled existence. This news had made absolute nonsense of all those years when, instead of straining with might and main to find her, I had curbed those instincts.

Whatever their motives, what difference would it have made from their point of view had they told me the truth? I was already confined.

It is almost dawn now. It feels so strange yet wonderfully comforting to have Coley here: strange, because since my childhood snuggling with my sisters, I have never before slept in a bed with another person – let alone a great big one like Coley Quinn, comforting at such a time to have the one person beside me who will understand how I feel.

When he fell asleep I tried to match my breathing exactly with his and each time he has turned, I turned too and fitted myself against his long back. At present he is half wrapped round me, one of his arms across my belly, his belly and chest close against my side.

I have decided what I will believe about the lie Mother and Father told me. I will believe they were acting with a type of perverse compassion: that by removing any hope I might entertain about reuniting with my daughter, and by making my existence in my prison cell as benign as they could, they tried to ensure I might in time settle into a peaceful life.

That is the only belief open to me, for to judge them capable of such deliberate cruelty is to make fiends of them and no child can believe that of her parents: it is against nature.

## 49

## SEYMOUR BRICK

Bob and I both sleep it out on the morning after our reconciliation, and in the hurry and fuss of getting ready for work, I don't take breakfast into Coley until almost eight thirty. It wasn't surprising that I hadn't heard him come in the previous night: I had slept so soundly I can still feel the relaxation in my calves as I rush round the kitchen.

His bed is empty and undisturbed.

Immediately I ring Bob on his mobile. 'Do you think something has happened to one of them?'

'They'd have rung. Or someone would – you always hear bad news. It probably just got too late.'

'You mean he stayed with her?'

'So what? Why are you surprised? They have a lot to talk about.'

'Are you being funny? Do you think they – you know?' I am letting my imagination run away with me.

'None of our business, Claudine.'

'I know that. But wouldn't it be great?'

'I'll see you tonight. In the meantime, let them alone.

They're adults. They have all their marbles.' He chuckles as he hangs up.

They get through to my mobile while I'm conducting a viewing of a semi-detached house in an estate in Balbriggan. 'Excuse me a moment,' I say to the client, a girl who already has a house in the same estate, but who's considering buying this one as an investment. She's single, in her early twenties and works in the lower tiers of the banking industry – it's the new Ireland.

It's Violet who speaks to me, soberly enough. She asks me in her genteel voice if it would be 'at all possible' for me to deliver Coley's belongings into the Gresham some time before the evening train at five thirty. 'He has agreed to come home with me for a visit. His ankle is much better. Could you tell his nurse, please? And we shall, of course, be returning the money you gave him for his taxi since he won't now be needing it. He will have to keep your stick, though. And is it all right if he also keeps Bob's clothes for the moment? I'll have the suit dry-cleaned before we return it.'

'Oh, Violet! Don't worry about any of that.' I look at my watch: it's just after eleven o'clock. I have another viewing at lunchtime but the afternoon is free. 'What are you going to do in the meantime?'

'We're going to spend a little time in Dublin.'

'I'll see you at about four, then. And I can drop you to the train.'

'That would be—' The phone goes dead; they've run out of credit.

I needn't worry about those two, I think, as I click off. They have all their marbles, right enough.

\* \* \*

They're waiting for me in the lobby of the hotel. I try to behave as if nothing unusual is going on, that they didn't sleep together for the first time in sixty years, and I'm just here doing a favour for two septuagenarians of casual acquaintance. But to judge by their exchanges of looks and their frequent use of 'we', whatever went on between them in the last twenty-four hours was significant, I think, as I load them into the back seat of my car and pass in one of Bob's travel bags containing Coley's bits and bobs. I was amused to see, as I packed for him, that he still had his keyring. Our own spare wasn't among them – but, of course, he would have had that one with him. I reckoned these were for Whitecliff: he would have had them on him when he fell.

As we crawl our way down the Quays to Heuston station, I bring up the subject of Whitecliff with Violet. Tommy O'Hare had been on my case about it again. 'Have you had any further thoughts on it, Aunt Violet?' I ask her, watching for her response through the rear-view mirror.

'I have been in a bit of a muddle,' she and Coley exchange another glance, 'but I promise I shall think about it seriously when I get home. And I shall consult Mr Thorpe. You understand I have to do that?'

'There's no pressure,' I assure her, while seeing Tommy O'Hare's outraged little face hovering in front of my eyes.

I get them to the platform just after five o'clock. Although the train is there and is already filling up, we loiter outside the ticket barrier. 'I'll miss you, Coley – take care of that ankle.' I'm having to shout because of the idling of so many diesel engines under the one iron roof. 'And you, Violet, it's been great to see you again.'

She hands me a piece of paper, the fruits of her trip to

the registry. 'I think this will be helpful, don't you?' She, too, has to yell.

'It sure will.' Full of admiration for her enterprise, I put it carefully into my handbag. 'I think you should go, if you want to get a seat.' Coley then tries to return the taxi money, but I insist they keep it. 'Bob would kill me if he knew I took it from you. Please. There's a dining car on that train. Use it to have a nice meal.'

He looks at her and she smiles delightedly. 'All right, so,' he says. 'But we'll definitely pay you back soon.' She thanks me 'for everything, Claudine', and I hug her, then shake his hand. They show their passes and go through the barrier, and for a couple of minutes, I watch them move slowly down the length of the train, stopping every so often to check through the window for seats to suit them, he limping a little, she walking like a queen.

Three days later, having made an appointment, Bob and I go to visit his private detective, a tiny New Zealander who rejoices in the fantastic name of Seymour Brick.

Rosemary's social worker and I had found it impossible to make a mutually convenient appointment to meet any time soon: the woman was run off her feet. And I, having bazzed off so much from work recently, was making it up to Tommy, working long hours, and hadn't ventured again into Dublin to consult archives. It wasn't hard, therefore, for Bob to convince me that, with his professional resources and experience, the detective would probably get results, if these were to be had, far faster than if we were to trust to my amateur fumblings.

'It's a delicate metter, Mr and Mrs Ehrmstrong,' Mr Brick says to us, from behind the scarred desk in his unremarkable office, one of several in a small building in a Dublin suburb. 'We heve a high success rate in finding people but we don't work outside the law. I hope you understend that? And if a pirson wants to stay missing, we try to convince him on behalf of our clients but in the end we have to respict thet too?'

'She's not missing, though.'

'We treat cases like yours as missing pirsons.' He remains matter-of-fact. 'Don't worry, Mrs Ehrmstrong, we know what we're doing.'

'Sorry.' I pass across to him the two names and 'inform-ants' Violet had found in the register, then give him the benefit of Bob's theory about the newspaper archives, emphasising that we'd like a priority to be made of the case. 'The parents are in their late seventies.'

'I understand, Mr and Mrs Ehrmstrong.' He sweeps the single sheet of paper into a file cover and writes our names on it, and somehow this official act, despite his unprepos-sessing appearance and his miniature three-piece suit, reas-sures and excites me. We pay him the deposit he asks for against his fee, and another sum to cover his initial expenses, then leave him to it.

Work continues to occupy me over the next few days: Tommy has recently acquired a licence as a mortgage adviser and there is a backlog of paperwork. Plus the Greenparks consortium seems to be getting its act together and the pace is hotting up there too. So, outside making a quick social call to my aunt every couple of days to enquire about her welfare – and Coley's – and to assure her that our detective is, in fact, working away in the background, I return to my life pre-Violet. She is not a telephone-chatter, I'd discovered early on, so our conversations are always brief and to the point.

Coley, she tells me each time, is getting on fine. And, despite Tommy's nagging, I don't bring up Whitecliff again: I've become protective of the two of them, and as far as my own ambition for the house is concerned, I'm coming round more and more to questioning whether I want it or not. I haven't given up the idea yet, but just as many people are reluctant to buy a place where someone has died, I'm beginning to doubt that, given what I know now about the house's history, I could be relaxed there.

On a Saturday morning, about ten days after I had seen off my aunt and Coley at the railway station, the telephone rings. 'Who's that?' I really don't want to answer it. I'm still in bed, listening to the radio – a rare luxury any morning – and still working on a cup of coffee Bob had brought me. He had been up and out already and was now shuffling through the newspapers, one of his Saturday treats. 'Will you get it?' I ask him. 'And if it's Tommy, tell him I'll ring him back.'

He reaches for the phone. 'Yes, this is he . . .' He listens. 'Uh-huh? Uh-huh?' He writes urgently on the air, signalling to me he needs a pen. I pass him one that I keep in the drawer of my bedside table and watch as he scribbles what seems to be a very long message in the margins and white spaces of the newspaper on his lap. Must be a client, I think lazily, and again pick up my cup.

'Thank you very much. We really appreciate it.' He seems to be winding up. 'We'll be in touch. And you'll send the account to this address?'

He says goodbye, then studies what he's written. 'Well,' he says, 'that worked well.'

'What did?'

'That was Seymour Brick. Pay attention now, Claudine. Your cousin's name is indeed Eve. Seymour says that once he tracked down that Newtown address – it was an orphanage, but defunct now apparently – things became relatively straightforward and he was able to find the trail. He found an employment history from when she worked as a domestic: fortunately her employer paid stamps for her. She was married early in life – he found her marriage certificate. She has three adult offspring, Arabella, Willow and Rowan. Got that?' He's grinning.

'Go on!' I'm clutching my cup so hard my fingers are throbbing.

'Weird names, huh?'

'*Bob!*'

'OK. Let's see now.' He relents and turns the newspaper sideways, peering at his scribbles. 'The first two are daughters and live in Dublin – Willow is married with two children. The third, Rowan, he's the guy, is currently in the US. So is Eve. She lives there. She goes by the name Eve Rennick now, for some reason, although that's not her married name and, would you believe, lives alone in a trailer park in Arizona. I have the address and the telephone number of the site manager.'

His grin widens. 'Good old Seymour says your cousin is more than happy to be contacted. "Thrilled at the idea" were his exact words.'

## 50

## MYSTERIOUS WAYS

Coley Quinn and I are speeding towards my niece's home in the back of Bob's car. He picked us up from the bus station in the centre of the city: we came on the express bus this time, since we had both been on the train already. I found it very comfortable – and it was interesting to travel through actual towns, instead of along the peripheries, which is where the rail tracks are laid. On the negative side, the tang of cheese and onion potato crisps was still to the fore. Bob says their house is only fifteen minutes away now, and I am more excited and nervous than ever, if that is possible, about what lies ahead. Not about Claudine, of course, but about going to the airport tomorrow with Coley to meet our daughter.

I would find it difficult to pick out any single event of the past two and a half weeks, other than, naturally, the extraordinary telephone call Claudine made to us that Saturday morning and the even more extraordinary one between our daughter and us later that day during which all three of us were so stunned, I think, that even the word 'gamut' could not cover the highs and lows of what we went through.

We have barely slept since. We have been by turns thrilled,

distraught and desperately anxious – and have spent many of the dark night hours gripping each other's hands for support while engaged in fevered speculation about how we would get on with Eve. Intellectually, I know I am exhausted and at one point considered taking another of Johanna's tablets but since I continue to feel as sharp and energetic as Father's fretsaw, I decided against it. I want to experience every last dart and shiver of the emotions engendered by this amazing discovery.

Initially, Coley was of the opinion that we should invite Eve to West Cork, but I felt she would want to stay in Dublin to be near her own daughters and her grandchildren – our grandchildren and great-grandchildren, still to be met too! We have an open-ended invitation to stay with Bob and Claudine but, as yet, have no idea how long that will be: it depends on Eve. We hope to see a great deal of her.

Ensconced in the warm, comfortable back seat of Bob's car, Coley takes my hand. We have hardly been apart for a single minute since that first night in the Gresham Hotel, and having him with me has changed the complexion of life in West Cork greatly. In a sense, we have reverted to childhood and are 'playing house'; apart altogether from our personal relationship, the earth-shattering discovery of our daughter, it is extremely gratifying to have my own man around to share, and even take over, some of the domestic tasks. We are having fun.

I have no idea what the good folk of our village have to say about us, but I give not a whit for anyone's opinion – although Coley, charmingly, continues to worry about my reputation! We have been the subject of many curious looks, as in the post office on the first pension day when he accompanied me to change the address on his own book. On pension day the place is always crowded, but we got through it and the two women there were as pleasant as ever and held their tongues.

Despite my preoccupation with what's going to happen tomorrow, I cannot but be fascinated with the changes in the topography around the car as we zoom along. In my childhood, I would have been familiar in general with this area of North County Dublin, now apparently named Fingal, but I remember it as a slow, green place, criss-crossed with little roads winding through high hedgerows and dotted with crossroads settlements and villages, not this vast open area of huge highways, housing estates and cranes. 'I'm sure everything has changed since your day, Violet.' Claudine's husband has noted my fascination.

'It certainly has.'

'We're not that far from Whitecliff, you know,' he says slowly. 'It would only be a few minutes out of our way. Would you like to see it?'

'No!' I can see my vehemence has startled him, so I amend it: 'No, thank you, Bob. Claudine will be expecting us.'

From necessity, as I have explained, and from the safety of Johanna's house in West Cork, it was relatively easy to discuss Whitecliff with Mr Thorpe and, however briefly, with Claudine and her husband. The very mention of the name, when I am in such proximity to it, strikes terror into me. Perhaps in the intervening years, memory has created an intolerable situation out of one that, while I was living it, seemed merely harsh. Anyhow, I do not want to go back there, ever. My view now is that when it becomes mine, I will sell the place immediately to whomever asks first and at whatever price he or she offers. If that is Claudine, well and good – but I doubt that I shall ever visit her there. I do not intend to say this to her, however, in case it might influence her decision. She has a soft heart, and must make up her mind about the house on her own terms. In a way, even though I don't want anything to do with it, it would be nice if it were to stay in the family.

Mr Thorpe has intuited these feelings and is urging caution: 'You would want to hold out, Miss Shine. You will be in possession of a prime land bank that will attract a lot of interest. You must not sell yourself short.' However, I am not without some wit and I am aware that, as an agent on percentage commission, his remuneration rises and falls with the price gained for the estate. He is hardly a disinterested party and I shall ignore his advice on that score.

I am also keenly aware of the irony inherent in this: as the person who has suffered most within Whitecliff (I think I am safe in saying this) it is rich that I shall now be its final bene-ficiary. The Lord, as dear Nanny used to say, works in myste-rious ways.

# 51

# CAN YOU SEE HER?

I n the Dublin airport arrivals hall, the electronic board has
just clicked over to deliver the news that Aer Lingus 104
from New York has touched down, but it's the Friday morning
of the August bank-holiday weekend and several other flights,
including another from the States, have also landed recently
or are due in the next few minutes. We might be in for a
long wait because if the huge crush of meeters and greeters
out here is anything to go by, it'll be chaotic in the baggage
hall. At least Bob and I have managed to bag a prime spot
near the front of the crowd among which, despite the
appallingly early hour, the atmosphere is festive – with otherwise respectable adults wearing funny hats and waving
balloons.

Violet and Coley, whose ankle has healed perfectly, are
sitting together away from the crush, she in a calf-length linen
coat and dress in mimosa, he in a blazer, camel-coloured slacks
and crisp white shirt: they had obviously gone shopping. I
notice that, as well as her handbag, she is clutching a manila
envelope, eight by ten.

There are only the four of us here; during long telephone

discussions with Eve's two daughters, Arabella and Willow – and with the agreement of Violet and Coley – we had all decided that their meeting with Eve for the first time would be emotional enough, without having to deal with so many other new people too.

And they sure do have a lot to cope with. In addition to meeting this woman after nearly sixty years, they also have to take in the ramifications of the life she has led, not least the discovery that, as Eve herself was abandoned, she abandoned her own three children and fled to America. This was from desperation, I gather, and a conviction that in doing so she was giving them a better chance at life. Although the circumstances were different, the parallel is astonishing. I gather also that, year after year, she had meant to come home to fetch them and 'make things right', as she says, but had never managed it. Although things are relatively stable between her and her kids now, she continues to be riddled with guilt and is carrying all kinds of emotional baggage.

So while the three of them have already talked some, there's a lot more to be said, and the current plan is that after this initial meeting, Eve will go to Arabella, Willow and her grand-kids this afternoon, and we will all get together tomorrow evening at our house. That'll be some party.

Now a frisson runs through the tightly packed crowd as the first wave of stunned-looking travellers comes through the Customs exit. It's not immediately clear from which of the US flights they've disembarked but, with their bum-bags and pallid, long-haul faces, they're definitely American: men pushing trolleys with suitcases stacked as high as Liberty Hall, women in pale lace-up shoes and pastel body-warmers.

The decibel count is rising all the time, with children

running, falling, swinging on the barriers, and a combination of high-octane chatter, constant ringing of mobile phones and a stream of announcements on the airport's Tannoy as a second wave of arriving passengers crowds in behind the first. The whole place is truly heaving now, and it's very difficult both for passengers and greeters to find each other. I'm concerned that Violet and Coley might be getting too stressed. Neither of them has been here before, or indeed at any airport, and Coley, in particular, is mesmerised. Looking over at the two of them, she seems the more composed, but only by a fraction.

I tell Bob I'm going to join them. 'Bring Eve over when she arrives, eh? You know what to look for?' We had exchanged photographs.

I haven't reached the old folk when I know their daughter has arrived. I know it from the look on Violet's face and the way her hand has flown to her mouth. I know it from the way the two of them are leaning against each other, his hand clutching her forearm. I turn but can't pick anyone out of the swarms of intermingling passengers and friends: 'Can you see her?'

## 52

# THE MOST BEAUTIFUL WORD

I had heard, of course, how busy Dublin airport could be, but I had not anticipated how busy. Nor had I imagined, despite reports in the newspapers, on the wireless and TV news to the contrary, how deeply unpleasant an airport can be. Somehow I had remained caught in the notion that flying off in an aeroplane is a glamorous experience.

We were both tense but excited. We were meeting our daughter at the airport, something that everyone else in Ireland seems now to take for granted – I am sure, however, that very few will ever have the privilege of doing so in our situation. For Coley in particular, an added fillip was the idea of going to visit a real live airport. 'Maybe some day you and I might even fly somewhere, Violet. How about Paris?'

'Time enough for that.' I could think of nothing and no one but Eve.

I had no idea how long we had been sitting, waiting. We had run out of meaningful conversation and had been reduced to exchanging inanities about how warm it was, or how time was passing so slowly – or flying to Paris!

Alongside my excitement, I was so apprehensive that I was

nauseous: while I was confident I could control myself in almost all circumstances, this was new ground, and I certainly did not wish to discomfit my daughter with a public scene.

As I have said, I hate using the telephone for anything except to impart essential information or make appointments. So rather than have Eve and myself 'catch up' totally on our lives on a very expensive transatlantic telephone line, I wrote her a long letter, telling her as much as I knew about her family and Whitecliff – with one glaring omission: I asked Claudine to fill her in about that business with the tower. For despite many attempts, and waste of good notepaper, I found I could not write adequately about it. The bare facts cast Mother and Father – and, indeed, the rest of my family – in a bad light and I did not want her to think too badly of them. If I filled in the margins around these facts from my own point of view I either sounded self-pitying, furious at the deceptions visited on me, or so brave and saintly that I was casting myself as a latterday Joan of Arc and I certainly am not, nor was, that.

In her reply, sent before Claudine telephoned her about the tower, Eve apologised for her lack of literary skill, explaining that while she had had a 'rocky' start to life in her orphanage, she was 'fine and dandy' now but that her poor education was still a handicap. Apparently she had spent a great deal of her life in domestic service because, she said, she was not fitted for anything better: she had teetered into alcoholism – Coley's legacy, I wondered? – but has been sober for many years.

She also confessed the saddest fact of all, which was that she had run away from her violent, drunken and philandering husband and her three 'lovely innocent children'; while they seem to have forgiven her for this, it is clear that she remains deeply upset about what she did.

It is hard to describe how badly I felt on reading that heartbreaking catalogue, so far from the life I had imagined for her – but all of that is obliterated now. I am standing. My heart is beating so fast it is choking me. Coley and I are supporting each other. She is here. Our daughter is here.

As she comes closer, I see my sisters and Coley – even Father – in her height, sturdy frame and handsome demeanour. Even at a distance of twenty feet, it is a shock to recognise the eyes of my mother – inherited by my twin brothers – a luminous pale grey with a rim of dark blue. Plans, control and decorum desert me. 'Eve!' I hold out my hands.

'Hello, Mother.' She takes them in hers. 'Thank God.'

Those eyes are on a level with mine but instead of being judgemental, as I had feared, the expression in them is loving, but also afraid: she is as nervous as we are. 'I've stayed alive for this moment, Eve,' I tell her, and my voice seems to belong to someone else. 'I did not know that until now. And I'm so sorry.'

'Please. Don't – I'm the one that's sorry – I've let you down so badly—' In danger of being overcome she turns to her father: 'You're Coley?'

He reaches out and grips her shoulder. 'I'm your daddy, Eve.' His voice, too, is unrecognisable and it is left to poor Claudine, who herself is in tears, to come to the rescue of us all and prevent the situation from descending into Grand Guignol.

'We can't all stand here weeping.' She beckons to Bob who, carrying Eve's suitcase, is hanging back. When he joins us, it is he who suggests, sensibly, that we all go straight home to breakfast.

As we make our way out of the airport to Bob's car, I have eyes only for my daughter who is walking a little ahead of me with Claudine. I drink her in, her movement, the inclination of her head, the curve of her back. In my imagination I hold her. I comb her hair. I clothe her in gold raiment – the biblical language of my childhood catches me by surprise. 'I have a gift for you.' I tap her shoulder and give her the envelope, warm from my hands, but she is distracted by something Claudine says to her, and puts it quickly into the outside pocket of her shoulder-bag.

'I'll open it later, thank you, Mother,' she says, for the second time using the most beautiful word in the English language.

# 53

# A VELVET HAMMER

We're driving against the flow of traffic into the city. I'm in the back with Violet and Coley; Eve, the honoured guest, is in the front with Bob. 'I guess Whitecliff isn't all that far from here?' She cranes her neck to address the three of us. 'I'd love to see it, if that's possible.' I'm puzzled. While the enquiry had sounded casual, it had seemed over-deliberately so.

But I can tell by the stiffening of Violet's body against mine that this suggestion is far from welcome. I'm sitting behind Bob and in the best position to see Eve's expression, but I can't read it. 'It's not much of a detour on the way to our house, that's true, but aren't you very tired? Jetlagged and all of that? I'd be very happy to bring you another day when you've acclimatised.'

'Oh, God, Claudine, thanks, but I wouldn't be able to sleep now if you hit me with a velvet hammer. I just thought that since we're so near . . .'

'There's really not much to see. It's a wreck, you do know that? And I'm sure Violet and Coley could do with a cup of tea,' I try again, looking at the two old folk, both of whom are unhelpfully gazing at their laps.

'It wouldn't take all that long. You wouldn't mind, Bob?'

'Not a bit.'

Bob, probably not fully understanding what's going on here, is concentrating on changing lanes. Why is Eve pushing this? But before I can say anything, Coley pipes up: 'If you really want to go there, Eve, I have the keys.'

I could kill him. And yet, of all of us in the car, he knows Violet best. I'm still desperate to save her from this, however. 'Let's think this through, eh? Whatever about getting into the house, Coley, how are we going to get everyone through those awful brambles?'

'I've a key for the gate padlock.' Coley glances at Violet.

She doesn't notice because her eyes are closed. Then, opening them, she astonishes me: 'If you really want to go there, Eve, I don't mind.'

I understand. They would do anything, anything at all, to please their daughter.

In less than twenty minutes we're pulling up outside the gates I remember so well.

Coley, bless him, makes short work of the padlock and then, driving slowly through the bramble walls, we inch up the bumpy corridor that once was the imposing avenue leading to Whitecliff.

'Wow.' Eve is blown away when, on rounding a wide bend, the house comes into view. 'I thought you said it was a wreck, Claudine?'

'It is – although the walls are sound, and so is some of the interior. For instance, there's a wonderful fireplace and a truly magnificent staircase . . .' Almost like a physical blow, I can feel Violet's reaction. I have no time to say any more because, like a broody hen, the car has settled in front of the house on the turning circle.

We all get out. It's a lovely morning, still and warm, if a little overcast, and Whitecliff's grey stone and graceful portico seem more imposing than ever.

Eve looks up at the crumbling gutters. 'I see what you mean. It's gorgeous, but it's a money pit.'

'I'm not going inside,' Coley mutters suddenly, giving me his keyring so abruptly that I drop it. 'I know what it's like, don't I? I have to see a man about a dog.' He hurries off towards the brambles.

I notice that, despite the day's warmth, Violet is shivering and, nice as Eve is, I'm angry with her: surely she must be able to see the effect this is having on her mother. 'How about you, Aunt Violet? Maybe you're tired after all the excitement and such an early start. Would you like to sit this one out in the car? I can bring Eve through the house.'

But I've been wrong about my cousin. She comes forward and gently takes her mother's hands between her own, which I now see are well shaped and strong, but red and ruined from physical work. 'This is going to be so hard for you,' she says softly. 'It's going to be hard for me on your behalf. That's why we have to do it together. We'll confront those demons in there. We'll trounce 'em, Violet, and they'll never bother you again. And you know what? Before I go back home, we're all going to have a party in there. A barbecue maybe. Trash the place good. So come on now,' she squeezes Violet's hands, 'don't you worry, you'll be safe with me. Are you ready?'

Violet smiles but her eyes are still wide with fright. 'Yes,' she whispers. 'I did vow I'd never come near Whitecliff again but, yes, I'm ready now.'

Eve turns to me. 'I think this is something we have to do

alone, Claudine. Do you mind? We won't be long, although we will take as long as we need. Have you the house key?'

'Sure—' I hand her the keyring. 'It's for the back door.'

Then I watch as the two of them, choosing to veer right, walk towards the house. They are of equal height, but Violet is more slender. After a bit, Eve puts her arm protectively round her mother, pulls her into a semi-embrace, and so, in step, they walk along the side wall, turn the corner at the back of the house and vanish from my sight.

## 54

# WHERE ONCE AN
# IMPERFECT FAMILY LIVED

My daughter turns the key of the back door and we enter Whitecliff.

I have never been afraid of mice, but when we come across the threshold and thereby panic the resident population, Eve, who had physically supported me as we walked round the side of the house, flinches. 'I hate 'em,' she says, remaining in the doorway. 'You'd think that with all my years scrubbing and sweeping into the corners of old houses I would've gotten used to them, but I never did.'

'You can come in now, they've gone.' She had been mother to me, and now it was my turn.

'Yeah, but they could come out again! That's what worries me – ah, never mind.' She comes in and goes to close the door.

'No, leave it!' I do not want to be shut into this house.

'You bet.' She opens it as wide as it will go and the blessed sunlight floods the entire kitchen, as far as the pantry.

Everything is as I remember it, structurally at least. The kitchen table, sporting Coley's larder, as he had described it, is intact but in my seventy-six years this is the first time I have ever seen a dirty floor in here or have felt no heat coming from the range, which is rust-brown and corroded around the outer edges. It is also painful to see, instead of Mother's bleached and starched nets, a thick lace curtain of cobwebs, grey and tangled, stretching in sagging half-circles across the dirty window-panes; and in the absence of her bright garden of geraniums on the sill, the whole place, despite the moderately clean sink, seems to have curled drably in on itself, a resigned old dog slinking into a corner to die. 'Is it what you expected?' Eve is looking upwards at the brown and peeling ceiling.

'Yes.' Slowly I cross to the far end of the room and open the half-door to the pantry where I hid to dress on the morning after the big party, and from where I forgot later to collect my wretched nightdress, stuffed under the colander. This latter is no longer in evidence, although the shelves still hold pots and other utensils. I relatch the door, then change my mind, pull it wide and open the bottom half as well. My daughter's instincts, that I should confront my demons, had been correct: my intention now is to throw open every internal door in this house and leave them so when we depart.

As a matter of fact, I am feeling the stir of righteous anger, which I had not felt for a long time, maybe not ever; I am undoubtedly more confident. Although I tried to think of the house as little as possible, when I did, it had grown into a fairground house of horrors. Being here, however, among the shabby, ordinary things that are of no use to anyone any more, restores it to what it is: just a house mouldering to dust – an impermanent dwelling-place where once an imperfect family lived.

I glance over my shoulder at my daughter, picking her way carefully across the floor, and experience a bubble of perfect joy.

My daughter.

Righteous anger has been short-lived. 'Shall we move on, Eve?'

Leaving the kitchen door open, we move into the half-darkness of the hall, where the shutters are all bolted. Yet the efforts Johanna and I – and whoever succeeded us – had put into polishing the flagstones seem to have paid off. They are not pitted as I had expected but, sealed with so many layers of polish over the years and even centuries, continue to gleam a little under their drifts of dust. 'This is gorgeous, Mother! What awesome stairs!' Eve looks up towards the mezzanine.

'I'd like to open the shutters.' I pull at the nearest hasp, but we struggle in vain with the heavy ironwork: it has rusted and needs stronger hands than ours.

Then I see the outline of Father's yew bench against the wall by the front doors. 'Have you got that envelope I gave you, Eve?'

'I sure have.' She pulls it out of her shoulder-bag. She had carried it with her, in spite of Claudine's urging to leave it in the car. 'Thanks, Claudine, but we might need tissues!'

'Why don't you open it? It's something I'd like you to see. Come into the light. As far as I remember, the french windows in the drawing room are not shuttered.'

Memory has not let me down: although the front bays are dark, the light through the french windows, though filtered by grime, is comparatively bright. Standing close, Eve draws out of the envelope a professional colour portrait of the yew bench outlined in the hall, lit from an angle that enhances its purity of line and depth of colour. I had commissioned it from a Béara photographer. 'What's this?' Her forehead wrinkles.

'It's for you. It's the one piece of furniture I have from this house. My father, your grandfather, made it with his own hands. We can arrange to have it transported to Arizona. Will it fit in your trailer?'

'Oh, Mother, it's beautiful. If it's ten feet wide and ten feet high, I'll get another trailer.' She hugs me hard. Then she pulls away. 'But if he made it, why did you want it after what he put you through?'

'That's hard to answer. Maybe it has something to do with knowing that no one could have created a piece so beautiful without pouring a little of his own spirit into it. I do want you to have something to admire about him, Eve, about both of them. I'll tell you about her too – about her industry and thrift, and the good things. I don't want you to spend the rest of your life judging them by what they did to me.'

In speaking about them like this, I am overcome, but not in the way I had feared: in spite of my genuine lack of bitterness, I had been afraid that in this house I should feel the remnants of a malevolent presence. Instead I am flooded with compassion for my parents. I feel they have been trapped here by their deeds and that they need me to release them. It is far-fetched, perhaps whimsical, and I am well aware of how impressionable I am at present, but I do sense strongly that they are watching and waiting in fear of me.

Suddenly I remember that first night at the Gresham when Johanna's sleeping tablet was taking effect and I saw that puzzling vision of my transfigured mother wearing the guardian angel's robes from Nanny's picture and hovering over my tower. I close my eyes and tell them I forgive them. I mean it. *Go free, Mother. Go free, Father. I love you both and I forgive you, as I am sure you forgive me.*

'Are you all right, Violet? You've gone very pale.' Eve's touch brings me back to reality.

'I am perfectly well. Shall we see the rest of the house now?'

On our way out, I open the double doors to the drawing room to their widest extent and, as we wander through the empty rooms upstairs, my daughter is clearly impressed with the scale and proportions of the house. 'If I'd only known I was so toney.' She giggles when I show her the massive claw-footed bath that must have been too unwieldy for Johanna to send to the contents auction after Father's death. Her American enthusiasm is infectious. I am even enjoying myself, gaining great satisfaction from the din as I go along the echoing landing – Crash! Crack! Crash! – slamming open all the doors as far as they will go on their hinges.

Then we come to the door to the attic. 'This is it.' I pull it open and am shocked to be hit with a blast of sunlight. But no stairs. No one had warned me. As I look at the neatly shorn remains, I know instantly who has done this.

'Oh, Mother.' Eve is dismayed as we peer up at the holed roof above the landing outside my prison door. 'I'm just as glad we can't go up there. What they did to you! I could barely believe it when Claudine told me. It sounded like something out of Grimm's fairytales.' It is the first time she has referred directly to my incarceration and, indirectly, to her own birth up there. I take her hand. 'But don't you believe in happy endings, Eve? Look at us now.'

'We've lost so much time . . .'

'All the better in some ways. More than most people, we shall probably appreciate and enjoy the time we have. How long are you staying?'

'I have an open ticket.' Then she hesitates. 'All my friends are in Arizona, Mother. It's my home now. It would be a very big step to move back here.'

'I know you won't do that. That is not what I asked.' My poor heart, already over-taxed, jumps in anticipation of saying goodbye to her again.

'Don't worry. I'm not going any time soon. It's not only you and I who have to catch up, Mother – something I never dreamed would be possible. We both owe Claudine a lot.'

'Dear Claudine.' I smile. 'She's so – so . . .' I search for the proper word '. . . so energetic!'

'Thank God she is. But as you know,' she adds slowly, 'I still have a lot of work to do with my three.' She speaks then, hesitantly, about Arabella, Willow and Rowan, whom I know only from their photographs. 'What I did to them – but at the time . . .'

'You left your children and your own hopeless, dreadful life in the expectation that they would enjoy a better life than you could give them.' I am trying to sound stout and comforting. In her letter, she had told me in heartbreaking detail about her husband's violence and fecklessness, and her abandonment of her children; she had blamed herself for her son's descent into drink- and drug-fuelled homelessness. 'They're doing fine now. You told me in your letter that even Rowan is making his way.'

'Yes, I suppose so. But Willow will never forgive me. I know she won't. Why should she when I can't forgive myself?'

'Willow will come round. You'll see.' Again, I know from

her letter – and from reports of Claudine's telephone conversations with her – that my second grandchild is still mired in resentment and anger. 'I'll talk to her. She'll listen to me, I'm sure . . .' Then my breath pools in my chest. 'You talk about abandoning them. I abandoned you too, you know, Eve. Can you forgive me?'

She looks at me in astonishment. 'Of course, Mother. The difference between you and me is that you had no choice. I did.'

'I could have sought you out earlier.'

'Oh dear!' She laughs. 'We're competing to see who has behaved the most horribly. What an oddball family we are, Violet! At least no one could ever call us boring.'

'Who is to know what a real family is?' I touch her face. With her carriage and her extraordinary eyes, she is still handsome but I can see how beautiful she must have been when she was younger. Her skin, though, is rough under my hand. 'Eve, my dearest Eve, I am truly sorry for what happened to you.'

'Listen to me.' She crosses her arms in front of her chest. 'No matter what happens in childhood, we make our own lives. There's no reason in the wide earthly world to blame anyone else. So you quit now. You quit blaming yourself for anything that might have happened to me. You hear?'

'Similarly, your children will understand too. You should stop blaming yourself, dearest.'

We stare at each other. Then she shrugs. 'Life's life, Violet. Sometimes it sucks. In your case, all you did was fall in love with a young boy and get caught out. That's happening every day in every town and village in this country – heck, it's happening in the US, in Afghanistan, everywhere.' She sees a frayed tassel on the floor, picks it up and runs it through her fingers, concentrating on it. 'As I said, you had no choice as to what happened to me.'

With great care, she separates one of the strands of the tassel from its fellows. 'I could have stayed and put up with things, Mother.' She's whispering now. 'Others in my situation did. I could have come back. I always meant to come back and collect them. But it's no goddamn use saying those phrases and doing nothing – sorry for the language, Mother, I know you're a refined lady – but the plain fact is I left those three little children to sink or swim.'

'Oh, Eve!' As I gaze at her bent head, I'm dismayed. My mothering experience being so sorely lacking, I cannot think of anything wise to say that will comfort her. My instinct is to hug her and for once I allow it to gain the upper hand on reticence and propriety. I hold out my arms. 'Come here, my poor, darling girl.'

'No, no, I'm all right, I'm fine—' She waves me away but then, abruptly, leans into me and dissolves into tears.

As I hold her stormy, shuddering body, I am flooded with pure emotion, as intense as flame; her pain hurts me physically in a way my own never did. I am angry, too, and helpless. I want to remove this chalice and I cannot. (Another biblical reference? Is today the day for the descent into second childhood?) I understand then that this is motherhood.

I wrap my arms tighter round my daughter and allow her to cry. And yet, buried somewhere is a small worm. I know that she and I will never be this close again. I don't know how I know it, but I do.

As if she, too, understands this, she draws away. 'Oh, God, look at us.' She laughs. 'This wasn't supposed to happen. I was supposed to be supporting you. I had it all planned. I must be real tired after the trip.' She roots in her shoulder-bag and takes out a pack of paper hankies. 'To get back to what we were talking about before that happened,' she blows her nose, 'now that we've found each other, you needn't worry, I'll come again. I'll come regularly. What's more, you will have to come and visit. You and Daddy together? The world is a small place, these days, Mother, and I'd love to show you our part of America. It's a wonderful place, especially in the desert where the air is clean. And the colours! I think you'd be blown away.'

Her recovery has been remarkable and I feel bound to match it.

No, I do not feel bound. It comes easy to follow her lead. It feels splendid. 'It sounds marvellous, dear, and thank you for the invitation.'

I am remembering Coley's flippant invitation to fly with him to Paris. Distances aside, would it be all that much more difficult to fly to Arizona? The act of boarding the aeroplane and taking off would be the hard part, I imagine. The rest would be a simple matter of putting in time and, Lord knows, I am accustomed to that.

I realise we have slipped imperceptibly, in Whitecliff of all places, from contemplation of the past to planning the future. Until Claudine burst into my life, my plans had been confined to organising some comfort for a solitary old age before I die. Now, with a daughter I never thought I would see, I am discussing the possibility of flying to a desert on the other side of the world with her father, my dearest Coley Quinn.

The sunlight beaming through the empty stairwell is warming both of us and, no doubt rebounding from all that emotion, I am light-hearted, even giddy. I cannot remember when last I felt giddy. Coley and I will be seen off at the airport by my extended family. I shall buy drink and forbid Coley to drink and I shall get tipsy in my aeroplane seat and Coley will have to look after me. We shall arrive at Eve's desert airport and our daughter will put us to bed and give me aspirin . . .

'What are you thinking about, Mother?' Only the redness of Eve's eyes betrays what has happened so recently as she smiles at me with obvious affection.

'Why do you ask?'

'You look like a mischievous child.'

'I was just thinking, dear, that I shall enjoy you while you're here and not think too much about what happens next.'

'Me too.' She looks away from our island of light, isolated from the dim mezzanine, towards the line of open doors, keys on a huge piano. 'Have you had enough here? I certainly have. Look, Violet,' she is rueful, 'sorry about that little exhibition of mine. I should have been the one looking after you.'

'I'll not hear the word "sorry" from you again, Eve.'

'OK. Same for you. We're going for a brand new day here. Whatever about me and my problems with my three, at least where you and me's concerned there's no looking back. Is it a deal?'

'Deal.'

'Grand. Are you ready to go now, Violet Shine?

'I am ready, Eve.'

'And we leave this door open too?'

I am delighted with her: she is observant. She is getting to know her mother. I am delighted with the way she interchangeably calls me Mother and Violet. I am delighted with the fizzy feeling I have in my chest. I am delighted, full stop. I take a last look up through this shaft, crowned with light, that no longer holds any sway over my life, past, present or future. 'We do.'

## 55

# A HAWTHORN TREE

'They've been in there a desperate long time.'

'Relax, Coley, they need to spend time in there.' While Bob is in the car reading his newspaper, I've been doing nothing much. Just enjoying the sunshine.

'Yes, but anything could have happened to them. That house isn't safe.'

'Tell you what, Coley, I'll go in to see what's keeping them. You all right here for a bit?'

'I'll come with you.'

We make our way towards the back of the house, choosing to go left. When we round the corner, past the blasted beech, I see that, with Eve in close attendance, Violet is bent over the padlock on the back door, locking it with Coley's key. Striding towards them, I call out, 'Hello there, ladies. Everything work out all right?'

A complicit glance passes between them and it's Eve who answers: 'Grand. That sure is an amazing property but whoever takes it on is going to have a tough job.'

Violet straightens up. I'd expected her to be pale and shaken, given the ordeal she's been through, but there is a spark in her eye and she is positively merry. 'Oh, our Claudine has plans for Whitecliff,' she says, 'she and her friends in real estate.'

What has happened in there? Something has shifted. While Eve — whose eyes are red — seems tired, even wrung out, Violet has been energised to the extent that, instead of her normal erect glide, she is pepping. This is the opposite of what I had expected. She has now spotted Coley, who is lurking by the ruined beech. She walks by me and looks up at him: 'You cut down that staircase, didn't you?'

'Violet, I—' He stops because she's looking past him.

'Oh! And I didn't see it until now — you set fire to my poor beech tree too, didn't you? That was a perfectly good tree, Coley Quinn.'

Behind her, Eve and I cannot see her expression, of course, but to judge from Coley's grin as he looks down at her, it is not severe. 'I just couldn't stick it. I didn't protect you when I should've and I suppose I took it out on a few things.'

'What else did you take it out on? I suppose if you couldn't find enough kindling you would have set fire to the whole house.'

He's horrified. 'That'd be terrible. They'd've sent me to jail, Violet.'

'But you thought about it, didn't you?' and before he could react: 'I always knew you were a goose, Coley Quinn!' Something very private passes between them as they look at each other, and in a sense Eve and I are trapped. If we turn and walk away, they will know we have seen.

'And listen, Violet.' They're not finished.

'What?'

He lowers his voice but it's a still day and it continues to carry: 'I went all the way over to that sea-field.'

'Yes?' Her back stiffens.

'That hawthorn tree's regenerated. It's as big as it was. There must've been seeds. Or maybe it's not the same one.'

Again he looks over her head. I pretend to be rummaging in my handbag and, as a result, don't see her response. But when I look up, they are both coming towards Eve and me, and many of the years Violet has lived have fallen away from her face.

# 56

# MY MOTHER WON'T MIND

We were all there when Violet died. Even Eve had made it from Arizona in time. They say that the dying always choose to go when they are alone. Violet Shine had been alone for most of her life and that was not going to happen if we could help it.

I wish I could relate that she uttered some memorable last words but that was not the case. Her speech, that elegant syntax, had been swallowed by the cancer in her last week but she was conscious almost to the end and was able to look lovingly from one to the other of us, her eyes always lingering on Coley, who for days had never left her side except to go to the bathroom. He would not have eaten anything if we had not insisted on bringing him sandwiches and cups of strong tea and standing over him while he consumed them. He slept under a blanket in a recliner that the matron of the nursing-home had installed beside Violet's bed.

On her last day, she slipped into a coma, out of which, we were warned, she would not emerge. Her kidneys were failing and the gaps in her breathing were getting longer.

Having been assured that we would be called if necessary,

except for Coley we kept vigil in shifts so as not to hamper the medics, two of us sitting with her and Coley while the others either hung about the nursing-home canteen or, in the case of Bob and Willow, attending to business. Tommy O'Hare could not have been more accommodating and I was free to attend to my aunt for as long as I liked. He credited me with his successful acquisition of Whitecliff, but that was not why he was being so decent: he was old-school Irish, where death and dying always take precedence over commerce.

I had let go my own dream of living at Whitecliff without a qualm and now considered that my zealous pursuit of it at the beginning had been a symptom of other needs. Gradually I had realised that I could not live in the rooms, however intrinsically beautiful, beneath that cursed attic. Violet may have harboured no grudges – and I didn't either, in truth – but no matter what internal changes were wrought, those eaves would always be there and so would that roof. It was a decision I took long before she fell ill and therefore had not been influenced in any way by that calamity.

She had shown no emotion when I told her. To her, the house and the estate were now simply a means of providing her – and Eve, she confided – with a secure future. There would also be a comfortable old age for Coley 'if I'm to go first'. She had taken Tommy's offer, against the wishes of her Mr Thorpe, who, she said, was advising her to take the place to auction. Now, depending on planning issues, my boss was considering all kinds of uses for the house: the front-runner at the time of Violet's death was its conversion to a restaurant, spa and clubhouse for a nine-hole golf course, around which he would construct a necklace of detached luxury residences. I wonder what my grandfather and, especially, my grandmother would have made of it.

It was June again and, as it happened, the month was unusually warm and sunny for Ireland. Violet's nursing-home was U-shaped, built around three sides of a large, well-tended garden. After a brief shower earlier that afternoon, the scent of roses was heavy in her small room where both windows were open. Actually, the roses all over Ireland in the month of Violet's death were as June roses should always be, so abundant and heavy that their stems bent under the weight. Even our own beds at home had put on a gorgeous show.

She told me about her illness before she told Coley. It was early in April. 'Pancreatic cancer is very fast, I believe. That's a blessing. But I don't know how to tell him, Claudine. He will die, too, and that is not fair.'

She found some way and the two of them came to stay with Bob and me for a few days before she was left with no choice but to accept round-the-clock care. During those days, as she failed, Coley uttered hardly a word. He ate little; he did not leave her room. He could not sleep in her bed, she was too ill for that, but he slept on the floor beside her, refusing even a mattress; it was as if by undergoing such small hardships he could alleviate some of hers. On her last morning with us, I went in to her early and found him using a soft towel, carefully blotting from her wasted breasts the terrible sweats she endured.

On the day of her death, I had been sitting at her bedside with Eve and Coley for more than an hour, and while Coley held and stroked her blackening hand, Eve had been telling me in a low voice about her life in Arizona. I was getting hungry – the mundanities do not yield even to crises such as these; we had been attending Violet for almost a month now and although we knew the end was near, an element of routine had crept in.

Still talking, Eve dipped a lollipop sponge into the pitcher of iced water on the bedside locker, then leaned over to moisten her mother's cracked lips with it. She stopped, holding the sponge in mid-air. Violet's head had not moved but her eyes were open and directed towards Coley.

'She's awake. Should I call the nurse?' Agitated, Eve turned to me.

'Not yet.' It was Coley who responded, although he did not take his gaze from Violet's. 'I've something to say to her in private, if you don't mind.'

'Of course.' I got to my feet and, followed by Eve, went out of the room. But we left the door slightly ajar, just in case.

The corridor outside, painted a pale pink with a thick green carpet underfoot, was hushed. It was tea-time and the ambulatory residents had all moved down to the dining room; there was no sound from those left to eat in their rooms, whose doors were made from heavy blond wood.

Eve and I were quiet. No doubt she was imagining, as I was, what Coley was saying to Eve, and thinking, as I was too, about the next twenty-four hours, the outcome of which we already knew.

The mind is like a rabbit and will not be confined, however, and in parallel with our situation, I was also thinking, oddly, about Violet's Mr Thorpe. When, at her request, he came to speak to us about the disposition of Whitecliff, I had been expecting a rotund, Dickensian figure, perhaps moustached, with carefully oiled hair. For some reason, this was how I had

Deirdre Purcell

always received the image she had projected of him.

Violet's Mr Thorpe drove up to our house in a low-slung, growling sports car. As he unfolded himself from it, I could see he was about six feet three inches tall and no more than twenty-eight years old; he was certainly under thirty.

He turned out to be as clever as Violet had always said he was because he had divined my astonishment straight away. 'It's the sports car, isn't it? You were expecting someone perhaps more mature?'

'Indeed I was. But I should like to thank you for looking after my aunt. You seem to have taken her somewhat under your wing.'

'From the moment Miss Shine first walked into my office, I could see there was something special about her. My parents were both only children, Mrs Armstrong. I have no aunts, uncles or cousins. Your aunt is a lady, the kind of aunt I would dearly have loved to have, the type who, fifty years ago, would have taken me on the Grand Tour of the European capitals.' He had smiled. 'Yet despite her apparent self-sufficiency, I could see she needed someone in whom to confide and . . .' he had hesitated a little '. . . to look after . . . shall we say the more worldly aspects of her life? That became my privilege. I mean that.'

I was smiling at the recollection when Eve clutched my arm. 'Can you hear something? Singing?'

I listened. Sure enough singing was coming from behind Violet's door. A man's voice.

'What'll we do?' Eve's eyes swam. 'Do you think she's already gone and he's singing a hymn?'

'That's not a hymn.'

With Eve at my heels, I pushed the door wide. We went

in and stopped just inside. Coley was leaning over Violet and singing softly, in an accurately pitched baritone:

> My young love said to me,
> My mother won't mind
> And my father won't slight you
> For your lack of kine;
> And then she went homeward
> With one star awake,
> As the swan in the evening
> Moves over the lake.

My aunt's eyes, red-rimmed, were still open and fixed on his. They were glassy with the sheen of tears she could no longer shed.

> She stepped away from me
> And she moved through the fair,
> And fondly I watched her
> Move here and move there,
> And then she came to me
> And this she did say:
> It will not be long, love,
> Till our wedding day.

Eve and I should have been running to fetch the others, I knew that. I couldn't see whether or not Violet's chest was rising or falling. But I found I couldn't move. Neither, she told me later, could Eve, as Coley, either unaware or uncaring of our presence at the door, sang on:

# Deirdre Purcell

> Last night she came to me,
> My young love came in.
> So softly she moved
> That her feet made no din;

We saw that Violet was not yet dead. Her eyelids flickered and her eyes slid upwards away from Coley's as still he continued:

> She laid her hand on me
> And this she did say:
> It will not be long, love,
> Till our wedding day . . .

Violet's chest moved. She expressed a long sigh, then did not move any more. Her eyes remained open. Coley stopped singing. He watched for the next breath, and when it did not come, reached over with infinite tenderness and closed her eyes, using his index finger and thumb.

Her mouth had fallen a little slack. He took her hand towel from the locker, rolled it carefully and put it under her chin to support her jaw. Then he stood, leaned over her, tidied away a strand of her hair and gently kissed her forehead.

One of us must have made a sound, because he looked round and saw Eve and me, holding each other. He seemed composed. He walked across the room to her windows – having sat for so long his gait was stiff – and opened them to their widest extent to give her spirit easy passage. 'I'll not be long after her,' he said, whether to himself or to Eve and me, I couldn't tell.

\*  \*  \*

472

Coley refused to go to Violet's funeral and we didn't insist. It was a small turnout, just her new family, Mr Thorpe, the two women from the post office in West Cork, Bob's aunt Louise and Tommy O'Hare, out of respect for me and for the dead. She was laid to rest in the lichen-covered and neglected Shine mausoleum, the rusted gate of which faces the rising sun and the sea, like the window in her tower.

Coley Quinn's prediction that he would not survive her for long was fulfilled. He died one lovely September morning, less than three months later, alone, but peacefully, to judge by the serene, almost jovial expression on his face when Bob found him, lying on his side as if comfortably asleep on the lawn of our back garden. He had been up early, picking red roses to bring into the house and, in his fall, must have tried instinctively to save them from being crushed or scattered because his fist had closed so tightly round them that his skin, pierced by thorns, had leaked blood through his fingers; the undertaker, when he came, found it impossible to pry the roses loose and Coley was taken away with them still in his hand. The doctor who certified his death said he had suffered a brain haemorrhage and that he would not have felt any pain.

On the instructions of Eve, and with the co-operation of the rector of Rathlinney, Coley now lies beside his Violet in the Shine vault, and he, too, faces the rising sun.

They had only a year together, less, if her months of illness are subtracted, but it was a full and joyful time, and if death could be said to be happy, she had a happy death, as did he.

I grew to love her in the short time we knew each other but never felt she allowed me to get close to her. Eve felt the same, I know. She tried. But she was living in Arizona, and although she came to Ireland twice after that first visit, the bridge proved too long, and their time too short, for them to reach the span at the centre. Violet's daughter knew that her mother's commitment to her was absolute, her yearning genuine, her emotion on their meetings truthful, yet she agreed with me that Violet Shine had reserved the full of her heart for only one person.

Her inheritance to me is a family, Eve, Eve's children and grandchildren. She also taught me private lessons about how to live my life.

The other day I went up to Whitecliff. The bulldozers and earthmovers, cranes, skips, Portaloos and scaffolds were being assembled outside the boundary wall and were just waiting for the off. The iron gates had already been removed from their pillars, and as I arrived, the contractors were unloading the warning signs and rolls of site tape. The gaffer said he would let me in for a last look round, but I didn't take him up on his offer.

There is only one sure thing in this life, and that is that nothing stays the same. In the time it takes for the second hand of my watch to move from 59 to 60, everything changes.